OUT OF DARKNESS

A NOVEL BY
W. G. PEAKS

Out of Darkness
Published: October 2019
Printed in the United States of America
ISBN: 978-0-578-55355-9

This book was published with the assistance of Self-Publishing Relief, a division of Writer's Relief, Inc.

Cover design by Self-Publishing Relief

TABLE OF CONTENTS

**AT NIGHTFALL WEEPING ENTERS IN
BUT AT DAWN, REJOICING.**

Psalm 30

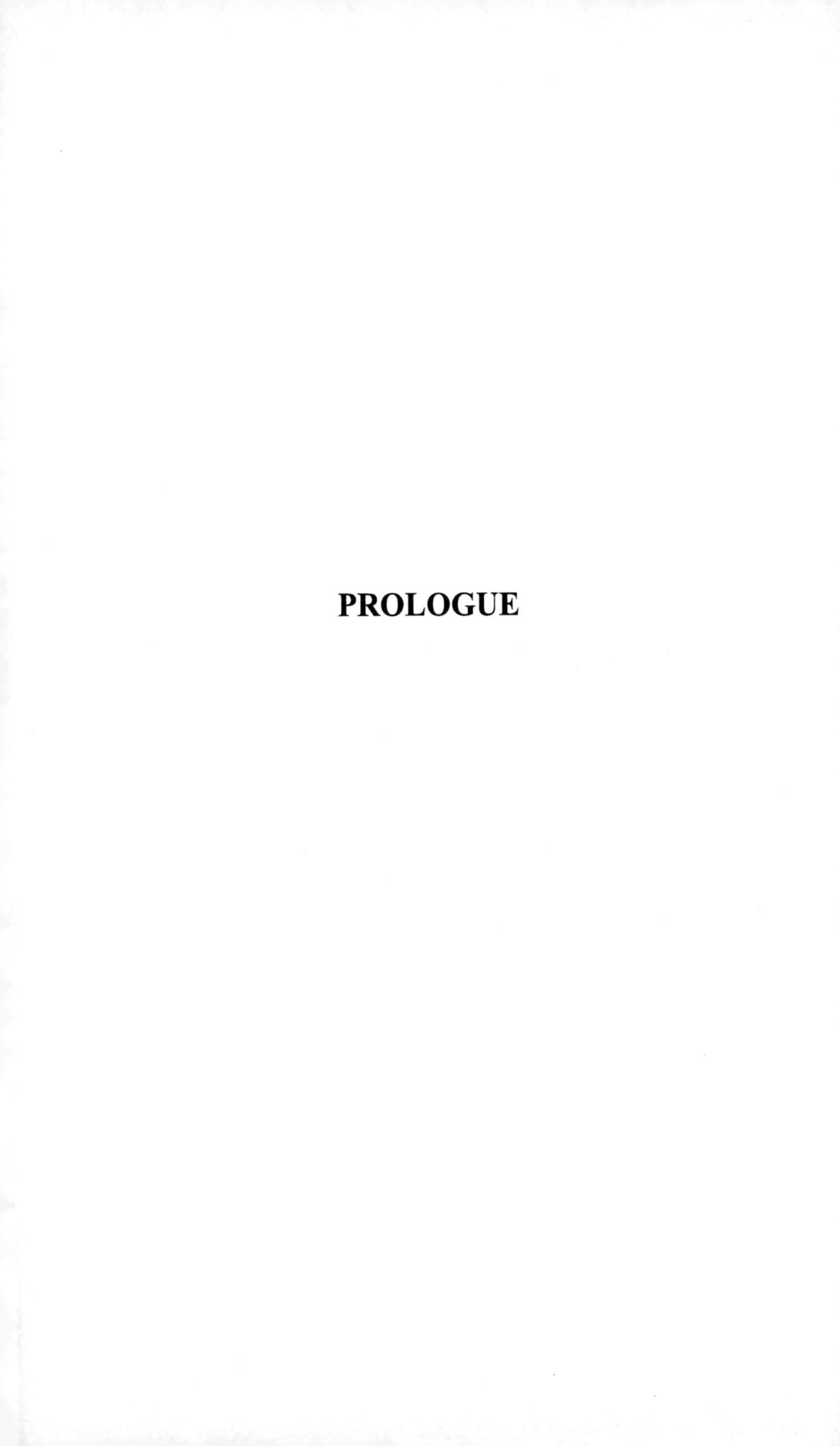

PROLOGUE

Mike occupied a stool at the local beaches' VFW, staring at his beer. It had been a good while since he'd been here, though as a young veteran he had once been a regular, trying to find refuge in alcohol from the grief and guilt he had brought back from Vietnam, the blood, the agony of death of young men, the stupidity of war.

He took a deep breath, refusing to indulge the old pain. He had been able to find a peace of sorts for much of the past forty years, thanks to good friends, good luck and the love of Molly, the magical woman in his life. Now there were only rare times when he felt himself being pulled back into that vortex in which there was no recognizable up or down, no certainty, no ending, no reason.

That wasn't why he was here today. He had come seeking a quiet place to digest the diagnosis of Parkinson's he had just received from Mayo. He watched his left hand tremble with morbid fascination as he sat the half empty beer mug on the counter. He thought it ironic he would catch a disease that would destroy the very thing that had been the mainstay of his life and sanity all these years—his art.

He cursed silently, but with resignation and almost no self-pity. He felt his frustration building however, because before the trembling in his hand had become too strong to ignore, he had started what he had planned to be his most important work, one that might be the culmination of his art.

He had made an obscenely large amount of money from his art. He was one of the most recognized and appreciated abstract expressionists in the modern art world. But throughout his career, he had felt something vital missing from his work, as though the meaning of life's ultimate value kept eluding his artistic view. Now, late in his career, he had finally begun to sense the beginning of some artistic clarity to his vision. But along had come Parkinson's. Now with his growing shakes, he doubted he would have the physical ability to realize his final creative expression.

He finished his drink, said his goodbyes to the few other drinkers at the bar, and walked outside to feel a noticeable change in the weather. A late March nor'easter had begun blowing in off the ocean. He thought the weather probably matched his mood, although he reminded himself how revitalized the sometime powerful winds made him feel, with their roiling dominance of the ocean waves.

At the same time, he admitted, he sometimes felt an uneasiness at the power of the storms and their ability to put the rest of nature almost into submission. With their power, they could sometimes cause him to question his own value, feeling as though he was merely a speck of sand in the universe.

Dismissing his mood with a shrug, he climbed into his truck to head home and find a way to share the news of his Parkinson's with Molly.

On the way, he saw two scruffy-looking young men walking toward him along the side of the road. They were coming from the direction of the local beaches charity house that helped feed the area's homeless. He knew the kitchen had been closed for a couple of hours, so he wondered if they'd missed a chance at a meal.

They each carried back packs with bedrolls on top, were dressed in faded jeans and nondescript t-shirts. Neither appeared to have shaved in several days, and while their hair was a little long, it was obvious that their accustomed style was high and tight. One had the edge of a tattoo showing on his arm beneath the bottom of his shirt's short sleeve, looking familiarly like part of a globe and anchor.

He was struck by an old but still familiar look about them. They walked in single file, with wary eyes alternately searching from side to side, then staring off into the distance.

Impulsively, Mike drove up next to the two men, rolled down his window and said, "Where you headed, Marines?" Startled to be addressed as Marines, the two stared at Mike with heightened suspicion.

"If you're interested, I know where there's some hot chili, a clean shower, and soft beds."

The two young men continued to stare wordlessly.

Sensing their confusion, Mike said, "Relax, guys. I'm harmless. Just trying to do fellow Marines a favor. Climb on in and we'll go find the chili."

The two young men looked at each other, suspicious of Mike's offer, but then with a shrug climbed into the back seat of the truck.

Mike turned in his seat. "I'm Mike Pallaso."

The older of the two briefly shook Mike's hand and said, flatly, "I'm Paul. This is Keith." They both continued to be suspicious and sat rigidly in the back seat, offering nothing more about themselves as Mike started the truck moving again.

"How long you guys been out?"

After a moment's hesitation, Paul said, "A few months." Keith said the same.

"We're about ten minutes from my house. It's on the ocean just a short way from here." Then, engaging the Bluetooth in his truck, he quickly dialed. "Hi there. I'm bringing a couple of fellas home for some of your chili. And maybe a hot shower and a bed for the night."

The woman answered without surprise. "Fine. I'll set a couple of extra places. See you in a few."

"That was Molly, my better half. You'll like her."

The young men remained unresponsive, as though speaking might open a crack in their fragile shields to this strange old man.

When they arrived, Molly met them at the door. She smiled and offered her hand.

Mike introduced them as they shook hands.

A beautiful collie came to the door and tried to insert herself into the group, eagerly sniffing the young strangers, begging for their attention.

"And this is Lady," Molly laughed. "She'll be a nosy pain, especially if you ignore her." Turning toward the kitchen, she said warmly, "I'm glad you're here. The chili's ready."

As they walked into the kitchen, Lady attached herself to Keith, nuzzling his hand with her nose. With a brief smile, he rubbed her head and scratched behind her ears. She didn't leave his side as they sat down at the table.

During the meal, everyone ate without talking. In an effort to get the young men to relax and open up, Mike said, "You're probably wondering how I knew you were Marines."

Paul nodded. "Yes sir, I guess. That was a little strange."

Mike smiled. "You know, I'm not sure. I guess it takes one to know one. And I thought I recognized the tattoo. But you looked like someone that had been where I had once been. Maybe it was the careful walk." He didn't add noticing the empty, anxious eyes or the stooped shoulders.

Paul and Keith remained largely unresponsive, save with nods of acknowledgement, eyes focused on their now empty bowls. After a moment Paul stood, followed by Keith, and gathered up their bowls to take to the sink. Paul paused to say, “Thank you, ma’am. That was awfully good. Now we better be going.”

Molly quickly said, “Please don’t worry about the dishes, guys. I’ll clean up.” She looked expectantly at Mike, urging him to convince the young men to stay the night.

“I wasn’t kidding about the hot shower and the soft bed, guys. You’re welcome to stay,” Mike said

Paul, who seemed to be the more vocal of the two, said, “Don’t think we don’t appreciate the offer, sir, but why’re you doing this?”

“You look like you’ve come a long way and could use a rest. We’ve got a lot of room and you’re not a bother. Molly’ll show you to the shower, and I’ll get you some fresh clothes from my closet. You can give Molly your clothes and we’ll get them cleaned up.”

Paul and Keith grudgingly nodded their agreement and followed Molly back to the bedroom area of the large, comfortable house.

After their guests seemed to have settled down for the night, Molly and Mike retired to their bedroom. As they slipped under the covers, Molly said, “They seem to be nice guys, and I’m glad you convinced them to stay. They look like they could use some TLC.”

“Yeah, they do. When I first saw them and that long, empty stare in their eyes, it was as though I was looking back in time, a time when a lot of other guys, including me, probably had that same lost look. It was like looking into a mirror of the past. Now that I think about it more, they look like guys that could seriously use some help.”

Molly reached over and hugged him softly. “You have such a good heart, which is why I love you so much.”

He hugged her back. “Thank God for your love. I couldn’t live without you. I love you. Good night.” He turned to his side.

“Not so fast, there, Mr. Slippery. I need to know what the doctor had to say today.”

He stayed on his side, looking away from Molly. “It was no big deal. Nothing to get excited about.”

"Uh-uh." She punched him firmly in his back. "I want to know exactly what he said! Mike, you're the most important thing in my life. I need to know!"

He rolled back to face her, reaching to caress her cheek. "The doc thinks I maybe have Parkinson's disease. That's what's making my hand and arm shake."

"Oh, Mike! You weren't going to tell me, like it's no big deal?" She punched him, again, this time more forcefully.

He hollered in mock pain, reached for her and folded her into his arms. "You know I'm not going to leave you out of anything important," he whispered into her ear. "I just didn't want you to start worrying before I get it straight in my mind."

She pushed back from him until she could look into his eyes. "You can't leave me out of anything affecting you, Mike. We're together in everything. Don't you forget it! Now what about treatment? What can they do?"

He stayed quiet for a moment. "There's nothing they can do to cure it. Only some drugs to try to slow it down. The doc gave me a prescription, but I'm not sure it'll help, and I don't like the side effects he said I might have. How about we talk about it tomorrow?

"You're telling me the truth, aren't you? I don't want to have to hit you again."

"I swear. I know I'm the luckiest guy in the world to have you in my life. I promise to keep you in the loop."

"Well, Mr. Lucky," she responded, "if you want to stay lucky, give me the prescription and I'll get it filled tomorrow. We're not going to ignore this. Understand?"

He sighed in resignation. "Yes ma'am. Now can we get some sleep?" With that, he kissed her softly and they turned over and drifted off to sleep.

During the night, they woke suddenly to the sound of moaning and frightened hollering coming from the bedroom where Paul and Keith had bedded down. They rushed into the room, turned on the lights, and saw Paul shaking Keith, whispering, "It's okay, Bro. Nothing here but us chickens. You need to wake up. It's just a bad dream."

He looked at Mike and Molly. "He gets the nightmares bad sometimes. Has trouble sleeping." He gently rocked his companion, and Keith finally seemed to wake up and began calming down.

Lady appeared, went to Keith and Paul, nuzzling their hands, and pawing at them. Mike started to call her away, but Molly softly touched his arm and whispered, "She knows they need her. Let her stay."

Keith slowly became fully aware of what had happened, looked sideways at Mike and Molly and mumbled, "Sorry. Didn't mean to cause any trouble."

Molly went to him and gently rubbed his shoulder. "It's all right, Keith. Mike still gets those kinds of dreams sometimes. But they go away. And we're here for you. So is Lady. I don't think she's going to leave you alone unless you'd rather we send her to her bed."

"No, she's okay." He petted Lady's head absently. "I'll try to get back to sleep."

Paul had remained quiet.

"What about you, son?" Mike asked him. "You doing okay?"

Paul sat silently, seemingly unable to respond. He looked off into the invisible distance, with what Mike recognized as the familiar stare of the combat soldier. He was gripping his backpack fiercely, in a strangely guarded manner. Finally, he whispered, "Keith has it worse than I do. I'll do okay. I can handle it."

Mike nodded thoughtfully. "We're right next door if you guys need anything. See you at breakfast." He looked at Lady. "Don't be a nuisance to our friends." He turned out the overhead light and with Molly walked out to their room.

Back in bed, Mike said, "Those boys need help. I know what they're going through, and they're having a tough time. I'm not sure which one is in more trouble, Keith with his nightmares, or Paul. He's wound pretty tight with his own pain."

Molly nodded in agreement. "I think you're right. I suspect they need more help then we can give them. Maybe some professional help."

"Yeah. You're probably right. I'm not sure what we can do, but I'll think on it. Look, I don't think I can get back to sleep. I'm gonna go get some coffee and go to the studio for a while."

He leaned over, kissed her, and treaded quietly toward the kitchen. With coffee in hand he opened the door to his studio and smelled the familiar scent of what had been his life's work for the past thirty-plus years. He took a deep breath, feeling the soothing calm as he turned on the lights and looked around at the comforting jumble in the large room.

He focused finally on a framed blank canvas, about six by four feet. It sat on two easels where it had been for almost a month, untouched except for a coating of white gesso he had applied earlier.

It was to have been the beginning of what he thought might be his final work, the ultimate in his quest to find completeness to his art while he still had time. Now as he looked at the blank canvas, its size seemed utterly inadequate to capture what he needed to create.

With a swift move, he pulled the canvas from the easels and tossed it into a corner of the studio, frustrated by the continuing feeling that he was still missing the focus he needed to proceed with his painting. He wasn't feeling empty of creative juices, but still confused by his jumbled vision. And now he had to deal with the Parkinson's.

He spent some frustrated minutes wandering about the studio, looking at works he had finished over the past year, feeling annoyed and slightly angry by their lack of completeness, by how unfulfilled he now felt with them.

Aimlessly he fingered the tubes and cans of the different colors of oil paint on his work table. He looked familiarly at the foreboding crimsons, explosive reds, angry blacks, bleeding yellows, phosphorus whites, and mournful grays whose unique, stark color creations had been a hallmark of his work. This morning, as had occurred so often in recent months, he recognized that his work only mirrored death, the end of life in all its painful iterations. But with his building vision, incomplete as it was, he felt there was something vital missing in his work, something that transcended death as an end point. If only he could capture that vision on canvas.

In a fit of frustration he tried to sketch with charcoal on a sheet of butcher paper what he felt he envisioned for his final work. The result was nothing more than another vision of death, a furious gathering of his mind's explosive pain, an uncontrolled series of swirls and slashes, stopped only by the pain in his arm and the tremor in his fingers. He tossed the charcoal across the room, feeling the failure in his mind looming before him. He feared he would have neither the time nor the strength to do what his mind demanded of him.

Slowly he regained his composure, refusing to give in to his frustration. He noticed the sky beginning to lighten and thought a run on the beach might clear his head and help him find a solution to his physical and mental palsy.

He left the studio and snapped his fingers to call Lady. She came quickly to him from Keith and Paul's room, anticipating their daily morning beach run. Ignoring the joint stiffness he had lately begun noticing, Mike led the way out the patio door and over the dune crosswalk to the beach.

As often happened when he ran, Mike's mind took him back through what he had come to call the swirls and slashes of his past. This morning, likely because of the familiar mental distress he had seen in Keith and Paul, his thoughts took him back to Vietnam.

It had been a place where darkness, drizzling rain, mud and death had ruled his young life. Even today, so many years later, the remnants in his memory of that time and place threatened to overwhelm his mind. In times of stress, the dormant cancer could still threaten to come, to destroy reason with pain and fear. Now, the still haunting memory of that time and place surfaced once again, unbidden into his thoughts…

PART ONE

THE DARK SIDE

MIKE – KHE SANH
CHAPTER 1

Mike felt the change in the rotors and roused himself from his numbness as the chopper settled on the runway at the Khe Sanh combat base. He looked around at the remnants of his squad, all of them staring bleary-eyed and motionless. They were returning from Hill 881 South, where Mike had lost four of his squad the night before –two killed and two badly wounded—while India, his company, was fighting to hold the hill from a furious NVA assault. The battle had been a bitch. India had been successful in driving the NVA back, but they'd been badly mauled. Now, with a pause in the fight, Echo Company was replacing India on the hill. They're welcome to it, Mike thought.

He and his squad had been ordered to stay behind on the hill to help Echo Company get squared away with the defensive positions. Afterwards, he had grabbed his squad a ride back to the Khe Sanh combat base on one of the Hueys.

As the chopper settled down he said, "All right, people, let's move. Grab your gear and head over to the battalion mess tent. Get some chow while I go find the Lt. and see what's up. Corporal Phillips, hold back a minute."

The squad, minus Phillips, shuffled off the chopper with their gear, all of them looking ragged in their filthy utilities and four or five days of dirty face stubble. They moved on stiff legs in a strange waddle as they ducked under the chopper's rotors.

Mike gave a desultory thumbs-up to the air crew and slowly followed his squad off the chopper. As usual, it was drizzling rain, turning the red dust of the combat base into constant frustrating sticky mud. He tried to wipe away the rain being blown into his face by the twirling blades, but soon gave it up as he headed for where Phillips stood waiting for him. Phillips, despite the mud and stubble, stood resolute, waiting for Mike.

"What's up, boss?"

Mike stared in exasperation at the irreverent Marine, who referred to him as boss, a totally unacceptable defiance of Marine protocol. But then he shrugged, as he remembered how Phillips and his team had stood beside him as they fought a determined charge by the NVA trying to break through the company's flank in the final moments of the battle for Hill 881.

"Corporal Phillips, how many times I gotta tell ya' it's Sergeant Pallaso, not boss?"

"I lost count, boss. Screw Marine protocol. We made it, didn't we?"

"Some of us didn't. That's what I want to talk to you about. Hadn't been for you and your team, we'd lost a lot more. You and your people helped save our bacon this morning. I wanted to thank you and tell you I'm recommending a commendation for all of you."

The muddied Marine, standing tall despite his obvious exhaustion, laughed at Palazzo. "Give your medals to the rest of the team. I don't need any medals from the fuckin' Corps. Just make sure I leave this shithole standing up when my thirteen are up."

"Go see to your team, Corporal Phillips. I can't take any more of your shit today,"

"Aye, aye, boss." Then Phillips did a smart about face and began trudging towards the mess tent. He paused, hearing Pallaso say: "Philly: Thanks. I owe you one."

"One piece, boss. One piece. My ol' man and mom would appreciate it." He winked and continued to the mess tent.

Mike stood in helpless frustration, watching Phillips walk away, wondering how he was supposed to keep him, and all the others in his command, in one piece and breathing in this shit-hole of a country.

Exhausted, he resumed trudging through the mud, looking around at the desolate landscape of the combat base. Shaped somewhat like a large aircraft carrier, the plateau on which the base sat ran roughly east to west, approximately one mile long and about a half mile at its widest part at the west end.

Seabees had constructed a single runway approximately three-quarters of a mile long, enough to accommodate the C-130s and C-123s used to resupply the base and to move wounded off and bring in fresh people. The runway was also used by the Marine CH-46 -Sea Knight helicopters for resupply and people movement when weather or NVA shelling kept the cargo planes away.

The entire perimeter of the base consisted of deep trenches, firing holes and bunkers for eating, sleeping, communications or even just hanging out if the Marines could find the opportunity. Each trench and firing hole was well sand-bagged. In addition, many had pieces of scrap lumber or pieces of spare or broken runway matting covering them for added protection from the sporadic shelling by the NVA forces around the base.

Out beyond the trenches by about fifty paces were the razor wire and tripwire defenses, wire-controlled claymore mines and hand-made explosive devices put together by the Marines.

These outer defense measures were consistent throughout the Marine enclave, including those used on Hill 881. But despite their general effectiveness they had still been penetrated by the fanatical NVA. The Gooks had run through parts of 881's trench defenses and close combat had taken its toll on India Company. Most of the night had been in fierce doubt for the Marines, and Mike and his squad spent most of the night running from one breached area to another to shore up the platoon's defenses.

Choppers had spent hours at the LZ collecting the KIAs and wounded for the trip back to Da Nang. The remaining members of India Company cleaned out the bodies of the NVA, tried to put their defensive positions back in shape, grabbed a bite of C-Rations and waited to be relieved by Echo Company. They were to move back to the combat base, pick up replacements, and find out what their new assignments would be.

CHAPTER 2

As Mike neared the battalion bunker, Gunnery Sergeant Joe Morgan spotted him. "Pallaso," he hollered, "you got your people squared away?"

Mike nodded. "Sent them over to the mess tent to find some chow while I checked in with Lieutenant Brandon."

"Sounds good. Pallaso, you look like shit. How you holdin' up?"

"Hanging in there, Gunny." Then he said in a matter-of-fact tone, "Rough night. What's the count?"

Morgan answered in the same flat tone, "Nine dead, forty wounded, twenty-four of those sent back to Da Nang. Not as bad as Con Thien but pretty rough."

Mike still experienced painful flashbacks about Con Thien, a Marine combat base just east and north of Khe Sanh. Con Thien, called the Hill of Angels, was a plateau located only about three thousand meters south of the DMZ. The Marine mission at Con Thien was to help block NVA infiltration into South Vietnam from the DMZ. India Company, on a company-sized search and destroy mission in hedgehogs just to the north of Con Thein, had experienced a brutal number of causalities from a bloody ambush by the NVA.

Mike's platoon, leading the mission, took the brunt of the initial ambush, and his squad had been in the thick of battle for almost eight hours. The fire from the NVA ambush had been relentless. The three platoons committed to the mission were pinned down with almost no cover and finally their only choice was to gather casualties and disengage. The battle had cost the company over seventy percent casualties, destroying it as an effective combat unit. What was left of the company, including Mike and six of his squad, was sent back to Da Nang for replenishment and complete reconstitution as a fighting unit.

After extensive replenishment of men and supplies, India Company had been deemed a capable combat unit and assigned to help defend the Khe Sanh combat base.

Shortly after its arrival at Khe Sanh, the replenished India Company had been sent to occupy and defend Hill 881S. The hill was one of the highest points around the base, located about four miles to the northwest, and would offer the NVA a decided strategic advantage in its efforts to dislodge the Marines from Khe Sanh.

Mike heard Gunny Morgan hollering in his ear and realized he had zoned out. "Pallaso," Morgan hollered. "You listening? I said Brandon is in with the other platoon leaders getting their marching orders from the Captain. He'll be a while.

"In the meantime, there's a bunch of new guys over in the mess tent. Here're the names of your four replacements. Go pick 'em up and get 'em squared away. Then tell the old guys –you included—to get cleaned up, draw rations and ammo as quick as they can, then you and your squad get back over here by 1600. By then, the lieutenant 'll be ready to brief you.

"Your squad and the rest of the platoon're going to head for the Gray sector trenches. You'll need to get your people settled in as quick as you can. Word is intelligence thinks the gooks're going to hit the base in force within the next twelve hours. Move your ass, Pallaso," the Gunny shouted, as he turned back to the bunker. "The war ain't waitin' on you."

Mike could only nod numbly. His fatigue was monumental, having not slept more than three hours in the last twenty-four. He, like the rest of the company, was living on fumes. Still, he turned resolutely and headed toward the mess tent in what would pass for a fast shuffle, not helped by the scrapes, cuts and bruises he had sustained from Con Thien or the new ones from the fight on 881.

As he moved, his thoughts turned again to the pain of Con Thien, and how that experience had increased his conviction that America didn't belong in Vietnam fighting a senseless war. Stronger still was the feeling of guilt beginning to consume him over the deaths of the young Marines in his squad. Only the discipline instilled in him as a Marine enabled him to continue carrying out his duties.

As he arrived at the mess tent, he saw his squad, and other members of the platoon sitting at one end of the tent, while at least a dozen new replacements were sitting at the other end. The older members of the platoon --those who had survived the last two months or more, including his squad-- were trying to ignore the sound of occasional firings from the base's Marine batteries.

Mike noted with battle-worn understanding, they were also studiously ignoring the new guys. Without exception, each surviving Marine had lost at least one buddy in the last week --and more in the last month or two. He knew from his own experience that the pain of that loss was eating at their guts and they had no interest in going through that experience with anyone else. Hence the derogatory, uncaring term adopted for anyone new – Fuckin' New Guys.

The replacements were looking anxiously around them and at each other as the firing from the Marine batteries continued. Most had put on their helmets and were clutching their rifles tightly as it was dawning on them that they were about to experience their first real combat. They all got quickly quiet as Mike walked up to them.

Shouting above the noise from the howitzers, Mike said, "Listen up, Devil Dogs. My name's Staff Sergeant Pallaso. Sound off when I call your name: Blume, Edward; Andrews, Gregory; Matthews, George; Pierce, James." Each one shouted out when hearing his name, and stood up, hesitantly moving toward Mike with their gear in hand. "You four come with me," Mike said. "The rest of you sit tight. Someone from the company'll be by soon to pick you up."

With that he turned and headed toward the rest of his squad. When he reached them, he called out, "Corporal Rodriquez, Lance Corporal Fisher, Corporal Phillips, these here're the replacements for your fire teams. Get 'em squared away with ammo and rations." He nodded towards the squad. "Then all you guys get cleaned up, get outta those rags into some fresh utilities, and meet me over at the company bunker at 1600. We'll find out what's going down then. Word is we might get hit by the Gooks in force soon, so look sharp." He turned and walked back toward the company bunker, ignoring the groans and curses to the news he had just given them.

CHAPTER 3

As he walked toward the bunker where his gear was stowed, Mike tried to sort out where he was, what day it was, and what the date was. He eventually calculated it was 20 January '68. It slowly dawned on him it was also his birthday. He was 23 years old. Except he reminded himself that birthdays were something you measured time with only in the real world. Here, time was measured in days or hours or minutes, or the time it took to eject one mag and jam in another. But in the secret, bad luck part of his brain he knew he'd been in this insane place for 180 miserable days. Only 189 days to go.

Then he remembered what had really made 20 January so unforgettable: A year ago his 64-year-old father had died suddenly from a heart attack while Mike was finishing up his training on Okinawa in preparation for Vietnam. He had gotten leave through the Red Cross to attend the funeral. It had been a starkly empty few days, culminating with the sparsely attended funeral, where his father was buried next to his mother's grave. Seeing the two graves together, he realized with profound sadness that he had no more family left. .

After his mother had died from ovarian cancer during his freshman year in high school, Mike and his father had continued to live in the family's mobile home by a quiet creek in the small Georgia town of Dalton. His father, a Marine veteran of the World War Two battles in the Pacific, chose to live a quiet reclusive life as a house painter. But with remarkable tolerance, he also found time to help guide Mike through the confusing experience of growing up. In the process, he taught him how to hunt and fish, and they spent numerous evenings skipping stones across the creek behind their mobile home while he offered Mike quiet advice about dealing with the world and about being a man.

Mike spent his teen years learning about girls, playing high school football, and doing remarkably well with his studies, considering how little time he devoted to them. In the midst of all this he had also discovered he had a unique talent for art, which he pursued with a secret passion.

He went back to Okinawa with a heavy heart, wishing there had been one more chance to skip stones with his father.

A few minutes of this dazed thinking brought him to the bunker where his gear was stowed. As he dug through the accumulation of personal detritus that marked his world of Vietnam, he saw his tattered sketch book. As he idly thumbed through it, he saw, not for the first time, that his early drawings had tried to capture those fading memories of Dalton –a time when there was no Marine Corps and no Vietnam. Lately, he knew, his drawings had evolved into the stark reality of war.

It was painfully clear from his sketches that in his short life he had existed in two totally different worlds between which there was no common language, vision, reality, order, purpose, or future. He also noted, with a critic's eye, that his sketches reflected his natural artistic talent, remnants of another time and place, which he thought had been replaced by the skill of killing. He asked himself, not for the first time, how had he gotten to this place in his life?

CHAPTER 4

He remembered it had begun on a late fall Friday afternoon, with the tortured sound of Pete Zacharias' 1960 VW Bug pulling into the graveled driveway of the double-wide Mike and his dad shared.

Mike ignored the sound as he put the final brush strokes on the landscape he was painting. It was a scene he had worked to capture for several days in which a dense stand of gnarled, dead-looking trees had been shedding an incongruous bouquet of bright red, orange and yellow leaves. He had been fascinated by the paradox in nature that life could appear dead and death alive.

"Man, that's beautiful," he heard Pete say as he walked up to peer over Mike's shoulder. "That's fucking fantastic. How the hell do you do that? And everything looks totally real, like you took a picture."

"It's called 'realism,' in art. We studied it in my art history class. The artist tries to mimic reality in his painting as though the eye was seeing a scene as nature meant it to be seen. I thought I'd try it."

"Well you've nailed it, man. Too bad you're not as good with a pen as you are with a brush."

"What're you talking about?"

"Bro, our grades just got posted for this quarter. We're busted. You got As in art history and lit, and Ds and Fs in everything else. I got a B in Spanish and math, but busted everything else. We'll be lucky if they let us back in."

Mike shrugged indifferently and bent to dab a dot of orange on a single leaf falling lazily through the air.

"Man, are you listening? We get kicked out, we're liable to get drafted!"

Mike shrugged again. "Yeah, I know. But I've been thinking. Maybe I'll quit school anyway and join the Marines. Dalton feels like a dead-end to me. The world's bigger than Whitfield County. I'm ready to move on."

Pete stared opened-mouth at his friend. "Bro, what're you saying? Never heard you talk like this before. Always thought you'd stay in Dalton and be an artist. And what's your old man gonna say?"

"I can be an artist anywhere, paint anywhere. Not just in Dalton. But I gotta' go see things up close. And my old man, we've talked about this. He says I'm almost a man now and need to make my own way. I know he doesn't want me to join the Marines. He doesn't talk about the war in the Pacific, but I know he and his buddies had it tough out there fighting the Japs. But I want a chance to see the world, and the Marines go all over the place."

"Dude, we need to talk about this. I'm really feeling bummed out. I brought a couple'a cold six-packs of Old Milwaukee. Think your dad would mind if we killed a few of them here tonight?"

"He won't care. He won't be here anyway. He called and said he'd be working late finishing painting a house he's working on. Let me clean this mess up and I'll be ready for a cold one."

The evening became a deep philosophical discussion, made bigger by the growing pile of empty cans at their feet. Before it was over, Pete had decided he wanted to be a Marine, too. In an inebriated pact, they agreed they would drive down to Marietta in the morning to the Marine recruiting station there and enlist. Pete left late that night, much too drunk to drive, but Mike, equally impaired, let him go, figuring the bug could find the way home even if Pete couldn't.

The next morning Mike woke and saw his father standing out by the creek, a cup of coffee in his hand. He turned at the sound of Mike opening the back door and waved him to his side.

He said, "I see all the empty cans. You and Pete must've had quite a night."

Mike nodded and proceeded to tell him about the grades and the decision to go see the Marine recruiter in Marietta that morning.

When Mike finished, his father reached down, picked up a flat stone and tossed it skipping across the creek. As almost always, the stone had danced across the water, skipping at least eight times before it sank. He picked up another stone, bouncing in his palm and said, "Like I already told you, you're 'bout grown, and big enough to make your own decisions. You got a lotta spring in your step right now, and the brains to go with it, so you oughta' do all right, whatever you decide. But you need to keep this in mind. Life's like tossing stones across the water. You have to spend a lotta time finding the right-shaped stone—sorta' like deciding what you want your life to be like, and then practicing over and over to get the right skip.

"Some folks count on luck to get the stone to skip right, but the really good ones make the stone skip the way it's supposed to with practice and hard work. Good luck ain't nothin' but what you get when you do the right things right."

And he added, "But ya need to remember, no matter how good you skip the stone, it's finally gonna stop skipping and sink, and then it's all over. Life's like that. A lotta times it'll run out on you long before you're ready. Point is, all you can do is try to do the best you can while you can. You understand what I'm saying?"

Mike nodded, feeling gratified by his father's low-key response to his announced plans.

"Good. Now pick up all these cans and come on in the house for breakfast. You look like you could use somethin' solid in your stomach."

Later that morning, Mike and Pete, both feeling like recovering alcoholics, climbed in Pete's Beetle and began the hour's drive down to Marietta to find the United States Marine recruiting station.

Pete moaned, saying, "You have any idea what my old man's gonna say when I tell him I'm gonna join the Marines, never mind what he'll do when he sees my grades?"

Mike glanced sideways at Pete. "Look, I know your old man. He's the last person in this town --hell, in this world, that's ever going to lose his cool. He'll just look at you with those calm, patient eyes and ask if you're sure this is what you wanta do."

Mike had spent enough time with his feet under the Zacharias' dinner table in the past twelve years that he thought he knew Pete's father as well as he knew his own.

He knew Mr. and Mrs. Zacharias had immigrated as a young couple from Greece to escape the civil war in that country following the end of World War II. And he knew, despite having a degree in philosophy, Mr. Zacharias could find no work in the States with those credentials. But fortunately, he had grown up working in his father's bakery in Athens and was able to find work in a cousin's bakery in Dalton. Over time, with determination and an unusual business acumen, he had eventually developed a small, but very successful bread company, with product distribution throughout northwest and north central Georgia. In the process, he had become one of the stalwart leaders in the Dalton community.

He also had the well-earned reputation of being one of the kindest, most generous men in the community, so Mike knew Pete's moaning had little to do with fear of his father's wrath.

Mike said as much to Pete and added, "Look, if you want to change your mind, I'll understand."

Pete had sworn, with a false bravado, that he was still ready to get on with their beer-induced pact. Mike failed to notice Pete's lack of real enthusiasm, busy in his own mind trying to weigh the pros and con of their decision. In the end, he felt a strong desire to look beyond Dalton for a change in his life.

As it turned out, Pete's weight problem --he was known affectionately as Jello by his high school classmates-- and his coke-bottle eyeglasses, quickly caught the attention of the Marine recruiter. In an uncharacteristically kind manner, he suggested that Pete go home and think again about joining the Marines. On the other hand, seeing Mike's 6-foot, 175 lb. frame, the recruiter quickly told him where to report for his physical, and to be prepared to sign on the dotted line.

On the drive back, Pete tried as best he could to hide his elation at being turned down, while Mike sat quietly trying to digest the enormity of what he had just done. He would spend most of the next three years second guessing the decision he'd made that morning.

CHAPTER 5

As he continued sifting through the pile of his personal stuff, he saw the letter from Pete that had finally found him in Da Nang. In it Pete told him he had gotten drafted by the Army, got sent to language school to learn Vietnamese and been sent to the embassy in Saigon as an intelligence analyst. He had urged Mike to look him up if he got to Saigon.

Mike hadn't bothered to reply. He'd been totally absorbed by the demons from Con Thien as he went about trying to help get the FNGs ready to deploy once the company was determined to be combat ready.

India Company had spent several weeks back at Da Nang after the shattering battle at Con Thien licking its wounds and trying to put itself back together. Mike went about his duties listlessly, finding it impossible to stop obsessing over the heavy loss of life the company had suffered. With no justification, they had gotten their ass kicked by the North Vietnamese with nothing to show for it but a bunch of body bags and ruined lives.

After observing Mike's attitude for a few days, Gunnery Sergeant Morgan cornered him one afternoon after company formation. "Pallaso, what's eatin' your ass? You're walkin' around here like a dead man. You've got the FNGs so up-tight they're pissin' their pants. Morale-wise, you're about as useful as a hemorrhoid in tryin' to get this company ready to go again."

Mike couldn't ignore the Gunny's challenge but didn't know what to say to get him off his case. Eventually he said, "I'm okay, Gunny. Maybe I got some malaria or something."

"Malaria, my ass. Whatever you got, you're infectin' the whole company. I want you outta here for seventy-two hours. I'm gonna get Lieutenant Brandon to give you a pass, and you *will* take it. Catch a milk run to Saigon and get drunk or get your ashes hauled but get yourself squared away. Got it?"

"Understand, Gunny," Mike reluctantly agreed. "I'll see if I can catch a ride in the morning."

"See that you do. Now get outta my sight." With that, the Gunny rigidly turned on his heel and marched away, leaving Mike feeling diminished and off-balance, wondering how going into Saigon could possibly help him sort out the pain in his head.

The next morning, he managed to catch a C-47 for the two-hour flight down to Saigon. Once there, he got directions to the embassy and told a Marine guard he was looking for Pete. Pete arrived at the gate shortly, and after a few minutes of excited back-slapping, he finally asked Mike what he was doing in Saigon. Mike remained non-committal, saying he was just looking for a good American beer.

So began a frenzied afternoon, with Pete as guide, chasing beers at several bars primarily frequented by U.S. military. As the beer flowed, Mike became increasingly morose, limiting his talk to monosyllabic responses to Pete's animated conversation.

Pete watched his friend, easily sensing his moodiness, and finally said, "Man, you haven't said a dozen words. What's going on? Talk to me."

Mike looked away, at first seeming to ignore his friend's entreaty, then leaned forward and said forcefully, "I'm just sick of this place and this senseless war, and the dying of good Marines for no reason. I can't keep my people alive." He pulled out the fist-full of dogtags he'd collected from his dead squad members at Con Thien. "This is what I'm talking about. This is what this insanity is all about! It's not about winning anybody's hearts and minds, it's about filling body bags. And I'm sick to death with it."

Pete could only provide a nodding understanding he didn't really have, knowing nothing he could say could relieve the pain his friend was experiencing.

Mike sat distractedly for a few minutes, pulling the damp label from his latest beer bottle, then said, "I shouldn't have come. I need to get back, even if Gunny kicks my ass. Help me find a place to crash tonight, and I'll try to catch a ride back to Da Nang tomorrow. I'm sorry, bro. Hell of a reunion, eh?"

Pete reached across the table and grasped his shoulder. "I wish there was something I could do or say to help, Mike. But all I can do is what

I've been doing all afternoon, and that's listen. Come on. I know a good place we can squat tonight, and if you feel like you have to get back tomorrow, I understand."

Mike left the next day, promising to get back to Saigon when he could. As he expected, Gunny reamed his ass, but reluctantly let Mike continue working with the replacements. Two weeks later, the company rejoined the war, this time at Khe Sanh, and Mike swallowed his anger, knowing he still had a responsibility to try to keep his new squad alive.

CHAPTER 6

Mike shook his head in a reluctant effort to bring his mind back to the reality of the moment. As he began stripping out of his dirt-filled utility blouse, he felt the dog tags in his pocket he had collected that morning from the dead squad members he had lost on Hill 881. Clutching them, he silently repeated the young Marines' names with a feeling of continuing guilt that he had failed them. He added the two tags to the four he had collected at Con Thien, carefully tying them all together with a blousing garter before putting them away in his ditty bag.

He stripped out of his dirt-filled utilities, moving zombie-like from total exhaustion. He attempted indifferently to sponge the biggest chunks of dirt from his body, shave the week's growth of stubble from his face, then pull on his last clean pair of utilities. He spent the next 30 minutes trying to brush teeth, clean his M-16, load his flak jacket with ammo and grenades, and fill his two canteens.

Finally, he climbed out of his bunker and slowly walked toward the company area. He saw his squad, including the new guys and beckoned them to him, as the rest of the company plodded up.

Shortly, Lieutenant Brandon walked out of the command bunker and called out, "First platoon, on me." The platoon gathered in a fairly quick shuffle and at his direction took a knee. Not yet twenty-four, Brandon was already into four months as a grunt platoon leader. He looks as beat up as the rest of us, Mike thought. Nevertheless, Brandon had put on his command voice and quickly began giving direction to the platoon.

He spoke in a loud, but tired-sounding voice. "Listen up. We're moving to Gray sector. That's over on the southwest perimeter. We'll occupy the trenches there, make improvements as needed, get the sixties set up, and make sure the razor wire, claymores and trip wires are working. Squad leaders and fire team leaders, make sure your people're set up with ammo and rations and fields of fire are set. I'll do a comm check shortly."

With a total lack of sincerity, Brandon then asked if there were any questions. Hearing none, he dismissed the platoon. "Ok, move out."

Mike led his squad through the perpetual clay mud toward the Gray sector, in what he'd begun to call the Khe Sanh shuffle. When the squad arrived the fire team leaders immediately began getting their teams set up. The new guys seemed to be getting their bearings, Mike thought, or at least they had their pieces pointing in the right direction.

He made a slow pass through the trenches and firing positions and went out with the team leaders to check the razor wire and claymore defenses. Satisfied that the squad was ready, he settled down and began a dispirited effort to get some food in his stomach from a can of C-ration fruit. He tried grabbing a few minutes of sleep but kept waking in sudden starts when the Marine batteries periodically fired off rounds toward what he assumed were targets around Hills 881 North or 881 South. Finally, blessedly, he was able to doze off despite the cannon fire, asleep from utter exhaustion.

CHAPTER 7

Mike jerked suddenly awake in the dark hours of the morning to the screams of "Incoming!" Simultaneously he heard the ear-splitting, smashing explosions of enemy artillery fire rocking the combat base. Then began the most relentless, devastating and frightening barrage of enemy fire any of the Marines had ever experienced. Round upon round of large NVA cannon and 122 mm mortar fire erupted on and over the base.

The continuous, deafening blasts quickly destroyed almost all above-ground structures, ripping them apart. Deadly shrapnel flew through the encampment, and cries of the wounded rang out, followed by loud cries of "Corpsman!"

An enemy shell made a direct hit on the larger of the base's ammo dumps, creating secondary earth-shattering explosions, filling the sky with a boiling caldron of fire and smoke. Adding to the murderous explosions of incoming enemy shells and exploding American 155 mm shells, mortar rounds and small arms ammunition from the dump began raining down on the Marines. Unexploded shells from the dump fell into the trenches and bunkers, causing serious impact injuries among the Marines. A shell landed in the bunker containing CVS gas containers, and the base was filled with nauseating, eye-burning gas.

Mike could only hunker down at the bottom of the trench he was in and wait for what he thought was going to be his last moment. He was totally deaf from the explosive concussions impacting the base, and the CVS gasses choked his throat and burned his eyes beyond anything he had ever experienced.

Mike's PRC suddenly erupted with the static-filled voice of Lieutenant Brandon. He realized his hearing had partially returned as he heard Brandon talking to all his squad leaders. "Listen up. Get your people up on the line. We expect the Gooks'll be coming at us any minute. Get set." Then he said, "Pallaso, I need you back at the command bunker now!"

With a mental groan, Mike pushed himself up and began a duck waddle through the trench where his fire teams huddled. "Rodriguez, Fisher, Phillips," he called out. "get your teams on line. The Lt. says the Gooks are coming at us. Make sure your new guys know which way to point their pieces."

Someone hollered. "Fisher ain't moving. I can't get him to say nothin'."

Mike moved toward where he knew Fisher and his fire team were supposed to be in the trench line. He saw Fisher's inert form lying in the mud at the bottom of the trench. Reaching to turn him over, he saw an unmistakable piece of mortar shrapnel imbedded in his head just below his helmet and his eyes staring sightlessly into the void. "Fuck," Mike murmured quietly. "Anybody else hit?" he hollered. No one responded.

"Jefferson," he called out to one of the more seasoned PFCs in Fisher's fire team. "You got the fire team. Get 'em on the line." Then he yelled over the continuing explosions, "Corpsman up."

A young corpsman came crawling up, took one look at Fisher, and said, "He's done for, Sarge."

"Yeah," Mike said as he undid one of Fisher's dogtags from the chain around his neck. He closed Fisher's eyes then said, "Let's get him out of here."

He turned to Jefferson, the new team leader. "Help get Fisher back to the aid station." Jefferson nodded and pointed to two of his team. They shouldered their weapons and grabbed Fisher's flak jacket and began pulling his body back through the trench. "Jefferson," Mike said, "secure his weapon. We might need it."

Mike began crawling and duck walking back through the trenches toward the company command post. The fierce enemy bombardment continued to pound the combat base, and he moved numbly through the trenches, noting the fearful looks of the Marines as he passed. He also saw the corpsmen desperately working on the wounded, many of whom appeared beyond help.

He reached the command post, or what was left of it. Lieutenant Brandon and the other platoon leaders were gathered around Captain Taylor, the company commander.

Without any preliminaries, Taylor said, "Khe Sanh village's under attack by a large NVA force. They're barely holding on, despite air support and our own artillery. We've been ordered to provide a relief force, and Lieutenant Brandon's platoon will try to reach the village. Sergeant Pallaso, Lieutenant Brandon says your squad will take point for the platoon."

The village lay to the South, about two or three kilometers away. Suddenly howitzers from the Khe Sanh combat base began firing toward the village. Their noise was deafening and continuous. The village defense force was sparse, consisting only of an Army Special Forces A Team, about twenty-five Combined Action Company Marines, a platoon sized group of Bru tribal militiamen and about seventy-five South Vietnamese soldiers.

Mike focused on what he was hearing from the captain about his squad being the spear and looked pointedly at Lieutenant Brandon. Brandon chose not to meet his accusing look, staring instead at his folded hands between his knees.

"Sir," Mike said to Captain Taylor, "I just lost one of my team leaders, and just got four FNGs less than ten hours ago. We're in no shape to lead the platoon."

Captain Taylor glared at Mike as though he'd just disobeyed a direct order, but before he could respond, an NVA 122 mm mortar almost scored a direct hit on the command bunker. Miraculously, no one in the bunker was injured, but as they picked themselves up --with more than a few wild-eyed looks-- they could hear the cries of the Marines around the bunker who had been wounded from the explosion and the desperate cries for corpsman.

In a measured deliberate tone, Taylor replied to Mike's protestations. "We all got our problems, Staff Sergeant. According to Lieutenant Brandon, you've got the most dependable people, even with the new guys, and he's recommended your squad take the lead. Now here's what we're gonna do."

Taylor went on to lay out the plan for the platoon to head out for the village. His plan was to send the platoon out through the perimeter wire single file, led by Mike's squad, followed by the rest of the platoon, through the elephant grass and swamp until they reached the road to the village with Mike's squad taking the lead. Call sign would be 'Red Sox.'

"Now let's get moving," Taylor said. "First sign of heavy engagement, move your asses back here. First priority is defending this ground, and we can't afford heavy casualties trying to bail out the village. Second and third platoons will be available if you get in serious trouble. Lieutenant Brandon, plan on crossing the LD in forty-five mikes. Now move."

CHAPTER 8

Mike moved quickly back to the trenches, newly energized by his growing apprehension. He called his squad together and hastily briefed them on what was about to happen. "Corporal Phillips' team takes the lead. Philly, I want you to take point. Take the shotgun. I'll be on your tail." He wanted Phillips on point because he had eight months in the field, had good instincts on point, and didn't panic when things started erupting around him. Besides that, he was damn good with the shotgun in close quarters.

"Jefferson," he continued, "you and your people take the middle. Rodriguez, you bring up the rear. Keep the intervals, stay quiet, but sing out quick if you see or hear anything."

"First squad moving out in one," he murmured into the radio and moved up to get in line behind Philly. "Okay, Corporal Phillips, let's take it nice and slow."

"Just remember, boss," Phillips mumbled. "Upright in 13."

"Move out, Corporal."

With Philly in the lead, the squad, followed by the rest of the platoon, began winding down through the razor-wire defenses, following the subtly marked path out of the defense line. The village lay approximately two-and-a-half kilometers to the southwest of the combat base, and the platoon would be moving through head- high elephant grass, knee-high, boot sucking swamp, and across narrow streams. Ambush by the NVA was in everyone's mind, and almost immediately Lieutenant Brandon passed word for the platoon to spread out into a wide v-shaped formation with the first squad at the point. Going was tough, with movement through the razor-sharp elephant grass slow and noisy. Hand signals were almost impossible.

Suddenly, fierce firing from AK-47s, machine guns, and RPGs hit the platoon, and casualties occurred almost immediately. Calls for "Corpsman up" began, while the platoon took up defensive positions in the elephant grass. It quickly became obvious the platoon was almost surrounded and badly outnumbered.

Lieutenant Brandon passed the word as best he could for the platoon to try to disengage, get the wounded to the back of the platoon's defensive line, and move back to the combat base.

Mike and Philly had taken the first blasts from the ambush, with Philly going down almost immediately with gunshots to the chest and belly. Mike had been hit in the helmet by a ricocheted piece of shrapnel from an exploding RPG round and he lay stunned beside Philly. He slowly regained his senses, as the firing around him intensified. He could hear calls to fall back, and "Corpsman up."

Seeing how badly wounded Philly was, Mike quickly started calling for a corpsman. None came, and he desperately began trying to staunch the bleeding from Philly's wounds. His efforts were futile, and Philly continued to moan and struggle to get up. Mike could see Philly wasn't going to make it, that there wasn't anything anyone could do to save him. He had a morphine syringe he'd pilfered from a corpsman's medical kit and injected Philly to try to help lessen his pain. Finally, he lifted Philly up by his shoulders and cradled him in his arms, saying, rather stupidly he realized, "Shh. It's going to be okay, Philly."

Philly stared up at him with vacant eyes, then mumbled, "Shit, boss. I don't wanna die." A moment later he whispered 'Momma, Momma,' then grabbed Mike's flak jacket, his eyes closed, and he was gone. As he slowly lay Philly down, Mike knew with absolute certainty that he had killed him by putting him on point.

The firing from the platoon was ragged, without targets, as they tried to hold the NVA at bay, move the wounded back, and reach the perimeter wire. Firing from the NVA ambush remained steady, as if anticipating over-running the platoon positions. Calls for corpsman continued, and Lieutenant Brandon's anxious voice on the PRC kept calling for situation reports and giving orders to move back to the perimeter wire.

Mike's PRC, as too often the case, was on the fritz. He could receive but not send. He realized the mess he was in, unable to call for help while hearing the gooks moving around him. He sensed that most of their movement and noise seemed to be coming behind him and the rest of the platoon, clearly trying to block their way back to the perimeter wire.

Moving as quietly as he could, he began to search around for his M-16 and Philly's shotgun. His hand touched the butt of his '16, but when he pulled it to him, he felt the crippled, bent housing. It was worthless. He figured it had been hit by some of the RPG shrapnel that had hit him. In addition, as hard as he searched through the roots of the elephant grass, he couldn't find Philly's shotgun. All he had for weapons were three grenades, his .45 and his K-bar.

Mike felt desperate because he knew he had no way to get back to the combat base, and because he knew he wouldn't be able to take Philly's body with him, no matter where he tried to move. Drilled into him as a Marine was the absolute rule that you never left another Marine behind. He lay quietly beside Philly, with his .45 ready should a Gook stumble on him.

He knew he had to move soon; daylight had begun to filter in through the ground fog, and he could hear the NVA forces settling in between him and the combat base. In despair, he decided he would try to make his way toward the village and hook up with the US forces there. As for Philly, he would try to cover his body with whatever river stones he could find, mark where the body lay, and plan on coming back to recover the body as soon as possible.

After covering Philly as best he could, he began to inch his way through the slicing elephant grass in the direction he hoped would take him to the village. He moved numbly through the suffocating jungle, heavy with guilt for Philly's death, feeling the desolation growing that had slowly been overtaking him for the past several weeks.

He felt no hope for the future and continued to move only through discipline and training. He thought of the death that was surely going to come to him as a relief he could welcome.

CHAPTER 9

After several hours of moving through the elephant grass, jungle undergrowth and rain swollen streams, Mike sensed he was finally near the road he would need to cross to get near the village defense perimeters.

Daylight had sent the NVA forces attacking the village into hiding, as Air Force and Navy jets plastered the suspected NVA positions with rockets and napalm. At the same time, out-of-sight B-52s rained 500 and 1,000-pound bombs in a fearful symphony of deadly explosions as part of a bombing strategy code named Arc Light.

Mike figured NVA casualties had to be high from the bombing and shelling, but he knew from his experiences at Con Thien and Hill 881 they'd still be relentless in trying to overrun the village. Once night, fog, and rain returned, their attacks would resume with increased intensity. He had the weary feeling he was just moving from one region of hell to another.

As dusk approached, he managed to cross the road undetected and began the slow, laborious effort to approach the village defensive perimeter. He knew he was in as much danger from the village's defensive forces as he was from the NVA.

Still, despite his desperation and exhaustion, he finally crawled to within what he thought was about twenty paces from the outer defensive perimeter wire. At that point, he hollered, "Red Sox! Marine here. I need help. Bring me in!" Then he added, "India Company, 1st Platoon, 1st Squad. Sergeant Pallaso."

At first, there was no reaction, other than the sound of a shotgun being cocked. Finally, a voice, filled with caution and skepticism said, "Where'd you do your basic, Marine? And what the fuck you doin' out there?"

Mike hollered back, "Parris Island. My platoon was sent out to help relieve you guys, but we got ambushed and I got cut off from my people. Now how about bringing me in."

After an agonizing wait, the voice from inside the perimeter said, "Stand up, so I can see you. Then I'll lead you in."

"Not happening," Mike shouted back. "I'll wave my flak jacket over my head, then you tell me how I get through the wire. You don't like what you see, then shoot. Just make sure you aim good!"

"Ok. Show me your jacket, then move where I tell you. Take it slow." Mike waved his jacket, then in a low crouch followed the shouted directions as he moved through the razor wire. Finally, he stopped at the edge of a sand-bagged firing position. He faced the business end of a shotgun held by a scrubby-faced Marine, a kid who somehow looked about a hundred years old. He lowered the shotgun slightly, saying, "Alright. Who the fuck're you?"

"Pallaso," Mike said. "Staff Sergeant Mike Pallaso. Who're you?"

"Corporal Keene, Sergeant, with CAC. Where'd you come from, Sergeant?"

Mike explained briefly, then said, "I could use some water." Keene handed him a half full canteen, cautioning that water was in short supply. Mike nodded, resisting the urge to empty the canteen, and after a few swallows said, "What's the situation here?"

"We're in deep shit, right now, Sergeant. Running real short on ammo, food and water. We've taken a lot of casualties, especially the South Vietnamese and the Montagnards, and the fog and rain have made air support hard to get. We really need backup or we're gonna' have to 'di di' outta here." Looking at Mike, Keene asked, "Where's your piece, Sarge?"

"Gooks broke it. You got anything I can use?"

"Might have, if you feel like Capone," and with that he reached back into his firing hole and pulled out an actual Capone-era Thompson sub-machine gun with a round ammunition canister.

"Where'd you get that," Mike laughed, adding "Does it work?"

"It works, Sarge. I got it off a wounded South Vietnamese."

Mike took the weapon, hefted it, examined the firing mechanism, and asked, "Got any more canisters?"

"I got three more," Keene replied and handed them to Mike.

"Okay," Mike shrugged. "Now, who's in charge?"

"First Sergeant Hannibal. He's out checking the defense perimeter around our sector, trying to make sure our people are ready for the Gooks to come again. It's getting on to 'dark thirty,' and the Gooks like that time of day. First Sergeant should be back shortly."

Presently a short, brawny Marine appeared in the trench leading up to Keene's firing hole. He stared at Mike with just a momentary look of puzzlement on his face, then said, "Who the fuck're you?"

Mike responded, "Staff Sergeant Pallaso, First Sergeant," then gave a brief account of who he was, where he'd come from, and how he got there.

"So you're our fuckin' relief, huh?" Hannibal muttered. "Those assholes at Khe Sanh promised us some relief, and this's the best they can do? Shit. Okay. I can use you. We've spotted about a hundred Gooks looking like they're getting ready to come party. You bring your toy there and follow me. We got to get ready for the show. Keene, put down that shotgun, man the pig, and cover our flank."

With that, he moved off down the trench, with Mike following. They moved about forty yards, where they joined two other Marines manning a machine gun and staring anxiously out past the perimeter wire.

"What're you seeing, Flowers?" Hannibal queried quietly.

"Can't see much, First Sergeant, but there's lotta noise out there."

"They're coming," Hannibal muttered. "I can smell it. Hold your fire 'til I say, but be ready to rock an' roll. If they get past our wire, we're fried."

Mike stood numbly in the trench, peering out through the sandbags, thinking, So this is where I die, in some god-forsaken village in some God-forsaken country that even the devil wouldn't have.

Suddenly the NVA forces started dashing out of their cover, running in what appeared to be a suicidal charge toward the perimeter defenses, while mortars and RPGs began firing into the village defenses. The NVA soldiers ran firing their AK-47s from the hip like some version of a John Wayne movie.

"Hold your fire!" Hannibal hollered. "Wait for my command!"

Mike thought, Hell, I can't hit anybody with this thing 'til they're dancing in the trench. Might as well wait.

Then Hannibal hollered, "Rock an' Roll!" And Flowers cut loose with the sixty, while the other two Marines began firing their '16s as fast as they could, slamming full magazines into their weapons like mad men.

Hannibal was firing his '16 in a more measured beat, and Mike could see the NVA infantry stumbling and falling in growing numbers.

Still, those on their feet continued to charge and Mike thought, What the hell, and began firing his sub-machine gun as well. Soon he'd emptied all of his canisters and watched as the last of the enemy soldiers collapsed at the wire. He looked in stupefaction at the multitude of bodies lying across the field of fire.

"Jesus," Flowers whispered.

"Good job," Hannibal murmured.

And Mike could only close his eyes in disbelief at the carnage before him.

It dawned on him that the NVA mortars and RPGs had grown silent, as if they too couldn't believe what had just happened. As the night fell fully on the village defenses, the moaning voices of the wounded NVA soldiers began to dominate the scene. Then they too were silent.

CHAPTER 10

The rest of the night was relatively quiet, with some hope on the part of the defenders that with continued air and artillery support, they might be able to hold the village. To add to that hope, they could hear a Spook aircraft hammering the NVA positions with its mini cannons.

But a resupply mission with several Hueys failed in the morning, due to relentless fire from the NVA guns, with one chopper and its crew lost. Later in the day, word was received from the Khe Sanh combat base that the village was considered indefensible and there'd be no more artillery support.

Two Hueys were sent to bring the Marines and Special Forces unit back to the combat base, but the commander of the SF team refused a ride. Instead he and the rest of his team organized the remaining South Vietnamese and Montagnard's into a force and began the three-kilometer hump to the combat base.

Mike elected to go with the Special Forces and their allies because he had promised himself he would recover Philly's body and return it to the combat base. With the help of some Montagnards and the cooperation of the Special Forces commander, Mike managed to find Philly's body, get it into a body bag, and onto a litter for the rest of the walk back to the base.

Miraculously, the entire contingent of Special Forces, South Vietnamese and Montagnard's made the walk back without encountering any NVA.

Once inside the base, Mike stopped briefly to shake hands with the SF captain, then followed the corpsmen who were carrying Philly's body to the aid station. After a few minutes of standing over the body with relentless guilt eating at him, Mike reached down and pulled one of Philly's dogtags off its chain and walked toward the company command bunker to report in. As he reached the opening to the bunker, the continuing bombardment of NVA artillery and mortar fire increased in intensity

He stumbled into the bunker, almost falling over Captain Taylor, Lieutenant Brandon, and a couple of the radio operators crouching on the deck of the bunker. In one corner, seemingly unaware of the shelling, stood Gunnery Sergeant Joe Morgan who looked up and shouted, "Pallaso, you still look like shit. Where you been?"

"On a long walk, Gunny," Mike hollered back. "Need to report in, and also report the loss of Corporal Phillips." He held up Philly's dog tag, and said in a flat, emotionless voice, "He's over in the aid station."

For the next five and a half interminable months, Mike and the rest of those at Khe Sanh continued to endure the constant brutal bombardment from the NVA. Survival was the primary focus for everyone –that and the continuing defense of the combat base. Air support from the Navy and Air Force, including the Arc Light Bombings from the B-52s, kept the NVA at bay, with no attacks in force, as had been anticipated by the base command.

Mike spent most of his time trying to keep his squad and himself alive, although defining living with the constant hammering from the NVA, was difficult. He had also tried to write letters to the families of those he had lost in the months the company had come first to Con Thien and then Khe Sanh, but he was poor at trying to explain why they had had to die. Mostly because he couldn't explain it to himself.

Sleeping and eating were far down his list of survival activities, and he spent most of his time hunkered down in the trenches simply staring at an earthen prison wall. The constant shelling from the NVA, along with the continuing cries for a corpsman for the wounded, became a dreadful symphony in his head, directed by the devil.

On the 360th day of his scheduled thirteen months in Vietnam, in a run to the company command bunker, Mike took shrapnel in his left side and left leg from an exploding NVA mortar shell. He vaguely heard the call for corpsman before he gave up consciousness to the pain.

He had no memory of the chopper ride back to Da Nang nor of the efforts by a surgical team to keep him alive. After a few days of recovery, he was loaded onto a plane for the trip back to the states. A pretty navy nurse, while strapping him in for the flight home, told him he'd been lucky; he'd only lost his spleen, which she assured him he could do without, and his broken left femur would heal in time. Best of all, she told him he was going home.

BEGINNING AGAIN
CHAPTER 11

Mike pulled the plug on his and Lady's run at about the half way point, deciding to take a breather after a good thirteen minute/per mile run. "Not bad for an old man," he said to his happy companion, who hardly looked winded. In fact, she ambled toward the water and was soon jumping over the smaller waves rolling onto shore.

"Show off," he hollered, and laughed at her antics, despite knowing he'd have to hose her down later.

As she trotted back to his side, Mike began picking up shells and tossing them toward the waves. As he did, he thought about his long dead father and his uncanny ability to skip stones across the creek.

Thinking about his father and his days back in Dalton served as a painful reminder of his return home from Vietnam. When he'd finally left Walter Reed with a medical discharge, he'd checked into a motel and spent several days wandering the streets of Washington with no direction or purpose. His nightmares, sleepless nights, his flinching at the normal sounds of civilian life, and the cold reception he could feel from most of the strangers he met, almost made him want to return to the upside-down normal of 'Nam.

In his saner moments, as few as they were, he had thought maybe he could find some peace and sanity if he could just go home again, even though there were few real friends there. Still, he felt a tugging loneliness pulling him back, so impulsively he bought a Greyhound ticket to Dalton.

After he stepped off the bus in Dalton, he decided to walk around downtown, looking for the old places of his growing up. He saw the library, the pharmacy with the marble-topped lunch counter, the Ritz theater and the Kress five and dime, but rather than looking familiar, they seemed alien, as though he had just landed on another planet. Rather than being able to reconnect to his past in the small town, he began to experience flashbacks to the more recent chaotic past of Vietnam. What should have been comforting memories of an innocent time morphed into mud and jungle and shell holes and the stink of napalm. People on the streets became NVA, running towards him with bayoneted AK-47s. In near panic, he finally dodged into an alley between the library and drugstore where he covered his eyes and tried to catch his breath, desperately working to overcome the insanity in his mind.

After about fifteen minutes he managed to find the courage to leave the alley and tried to see the town for what it was. He walked stiffly down the sidewalk, passing people who looked at him strangely, some abruptly crossing the street to avoid passing him. As he neared the outskirts of downtown he saw an idle taxi and ran to claim it, giving the surprised driver the address of his old double-wide.

When he arrived and paid the driver, he stood looking at the aging property he had shared with his father, seeing the mildewed walls, crooked-hanging shutters, and hip-high weeds covering the front yard. It was obvious the place was in bad shape, but the sight of it gave him a momentary sense of calm. He found the front door key where it had always been hidden under a fake rock and entered the dust-covered front room, undisturbed since he had last been there for his father's funeral.

After dumping his duffle, he walked around the inside of the double-wide, idly fingering the once familiar furniture, kitchen table and knick-knacks his mom had collected. He saw the bookcase filled with the books his mom loved and which she had taught him to love as well. In his bedroom, he saw the painting of the trees and fall foliage he had finished before leaving for the Marines.

He stepped out the back door and walked to the edge of the creek. Aimlessly, he picked up a stone and tossed it across the water's surface. It sank almost immediately and he laughed derisively, but then felt his eyes begin to water. He turned slowly and walked back to the house, feeling stupid to think he could come back here and find any comfort.

In the early afternoon, he decided to walk the mile or so to the cemetery to visit his parents' graves. When he arrived, he saw the grave sites were overgrown with weeds, so he spent the next hour clearing the plots.

He thought he ought to be saying a few words to them, but nothing would come and he felt the now familiar numbness overtaking him. Finally, he sat down between the sites with a hand extending to each gravestone. He sat there for several minutes, feeling some peace without any understanding of the source. All he knew was he felt less alone there then he had in a long while.

Suddenly he heard a strange noise, and instinctively ducked down. Then it dawned on him he had heard a car over in the newer part of the cemetery. It stopped, and he heard a door open, and then a strangely familiar voice murmuring, "I brought you some fresh flowers, son."

Mike sat in disbelief, trying desperately to make sense of what he had just heard and to deny the possibility: he had heard the familiar voice of Nicholas Zacharias, Pete Zacharias' father. The only conclusion he could draw defied all his denials. Nicholas had only one son – Pete.

Bewildered, he ran toward where he had heard the car and the voice, then stopped abruptly as he saw Mr. Zacharias kneeling beside a grave site.

In confusion, Zacharias rose and looked up at Mike standing in the roadway. , He called, "Michael, is that you?" then walked quickly to his side and gave him a fierce hug.

"Mr. Z, what are you doing here? What's going on?"

"Ah, Michael," Pete's father said softly. "You don't know, do you? Peter was killed in Saigon during the Tet Offensive. They say he was trying to get back to the Embassy during the night when he was shot by the Viet Cong. I'm so sorry to have to tell you."

"God, Mr. Z," Mike said, wiping his eyes. *They just keep falling*, he thought. *Everyone I touch or care about.*

Zacharias took his arm and steered him to a concrete bench near Pete's grave. "Come," he said. "Sit with me for a moment." As they sat, Mike buried his head in his hands, staring at the ground.

"We buried Peter about six months ago. His mother and his sisters and I drove up to Dover to meet the plane he was on and hired a funeral home to drive him back here. Almost all the town came to the funeral service and to the cemetery. It was a lovely ceremony, with taps on a bugle and a flag for his mother and me. We try to get out here at least once a week with some fresh flowers."

With the impassiveness he had armed himself with in Vietnam, Mike only offered, "I'm sorry, Mr. Z. I wish I could've been here."

"Peter would have liked that, Michael, as would his mother and I," he replied. "But we know there was no way. Now tell me what's going on with you. Are you out of the Marines?"

"Yes, sir," Mike replied flatly. "A medical discharge."

"You were wounded?" Zacharias exclaimed.

"Yes, sir," Mike replied, and then went on to explain tersely the circumstances of his wounds and treatment.

"My God," Zacharias whispered. "War is such a cruel and painful invention of man. How can we go on this way?"

They sat quietly for a long while, then Zacharias said, "Michael, you must come home with me for dinner. I know Peter's mother would insist that I bring you."

"I appreciate the offer, but I wouldn't be good company. Too much going around in my head. Maybe another time. Right now, I just feel like I need to be alone. You understand?"

Zacharias patted him on the shoulder and said, "I understand, although I don't think it's such a good idea. Promise me you'll come visit with us and have dinner very soon. By the way, where are you staying? You know, of course, you're welcome to stay with us."

"Thanks, Mr. Z, but I plan to stay at our double-wide tonight. Then I'll just have to see."

"All right then. But wait, what about transportation? Why don't you use Peter's old VW? It's just sitting there gathering dust. In fact, why don't I drive you to the house, you pick up the car, and be on your way?"

Reluctantly, Mike agreed, and after he and Zacharias spent a few quiet minutes at Pete's grave, they climbed into Zacharias' station wagon and made the ten-minute trip to the Zacharias' home. After a few minutes with a tearful Mrs. Zacharias, he politely and repeatedly turned down her insistent invitation to stay for dinner, climbed into Pete's VW and drove back toward the double-wide. On the way, he stopped at a café for a hamburger and then at the liquor store for a fifth of Kentucky Gentleman.

Back at the double-wide, he opened the bourbon and walked out to the edge of the creek. It flowed sluggishly as though it was reluctant to get where it was going. A shadow brushed the creek and Mike looked up to see a single crow floating by seemingly without purpose in the late afternoon air currents. He took a long drink from the bourbon and picked up a stone. He bounced it a couple of times in his hand, then tossed it across the water. He watched it bounce twice, then quickly disappear beneath the surface.

He shrugged and sat down heavily on the creek edge. After a few minutes of silent staring he reached down and picked up a hand full of stones, thinking perversely that he would throw a stone for each dogtag he had brought back from Vietnam. For each stone that failed to make it to the other side, he would take a drink of bourbon. He started with Philly. Ten stones later the bottle of bourbon was almost empty and he was feeling the pleasant numbness of being drunk. Eventually he lay back and watched stars begin to appear as the darkness overtook the day. He remained there through the night, finding a small comfort that his nightmares were drowned in the alcohol.

CHAPTER 12

The next few weeks were a kaleidoscope of senseless confusion for Mike. He moved by rote and deeply ingrained Marine discipline, trying to bring order to his surroundings in a failed effort to ignore the weight of his survivor's guilt and the recurring nightmares. His days were consumed with cleaning and repairing the double-wide and the surrounding property. His nights consisted of a drink-induced numbness with only snatches of exhausted sleep, too often interrupted suddenly by shouts of incoming and cries for corpsman.

One afternoon around the fourth week of his self-induced hermit existence, as he was taking the first drink of his nightly bourbon dinner, he heard a polite knocking at the front door. He stood with the drink half-way to his mouth, tempted to ignore whoever was there.

Then he heard Zacharias calling, "Michael, are you there? May I come in?"

Reluctantly, he put the full glass on the counter and opened the door. "Mr. Z. What're you doing here?"

"Michael, I just stopped by to see how you're doing. Do you mind if I come in?"

Mike was torn. He didn't want company, especially not Mr. Z, who he knew had already noticed his unshaven appearance and the smell of whisky permeating the double-wide.

With growing insistence Zacharias said, "Are you going to invite me in, Michael?"

"Sure, Mr. Z. Come on in." Mike opened the door wide and stepped back. He walked back to the kitchen, picked up the glass of whisky in defiance of what he knew would be Zacharias's disapproval and said, "I'm just about to have a drink. Would you like one?"

"No thank you, Michael. Do you mind if I sit?"

"No, of course not," Mike said, realizing he was behaving like a jerk. "Sorry about my poor manners, Mr. Z. It's just been a rough day."

Zacharias settled onto one end of the couch. "I understand, Michael. We've worried about you, hoped you might stop by, have dinner with us. I can see you are having a hard time getting past the war and becoming a civilian again. I'd like to help if I can."

Mike stood in the middle of the living room, whiskey glass in hand, staring off into some unknown space. He really wanted Zacharias to leave so he could get on with his nightly ritual of drowning the demons in his head. He finally said, "Mr. Z, I'm crazy with the pain of that place. I'm carrying images in my head that are rotting my brain, images that no one who wasn't there could ever understand. I don't think you or anyone can help. This," he said, holding the glass of whiskey, "is all that's helping."

Zacharias sat quietly, hearing the agony in Mike's voice and watching him drain the last of the whiskey. Then he said, "Have you done any painting since you returned? Peter used to talk about how talented you were, how much you loved your art."

Mike stared at Zacharias in confusion, unable to understand what he was asking in the middle of his agonized disclosure. "Painting? I haven't touched a brush in three years. I don't intend to. My art is all done." *Why do you ask such a stupid question?* he wanted to add.

"It just occurred to me that painting might be a way for you to relieve some of the stress you're under right now. In fact, maybe you and I could get some materials for you to get started with, you know, brushes, paints and canvases, that sort of thing."

"Look, Mr. Z, I appreciate your trying to help, but I got no interest in painting. Art takes vision, and there's no vision in my head other than all the shit I brought back from that God-forsaken country. I don't want to be impolite, but I'd appreciate it if you'd just go."

Zacharias rose. "All right, Michael. I'll leave. But I'll be back. You need help, and I'm going to help you find it. The demons in your head aren't drowning in your alcohol. They're only growing stronger. I wish you peace, son. Good evening." He walked to the door and said, "I'll let myself out."

Mike watched the door close and absently tried to find a last drop in the empty glass. He shook his head, mentally chastising himself for the way he had treated Zacharias, then turned back to the kitchen and refilled his glass. He took a strong drink of the whiskey and waited impatiently for the numbness to reach his brain.

He wandered aimlessly about the double-wide, soon finding himself in his bedroom staring at the last painting he had done. A part of his brain impartially critiqued the work, accepting it as a decent rendering of the trees and the brightly dying foliage they were shedding. But the larger part of his brain refused to think that any art could be a part of his dismal future, and that Zacharias, for all his desire to help him, was full of shit to suggest paints and brushes could cover over his misery.

He left his bedroom abruptly, angry at himself for even entertaining Zacharias' suggestion, and after picking up the bottle of bourbon, walked outside to sit by the creek. He took another large swallow of the hoped-for anesthetic and glanced across the creek at the same black trees he had painted before. Their branches were swollen with buds of green, but even now he could see glimpses of rusted red and yellow signaling the beginning of dying and the end of a season. Helplessly he felt the tug of what had been a long dormant artistic challenge as he held up a mental thumb to visualize how his brush strokes might fall.

He shook his head, angry at himself for allowing Zacharias' suggestion to seduce him into believing there might be a way out of the mental swamp he was lost in. He took several deep swallows of whiskey and felt the comforting numbness begin to overtake him. He lay back in the weeds into welcomed oblivion.

Late in the night, he woke to the sound and flash of artillery fire. He jumped up in confusion, searching in the darkness for his bunker. Suddenly he began to feel the pelting raindrops on his face and it slowly dawned on him that the artillery fire was the thunder and lightning of a rainstorm and that he was standing next to his double-wide. He stood for a time with up-turned face, trying to let the rain wash away the smell of Vietnam from his brain. He finally stumbled into the double-wide where he sat for the rest of the night holding his collection of dogtags wishing he had another bottle of liquor to deaden the memories.

CHAPTER 13

The rest of that week, Mike drifted through the same routine, trying to drink himself into oblivion at night, and working at a punishing pace during the day to clean up the double-wide and surrounding yard. Perversely, he welcomed the pounding hangover in his head as he worked with hammer, mop and scrub brush to help silence the sound of Philly's dying in his arms, or the sight of Fisher's lifeless eyes as he lay in the mud of Khe Sanh. Similarly, he accepted, like a monk indulging in self-flagellation, the stabbing pain in his still-tender stomach and leg wounds from swinging a sling at the hip-high weeds in the yard.

It was the Saturday of that week, as he was leaning on the sling to catch his breath after attacking the front yard, when Zacharias pulled up. Mike looked at him without greeting as he climbed out of the car, waved to Mike, and walked up the stones that served as a walkway.

Zacharias pointed at the cut weeds. "Hard work, but it's looking better. How are you?"

"Doing okay," Mike said noncommittally, but wanting to say, *Why are you here again?*

"I know you're not happy to see me, but I have some things in my car I wanted you to see, to make sure I made the right purchases."

Mike looked puzzled at Zacharias. "What're you talking about Mr. Z? What purchases?"

"Come see," he said, and walked back and opened the trunk of the large car.

Mike tossed the sling aside, feeling more irritation than curiosity and followed Zacharias. When he looked in the trunk he saw a large roll of canvas, numerous tubes of different colored oil paints, a variety of different-sized brushes, a couple of palettes and a bundle of rags. He shook his head in exasperation. "Mr. Z, what are you trying to do? I told you I couldn't paint again. You've just wasted your money. I've got nothing in my head for this kind of thing. There's nothing there but the shit I brought back from 'Nam. I can't believe we're even talking about this again."

"I understand you're upset with me, that you feel I'm interfering with your life. And that's okay, but you need help and that's why I'm here again. I happen to believe that getting involved in your painting is one of the ways you might be able to start dealing with the pain in your head, in a much better way than with whiskey. Why don't we go inside and let me tell you more about my ideas?"

Mike just shook his head in silent resignation at Zacharias' persistence, turned and walked to the front door, feeling angry at himself for his growing curiosity to hear what Zacharias had to say.

Zacharias sat on the couch, looking expectantly for Mike to join him. Mike slouched on the edge of a chair across from him, not bothering to wipe away the rivulets of sweat running down his face as he waited for Zacharias to start.

"Peter used to talk about what a wonderful artist you were and about how much you enjoyed expressing yourself on canvas. My thought is that you use that artistic talent to pull the pain and the demons of war from your mind and capture them on canvas so they can't get back into your head."

Mike threw up his hands and said derisively, "First, I haven't touched a paint brush or a canvas in over three years. I'm not sure I even know which end of the brush to hold. And even if I did, there's no way for me to visualize what's in my head. It's all so mixed up, so muddled, so without shape or form. How can I possibly put such a shapeless image on canvas? How can I recreate this pain in my head?"

"How do you know whether you can or can't until you try? And think of this-- You've just come through what must have been the most horrific experience in your life and you managed to survive. Surely you have the strength and the courage to put paint on a canvas. Surely, you'll be able to recreate the demons and pain in your head in some recognizable form, even if only you can recognize them. And in the end, the only important outcome will be the purging them from your head.

"You must close your eyes to the recognizable world and open your mind to those unique images. Let those images flow down your arm into your brush and onto the canvas. It won't be easy, but I believe it would be essential in helping you purge them from your mind."

"How can you possibly know this?"

Zacharias laughed. "Michael, don't you know that Greece, my homeland, is the birthplace of wisdom and healing? Have you not heard of Plato, Diogenes, Socrates, Hippocrates, and all the hundreds of other great thinkers of the Greek world? And you ask how I can know this? Trust me.

"Your canvases will be a mirror of your pain. You will be able to empty that pain from your mind onto the canvases and perhaps one day the world will look with astonishment at what you have created. They may not fully understand what they are seeing, but they will know they are seeing a totally unique vision of a part of this life we must overcome. More importantly, you'll have healed your mind –you will have emptied it of the pain and sorrow you now live with."

"Mr. Z, I still think you're full of shit."

"Look at yourself. What Vietnam couldn't do, you're doing. You're killing yourself. And why? Is it because of the guilt you are carrying around with you –the dogtags I've seen you clutching? Are you deliberately punishing yourself because you have survived and those young men didn't? Don't you see, you must survive, you must get beyond your pain in order to honor them, and all those who have died in this senseless war. Like my Peter." As he said this he looked off into the distance, fingering the single dogtag he wore around his neck.

Mike sat with his hands hanging down between his legs, trying to come to grips with what Zacharias was saying. Was he really trying to kill himself? Did he even care? Wouldn't dying end the pain? And if he lived, how would that honor those that didn't?

He looked up at Zacharias, who had been watching him with a pain of his own. "I don't know Mr. Z. Maybe what you're saying makes sense, but I just feel so numb, so mixed up. It's like I'm trying to walk through the swamps and mud of that place, trying to put one foot in front of the other without even knowing where I'm going? I don't see how my trying to paint is going to help me get out of that swamp."

"Michael, my idea might not be the best, but what do you have to lose? Tell you what. Let's give it a month. If you still feel the way you are feeling at the end of a month, I'll stop bothering you."

"I don't know…."

"Please, trust me on this."

Mike shrugged in capitulation. He felt stupidly lonely. The presence of Zacharias, despite the craziness of his suggestions, was oddly comforting. “Okay,” he said. “One month.”

Zacharias clapped his hands. “Good. But I don’t want you to be alone. I have an apartment over our garage I want you to stay in. There is good lighting there and plenty of room for you to use as a studio while you’re painting. And Mrs. Z will insist that we feed you.”

“Mr. Z, I’ll try, but no guarantees. If the pain gets bad ….” He drifted off, wishing right then that he had a bottle. He stood, motioning to the bedrooms of the double-wide. “I need to get cleaned up.”

“I’ll be here, Michael. Go get cleaned up. It’s a beginning.”

Mike reappeared after almost thirty minutes, minus his beard, with clean, though long and stringy hair, dressed in an olive-colored tee-shirt, Marine utility pants and flip-flops.

“Well, you’ve cleaned up pretty good,” Zacharias observed, with a slight smile of humor. “Shall we get started? I’m hungry for a hamburger from the café before we do anything else.”

“Mr. Z, I’m not feeling like eating….”

“I’m sure not, Michael, but you need some decent food in you. Now let’s go find the café.”

CHAPTER 14

They ate in silence at the café. Mike surprised himself with an appetite as he attacked a hamburger, fries and a large milkshake. As he was finishing, Zacharias said, "You've seen what I bought for the painting. Is there anything else we need?"

Mike absently picked at crumbs on his plate, wishing he hadn't given in to Zacharias' persistence. But finally he said, "Yeah. I'll need to frame the canvases, so we'll need some wood for that. And I'll want to coat the canvases so we'll need some titanium white. I'm guessing you got the stuff from Mr. Franklin's art store, so we can get the other stuff there too."

Okay, we'll pick that up before we go to the apartment. But before we do that, I want to show you something at my office. It won't take but a few minutes."

By now, Mike had relinquished control over what was happening to Zacharias, and only nodded in silent acceptance.

They drove to Zacharias' bakery office in the far western part of Dalton. Zacharias led Mike into the reception area to a large aquarium in which several tropical fish swam around an artificial reef.

Most of the fish swam rather placidly, but one fish, a darkly iridescent blue about the size of Mike's hand, swam frantically back and forth from end to end in a continuous pattern of crazy eights.

Mike watched the fish almost hypnotically as it swam the same frantic pattern over and over. Finally, he looked at Zacharias, who had been watching him closely. "Are you saying that's me?"

"Not just you. I think the fish represents all of us, Michael, when we are trying to deal with the pain that life sometimes gives us. As you can see, there is no purpose in the fish's movements; he gets nowhere, has no hope or relief in sight. When I first learned of Peter's death, I found myself behaving like this fish. I was going crazy with my grief, and even now, I occasionally fall back into that same senseless pattern of behavior.

"Fortunately, I have Mrs. Zacharias and our daughters, who have helped me regain my sanity, and I know Peter wouldn't want me to roll around in self- pity. Finally, you have shown up, and I see that as a special blessing. It has helped me focus on a wound besides my own, one I feel we can find a way to heal. And as we heal your wound, I strongly believe we'll also be able to further heal our own."

Mike nodded slowly, not in total agreement, but in recognition that the fish and he were not that different. "What if the fish can't change?"

"The fish may not know it needs to change, or how to change. But I think we do. We just have to want to enough to find a way. But let's not forget the lesson the poor fish has taught us; we can't waste our lives swimming in senseless patterns of pain. Now come, let's go get the wood and paint you need and go see the apartment."

As promised, the apartment had good potential, including decent light, Mike had to admit. He stood looking around, thinking about where the easel might go, while Zacharias disappeared only to reappear shortly with an arm full of the equipment and supplies they had purchased.

Without thinking, Mike reached to take some of the supplies from Zacharias. "I've got this," Zacharias said. "You get that roll of canvas and the easels. In fact, why don't you put the canvas and the wood for the frames in the garage? We can do the framing there."

As he went downstairs, Mike realized he was responding to Zacharias' instructions in the same disciplined way the Marines had pounded into him. He couldn't help but think that Zacharias would have made a good drill instructor. He felt himself momentarily accepting the familiar comfort of discipline and order.

They managed to get the apartment studio squared away by mid-afternoon, then went down to the garage and began building the frames for the canvas. Once they had a half-dozen frames completed they began cutting the canvas into appropriate sizes and Mike showed Zacharias how to stretch and staple the canvas to the frames.

When they finally finished it was late afternoon. Zacharias mentioned they would be eating in about an hour and that Mike was expected.

Mike half-heartedly tried to talk him out of his joining the family, but Zacharias remained insistent, and Mike finally agreed. Then he reminded

Zacharias that he'd need to go back to the double-wide to get his duffle bag, toothbrush and other stuff he had accumulated.

"Fine. We'll go now. You can drive the VW back, and we'll be back here in time for dinner. "

After dinner Mike gave his thanks to the family and quickly retired to the apartment. He stood helplessly in the area designated as the studio, surrounded by the empty canvases, feeling them staring challengingly and somehow accusingly at him as he struggled with where to begin.

He thought briefly about just going to bed and waiting until morning to begin. But he knew that sleep would be painful at best and filled with nightmares and those mind-blasting images he carried with him constantly, ready to pounce on him the moment he let his guard down.

Instead, he decided to begin with the mechanics of his art to help get him past his inertia. First, he set up an easel on which he placed a five by four-foot framed canvas. Next, he prepared the canvas with a coating of titanium white paint, feeling intimidated as he did so by its huge emptiness. Eventually he set about squeezing out a multitude of different colored oil paint tubes onto one of the newly purchased palettes. Then he began to sketch what he thought would be his beginning images.

It wasn't long before he found himself rubbing off image after image in growing frustration at his inability to transfer the burning memories onto the canvas. In the end, he sketched out a guilt-ridden memory from the recesses of his mind, and with the care of a Michelangelo, began to fill in the images he had sketched. After hours of meticulous brush strokes, he looked a final time at his work and finally collapsed into his bed.

CHAPTER 15

He awoke in the late morning from a fearful nightmare in which he had been struggling through strangling elephant grass with bloody tears slowly dribbling down each razor-sharp blade. He finally became aware of an insistent knocking and stumbled to the apartment door to find Zacharias standing with a large coffee and a bag of pastries.

"Food for the starving artist," Zacharias said as he stepped into the apartment, but quickly saw the painful emptiness in Mike's eyes and asked in a sympathetic tone, "Rough night?"

"Yeah. I'm not sure I can do this, or that it'll help."

Zacharias nodded. "It's got to be very hard for you, I know, but you're just getting started. I see you've covered the canvas. Were you able to paint at all? Can I see what you've done?"

Mike shrugged, turned back to the canvas and uncovered it.

Zacharias stared at the strange images on the canvas, not sure he understood what he was seeing. In the center stood a gnarled black tree. Hanging from some of its branches were several scarlet-colored, rectangular leaf-like objects, each outlined by a thin gold-colored band. Other similar-shaped objects were in mid-air like falling leaves. And on the ground beneath the tree were still others in varying shapes of decay, some curled up, some crumpled and broken. The images were meticulous in their rendering, as though from a photograph.

"I'm not sure what I'm seeing, but the image is startling. Is this part of the vision you've brought back from Vietnam?"

"I don't know, and it's not something I can talk about. But I don't feel like it's helped free me from the crap that's in my head, like you said it would."

"Perhaps not, but it's a beginning. Granted, it's strange looking, but not unexpected. The images haunting you are coming from your war experiences and there's probably nothing in the sane world you can relate those images to. It doesn't matter.

"You must close your eyes to the recognizable world and open your mind to those images. Let those images flow down your arm into your brush and onto the canvas.

"Now, I suggest you take the morning off. Go for a walk around Dalton and try to capture the images of this place that has been your home.. Maybe they'll help crowd the Vietnam images from your brain. I'll see you at dinner."

He turned and left Mike staring at the painting, totally frustrated by the clashing thoughts in his head. Did Zacharias really know what he was talking about? Could a canvas and brush truly help rid him of the pain in his head? Would he ever be able to sleep a normal sleep again?

And why was he feeling so uneasy about Mr. Z's friendship? Admittedly, it was comforting to have him and Mrs. Zacharias reaching out to him. But he felt an irrational fear that he could lose them, as he'd lost so many others that were close to him, as though he might be some kind of bad luck instrument of the devil.

In resignation, he decided to take Zacharias' advice and get out of the apartment and go into town. On Main Street, he walked about as he had when first arriving back, seeing all the places he remembered from his youth. The places still looked familiar, but there seemed to be a subtle change. The atmosphere was different, as though the war in Vietnam was infecting all the rest of the world, even Dalton. There didn't seem to be the same openness he remembered. People seemed to be in a hurry, not willing to stop and chat, say hello, or even talk about the weather.

He passed a familiar barbershop, and on impulse went in, knowing he could use a haircut, and maybe a shave. He recognized the barber, Mr. Babbitt, who put down his paper, pointed at the barber chair. "Yes, sir. What can I do for you?"

"I'd like a trim, fairly short and maybe a shave, too."

"We can take care of that. Have a seat." As he placed a hot towel on Mike's face, he said, "Say, ain't you the Pallaso boy? Heard you was in Vietnam. Must 'a been rough over there. Too bad 'bout the Zacharias kid. You go to the funeral?"

Mike began to feel nauseated and dizzy, knowing he had to leave. He stood up abruptly, saying, "I've got to go," and left the shop without further explanation. He walked rapidly down the street with no direction. Knowing he just had to get away, he finally broke into a stiff-legged jog, still favoring the wounded leg. He continued without conscious destination for several miles, until his leg began to protest.

As he began to realize where he was he turned deliberately back towards town until he found a remembered liquor store at the end of Main Street. He counted the few bills in his pocket and figured he had enough for a pint of bourbon. With a furtiveness born of guilt and pain he made his purchase and headed back to the apartment.

Once there, he quickly broke open the bottle and with eyes closed took a long gulp, then another. He shuddered both from the rawness of the alcohol and the release he felt begin from the pain in his head. He sat on the bed, continuing to drink from the bottle until it was empty. He let the drained bottle slip to the floor as he lay back, arm thrown over his eyes, and began to drift off in an alcoholic oblivion.

CHAPTER 16

That afternoon he woke to a persistent knocking at the apartment door. He stood groggily and stumbled to open it. Marsha, one of the Zachariases' daughters, stood there and announced shyly, "Daddy said to tell you that dinner would be in about thirty minutes and to please come and join us."

Mike struggled to comprehend the message through his alcoholic fever. When it became clear what she was saying, he could only say, "No, tell your dad I don't feel too good. I can't make it."

"Yes, sir. I'll tell him," she said, and skipped down the stairs.

Mike retreated to the bathroom, where he tried to throw up, but only produced drive heaves. Eventually he splashed cold water on his face and returned to the bed, wondering guiltily what Zacharias would be thinking. Screw it, he thought. Just let me die and get past this exploding head and collapsed back onto the sweat-filled sheets.

The next he knew there was more persistent knocking on the door and he woke to a darkening room, realizing that night was overtaking him, but not yet total darkness. "Yeah," he hollered. "It's open."

He wasn't surprised when Zacharias opened the door and turned on the overhead light. "Mr. Z. What's happening?" he asked in feigned surprise, as he stood up from the bed.

"Marsha said you weren't feeling well. Mrs. Zacharias thought some soup might help you feel better."

"Oh, no thanks, Mr. Z. I probably shouldn't put anything in my stomach."

Zacharias couldn't help but see the empty bottle, but refrained from mentioning it or suggesting Mike had already put too much in his stomach. Instead, he said, "I'll leave the soup in case you change your mind. In the meantime, I brought you some hot coffee. I suggest you try to get some of that in your stomach."

Mike nodded shamefully, understanding Zacharias's pointed suggestion, and took a tentative sip, almost relishing the pain of the hot liquid in a kind of penance.

Zacharias continued. "I understand you made it into town today, but maybe it wasn't such a good suggestion on my part. John Babbitt said you didn't finish getting your haircut, and some other folks said you went running past them without speaking. Something happen to set you off?"

"Mr. Z, no sense pretending. I guess you know I kinda went a little crazy in town. I apologize if I upset anybody."

"Michael, you don't owe me or anyone either an apology or an explanation. You just had a little slip. But just remember the desperate lesson our poor fish gave us. Now is there anything I can do for you before I go and stop interrupting you?"

"No, Mr. Z. I appreciate your concern. I'll be all right." He wanted to add, just go. I don't need anyone standing around watching me die.

"Fine, Michael. I'll leave you alone but eat your soup before it gets cold." With that, he turned and went quietly out the apartment door.

Mike sat unmoving on the edge of the bed after Zacharias left, equally torn by the lingering nausea in his gut and the sense of failure Zacharias' visit had generated. Hopelessness consumed him, that and the consuming, dominating pain of Vietnam.

He reluctantly tasted Mrs. Z's soup, and while he knew it had to be good, it sat like dry paste in his mouth. He sat the bowl aside and cast about the apartment looking for anything that would clear his confusion as he tried to digest the day's events. He settled on the one canvas he had completed.

Examining it, he knew it was too full of the recognizable world. It didn't begin to reflect the alien insanity swirling around in his head, the insanity Zacharias said he had to empty from his mind onto his canvas to find freedom from the hell he had brought back from war.

With no thought other than a desperate need for mental relief, he searched through the empty canvases he and Zacharias had prepared until he found a large one, about six by four feet. He tossed it onto a tarp he had spread on the floor and began stalking its emptiness with a large brush and a palette filled with the colors of the madness in his mind.

At the beginning, he felt overwhelmed by the emptiness of the canvas. Then, recalling Zacharias's prompting, he closed his eyes and began trying to visualize the shape of the craziness in his mind. Slowly, unique images he had brought back from Vietnam began to form behind his eyes. He realized, as Zacharias had prophesied, the images had a reality of their own, but were also a total aberration of the natural world.

He tentatively touched brush to canvas and began to spread a tint of color not unlike the rust and orange color of the wet Vietnamese mud that had been so dominant during the monsoon season.

Soon, he had covered the entire canvas with the mud coloring, and with growing intensity, using both brush and palette knife, began overlaying it with exploding slashes and swirls of boiling black, crimson, orange and yellow, creating a chaos of mind-numbing eruptions across the breadth of the canvas. In the midst of the chaos, he had planted, without conscious thought, images of screaming mouths and terror-filled eyes.

After several hours, when he finally dropped the brush and empty palette, he had spilled a vision of the raucous sound of death from his tortured mind.

As he stepped back in exhaustion and viewed his work, he felt a sense of calmness and partial peace that he couldn't remember having in a long time. He finally fell into bed as the fading night began to give way to the morning.

CHAPTER 17

Late that afternoon he woke with a blinding headache, and after several minutes of sitting on the side of the bed stumbled to the shower and stood for as long as he could under a cascade of cool water. As he toweled off, he heard a tentative knock at the door and guessed it was Marsha again. He called out, "Yeah?"

Marsha responded, "Daddy says, if you feel like it, come join us for dinner. We'll be eating soon."

"Okay," Mike responded in resignation. "I'll be over in about fifteen minutes."

"'Kay," she acknowledged and skipped down the stairs.

He dressed, then looked critically once more at the painting. He shrugged his acceptance of it as a beginning, knowing that artistic perfection was not what he was trying to achieve. As Zacharias kept drilling into him, his painting was just a means to try to empty the craziness from his mind. Still, he couldn't ignore the glimmer of creative excitement the painting was generating in him, and he was already visualizing other variations of the same theme.

With a last shrug he left for the house and rang the door-bell.

"Come in, Michael" Zacharias called. Mike opened the door to a delicious medley of familiar smells coming from the kitchen, one of which told him they were having Mrs. Zacharias' famous stuffed grape leaves. He could feel his stomach rumbling.

Zacharias invited him into the comfortable family room and smiled. "You actually look rested, a good change from earlier. I trust the painting is going well."

Mike nodded non-committedly. "It's a beginning. We'll just have to see. I finished a canvas last night. Don't know if it's any good, but at least I got a little sleep afterwards. Maybe your idea is working."

Zacharias waved away Mike's comments. "The important point is whether you have found a way to empty your mind of the poisons you've brought back from Vietnam. If so, then the artistry of your painting will be a bonus. In any event, I'm glad if we're able to support you. Now, would you care to join me with a glass of red wine?"

"I don't know. Alcohol and me, we're not doing too good."

Zacharias smiled. "Michael, I think your drinking yesterday was just an aberration, a slip back. I don't think you're an alcoholic. If I thought that I wouldn't offer the wine. I think, now that you have canvas and paint, you don't need alcohol to chase your demons. Now you can simply use alcohol as a way of enjoying some social company. Please join me." With that, he handed Mike a glass of wine and raised his in a silent toast. "Come, my nose tells me it's time to sit down for our dinner."

After dinner, Mike and the Zacharias retired to the family room. He complimented Mrs. Zacharias on dinner and thanked her again for the meal.

She graciously accepted his compliments. "Having you here helps us in our grief over losing Peter. It helps us to try and fill the emptiness in our hearts."

Mike looked away to hide his filling eyes, angry at his display of weakness. "Yeah, I miss him. Really sorry for your loss. Our loss." he quickly added.

The room grew quiet, each with his own thoughts. Mike, trying to ease the awkwardness of the moment, asked if they had a picture of Pete he might have. Mrs. Zacharias nodded and quickly went to the desk in the corner of the room and brought back an envelope filled with family pictures.

She handed Mike several photos of Pete, telling him to please take whichever one he'd like. After a few minutes Mike chose one of Pete taken his senior year of high school. It was a surprisingly good picture, one Mrs. Zacharias said was her favorite, and one of which she had several copies. Mike slipped it into his shirt pocket, then thanked them for their hospitality and excused himself.

Zacharias walked Mike to the door and bid him good night, after first reminding him that they had framed several canvases and they all needed to be filled up. Mike nodded his understanding and walked back to the apartment.

As he climbed the stairs, he knew he probably needed to try to sleep, but couldn't shake the edginess he was feeling, a feeling that he needed to attack another canvas. Once back in the apartment, he moved the finished painting and rested it against a wall. He picked another canvas about the same size as the last, sat it vertically on an easel, and began covering it with a coating of titanium white. While waiting for the canvas to dry, he began looking at the colors of paint he had available. Without conscious purpose, he began selecting colors and loading his palette.

Hours later he stepped back to view the almost completed canvas, seeing a blossoming explosion of crimson rising like some flower spawned by the devil, spewing streaks of blacks and yellows and whites like stamen waiting to spread their evil. It was from a vision embedded in his mind of a single earth-shattering explosion of death at Khe Sanh. He found it damningly ironic that such evil could spawn beauty on a canvas.

CHAPTER 18

The first month passed without acknowledgement by Zacharias or conscious awareness by Mike. In the following months, he attacked a new canvas every few days with a compulsive need to try to empty his mind of the dominating pain there. Some canvases he rejected out of artistic impatience, finding them inadequate to fulfill his creative direction. For others, he found more fulfillment and more release when they were completed. He could not yet feel, with any of his painting, complete satisfaction or release from the painful memories of Khe Sanh and Vietnam. Only now he felt he could control them, could keep them in check, to not allow them to dominate him.

He believed he was healing through his painting and he marveled at Zacharias' ability to visualize such an outcome. Now sleep often went undisturbed by nightmares, and when they still occasionally came he could wake with little residual fear, believing instead that life was changing for him, that the demons of war were being purged.

For a release from the intensiveness of his efforts, Mike decided to try painting a portrait of Pete, based on the photograph he had gotten from Mrs. Zacharias. He intended it to be a gift to them for all their kindness to him.

He had been with the Zachariases for more than six months and had begun to feel a restless desire to move on. The feeling was heightened by the continuing fear that somehow his presence endangered those he was close to.

It was the recurrence of how he had felt in Vietnam at Con Thien and Khe Sanh with the loss of so many of the Marines in his command, of the death of his father, and lastly, Pete. Irrationally he felt he had to leave the Zachariases before some harm might happen to them.

He found a realtor in Dalton who agreed to try to find a buyer for the double-wide and the acreage it sat on. He priced it to sell quickly and a local developer bought it with little hesitation. With that money and what he'd saved during his deployment in Vietnam, he found a half-way decent pick-up and began planning his departure.

On the eve of his leaving, he gathered up three of his paintings and the portrait of Pete and carried them to the Zachariases' house when it was near time for the evening meal. Zacharias met him at the door, looked at the canvases he was carrying and said knowingly, "You know how sad this is going to make Mrs. Zacharias and me." Before Mike could protest, he added, "Never mind. Come on in and have a glass of wine while we try to deal with this."

Mike brought the canvases in and leaned them against a wall in the foyer. He looked at Zacharias and said, "I felt it was time I left, but how did you know?"

"Michael, this is a small town. There are no secrets. Besides, Mr. Clayton at the used car lot where you bought your truck saw me at the pharmacy and mentioned you had been in. So tell me, what are your plans? Where are you going?"

Mike sighed, then explained, "I've been looking at maps, and decided I'd like to find a flat part of the world. As much as I have my roots in Dalton, I need to be on flat ground. Hills and mountains, even the small ones around here, remind me too much of Vietnam. I know it sounds crazy, but that's what I'm feeling. I've found a place in Florida—Jacksonville—near the ocean, and that's where I'm heading."

Zacharias nodded his understanding. "You need to follow your instincts, Michael. I know that. It's probably part of the healing process. Nonetheless, I hope you know what an empty place it will leave in our hearts. You've been a part of our family all these years, especially these past months, and it will not be easy to see you go. You must let us know where you are and how we can reach you."

"Yes, of course," Mike said, beginning to feel uncomfortable with trying to say meaningful goodbyes to these people who probably saved his life. "Now could you ask Mrs. Z to come in for a minute? I have some gifts for you."

Mrs. Zacharias came into the family room at Zacharias' beckoning, gave Mike a hug, and said, "I can tell this is not going to be good news, Michael. Nicholas has been moping around all afternoon. Please, tell me what's going on."

Briefly, Mike told her of his decision to leave, and where he was planning to go. Then, as he saw the tears begin to form in her eyes, he quickly added, "I know there's no way to repay your kindness, but I have some gifts for you and Mr. Z," and with that, he first uncovered the portrait he had painted of Pete, then the three original paintings he had completed.

The Zachariases stood staring at the paintings, tears running down their cheeks, unable to speak. Finally, she whispered, "Oh, Michael, they are beyond beautiful," and reached to hug his neck. "We'll never be able to repay you. Thank you so much."

At that, Zacharias came and circled his arms around them both. "Michael, I'm no art critic, but I can see these are extraordinarily powerful works. We will treasure them forever. Now, I suggest we have a glass of wine to help celebrate this moment." He moved to the cupboard where the wine and glasses were kept. He poured each of them a glass and they touched their glasses to one another in silent salute.

Finally, with another hug, Mrs. Zacharias excused herself to go check on dinner. Mike and Zacharias stood looking at the paintings, with Zacharias softly touching the edge of the portrait of Pete, unable to speak.

After dinner, and a tearful good bye, Mike went back to the apartment, finished packing and loading his truck and fell into an exhausted, restless sleep. Early that morning he went out to his truck to find Zacharias standing there with a large cup of coffee and a bag full of pastries. He hugged Mike one last time, and whispered, "Don't forget to let us know where you are and how we can get in touch with you. God speed."

FAME BEGINS
CHAPTER 19

Mike's trip down to Florida had been long but uneventful. As he approached the Atlantic coast in lower Georgia, he smelled the unfamiliar but intoxicating odors of the tidal marshlands and found it oddly appealing. That evening he made his way into Jacksonville and, after getting directions, made it to Jacksonville Beach.

He felt comfortable and strangely at home as he drove slowly around the beach community. He located a small motel and after quickly unpacking, walked down to the ocean through the firm sand left at low tide. He watched hypnotized as the waves broke on the shore in an unending pattern. Although he didn't know why, the waves and the limitless horizon formed by the sea and sky seemed to be giving him a sense of calmness he had not known for a long time.

The next day, armed with a newspaper turned to the rental section, he set about looking for an apartment. After several stops, he found a small upstairs apartment near the beach with a view looking east, at least within hearing distance of the ocean. The monthly rental would be challenging, but the lighting was good, and the lady renting the apartment seemed pleasant. So despite his dwindling money, he signed a six-month lease, and handed over a first and last months' rent and breakage deposit.

He arranged for power to be turned on and a phone installed. Then, remembering Mr. Z's request to let them know where he was, mailed a short note with his address and telephone number and a thank you again for their caring and hospitality.

The next year was an anxious and exhausting time for Mike. Anxious because of his continuing, albeit lessening nightmare of Vietnam, and exhaustion from his feverish efforts to fill his canvases with the visions in his mind.

In addition, he had taken the time to paint some commissioned portraits to help supplement his money supply and had even painted some apartments for his landlady in lieu of his monthly rent.

Despite his money situation however, he was able to devote most of his time and energy to his paintings. He unashamedly marveled at the creations he was able to produce on his canvases -- the artistic depictions of the visions in his brain. He knew few, if any, would recognize his art as meaningful representations of reality, but thought it might still create a primitive understanding of the emotional depths from which it came.

He began to feel the beginning of a sense of peace in his life. His love of the ocean grew, and he spent almost every morning and late evening running on the wet shoreline or swimming in the surf. He loved the northeasters that blew up occasionally in the fall and early spring, feeling invigorated and energized by the pounding waves and the wind in his face.

One morning, as he had set to work completing his sixth canvas, his phone rang. Only Zacharias had his number and he assumed he was calling to check on him, as he had done periodically over the past few months. Mike wasn't annoyed by his calls, but they were always the same:

"How are you, Michael?"

"Good."

"How's your health? How's your head? What about the nightmares? Have they gone away?"

"Health's good. Head's good. Nightmares still happen, but I handle them."

Unasked, but Mike knew Zacharias wanted to know, was he drinking? And he would have been able to say it wasn't a problem. Maybe a beer once in a while, but a limited budget made them infrequent.

With all that, Mike was unprepared for the excitement in Zacharias's voice.

"Michael how is your painting going?"

"Some good, some bad. Mostly good. What's up, Mr. Z?"

"Michael, you remember the three paintings you gave me? Well I finally got around to hanging them in the reception area of my office. John Cavanaugh, one of my company's new board members, is a well-known art connoisseur from Atlanta. After seeing your paintings, he has said he'd like to speak with you. John, among other things, owns several art galleries around the country, the largest in Atlanta. Would you mind if I give him your telephone number?"

Mike put the phone to his forehead as he tried to think through the implications of why an art connoisseur wanted to talk to him. Finally, he said, "Sure. Give him my number. But what do you think he wants?"

"Michael," Zacharias said, still with excitement in his voice, "I don't know exactly what John wants, but I have a great deal of respect for him, and I've seen the enthusiasm he's shown after seeing your paintings. I think you should speak with him soon. I'll give him your number, and you must promise to call me and let me know what he says."

"Okay, I'll let you know," Mike agreed and hung up, still perplexed by what had taken place. Despite the fact it was only 10:30 in the morning, he decided he needed a beer to help him think.

With beer in hand he began pulling paintings from where he had stored them in a corner and lined them against the apartment walls and furniture. He sipped his beer as he looked at each critically, feeling an enthusiasm growing as he tried to imagine them being exposed to a discerning art connoisseur.

Then he stopped abruptly and thought about what had inspired and driven his painting. About the pain he had squeezed from his brain onto the canvases. Did he have the right to even think about profiting in any way from that pain and all the suffering and dying it represented?

He had no answer and was finally distracted by his ringing phone, having no concept of how his life was about to change when he lifted the receiver.

CHAPTER 20

An excited voice said, "This is John Cavanaugh. Is this Mr. Pallaso?"

"Yes. This is Mike Pallaso. Mr. Zacharias told me you might be calling."

"Michael –may I call you Michael?" he said.

"Sure, or Mike is fine."

"Good. And please call me John. Mike, I've seen your paintings in Nicholas' office, and I must tell you I was very impressed. In my opinion, you seem to have a prodigious talent.

"Nicholas tells me that since you left Dalton last year you have completed several more paintings. I'd like to come down and see them. If you're in agreement, we might eventually be able to arrange an exhibit of your paintings at my gallery here in Atlanta, and perhaps even arrange for their sale. What do you think?"

"I don't know what to think. I've never painted for anyone but me. It's a private thing."

"I think I understand. Nicholas has told me about your history, especially about your experiences in Vietnam, and how your paintings have been part of your healing process. I respect that, and don't want to do anything to interfere. But maybe sharing your work would help you in that process.

"It might be important for others to visually experience the emotional depths you display in your art. It might help remind people of how lost we can be in the dark depths this world can create. Let me come down and see your other canvases. We can talk later about what might happen next."

Mike took a deep breath as he tried to order his jumbled thoughts, then grudgingly said, "Okay, I guess. When do you want to come?"

"How does tomorrow sound?" Cavanaugh replied immediately. "I can be there tomorrow afternoon. Just give me your address and directions."

"Fine," Mike muttered, and dictated his address and general directions.

"Good. I'll call you when I arrive. I look forward to visiting with you," Cavanaugh said, and hung up.

Mike stood staring at the phone for several seconds and then called Zacharias as he'd promised to let him know what was happening.

CHAPTER 21

Cavanaugh arrived the next day as promptly as he had promised. Mike flinched at his knock and wondered again where this was all going as he opened the door. He found a diminutive gentleman who nonetheless presented an imposing persona of both command and excitement as he introduced himself.

"Hello, Mike," he said. "I'm John Cavanaugh, and so very delighted to meet you. May I come in?"

"Sure. Come on in. Want something to drink?"

"A beer would be good if you have it," Cavanaugh replied, surprising Mike by his seemingly plebian request.

Mike offered him a seat on the room's single couch, and got two beers from his refrigerator.

As he handed the beer to Cavanaugh, he said, "How do you want to begin? I've never gone through something like this before."

"Relax, Mike. Believe it or not, I am more nervous about our meeting then you can be. I am always that way in the presence of someone I think is truly gifted. Why don't we start by looking at your canvases?" He took a sip of his beer, and then walked over to where Mike had lined his covered paintings against two walls of the apartment. "Mike," he said, "would you uncover them all? I'd like to see them all together."

Nervously, Mike pulled the sheets from each painting, until all were exposed.

Cavanaugh stood in their midst, his head and eyes taking in the total display. Then he walked slowly down the line of paintings, spending several minutes before each.

After long minutes, he walked back to Mike and stared intensely into his eyes. "Magnificent," he exclaimed. "You are truly gifted, Mike. Let's sit while I gather my thoughts."

Mike only nodded as he took a seat across from Cavanaugh, trying to digest what he was hearing. He refused to let himself be seduced by

Cavanaugh's enthusiasm. Things were happening too fast, threatening to spin out of his control, a control he had fought hard to achieve over the past two years. Still, Cavanaugh's reaction to his work was beyond anything he could have imagined. He tried to visualize what there was about his art that could provoke such a reaction, but could not.

Finally, Cavanaugh roused himself. " Mike, if you agree, I'd like to arrange a future exhibit of your work in my Atlanta gallery. First, though, I have a few suggestions. The quality is unquestioned, but I have two thoughts regarding an exhibit. First, if I've counted right, you have eight finished paintings; if possible, I would like to have a minimum of ten or eleven paintings from you to display. Second, I would like to see some of your work on larger canvases. The size of your current canvases seems too confining.

"I don't in any way mean to sound crass or unmindful of the creative effort that might be involved in what I'm suggesting. But I feel confident that your creative potential is boundless, and that the art world will be clamoring for your work. You'll need to get mentally prepared for that. What do you think, and if you are agreeable, how long do you think it would take for the additional works? "

After a few moments trying to absorb the implications of what Cavanaugh was suggesting, Mike finally nodded his agreement and speculated he would need about six months to complete the additional canvases.

"Mike, I know what I'm asking of you is very difficult to predict. I'm just very grateful you are willing to try. In the meantime, I'll be putting together the plans for the exhibit," and he proceeded to outline those plans for Mike.

As they talked, it dawned on Mike he was being seduced by Cavanaugh's excitement after all, and that he was slowly relinquishing the very control over his life he had fought so hard to gain. Later he would have doubts, wondering if he had started a journey of betrayal of Philly and Pete, and all the others he had lost in that god-forsaken country.

When they finished talking, Cavanaugh indicated it was time for him to go and asked Mike to call a cab for him. Then he walked slowly by the canvases again, shaking his head in wonder. Finally, he shook hands warmly with Mike, promised to be in touch, and left the apartment at the sound of the cab's horn.

CHAPTER 22

Eventually Mike called Zacharias and in flat tones recounted what Cavanaugh had proposed. Hearing the lingering doubt in Mike's voice, Zacharias asked, "Tell me, Michael, how are you feeling about all of this? Clearly, John's visit has created some turmoil in your mind and it's going to cause you to step out of your comfort zone. I think it's a wonderful opportunity for you, and can even be a new step forward in your healing. But I can hear you are torn in some way. What's going on in your mind?"

"I don't know how I should be feeling. Cavanaugh's reaction to my paintings was something I never expected. And I know nothing about the art world or whether I even want to be part of that. And there's this continuing feeling of betrayal--that I'm about to get something I don't deserve because I survived and all those that didn't –the ones that should be breathing the air I'm breathing—aren't."

"Michael," Zacharias answered, "I truly understand the thought of betrayal you're feeling. We've talked about this before, and I asked you then what you felt Peter would think about you and any success you might have with your art. We both agreed that he would be delighted for you. And I strongly suspect all the other lost ones would feel the same way. Think about achieving success with your art as a way of honoring their memory.

"You know, Michael," he continued, "you can certainly change your mind, and tell John you don't want to display or sell your paintings. I know he would be greatly disappointed, given how much he admires your works, but I'm certain he would understand.

"On the other hand, I agree with him that displaying your paintings and letting the world see the pain and anguish they represent can be a very positive part of your healing process."

"How? I don't understand."

"By letting the rest of the world see what they represent and understanding the depth of the pain you and so many others have brought back from the dark side of human experience. The world needs to see and feel the human stupidity this experience represents. It's something only you can decide, but please know that Mrs. Zacharias and I will support you, regardless of the decision you make."

"Thanks, Mr. Z. If I do go to Atlanta with my paintings, think you can be there too?"

"We wouldn't miss it. God bless, Michael. We'll talk soon."

After hanging up, Mike rose quickly, ran down the apartment stairs and raced toward the beach. It was low tide, and he began sprinting down the firm wet sand, trying to empty his mind of all the emotional fatigue he was feeling, thinking about the possible future he was facing.

At the end of his run, he stopped, sat down on the wet sand, and stared out at the endless ocean. A thought occurred to him that, despite its vastness, the ocean was only a miniscule part of the universe. Thinking this, he wondered where his art fit, how it possibly could have any significance. Then he thought, the world --the entire universe-- was made up of an infinite number of pieces, like a jigsaw puzzle, and each piece-- no matter how small-- was equally important to its completeness. And that maybe he and his art were one of those pieces. With that, he rose with growing resolution, beginning to rummage in his mind to plan what he would need to do to satisfy Cavanaugh's request and began a determined jog back to his apartment.

CHAPTER 23

The following months were equal parts frustration, fatigue and artistic doubt for Mike. He was continually plagued by trying to balance his creative intuition about what should appear on his canvases with the tentative time frame he had offered to Cavanaugh.

Cavanaugh kept his calls to check on progress infrequent and short. Nevertheless, they were filled with continuing excitement, which only added to Mike's uncertainty about what he'd committed to. But finally, just weeks after the six months he had originally promised, he called Cavanaugh to tell him the additional canvases were finished.

Cavanaugh was ecstatic and asked –almost demanded—that Mike let him come down and see the completed collection immediately, saying he could be there the next day. In his exhaustion, Mike was more than happy to let Cavanaugh come and take over, feeling that his work, though perhaps not his best, was nevertheless ready for display.

The next afternoon, Cavanaugh stood at Mike's door, his eagerness visible as he shook hands and cast his eyes about as he stepped into the apartment. In anticipation of his arrival, Mike had uncovered and spread all his canvases along the walls of the apartment, and Cavanaugh immediately began walking towards them.

Finally, after nearly an hour of scrutinizing Mike's work without comment, he sat down on Mike's couch, wiped perspiration from his face and said delightedly, "Unbelievable. I think I could use a beer."

Mike felt the need for a beer himself and shortly returned with two. In a solemn gesture, Cavanaugh raised his bottle in salute, saying, "Here's to true genius. Magnificent work, Mike. Now let me tell you my plans for the gallery display."

With more than a passing interest, Mike gestured for Cavanaugh to continue.

"First," Cavanaugh said, "we need to get the canvases to the gallery. If it's all right with you, I have a firm that will come in and pack and deliver them. I would like to plan for their display in two months, after I have notified my patrons and arranged for coverage in the *Atlanta Constitution* and the important art magazines, such as *Art News*. Of course, I'd want you to be there. I'll make arrangements for your flight up and your lodging."

By now, Mike was beyond numb as he tried to absorb the plans Cavanaugh was laying out. He had no knowledge of the art magazines nor did he understand why they might be important in Cavanaugh's plans. He could only nod in silence as the details rolled over his head.

Sensing Mike's confusion, Cavanaugh began writing an itinerary of events he planned to happen in the next few weeks, beginning with when the paintings would be prepared and shipped to his gallery and Mike's expected arrival in Atlanta. He chose not to share his plans for Mike to meet with any art critics prior to the actual showing at the gallery, seeing no reason to add to his obvious anxiety at this moment.

Finally, with details agreed upon, Cavanaugh took his leave, but not before he walked around Mike's paintings again, displaying the same eagerness he had initially shown. As he left, he took Mike's hand in both of his, saying over and over, "Thanks, Mike, for sharing your wonderful talent with me!"

After several minutes, Mike slowly began to try to process what had just happened. He remained unable to totally define his thoughts, still torn by what was being offered by Cavanaugh. He continued to have feelings of betrayal that he might profit from his painting.

As he had promised, he called Zacharias and began relating all that happened with Cavanaugh's visit. When he finished he reminded Zacharias of his promise that he and Mrs. Zacharias would be at the gallery for the showing.

"Absolutely," Zacharias said. "We'll get the details from John. In the meantime, I suggest you have a large glass of wine and try to settle down. You sound tired and wound up. I will talk with you soon."

CHAPTER 24

The next few weeks were a blur for Mike, starting with the knock at his door barely twenty-four hours after Cavanaugh had left. Three young men were waiting to wrap and transport his paintings to Atlanta. Shortly after that he received a Western Union message from Cavanaugh laying out the details of Mike's visit and the gallery's itinerary for the showing. This was followed by a telephone call from Cavanaugh, telling Mike that a ticket for a flight with Eastern Airlines was on its way, and that he would be meeting with a writer/art critic from *Art News* the afternoon of his arrival.

Mike arrived at the Atlanta airport as Cavanaugh had arranged, dressed in newly purchased khaki pants and a button-down plaid shirt. As he walked through the gate, he was surprised to see a gentleman dressed as a chauffeur holding a sign with his name on it. The man, who introduced himself as James, took his small suitcase and led him to a large Lincoln Town Car double-parked at the curb.

After depositing Mike in the back seat, James announced that he was to take him to the Hyatt Regency and then to Cavanaugh's gallery for an early meeting. Mike nodded his understanding and then sat silently as James maneuvered through the downtown Atlanta afternoon traffic.

As they pulled into the hotel's circular drive, James announced, "I'm to wait on you, Mr. Pallaso. Mr. Cavanaugh said to remind you that you have a reservation with the hotel, courtesy of his gallery. As soon as you have registered he would like you to come to his gallery for an early afternoon meeting with the representative from *Art News* magazine. I 'll be waiting for you here."

Mike acknowledged the information, indicated he'd only be a few minutes, then quickly entered the hotel lobby, the center of which was a towering atrium reaching skyward for twenty stories. He registered at the reception desk, then, with key in hand, began searching for an elevator that would take him to the tenth floor.

As he lifted up in the glass-enclosed elevator with an ascending view of the atrium, he couldn't help but be reminded of the many chopper flights he had been on in 'Nam and began to feel the now familiar tension he had experienced so often in those flights.

He exited the elevator on his floor, oriented himself with the directions and found his room. The key in the door worked smoothly and he quickly looked around at the spacious suite of rooms in mild surprise. He shrugged in acceptance of the extraordinary experiences he seemed to be having, threw his suitcase on one of the beds, and headed out again to find James.

CHAPTER 25

The ride to the gallery took only a few minutes despite the traffic, and Mike stepped out of the town car to see an imposing edifice with a discreet bronze placard that said Cavanaugh Art Gallery. As he opened the door, he was met enthusiastically by Cavanaugh. "Mike, I'm so delighted you're here! Come on. I want you to see the display we've set up in the gallery, and then I'd like you to meet Anthony Beloise, a writer from one of the most prestigious art magazines in America."

Cavanaugh led Mike into the main gallery, where his canvases had been hung, each with a small placard with his name, 'Michael Pallaso,' and the inscription, 'untitled.'

Mike had to admit the setup was inspiring. As they walked around the display, he was reminded again of the pain he had experienced in their creation. Still, he remained curious about how his work would be viewed, which was increased by Cavanaugh's reminder that the art critic was waiting to speak with him.

Cavanaugh stopped him as they were leaving the gallery, "You need to be prepared for some difficult questions about your art. Antony Beloise is a genuinely knowledgeable young art critic, but he has an ego problem. He wants to be sure he has not been seduced by some flash-in-the-pan artist, which I know you're not of course, so he may tend to be hyper-critical of your work during his interview with you.

"Be as candid with him as you can but try not to take offense if his questions or statements seem to be challenging. He's already viewed your work and I can tell you he was impressed by their creativity. But his questions may be driven by a caution not to be overly influenced by that initial reaction."

Hearing Cavanaugh's cautions, Mike wondered again what he was doing here. Why was he allowing himself to be subjected to a situation in which his art, regardless of how it was being reviewed now, was only meant to help him reduce the pain in his head? Still, he knew he was too far committed to back away, so he reluctantly moved forward to the meeting with the writer with no idea of how he might respond to his comments and questions. He followed after Cavanaugh with the feeling he was dragging a 105mm howitzer shell behind him.

As they neared the conference room Cavanaugh pulled him aside and whispered, "Don't forget. Beloise can be difficult. But stay calm. He can be very influential in his criticisms."

Mike could only remind himself of what he had survived in 'Nam and walked into the conference room feeling no fear –in fact, feeling nothing but a desire to be done with the whole thing.

Cavanaugh led him to the table where Beloise sat in one of the conference chairs with a note pad and several sharpened pencils before him. "Anthony," Cavanaugh said, " meet Michael Pallaso. Mike has agreed to meet with you for a few minutes before the gallery opens this evening."

CHAPTER 26

Beloise had curious, penetrating eyes and an aloofness about him that suggested a challenging intellect. He was a fairly young man, although his age was somewhat belied by his unruly head of hair and a salt-and -pepper-colored mustache. He stood and shook hands briefly with Mike, and said in a somewhat perfunctory manner, "Nice to meet you, Mr. Pallaso."

As they sat, Beloise spent several seconds looking down at the notes on his notepad, then looked up at Mike, and said "I've seen your paintings, Mr. Pallaso. Quite unusual. How long have you been painting?"

Mike, sensing the challenge implied by Beloise's question and attitude, felt himself stiffen but remembering Cavanaugh's warning, made a conscious effort to relax. "Please call me Mike. And I have only been seriously painting for about three years. But I've had an interest in art most of my life and have been encouraged by some folks to pursue whatever talent I might have."

"What made you decide on oils as your medium and why abstract expressionism as your technique?"

Michael, answered as candidly as possible. "I have only worked with oils, mostly because you can cover up your mistakes more easily than with any other medium. And I chose abstraction because that is how my mind sees the world. It's the way reality comes out of my head. I guess you could say my brain has a mind of its own."

Beloise made a few notes then said, "You seem pretty young to be a rising artist. Where have you been before you arrived on the art scene? Where have you been honing your art?"

Mike felt his gut tightening. "Why is that important? What does that have to do with my art?"

"Every artist has a history, a past that informs his art," Beloise responded. "I'm just trying to learn about you. Your art has a very definitive signature, full of dynamic creations of abstract swirls and slashes unlike any I have seen before. Quite frankly, it seems to be tortuous in its design, uncommonly disturbing, yet there seems to be some redeeming virtue in it. Where does this come from?"

"It comes from my head!" Mike responded, just short of shouting. He could feel his anger rising, with an almost uncontrollable urge to reach across the table and slap Beloise across the mouth. Cavanaugh, clearly sensed Mike's anger and squeezed his leg. With effort, Mike pulled himself back, then answered tersely, "I was in a dark and painful place and I am working my way back from that place, using my art."

Beloise sat quietly saying, "I understand." Then he said in an uncharacteristically unchallenging manner, "Mike, clearly there seems to be a repetitive theme in your work, one that I can imagine could become difficult to maintain creatively. How do you see your art progressing?"

Mike stared at Beloise for a moment without reacting. Finally he said, "You're probably right. There may be a repetitive theme in my work. However, if there is, I can't define it or describe it in any understandable fashion. But in my mind, I can see an infinite number of variations, so I'm really not concerned with any limitations in my painting."

"I see. Clearly your work is unusual, refreshingly so. But how do you think it will be accepted by the art world?"

Mike shrugged. "I guess acceptance will depend on how people are able to relate to what they think they're seeing. And anyway, I'm not sure I care what anyone else feels about my work."

Nodding with apparent understanding, Beloise asked a few more questions regarding background and technique, then closed his notepad and said, "I appreciate the opportunity to speak with you, Mike. Your work is extraordinary. I would like to have the opportunity to talk with you again."

"Thanks. Mr. Cavanaugh's my representative, so talk with him."

Cavanaugh took this opportunity to end the interview, reminding both Mike and Beloise that the gallery was about to open for invited guests to view Mike's work. He invited Beloise to stay and enjoy some champagne, then took Mike's arm and guided him out of the conference room toward the gallery where his paintings were on display. Cavanaugh commented, "Well, I thought that went pretty well, didn't you?"

Mike, in a fit of fatigue and frustration, said, "If you say so. But I'm not sure that fellow Beloise would think so. He didn't look too impressed."

Cavanaugh laughed. "Actually, Michael, he seemed to have kept his claws pulled in for the most part. I believe he's quite taken with your work.

I've seen him much more aggressive with some really talented artists, but with you I thought he was actually almost subdued. I guess we'll just have to see what he writes. In the meantime, let's go see what the general art lovers think of your work."

CINDY
CHAPTER 27

The first people Mike saw as they entered the exhibit room were the Zachariases. He hurried to their side giving each a warm hug, then whispered in Zacharias' ear, "What have you gotten me into? Get me out!"

Zacharias laughed, wrapped his arm around Mike's shoulder, then whispered, "I'm sure you have experienced worse in Vietnam, so I have confidence you'll get through this. Come, Mrs. Zacharias and I will walk with you through this horde of people and make sure you survive the evening. I must tell you, Michael, the paintings here have left us speechless. We are so awed by your talent. But tell me, how is the healing process going? Is the painting helping?"

"Truthfully, Mr. Z, I have good days and then not such good days, but yeah, I think the painting has worked like you said it would. I'm better than I was. But I still feel guilty, thinking that if I get money from my painting it'll be a betrayal."

"I understand, but as I've told you before, you and I know Peter must be proud of you and any success you might enjoy. And so, I think, would all the others who didn't come back. Now go and enjoy your success in their honor and believe this is how God intends for you to find your way out of the darkness. Just as important, through your painting perhaps you can remind the rest of the world of the pain we humans have created."

He paused for a moment, gathered himself, then said, "Forgive me, Michael. I got carried away, thinking about Peter. You go and enjoy the evening, knowing that those here tonight will be moved by your art, as they should be."

At that moment Cavanaugh appeared and grasped Mike's arm. "Mike, two things. First, I've already had offers for four of your paintings. Do I have your permission to sell them tonight? I can almost guarantee most will sell, and the prices I expect to negotiate will be astounding. What say you?"

Mike shrugged. "I don't have any idea what's involved with people wanting to buy my work, but if you think someone would like to buy what I've done at a fair price, then yeah, I agree. What kind of commission is good for you?"

"We can talk about that later. My usual commission for established artists can be as much as forty percent, but for a newly discovered artist I'm certain we can agree on a reduced amount. "

Watching him, Zacharias chuckled. "Your work is in safe hands, Michael. He's in his element. Now let's go find some champagne and let you share your work with us."

"Wait," Cavanaugh said. "I said two things, Mike. The other is that I want to introduce you to a lovely young lady, Miss Cindy Collins, who's asked to meet you. She happens to be the daughter of the junior US Senator from Georgia, who's been mentioned as a possible candidate for Vice President of the U.S. He's also the heir to one of the richest fortunes in Georgia. She seems anxious to meet you."

Mike rubbed the back of his neck, feeling the fatigue accumulating from the past hours. "Why do we need to meet?"

"Why? Because, one, she can afford to buy this entire gallery of paintings, and, more importantly, because she likes your work and wants to meet the artist."

"Go, Michael," Zacharias laughed. "What can it hurt? You did bathe today, didn't you?"

Mike nodded absently, then allowed Cavanaugh to take his arm and guide him across the gallery floor where a young woman stood looking at one of his paintings.

Looking at her, Mike felt a visceral burn charging through his veins. Had he been asked to describe her at that first moment he would have been reduced to mindless jello. Despite his artist's eyes, he could not have described her five-and-a half-foot athletic frame, her sleek curves, the high cheekbones of her face, full lips permanently curved in anticipation of a smile, the iridescent eyes, or glistening shoulder-length hair. It didn't register with him that she was without noticeable make-up save a splash of light lipstick, or that she wore her short black sheath and string of pearls in careless elegance. But he knew he was staring at astounding beauty.

As they approached, she stood with hands on hips about six feet back from one of his larger earlier paintings, done when the pain in his mind from Vietnam had been especially raw. The explosiveness of hammering blacks, reds and yellows, and streaks of phosphorous whites erupted across the canvas in demonic fashion. She slowly moved her head back and forth, as though trying to decide where she would jump into the canvas.

"Oh, Lord," Cavanaugh murmured. "She's still focused on that one painting, trying to talk me into letting her outbid the new owner."

She finally noticed their presence and immediately turned on Cavanaugh. "John, are you sure this isn't available? You know I'm willing to offer whatever it takes."

Cavanaugh slowly but emphatically shook his head. "Cindy, you know I can't do that. I am truly sorry for your disappointment."

She sighed, did a perfect imitation of a six-year-old's pout, then turned to Mike with a brilliant smile quickly replacing the pout. She thrust out her hand to him. "You must be Michael Pallaso, the creator of these marvelous works. I suppose I have you to blame for my disappointment."

Myriad thoughts tumbled through his head as he tried to grasp this bubbling young woman's appearance in the Alice In Wonderland night he had been experiencing. He wondered when the Mad Hatter would appear as he managed a mumbled "Hello" and shook her hand.

Cindy looked at Mike like a shark zeroing in on a pod of bait fish, totally focused on the rakishly handsome young painter. In her brash manner she said, "Obviously, you paint better than you talk. It must be all the noise and confusion of one of John's gatherings." With that, she took two glasses of champagne from a tray being circulated through the gallery and said, "John, is there a quieter place where Mr. Pallaso and I can talk?"

"Of course," Cavanaugh replied. "Come, I'll show you to one of our conference rooms," and led them down a hallway to a small room. "Please make yourselves comfortable. I'll be around if there is anything you need."

As the conference room door closed, Cindy said with a sultry laugh, "You look like a mouse hunting for a place to hide. I promise I don't bite, at least not on the first date."

Mike stared at her with confused fascination as he waited for his brain to interpret the surprising signals she seemed to be flashing. It was another in the series of recent events in his life in which the walls he had so carefully constructed were crumbling. Finally he said, "Is this a date?"

"Depends."

"On what?"

"If you want it to be."

"I don't know what I want. What do you want from me?" He knew he was being impolite, but his fatigue was great enough that he didn't care. Still, he was intrigued by her brashness and her beauty.

Cindy seemed to have a bottomless *joie de vivre* to go with her beauty. "I just wanted an opportunity to meet the person with the talent you certainly have, especially one with the deep secrets you seem to have buried in your work.

"I needed to meet someone who could put shivers down my spine, and you've absolutely done that with your paintings. Somehow I felt in looking at your work, that you have been to the edge of the world. An edge from which you can see some of the mysteries of this life and understand them. I want to get to that edge."

Mike replied quietly, "The only things I think I've been able to see from the edge you're talking about are darkness, pain, and confusion. You don't want to go there."

"I think I understand. I've asked John about your background and experiences, especially in Vietnam. He was pretty closed-mouth, but he did tell me you received some medals, were seriously wounded and had some pretty tough times over there. Looking at your paintings tonight it seems obvious that experience has colored your art.

"But I think your paintings suggest something more –maybe a contradiction that says underneath all the darkness is a bright, more positive vision. One that says beneath the darkness and pain there's a brightness and beauty in life. That's what I want to experience when I get to the edge."

Mike sat quietly for a moment, feeling exhausted by his day but strangely refreshed by listening to this young woman. Finally he said, "And how do you plan on getting to this edge?"

"I'm not certain. Maybe it'll just be through the osmosis of knowing people like you. But in the meantime, I'm a flying nut. I love flying. I can't get enough of it, especially aerobatics. Right now, I'm experimenting with a couple of crash-capable aircraft --don't tell my father-- that, when flown half-way right, seem to give me an outrageous excitement with life and, I think, gets me close to the edge. I've been flying, before my father finally put his foot down, in almost every aircraft available, and loving every bone-freezing moment of it. I've even thought about applying to

NASA to be an astronaut. Call me insane, and you'd probably be twenty points too close to center."

"So what you're telling me," Mike responded, helplessly intrigued by this beautiful woman, "is you're warped-nuts crazy. And all I'm trying to do is get back to half-way normal. So we don't have anything in common. We're just two ships flashing by, neither of which knows where the hell it's going."

"Maybe," Cindy conceded. "But we --you and I-- might just have found a flat place in the sea where we can float free for a few minutes. Want to give it a try?"

Beside himself with all kinds of confused emotions, Mike said, "What're you thinking?"

"Well," she said, "I've got a Cessna 172 sitting out at the airport. We could take a ride for an hour or so while we get more acquainted. I promise no loop-de-loops. Just a few moments of peace and quiet. What do you say, Michelangelo?"

"I don't know."

He sat perfectly still, his mind focused with distrust on the possibility that life, after all he had been through, could actually be offering him a new beginning, first with the success of his paintings and now this captivating woman. A beginning he desperately wanted, but which he feared was totally undeserved and doomed to failure.

"Tell you what," Cindy said, ignoring his obvious hesitancy. "This dress doesn't fly well. Why don't I leave and get changed and then pick you up in, say, two hours?"

Her enthusiasm was contagious, if totally misguided, he thought, but before he could stop himself he agreed, with rising excitement.

"Fine," she said as she got up from the table. "Be prepared for a fun ride," and with that brushed his lips lightly with hers and walked out of the room.

Mike watched her leave and sat in confused silence for several minutes, marveling again at all the positives suddenly happening in his life. But with a certainty, born at Khe Sanh, that bad follows every good thing, he was filled with foreboding. Wondering if he shouldn't just disappear into the woodwork like the mouse Cindy said he reminded her of. Finally, too intrigued by the beauty the future seemed to be promising, he pushed the fear from his mind and went with determination to find the Zachariases.

CHAPTER 28

The gallery was crowded with invited guests throughout the evening. They stood before each of Mike's works, champagne glasses in hand, excitedly exclaiming with glowing remarks at what they were seeing. Mike, at the urging of Cavanaugh, made himself available to those who wished to press the flesh of the artist and politely attempted to answer their many questions.

Finally, a soft tone announced the imminent closing of the gallery. Mike walked around the exhibit, noticing for the first-time small placards on several of the paintings with the word 'sold' and the name of the purchaser. Cavanaugh joined him and said gleefully, "Mike, six of your paintings have been sold. Two at $5,000 each, two at $7,500 and one, after a bidding war, at $15,000. And what I hadn't told you earlier is that one of my patrons, a very prominent -and wealthy- art collector, could not be here tonight, so I gave him a private viewing a few days ago. He immediately chose one of your larger canvases to be his. I told him I wasn't sure you'd part with any of your paintings, but he demanded I put his name on the one he had chosen and gave me a check for $30,000. How could I say no?"

Mike was too stunned to reply. Instead he found a chair, sat down heavily, and buried his head in his hands. Cavanaugh and the Zachariases gathered around him, and Cavanaugh signaled one of his gallery assistants to bring a bottle of champagne and glasses. When the glasses were filled, he handed one each to Mike and the Zachariases, raised his own and said, "To the artist, and to our good fortune to be a part of this unique moment."

Mike sipped his champagne, then said, "I'm pretty bushed. I'm going to excuse myself if you don't mind."

At that moment, a gallery attendant arrived, saying, "Mr. Pallaso, there is a Miss Collins here with your ride."

Mike attempted to hide his embarrassment and said, "Tell her I'll be there in just a minute."

“Ah,” said Cavanaugh gleefully. “So, Miss Collins has her talons in you already. Wonderful!”

Seeing the quizzical looks from the Zachariases, Cavanaugh continued, “Michael has met Cindy Collins, a young woman who apparently has charmed our young artist into a late-night affair of sorts.”

“Wonderful, Michael,” Mrs. Zacharias exclaimed. “I’m so pleased for you. I hope you have a wonderful time. You deserve it. Now, Mr. Zacharias, it’s well past our bedtime, so I suggest you get us to the hotel so we –I mean I—can get my beauty sleep.”

“Yes, dear,” Zacharias smiled. “Shall we plan on a late breakfast at the Hyatt, just to wrap things up?”

“Good idea,” Cavanaugh replied. “What about 10:30?” They all agreed and with hugs and kisses said good night.

Mike quickly excused himself and moved rapidly towards the gallery entrance.

Sitting outside, Cindy lounged comfortably in a late model Jaguar roadster and beckoned Mike to get in. As they drove off just below tire-peeling speed, she said, “Where are you staying?”

Mike looked quizzically at her.

“Relax, Mike. I thought since we were going flying anyway, we might as well fly to Jacksonville. We can stop by your hotel and get your stuff on the way to the airport. What do you say?”

“I think we need to slow down. I’m not sure where this is going. We just seem to be winging it without knowing how things are going to end up. If we don’t know where we’re going, we’ll never know if we get there.”

“Wow. That’s the most words I’ve heard you put together in the same breath since we first met. Mike, are you afraid of me and my wild ways?”

“Maybe. No. I just don’t trust how this might end up. You don’t know me. You don’t know how screwed up my head is. You don’t know how many people’s lives I’ve screwed up. It’s like I’m toxic. I should tell you to turn this thing around and dump me back at the gallery.”

Cindy pulled over to the curb but kept the motor running. She turned to look at Mike who stared straight ahead. She said softly, “But you haven’t told me to turn around, have you? You’re feeling the spark too, aren’t you? Take a chance with me, Mike. Let’s see if we can get this off the ground without crashing and burning.”

“Damn you, woman. I’m at the Hyatt on Peachtree.”

She laughed wickedly, put the Jaguar in gear and quickly jockeyed back into traffic. Shortly she had them sitting in the Hyatt's valet parking circle. "Hurry up," she said.

Mike stopped at the desk long enough to leave a message for the Zachariases regarding his change of plans, then waited distractedly for an elevator, wondering as he had so many times in 'Nam, how he had ended up in this place. With packed bag he returned to the idling Jaguar, tossed the bag in the back seat and climbed in.

"Wasn't sure I'd see you again," Cindy said. "Ready?"

"Yeah. Let's go. Just try not to kill us before we get to wherever we're going."

He grabbed the dashboard as she sped off, expertly maneuvering the sports car through the traffic. With a whoosh of breath, he finally acknowledged her skill at the wheel and managed to ease the tension in his back enough to half-way relax in his seat. He glanced at her, seeing the unconscious joy on her face as she drove and realized once again that he had lost control of his carefully structured life and was putting it in the hands of this beautiful, mysterious woman whom he knew nothing about.

He said, "You know, other than the little bit Cavanaugh told me and the few tidbits you gave, I know almost nothing about you."

"So, what else would you like to know? You know I'm crazy, would rather be in the air than on the ground, am passionate about the excitement of living on the edge, and lately have become an avid art connoisseur."

"Well," Mike said, "I guess that pretty much wraps it up. I do see a current parking sticker for Emory University on your windshield, so I guess you don't spend all your time in the air. That also tells me that you probably know how to read and write. So, when you're at Emory, what are you studying?"

She laughed as she turned into a gate allowing access to a private airplane facility including hangers, aircraft services and security. "Would you believe I've graduated with a major in anthropology and now I'm working on my master's, still trying to dig into somebody else's dirt. I know I'm no Margaret Mead, but I'm awfully curious about what makes this world tick, so I thought looking at our ancestors' cultures might give me a clue."

Mike, despite his continuing discomfort at losing control to this reckless young woman, nevertheless remained fascinated by her. "So what have you discovered about what makes this crazy world tick?"

"Hold on for a sec," she replied, "while I go in the office and do the paper work, check the weather, and all that crap so we can get off the ground. It won't take but a couple of minutes."

Mike watched her head into the office, paying more than a little attention to her rear end as she walked. No question about it: despite his continuing discomfort with the situation, he could feel his long-sleeping hormones beginning to stir.

CHAPTER 29

In less than five minutes she was back, saying as she climbed into the driver's seat, "We should be out of here in about ten minutes." She drove toward one of the hangers as its door was opening, and a gleaming single-engined aircraft began to be pushed out. She stopped about ten yards short of the aircraft and said, "There's my baby. Grab our bags; we can stow them in that forward hatch in front of the passenger door on the right."

With that, she climbed out of the Jaguar, tossed the keys to one of the maintenance people, and began a slow walk-around the aircraft, moving parts and peering into several orifices.

After a few minutes, she called to Mike. "Okay, let's get in the air."

She showed Mike how to strap himself in, then began an efficient pre-flight routine, checking a myriad number of gauges and switches before starting the engine. When satisfied the engine was running right, she called the airport tower to check in, identified her aircraft, and requested clearance for take-off.

In a matter of minutes, they were moving swiftly down a well-lit runway, and Mike felt the still familiar gravity change from Vietnam in his belly as Cindy lifted the Cessna off the runway.

At about 6500 feet, she settled back and said, "Now, where were we? Oh yeah, you wanted to know why a wild, senseless woman would want to waste her time in something called anthropology. Truth is, Daddy wouldn't pay for advanced flight school training at Embry Riddle, but he would pay for anthropology at Emory, which turned out to be a pretty neat school. Anyway, I began to dig anthropology."

Mike remained content to just listen to this fascinating intruder in his life. "And what made you get interested in anthropology?"

"Well, I've always wondered what makes people tick–what makes them behave the way they do. Anthropology has helped me look at how different cultures behave, and I've begun to see that, despite their differences, all cultures seem driven to behave by the same basic motivations."

He said skeptically, "Like me and the Viet Cong?"

She made some minor adjustments on the aircraft controls, then said, "Probably not a good idea to go there, but you might be surprised. Anyway, from what I've been able to see from my studies, people in all cultures –past and present-- seem obviously driven by an instinctive biological need to survive. And that need is so great it creates a primal fear of anything or anybody they think threatens that survival.

"So, fear of anything threatening his survival becomes man's primary motivation –the emotion that drives all his behaviors –good and bad. And we tend to hate what we fear, so hate has the potential to dominate the way we act. Just think of all the wars, all the killing, all the base behaviors that have dominated man's history and you can see how fear and hatred have driven our behavior toward each other."

Mike sat quietly, absorbing the depressing impact of what he was hearing. He thought about what had driven his paintings, the disturbing reality of the pain he had brought back from Vietnam and his own hidden fears. It was not a discussion he wanted to have, but helplessly heard himself saying, "What are you afraid of?"

She laughed. "I started to say nothing, but that would've been a stupid lie. The truth is, I don't know, or at least can't describe, what I'm afraid of. Maybe all my craziness is just a way of hiding my fears. Does that make any sense?"

"You're asking the wrong person about what makes sense. About anything. Like what am I doing up here a mile from solid ground with some wild woman I just met who's too crazy to be afraid of anything?" He sat staring out into the darkness, sensing more than seeing the steady whirling of the small propeller on which their lives depended.

Cindy looked at him, hearing the sudden tension in his speech.

Hesitantly, she asked, "What about you, Mike? What are you afraid of?"

For a long moment he said nothing, continuing to stare out at the propeller he couldn't see. Finally, he looked at her in the dim light of the instrument panel and said, "I don't know. Everything's all jumbled up in my head. It probably sounds crazy, but I think I'm always afraid of getting too close to good things in life. Because from what I've seen the rules in this crazy world say the good always has to be balanced by the bad." He shook his head. "I can't talk about this anymore."

"Okay. Didn't mean to upset you with my stupid chatter. I'll just shut up and fly this little plane. We should be in Jacksonville in about another ninety minutes or so."

He waved his hand in resignation without looking at her, feeling trapped in the small cockpit, and regretting letting himself be seduced into talking about the pain in his mind.

They flew in silence for the next few minutes until Cindy, unwilling to let the discomfort between them linger, said, "So tell me about Jacksonville Beach. What made you decide to go there to live?"

"No mountains, and there's a beach and an ocean," he said flatly. He knew he was being borderline rude with his terse response, but he didn't trust revealing more of himself to this woman in whom he was developing an uneasy attraction. He felt the irrational fear that he could somehow become a threat to her if he let her become important to him.

Cindy chose to ignore his moodiness. "I understand how the beach and ocean would be attractive. My family has had a summer place on the Outer Banks for years and I love the ocean. But why is flat an attraction? I mean I love to hike in the Piedmont hills and the Appalachians."

Mike looked at Cindy's profile. Maybe for the first time really looked. The earphones draped around her neck were slightly disconcerting, but they only added to the contrast of a beautiful woman totally wrapped in the kind of competence and assurance he hadn't seen since Gunny Morgan. He laughed at the thought, then finally responded. "I've seen too many hills going up into shit and coming down into more shit. I need to see where I'm going."

"I'm not going to get a straight answer from you, am I? But I've seen your painting, and your insides are vividly exposed. Only a complete fool could miss the complexity of your pain. Please don't shut me out. I feel a connection with you that's getting *my* head all screwed up. Can't you feel it?"

Mike met her eyes in a moment of intense nakedness, then looked away, feeling the shield of denial slowly falling away, to be replaced by a longing he had never felt before.

"Just fly the plane," he said. "Get us where we're going, even if you don't know where that is."

Cindy nodded and remained silent, not willing to touch the fragile moment. A short time later she called the tower at the small private airfield in Jacksonville requesting landing instructions. As she lined up for their final approach, Mike could feel the plane trying to yaw to the left as they began to settle, which Cindy corrected as though she and the small plane were one. "A little wind up here," she said. Shortly they were on the ground with scarcely a bump and she began taxing to a marked tie-down near the airport office.

As they climbed out of the aircraft, she stretched, smiled at Mike, and said, "Why don't you get the bags and call a cab for us while I check in at the office."

Mike nodded, then opened the forward hatch and gathered the bags. He walked into the office as Cindy was finishing arrangements for having the plane serviced and fueled for a Sunday afternoon departure. She pointed to the phone on the desk and mouthed "cab" to Mike.

CHAPTER 30

In about ten minutes the cab arrived and as they settled into the backseat Mike gave the driver directions to his apartment. On the ride to the beach, with no conscious thought on either's part, they sat with hands clasped together and Mike could feel the comforting sensation of her thumb rubbing possessively over the back of his knuckles.

As they climbed the stairs at the apartment, Cindy said, "I certainly hope you've got something stronger than a beer up here."

Mike unlocked the door and said, "Yeah, I can dig something up if you don't mind cheap bourbon." He swung open the apartment door, and they were met by the strong odor of paint and all the accompanying odors of his artwork.

Cindy wrinkled her nose, and Mike walked around throwing open several windows. They were blessed by a good breeze from the ocean and soon the smell was tolerable.

Cindy pulled off her flight jacket, then held out her hand to Mike in the shape of a glass. Mike walked to the small kitchen and pulled down a nearly full bottle of bourbon. He grabbed two tumblers, filled them with ice, then poured generous amounts of bourbon. "Water?" he asked.

"No way," she said, shaking her head vigorously. "This is definitely a no water night."

She took a generous swallow, sighed almost contentedly, then began wandering about the apartment. "So where are your masterpieces?"

"They're all at the gallery. I only have a few unfinished ones here."

"Well," she said in a tone Mike would only be able to describe as a mental foot stamping, "can I see them? It's the least you can do to pay for the ride down here, although maybe not the only thing," she said wickedly.

Mike took a large swallow of bourbon himself, suddenly glad for the diversion of the unfinished paintings from the sexual tension beginning to grow in the small apartment. "They're in the spare bedroom. Give me a minute and I'll get them."

Shortly, Mike brought out three partially completed canvases and arranged them against a wall of what would have been the apartment's dining room before he had converted it into a small studio. He turned the lights up for better viewing and Cindy walked slowly in front of the array. Finally, she pointed to the one in the middle. "I want that one. How much, and when will you have it finished?"

The painting was a variation of one he had once given to the Zachariases, a vertical explosion of crimson in the shape of a blossoming flower, with tendrils of yellow and black streaking out from its center.

He walked to her side and stood looking broodily at the tall painting, remembering still the feeling of life being sucked from his lungs by the fierce, compression of exploding munitions.

"Why?" he said, continuing to stare at the almost completed painting. "Why do you want this one?"

"Am I allowed to say I don't know for sure? It's just… haunting, somehow. I think I see in it a strange contradiction. I mean, I know it's supposed to be a depiction from your mind of the deadly explosiveness of war, but at the same time I think I see… I don't know, an explosive rebirth of some kind."

She touched his arm lightly and stared up at his bearded profile. "Does that make any sense?"

The electric warmth of her touch startled him and for an instant he was unable to respond. He saw the sincerity in her eyes and felt his carefully built defenses against any caring relationship beginning to crumble.

"If it does," he responded, "it wasn't conscious. I never saw any rebirth over there. Only death and dying." But If you want the painting, it's yours. It'll take a couple of weeks to finish then I'll ship it wherever you tell me."

"Oh, I want it! Tell me how much and I'll write you a check before I leave."

"We can talk price later. I really don't know what it's worth. Right now, I could use another drink. You want one?"

"Yes, please. But first I need to use your john. Where is it?"

Mike pointed to the bedroom door. "Through there. You'll see it. Ignore the mess."

She smiled her thanks and moved quickly to the bedroom.

Mike went to the kitchen and refreshed their drinks, wondering as he poured the bourbon what was going to happen next. He thought he knew what all the vibes between them said could happen, and he marveled at what he felt sure would be an unforgettable night. He forced himself not to think beyond that.

Forty-eight hours before he couldn't have imagined he might be beginning a romantic relationship with a beautiful woman. In fact, he reminded himself, he had vowed strongly since returning from Vietnam to avoid any attachment, fearing the toxicity of that place might poison anyone he dared care for. Now the irrationality of that mindset was about to be displaced by a different irrational possibility, one he was growing powerless to resist.

He shrugged with both resignation and anticipation as he took a large swallow of the undiluted bourbon. He heard the toilet flush and anticipated seeing Cindy reappear momentarily. Except she didn't. He heard nothing and saw nothing for several minutes and curiously picked up her drink and his and walked to the bedroom door.

He saw her standing at his dresser holding his collection of dogtags in hand, slowly shuffling through them, reading the names of the dead Marines.

"What are you doing!?" he demanded.

Startled, she looked up, frozen by the pinched anger in his face and quickly put the dogtags back on the dresser. "I'm sorry. I didn't mean to pry, didn't mean to upset you."

Mike turned abruptly and walked into what passed for the apartment's living room. Cindy followed, calling softly, "Mike, please wait. I had no idea my looking at those tags would upset you. Won't you tell me what's going on?"

He stood staring at nothing out the room's single window, hands clinched in white-knuckled fists.

Cindy walked hesitantly to his side. "Mike. Please. Tell me what I've done. I don't understand. One minute I thought… well, I don't know what I thought, but something good seemed to be happening between us. But suddenly you're filled with anger because I touched those tags. It doesn't seem to be me you're angry at, but somehow my touching those tags has set you off. I just don't understand. Talk to me, Mike."

He turned to her abruptly. "Wait here," and stalked into the bedroom, returning shortly with the dogtags clutched in his hand.

He pulled the first tag from the pile in his hand, saying. "PFC John Kirillo. Eighteen. Fire team member, First Squad, First Platoon, India Company. Killed 2 October 1967, Con Thien.''

He pulled a second tag. "Corporal William Parks, Nineteen. First fire team leader, First Squad, First Platoon, India Company. Killed 2 October 1967, Con Thien."

"PfC Harry Lynch. Eighteen," he read from a third tag. "First Squad, First Platoon, India Company. Killed 2 October 1967, Con Thien."

Cindy realized, watching Mike, that he had no need to read anything but the name on a tag. After that he recited, in a dead voice, all the other details of the young men's deaths.

Mike continued to sort through the tags, reciting the same stark details for each: name, unit, date of death, place of death. He finally finished with Philly, saying, "PFC Charles Phillips, Twenty. Second team, First Squad, First Platoon, India Company. Killed 21 January 1968, Khe Sanh."

"Mike, what's going on? Are these the friends you lost in Vietnam? I don't understand."

"Weren't you listening?" he demanded. "They were all in the same squad, the First. My squad. I was their squad leader. They died because of me! I was supposed to lead them, to keep them whole while we rooted out the NVA! And these were the ones that went back in body bags. Never mind the ones who went back without legs or arms or brains!"

"Oh, Mike! You're carrying around all this terrible burden, and I had no clue! She jumped up and rushed to him, sweeping her arms around his chest. He stood there, unable to acknowledge her, with arms hanging down, the dogtags dangling from his fingers.

Cindy clung to him, feeling the rapid beat of his heart as he stood in the nakedness of his guilt.

Finally, she said, "Mike, what about all those other men in your squad? Did they survive? Did you keep them alive?"

He remained standing, closed to her entreaty. "No. Luck kept them alive. It wasn't leadership. It wasn't me."

"So," she said, "it was your poor leadership that caused those young men to die or suffer terrible wounds, and just luck that kept the others alive?"

He heard her pointed logic, but the guilt he held in his hand was too heavy to lift. He said in a muffled tone, "That's right. My poor leadership got those people killed. And dumb luck kept the rest alive."

Ignoring his resistance, Cindy pulled him to the couch to sit beside her and gently took the dogtags from his hand. She gathered his face in her hands, demanding that he look at her. "Mike, I don't know what I can do to make this terrible anguish go away, but please let me help you. You seem to be carrying this guilt around with you as some kind of punishment for what happened over there. But you didn't kill those men. The enemy did. War did."

"No, you just don't understand!" He picked up the dogtags and rattled them in anger, saying, "Here's proof. I'm poison for anyone who gets near me. I still see their faces in my nightmares and hear their cries. I can't add anyone else to the list. You should leave before I poison you!"

"Mike," she said, grabbing his hand to quiet the rattling of the tags, "I'm not afraid of you. I'm afraid *for* you, but not afraid *of* you. I'll leave if you really want me to, but then we'll both just be running away. Trust me. Let me help prove to you your fear is unreal." She stood and pulled him to his feet. "Put these tags away in a safe place and bury their memories. And then let's go find out if what we're feeling for each other is real."

Her touch as she led him into the bedroom seemed a soothing balm, washing away the guilt that had surfaced so quickly with the tags. Then, as she turned and pulled the spread down to the foot of the bed, a long-simmering passion began flooding his mind, washing away all thoughts but the promise of what was to come.

She turned back to him, reached up and laced her hands around the back of his neck and whispered, "Mr. Pallaso, I'd really like you to put your arms around me and kiss me."

CHAPTER 31

Mike woke to the smell of coffee perking and felt the empty side of the bed. He stretched languidly, noting with surprise how rested he felt. He lay with eyes closed, reliving the night with Cindy, knowing he had never before experienced the passion they had known. It had begun with gentle kisses and explorations but built quickly to a blinding passion, finally ending in a climax that left them exhausted. They had fallen asleep in a spooning embrace, but during the night woke to new arousal, culminating in an explosive repeat of passionate love-making. Deep sleep came to him then, a sleep he had not known since before Parris Island.

He slipped on a pair of shorts and padded to the kitchen door. He watched Cindy standing at the stove with her back to him, cooking bacon while she blissfully hummed some music that sounded like the Air Force hymn. She wore one of Mike's tee-shirts with unconscious grace, occasionally brushing a stray strand of her hair from her eyes as she turned the bacon.

Watching her, Mike felt sensations of unfamiliar contentment and a residual uneasiness battling for dominance in his mind. He had let this beautiful creature into his life and experienced unbelievable joy, but at what price? What peril was he placing her in by letting her into his toxic life?

She turned from cooking the bacon, sensing his presence, and gave him a mischievous smile. "I was coming to wake you shortly. How did you sleep?"

"Like the dead, the happy dead. What about you?"

"It was a marvelous night. First time sleeping with a man. You snore beautifully. Think you could eat some breakfast?"

"God, yes. I'm famished."

She walked to him with a steaming cup of coffee. "You can start with this, but first I'd like a taste of last night. May I have a kiss?"

He pulled her to him and they were lost for a moment, entwined together starting with a gentle kiss that quickly grew to passionate proportions.

She pulled back, laughing, and said, "Keep that up and you'll be eating black bacon and eggs. Take your coffee and go sit down. How do you want your eggs?"

"Any way you want to fix them, as long as I can sit and watch you."

"You animal," she said with mock severity. "All you care about is my body. What about my brain?"

"Brain? You have a brain?"

She threw a wadded-up paper towel at him and turned to the refrigerator, bending over with a saucy shake of her behind.

Mike groaned. "Stop, woman, or we'll never get any food."

"Poor baby," she laughed. "Scrambled eggs coming up. Meantime, just close your eyes and think about last night."

She busied herself with finishing the breakfast preparations while he sat reliving not just the night of lovemaking but all that had preceded it the evening before. He still couldn't believe he had allowed this raven-haired beauty to knock down all his carefully constructed defenses, his vow not to allow anyone to become a victim of his caring. He felt uncertainty eating at the edge of his consciousness even as he sat basking in the happiness of the moment in her presence. His thoughts were interrupted as she approached the table with two plates piled with eggs, bacon, and toast.

"Okay, Mr. Pallaso, breakfast is served. But I was disappointed you didn't have any strawberry jam. We'll need to get some."

He quickly dove into the meal with unashamed hunger and it was several minutes before the implications of her comments about the strawberry jam registered with him. It smacked of a commitment to a relationship he'd not had the courage to consider. He looked across at her with fork and knife poised in mid-air as he tried to absorb what he'd heard.

She looked at him with a puzzled smile. "What? Do I have egg on my face? What're you looking at?"

"Your beauty. And trying to grasp what's going on here, with us."

"Mike, are you feeling happy? If you are, as I am, then that's all that matters right now. We'll just take it slow and see where that happiness takes us. Okay?"

He nodded. "Works for me. What would you like to do after breakfast?"

"I don't care, as long as we do it together. What do you do on a Saturday morning?"

"I like to walk on the beach. Let's do that."

She beamed. "That sounds great. Give me a minute to clean up the kitchen and brush my teeth and I'll be ready."

"I'll help with the kitchen," he said and grabbed up their plates. In minutes the kitchen was presentable and shortly they stood side by side in the bathroom brushing their teeth and laughing at each other in the mirror.

When they reached the beach, it was low tide. They stood for a moment watching the waves curl to the shore. Cindy reached for his hand, brought it briefly to her lips, then whispered, "Feel the happiness surrounding us? I'm right where I want to be right now, even if we're on the ground and not in the air. What about you?"

He looked down at her upturned face, nodded and gently kissed her lips. "Let's walk," and they set out on the packed sand with a determined stride.

That afternoon they spent napping and in languid love-making. Finally, hunger overcame them, and they walked to a small Italian restaurant where they ordered veal parmesan and a bottle of red wine, the name of which neither could pronounce.

They sat in silence, waiting for the meal to be served, with Cindy caressing the top of his hand. "What are you thinking?" she asked. "You've gotten so quiet, even for you."

He looked away for a moment, unwilling to break the spell they were in, but still feeling restless from the uncertainty for the future they might experience. The fear he had brought back from Vietnam had not relinquished its hold on him, despite the contentment he was feeling. He could not shake the certainty that bad stalked the good.

"I'm just thinking about where we go from here. Is there a future for us? What happens when you fly away tomorrow?

"Mike, remember what I said about the happiness we both have been feeling, being together like this? Why can't we trust our instincts that this happiness will lead us together to more happiness? I want to continue experiencing the joy of being with you, and I hope you want the same. Besides, my airplane knows the way back here."

At that point, their waiter brought the wine and two glasses, and after Mike nodded his approval, poured a full portion of wine in each glass. Cindy raised her glass in a toast, saying, “To our future, wherever it might take us, including to the edge.”

CHAPTER 32

Mike stood watching the Cessna gathering speed down the runway, slowly lifting into the afternoon air and then beginning a banking turn towards the northeast. He continued watching the sky even after the plane became a speck and then disappeared.

On the drive back to the beach he tried to sort his thoughts about the past three days into some coherent pattern, but coherency evaded him. Instead, random, disconnected thoughts bounced around in his brain in a strange pattern of their own, providing flashes of love and passion one instant, then denial and fear the next.

He fought to rebuild his armor of uncaring detachment that had crumbled so easily from the onslaught of her joy and enthusiasm for life. He failed, however, left instead with a cautious contentment that the future might be promising a happiness he had lost all hope for. He dared to ignore the lingering fear that the good he was feeling continued to be stalked by the bad.

Cindy and he had agreed she would fly down again in two weeks for the weekend. In the interim he'd work on completing her painting. By Wednesday of that week he had added the finishing touches. He stood critically, examining it for any blemishes, feeling stupidly anxious, anticipating her approval. It reminded him of how deeply he had allowed her to invade his psyche in the short time they had known each other.

He found enough busy work to help pass the time before she was due to fly back down. When she landed and exited the plane he managed to restrain the desire to rush to her side, choosing instead to wait at the office door, not certain that he hadn't misinterpreted where their relationship stood. She ignored his hesitancy and wrapped him in a tight embrace.

She leaned back, pinching his belly mischievously as she looked up at his wincing face. "Miss me?"

"Maybe. We can go find out," he said, and kissed her welcoming lips.

They finally broke breathlessly, and she said, "I'll take that as more than maybe. Grab my bag while I check in with the office, and then see if you can make that truck fly."

They filled the weekend with passion in the bed, long walks on the beach, and a laughing Saturday afternoon drinking beer and playing intensely competitive pool at a local bar called Pete's. That Sunday morning they enjoyed a late breakfast at the apartment, with Mike half-listening in lazy contentment as Cindy chatted away. It wasn't until she began talking about improvements they needed to make in the apartment, such as new curtains for the windows, maybe a better breakfast table, a floor lamp for the living room, and so forth, that he began to pay full attention.

Up to that moment he had been able to stay fully focused in the present, unconsciously ignoring thoughts of a future in their relationship. Now the possibility of that woke a wariness in his mind, a sudden need to pull back.

The weight of those thoughts was too heavy to be unnoticed by Cindy. She put down her coffee cup and stared curiously at Mike, seeing the curtain that had suddenly dropped down on what a moment before had been a happy smile of contentment on his face.

"What?" she said. "What did I say? Suddenly you were gone. You're still gone. Was I assuming too much, with my prattle about fixing this place up? Oh, God. I feel like such a fool. I thought we were on the same page, that we were feeling the same vibrations. I guess I was wrong."

She got up from the table, gathered the dishes and walked to the sink. She resolutely began rinsing the dishes. "Maybe I can get an early start back to Atlanta. I should be ready in about an hour."

Mike sat in stoned silence, torn between the guilt of realizing how he had managed to hurt her and what he thought was a rational belief that she would be better off if he could put distance between them.

But the guilt was too great. His feelings for her too strong. He pushed back his chair abruptly and walked over to stand at her back, wondering how he could explain his feelings to her. Tentatively he placed his hands on her stiff shoulders.

"I'm sorry I upset you. It's just that things between us seem to be moving so fast. I'm afraid to trust it. I came back from Vietnam believing that good things can't happen without bad things. It's stupid, I know. But that's the way I'm wired right now."

She leaned back against him, placing her wet hands on his. She turned to face him and put her hands behind his neck, kissing him softly.

"I'm sorta wired funny, too. I can't stop pushing the envelope. I can't stop feeling we're close to where I want to be with you. Why don't we call a truce? Let the future take care of itself. "

They stood embracing each other tightly, Mike resting his chin on her head, eyes closed in surrendered resignation. His desire for her, despite the warnings circling in his brain, was too strong. He couldn't find the strength to push her back from the edge. Instead, he leaned back, brushed a strand of hair from her moist eyes. "Why don't we go do some shopping this morning? Get some curtains and other stuff to fix this place up."

"Mike, come on. I got carried away this morning. We don't have to go this way. I'm sorry if I pushed too hard. Let's just go for a walk on the beach."

"No, I'm serious. We can spend the morning arguing about fabric and colors, or whatever couples do when they're playing house."

"Is that what we are? A couple?"

"I really don't know what being a couple feels like, but yeah, I think we must be. You want to be a couple?"

She leaned back so she could look him full in the face. "I don't think this is something you talk yourself into. And I'm not sure it's something *you're* fully committed to yet, whatever you think being a couple means. I keep feeling there's a lot of push-pull between us, like you can't decide what you want out of this relationship, or what the next steps should be."

Mike took a deep breath, running his hand through his hair, wondering how he could respond truthfully without creating hurt feelings.

She saved him from replying, saying, "I said let's call a truce and slow down. We're not sure where this is going, and I don't think you know where you want it to go. I'm a big girl, and if disappointment happens, I can take it. In the meantime, this place could still use some fixing up, so okay, let's go shopping and see what playing house feels like. Okay?"

He smiled his relief and pulled her to him. "I'm pretty stupid. I'm sorry. I guess you know you've gotten yourself mixed up with somebody missing some cards from a full deck. Maybe you can help me find them. In the meantime, let's go shopping."

Late that afternoon he watched the Cessna lift off, heading back to Atlanta. In the back of his truck were packages of window curtains, curtain rods, a small kitchen table and a floor lamp for the apartment's tiny living room. His assignment for the two weeks before Cindy returned was hanging curtains, house cleaning, and rearranging furniture. He also planned to start a new painting. As he drove back to the beach, he thought they might not be a couple, but they seemed to be acting like one. He knew he was already missing the possessive warmth of her arm around his waist, her hand in the back pocket of his jeans as they had walked around the local Pic N' Save, and he allowed himself a feeling of cautious contentment.

CHAPTER 33

One afternoon, a few days before Cindy's next visit, he received a letter from Cavanaugh, to which he had attached an article from the latest issue of the *Art World* magazine, written by Anthony Beloise, titled "Extraordinary New Talent of Abstract Expressionism."

Cavanaugh's note said, "I couldn't wait to share this with you! I told you I was sure Beloise was taken with your work. I just didn't realize how much until I read his article. Please call me after you have had a chance to read it!

Beloise's article began:

Recently, I had an opportunity to view the work of an extraordinary new talent in abstract expressionism at John Cavanaugh's gallery in Atlanta. His name is Michael Pallaso and I, quite frankly, found his work breath-taking.

What he has done with colors, despite their being primarily dark and somber in tone and with shapes beyond unique, was astounding. None of his paintings were titled, yet each was distinct from another, even though there seems to be a repetitive theme in them. When I asked him what informed his vision he said, "It's a pattern in my mind over which I seem to have almost no control. It is as though an alien being occupies me and demands to come out on my canvas. I can't say it's a pleasant feeling, but I know I feel relief when I'm able to splash the canvases with it."

I asked him where the extraordinary mix and use of colors –the dynamic blend of oranges, reds, blacks and yellows, with the subtle mix of whites and deep blues—comes from. He responded, "It's something over which I seem to have almost no control –as though my brain has a mind of its own."

Pallaso, in this interview, was very unassuming, seeming to be totally surprised by the high level of excitement his work has created. I cannot predict with certainty what the future holds for this young man and his art, but I feel certain the art world will be astounded by the extraordinary beauty and passion he is able to put on canvas. Some may think him a modern-day Jackson Pollock, but I think he will go far beyond that. He is truly uniquely sui generis!

For your viewing pleasure, I have included color photographs of his paintings that were displayed at John Cavanaugh's gallery. But don't bother trying to see them up close or attempt to purchase one. I have it on good authority they've all been claimed. And no, I was not quick enough to put my name on a sold tag nor could I have afforded one anyway. But fear not. I am sure that there are more in the works.

Mike sat in shocked silence, reading the article over three or four times. Finally, he picked up the phone and dialed Cavanaugh's number.

Cavanaugh's secretary answered, and when Mike told her who was calling, she said, "Oh, Michael, Mr. Cavanaugh was hoping you'd call. I'll tell him you're on the line. Wasn't that a wonderful article by Mr. Beloise?"

Before Mike could respond, she had put him on hold, then Cavanaugh came on the line. Excitedly, he exclaimed, "Mike, what a wonderful article, totally unexpected from such a stern art critic as Andrew Beloise! Tell me: What do you think?"

Mike replied, "I'm dumbfounded, as I have been by the whole experience. But tell me: What the hell is '*Sui Generis*'?"

Cavanaugh laughed explosively. "Michael, that's Latin, meaning unique. It was Beloise's clever way of saying your art is uniquely unique! Now, you best get busy with your next paintings. I feel certain I'll be getting numerous calls after people read Beloise's article. Congratulations, Mike. I'll talk with you soon."

Mike sat rubbing his forehead with the silent phone, as jumbled thoughts coursed through his mind. What did it all mean, these transforming events –Cindy, most of all, and now, fresh evidence that his art was being seen as unique by those who should know? Dare he risk believing that his life could be changing so dramatically for the good? Could not some ultimate evil be lurking, waiting to slap him down, laughing manically at his stupid ignorance? Clearly, he would need to keep his guard up.

He tossed Cavanaugh's note, with Beloise's article, on the telephone's side table, realizing he needed to get to the airport to meet Cindy's flight.

At the airport they embraced with their usual fervor and walked arm in arm to his truck. Cindy snuggled against him in the truck cab, saying, "So how much have you missed me, Mr. Pallaso?"

"More than you could ever know, woman! I've counted the seconds."

Despite his pronouncement, as astute as she was to the atmosphere around them, she sensed a reticence. "How come you're so pouty, Mr. Sour Puss? What's got you wound up when you should be wound up with your arms around me?"

Mike was quick to squeeze his arm around her shoulders as he steered his truck onto Atlantic Blvd. "Why do you think something is going on? Why 'sour puss'?"

"Listen, Mister, I think I know you. What's got you up tight?"

Mike was astonished by her sense of him, even though she had no way of comprehending the depth of his confusion. He decided on denial as his best strategy. "Nothing's going on, my beautiful lady. Just can't believe I'm so lucky. So glad you're here with me."

That seemed to satisfy Cindy as she snuggled more deeply into his arm. "So, what exciting things do you have planned for us this weekend? Are you planning to sweep me off my feet with another round of pool at Pete's, or try to get me into a week's worth of love-making in a week-end? I vote for the week's worth!"

Mike, unable to stay distant from her enthusiastic wantonness, laughed in happiness. "Motion carried, unanimously. Hope we have enough time left over for eating."

"You goofball. I'm so glad to be here with you. Seriously though, what's going on in that silly head? I feel like you're hiding something, When I first got here, it felt like you were mentally pushing me away, like you were afraid I had a disease, or maybe you had one you didn't want to give me."

Mike again relied on denial. "I think you've sucked up too much oxygen on the way down here. There's nothing going on in my silly head except visions of you in bed with me. Now shut up and let me drive this bus."

She sighed with feigned contentment, snuggled closer into him, and whispered, "Just wait till I get you in that bed. You'll be sorry you've been so insulting to me."

Mike found himself driving at a fevered pace, anxious to rid himself of all the negative thoughts he had been experiencing, willing himself to surrender to the love he was feeling with Cindy by his side. Only a whisper of continued dread wormed its way into his head.

When they arrived at the apartment, Cindy ran quickly up the stairs, leaving Mike to follow with her bag. She pushed the apartment door open and teasingly said, "Oh, you even straightened up the place for my arrival. How sweet. Just put my bag on the bed while I try to think of an appropriate tip for you."

Mike grinned wolfishly, saying, "Yes ma'am," as he passed by her into the bedroom.

While she waited, Cindy glanced around the living-room, nodding approvingly at Mike's efforts to straighten up for her arrival. She noticed the letter from Cavanaugh on the phone table and feeling only slightly nosy, glanced at the writing and the accompanying article by Beloise. She dispensed with all nosy guilt and read both Cavanaugh's note and Beloise's article with growing delight.

"Mike," she hollered. "You weren't even going to mention this!"

"What? " he said, as he sauntered back into the living-room.

"This letter from John Cavanaugh and the article by Beloise. You're a famous artist! And I discovered you first! She grabbed his arm and pulled him toward the bedroom. "Now I have to find a way to congratulate you. Forget the tip!"

They stumbled into the bedroom, pulling off each other's clothes as they fell into bed.

CHAPTER 34

The following months were filled with Cindy's frequent fly-ins almost every weekend. They followed a routine of exploratory strolls around the beach community, intimate walks on the beach even when they had to brace against the chilling winds of late fall nor'easters, and of course, hours of passionate love-making. And there were times when Mike was deeply into a painting and Cindy would sit watching him for hours as he moved around a canvas in focused creativity, armed with palette, knife, brushes gripped in his teeth and looks of frustration.

In the beginning, their times together were a source of continuing bliss for Mike, knowing he was falling deeply in love with this exciting woman, and finally beginning to believe that thoughts of their having a future together were legitimate.

But in time, the fear he had kept at bay in his subconscious, that evil would demand its ransom for the good, began to stalk him anew, drawn by the scent of his happiness. It was the over-powering fear that evil would ultimately strike those he cared for as it had so many times before.

With increasing frequency, he would wake from a fitful night lying beside Cindy, rise quietly and go to the box in which he stored his collection of dogtags. He would finger the tags as he would a secret talisman.

On the mornings following those fitful nights he would sit morosely at the breakfast table, nursing a cup of coffee in a detached mood. Cindy would at first try to ignore his mood, although she found his indifferent behavior more than a little irritating. She tried to disguise her feelings with aimless puttering in the kitchen and chatter about plans for the day, to which Mike remained unresponsive. Cindy would pass it off as the moody behavior of the artist fighting creative block, and as the day progressed, Mike would usually become more human.

In between their weekends together, Mike tackled his painting with a desperate effort to empty his mind of the paralyzing fear for Cindy that had begun to consume him. The logical part of his brain tried tirelessly to convince him that his fear was irrational –even crazy. That it made no sense that his love for her could possibly put her in danger. But the craziness dominated his mind, wrapping it in constricting tentacles of fear.

He attacked his canvas (actually a four-by-eight-foot hard wood board) with fury, attempting to follow Zacharias' prescription that the pain in his mind could be oozed down his hand through his brush and captured on his canvas. Instead, as he threw paint onto board, he could only see irrational visions of skeletons begging for absolution.

The painting became a layer of oozing Vietnam mud covered over by a grey sludge of sky slowly moving across the horizon like a ridge of rain-laden mountains. Interspersed in the sludge were red and yellow specks with no form or substance save their vividness of color, like peace in the midst of pain. Above the ridge of sky-mountains flashed distant explosions of dark yellows, reds and purples, as though the skies themselves spewed anger.

Exhausted, Mike could only stare at the finished painting with no sense of what had squeezed from his brain. He only knew, contrary to what Zacharias had predicted, he had no sense of calm, no peace. He had only turmoil, trying to make some sense of the conflict between the love he felt for Cindy and the fear for her it generated.

That night he woke, drenched in sweat, unable to escape from a gut-wrenching nightmare in which NV shells were bombarding Khe Sanh in a fierce barrage. The night was rocked with ear-shattering explosions, interspersed with the cries of wounded and dying. Despite the fiery noise of the attack he heard the frightened cry of Cindy, calling, "Mike, Mike, where are you?!" He looked up from his bunker to see her running across the exploding landscape of the combat base.

"No! No! Cindy! Get down!" He had shouted. But she had continued to run, only to be swallowed up in a gigantic explosion, leaving only a deep hole where she had been standing.

He finally was able to throw himself from the bed and stumble into the bathroom where he knelt over the toilet with the drive heaves. After an immeasurable amount of time he rose, threw water on his face and went in search of the bottle of bourbon. He poured a water glass full and sank onto the living room couch where he spent the rest of the night, eaten up with the sure knowledge that the nightmare was a harbinger of the danger he was surrounding Cindy with his love for her.

CHAPTER 35

On about her tenth weekend down, Cindy brought a large cardboard storage box with her. Mysteriously, she refused to give any explanation for its purpose to Mike, simply urging him to quickly carry it up the apartment stairs. Inside, she opened it, revealing numerous items of clothing and a handful of hangers.

"Here," she said. "Find me a space in your closet and help me hang these up."

He moved robotically, taking the clothes from her, sensing an irrational fear that events were quickly falling out of his control. He was letting Cindy get too close, but felt powerless to avoid it.

As they finished hanging the clothes she said teasingly, "I hope you don't mind. My closet was getting too full."

He smiled dutifully as she stepped into his arms, finding it impossible to ignore the heating passion of their closeness. Later they walked the beach, eventually ending up at Pete's Bar where they drank beer and shared pizza.

The next morning, after another sleepless night, Mike rolled over on his side next to Cindy, staring at her sleeping, peaceful face. He wondered how she could be so ignorant of the poison surrounding them. Somehow, he had to make her aware of the danger she was in. As she stirred into wakefulness she looked with alarm at the pain in his eyes. She rose quickly on her elbow, saying "Mike, what's wrong? Are you okay?"

He flopped back down, staring sightlessly at the ceiling. "So where is this going with us? What's happening? Are we going to have a future together?"

"My God, Mike! What do you think has been going on for the past months? I fly down here almost every weekend to be with you. We spend hours together, not to mention in bed. And next week we're scheduled to fly up to meet my parents. Where do you think we're going? You getting tired of me? Is there someone else?"

"God, Cindy. How could there be anyone else? It's just my mind. I'm all screwed up. Afraid to trust the good."

"Damnit, Mike," she cried, leaning over his rigid body. "All we've known together has been beyond good. Can't we trust that?"

He pulled her close, breathing in her early morning fragrance then pushed her back to stare into her eyes. "God-damnit, Cindy. Don't you see? It seems like everyone I've ever cared for ends up dead, or gone, or mangled. I can't stand the thought of something happening to you!"

"Mike, can't you see how irrational your thinking is? What happened to you in Vietnam has nothing to do with us, with our future together. I don't know what I can say or do to chase these demons from your head. All I know is, I'm afraid your fear will destroy us. Do you think you need to talk with someone?"

"You mean like I'm crazy or something?"

"I don't know what I mean, Mike. You're not crazy. We both know that. But maybe there's someone who can help."

Mike pushed away from her, climbing from the bed. "Ah shit, Cindy. My mind's so fucked up. You know I love you, but I feel like there's vultures sitting on a limb just waiting to drop down if they sense the way I feel about you."

She lay back down, clutching the sheet in frustration. "So, Michael, what do you want? Where do you want us to go from here? I can't take this back and forth, this pulling and pushing."

"Cindy," he shouted, "you need to get away from me! Can't I make you understand? The more I love you, the more I'm afraid for you. You need to just run away, get away from me before you die. I need you to go. My brain says I need to stop loving you!"

Cindy sat up, hands clutched together between her knees, tears rolling down her cheeks. "Oh, Mike, you *are* sick. How can you think that what you feel for me is a poison apple? How can you believe that what we have shared is nothing but a roost for death to come swooping down on us? I can't stay here, wondering what grotesque distortion of reality you will think of next. Either you love me, or you don't. Do you love me, like you say you do, or are you more in love with your pain, your guilt?"

"I need you to go, to be safe. I know I'm crazy, but I can't stop thinking that if we're together then you are only a step away from the poison I bring to those I care about. And those I care about the most are in the most danger."

She slammed her knees with balled fists in a growing rage. "Fuck you, Pallaso! You're right. I need to go. There's no way I can stand this craziness, this pain. I came here filled with love for you. With the happiness we were sharing. Now it's all dying, strangled by the absurdity of your fear. I'll gather up my stuff and be out of here in just a few minutes. Call a cab."

She stormed into the bathroom, leaving Mike feeling crazy relief . He heard her sobbing, "shit, shit, shit," as she slammed her toiletries into her overnight bag. She came out of the bathroom wrapped in a large bath towel, not looking at Mike. "Would you please leave," she murmured, "So I can get dressed."

"Cindy," he began…

But she demanded, "Just leave."

He left, heading into the kitchen where he automatically put on a pot of coffee. He stood at the sink as the coffee perked, staring sightlessly through the new curtains he had hung the weekend before.

Shortly Cindy entered the kitchen carrying two carelessly packed bags, wearing only a smudge of pale lipstick, with her hair in a ponytail held in place with a black rubber band. She was dressed in blue jeans and a stark white blouse.

"Did you call a cab?"

"No. I thought I'd drive you into the airport."

"No," she answered brusquely. "I prefer a cab. Never mind. I'll call." She dialed the phone and gave the address. Then she said, "I left some money on the dresser. It should cover the cost of shipping my clothes in the closet up to Atlanta. I'd appreciate if you'd take care of that."

He nodded, feeling the sudden emptiness in the apartment, with all the air sucked out . Only the certainty of danger, irrational as it might seem to those who hadn't walked in the swamp of his mind, sustained him in the agony of losing her.

They stood in isolation from one another, Cindy in her anger, Mike in pain-filled resolution. The sudden beep of the taxi horn stirred them into an unspoken finality. Cindy shouldered her bags, looked one last time at him with a shake of her head, and walked out the apartment. Mike could only watch her go with an odd mixture of pain and determination to see her safely gone.

He heard the taxi drive away, its fading exhaust signaling an ending of a fear that had been swallowing his mind and the beginning of a grief he could not have imagined. He grabbed a knife from a kitchen drawer and began slashing his recently completed painting, finally kneeling in exhaustion with tears dripping down his cheeks.

Finally he stood, threw on a pair of shorts, and ran bare foot down the apartment stairs and on to the cobble-stoned road heading to the beach, unmindful of the pain on his feet being inflicted by the rough surface. When he reached the beach, he turned north into the wind and began a three-hour, chest-bursting dash down the beach. It ended only at the jetties, built to guide the St. Johns River into the sea. He thought, as he stood on the jetty rocks, that the river seemed unable to wait to drown itself in the sea. He envied the river its release.

At last, he turned back, facing the south and began the slow trudge back to where he had entered the beach miles away, unconscious of the relentless, unending wash of waves attacking the shore.

CHAPTER 36

He was refilling a large tumbler with straight bourbon late that evening when the phone began to ring. He had no desire to talk to anyone and walked out onto the small veranda, trying to ignore the insistent ringing for his attention. The ringing stopped abruptly and as he took a large swallow of bourbon he began to imagine who had been calling . He almost wished the phone would ring again so he could quiet his curiosity. He was startled then by the phone beginning a new round of demands.

With resignation he took another large swallow of bourbon, went back inside, picked up the phone and placed it at his ear, saying nothing.

Zacharias said, "Michael, is that you? Are you there?"

Mike answered in a voice devoid of feeling. "Yeah, I'm here. What's going on?"

"Michael, I just got a call from John Cavanaugh. He just got a call from Cindy, saying she was in a hospital in Atlanta. She had an accident earlier today driving back to her apartment and has a concussion and two broken ribs."

A cold chill spread across Mike's chest and he realized he'd stopped breathing. He was struck with the paralyzing thought that evil had once again come to collect its due.

"How… how is she?"

"According to John, she says she's just banged up and probably would be discharged in a couple of days. John said it was a strange conversation. She didn't want her parents to know –she gave John as next of kin—and didn't want you to know. What's going on, Michael?"

"We've broken up," he said tersely. "What hospital is she in?"

"Michael, I've already broken a confidence by calling you. Do you think you should try to go up there?"

"Just tell me where she is, god-damnit!" he shouted.

"Alright, Michael. She's in Mid-Town Emory hospital in Atlanta. Just so you know, John talked Cindy into calling her parents, so I expect they'll be there soon."

"Okay. Gotta go," Mike said, and hung up the phone. He stood for a moment, unable to get past the omen of evil Cindy's near-miss represented, knowing without doubt that his decision to send her away had been right. Still, he had to go and make sure she was okay.

In less than thirty minutes he was cranking his truck and tearing out into the darkness. He made the drive to Atlanta in just over six hours. Quick directions from a gas attendant took him to the hospital, where he sat in the parking lot waiting for the published visitor hours to begin.

The energy that had brought him to Atlanta overnight had washed away, leaving him unable to make sense of why exactly he had come. With Cindy's leaving as she had, he was left with a feeling of not belonging here. That he had, in the process of freeing her from the toxicity of being with him, severed any rights to see her now. Resolutely however, he finally settled on the need to make sure she was okay.

He entered her room without knocking, afraid he would be banished if he announced himself. Cindy looked up with astonishment from a dispirited effort to coax a piece of pineapple from a fruit cup on to her spoon.

Several emotions flashed across her face at the sight of him, but she quickly settled on an angry dismissal. "What are you doing here? Did you come to gloat, to say 'I told you so'? Well, you're right. You did cause this. Because I was so angry and disgusted I didn't pay attention to my driving. I guess I'm lucky the plane found its way back to Atlanta. Now please leave."

He stood, flinching at the verbal whipping. When she took a breath of anger, he said quietly, "Are you okay? That's what I came to find out."

She laughed derisively. "Do I look okay? With my head wrapped in bandages and my ribs bandaged so tight I can't breathe? But not to worry. They're letting me out tomorrow, thank God. Prisoners get better food than they serve here. Now please go. I don't need you moping around here. If I'm lucky the pain pills'll knock me out. By the way, tell your buddy John Cavanaugh thanks for keeping a secret. Now go." With that she turned painfully so her back was to Mike and he couldn't see her tears.

Mike stared at her back, feeling the verbal stabs as he had felt the elephant grass slicing his face so many months ago. He murmured, "Cindy, I'm sorry," and eased out of the door, still feeling the conviction that he had done what had to be done.

He found a motel not far from the hospital, planning to catch up on his sleep and waiting to make sure Cindy was discharged the next day. Sleep proved evasive. He lay on the hard mattress, tossing and turning most of the day, finally giving up and going to find a meal and a beer.

After a tasteless sandwich and two beers he drove back to the hospital parking lot with no purpose in mind but to be close to her.

He dozed off and on through the night, cold but accepting the discomfort. At about eight-thirty that morning he watched a cream-colored Cadillac sedan arrive at the main entrance of the hospital. A lovely older woman exited the car while the driver remained. In a few minutes she returned walking beside a wheelchair in which a bandaged Cindy sat. The driver quickly went to Cindy and gave her a fierce hug, then helped her out of the wheelchair and into the car. Obviously her father, Mike thought, as the Cadillac drove away. It would be the last time he would see Cindy, and he sat in miserable silence as the realization sunk in.

His drive back to the beach passed in a hypnotic state, broken only by requirements of the bladder and gas tank. He arrived as a late nor'easter began demanding penance from the shore with whipping winds and smashing waves. Mike trudged up the apartment stairs with a blinding headache, aching for a large glass of alcohol, only to find a near-empty bottle of bourbon, left from Cindy's departure. Instead he stripped off his clothes, slipped on a pair of shorts and stumbled down the apartment stairs to the beach.

Rather than run the beach as he had so many times before, he chose to sit at the shore line as the intensity of the waves grew. Soon he was soaked, but felt nothing, sitting stoically as the waves began buffeting him.

He stood finally, and with a last look back at the dunes, began plowing through the waves toward the disappearing horizon. He walked until his feet no longer could keep his head above water, letting the rushing waves wash over him. But suddenly, his feet touched bottom again, raising his head above the waves. He had stumbled upon a hidden sandbar, and now the waves were only crashing against his chest.

He had failed. Failed to join all those to whom he owed a final allegiance, those whose tags he had held so close for so long. He turned with total dejection back towards the shore, looking for, but finding nothing that would give him a sign of finality, of peace.

That evening, dressed uncaring in only a tee-shirt, shorts and sandals, he drove to the local VFW with no purpose but to drown the devils swimming in his brain and raise a salute to those whose tags he still held. He dared not think of Cindy, nor the sacrifice he had made for her. Thus began a nightly ritual that would slowly turn him into a ragged caricature of himself, a derelict of the man he had tried to be. He became a near hermit, maintaining only the minimum accoutrements of a civilized life. During the day, after a rugged hour in the early morning running the beach, he would spend the day throwing gobs of paint on large canvases.

The paintings repeated his earlier themes, but were darker, more foreboding than any he had previously completed. When he attacked his cavasses, he did so with an artistic viciousness, slinging paint-filled brushes and pallet knives with no plan, no script. Yet there appeared a vision of repeating pain and desperation, of death and destruction born from the demons in his mind. And unlike Zacharias' predictions that those demons would seep from his mind, they stayed, demanding of him a penance he could not give.

Calls from Zacharias and Cavanaugh went unanswered and their letters piled on the floor along with overdue bills. Mike had no mental life preserver to which he could cling that would keep him from drowning in his anguish.

PART TWO

THE PROMISE OF DAWN

SAVING GRACE
CHAPTER 37

Months went by with a daily ritual of exhausting runs on the beach, intermixed with defiant dashes into the deepest waves, followed by slashing attacks on canvas, ending with evening visits to the local VFW for jiggers of raw bourbon and beer chasers.

At the end of his fifth month of self-flagellation, as he was returning from his morning run, Mike passed a tidal pool that he had not noticed when starting out. Now, in the brightening light of dawn, he stopped, alerted by the splashing sound and movement of numerous small bait fish in the pooled water. They seemed to be moving in a frantic effort to get back to the freedom of the ocean, only to be blocked by the lip of the pooled water.

Mike stood watching the fish in their frantic efforts and couldn't ignore the memory of Zacharias' aquarium and the irrational back and forth crazy-eight pattern that the iridescent-colored fish had been swimming. He remembered Zacharias' sobering lesson that he –and everyone swimming in the pain of darkness and loss-- were like the crazed fish in its frantic effort to find a way out.

Now, he was back swimming his own crazy-eight pattern, without direction in a hopeless effort to escape his pain. He sadly shook his head, feeling a vague sense of shame and self-ridicule as he continued his slow trudge back to his apartment.

One Sunday evening, as he was following his usual path back to his apartment from the VFW down the doubled-laned A1A highway through the center of the beaches, he found himself behind a lumbering dinosaur of a church school bus. He was in no hurry and assumed the bus would be turning out of his way soon into one of the small churches clustered ahead just off the highway.

Suddenly he heard the full-throated roar of what had to be a souped up muscle car behind him, impatiently waiting to zoom out into the left lane to pass him and the slowing church bus. A small opening in the traffic in the lane opened up and the roaring muscle car dove out from behind Mike, clearly intent on passing him and the bus. But when the impatient driver of the speeding car turned back into the slower lane, he misjudged the clearance in front of the bus, causing the bus driver to slam on his brakes and jerk the bus sharply to the right. The bus's front wheels slammed into the curb, causing it to crash onto its left side, shattering windows as it slid to a crunching stop.

Mike slammed on his own brakes and skidded to a stop close behind the bus. It was then he heard the frightened crying of children, some screaming for help. He ran to the back door of the bus, but found it wedged shut. He ran back to his truck, thinking a tire iron might help pop the door free. As he ran he smelled the unmistakable odor of fire, and memories of flaming Khe Sanh flashed through his mind.

He threw open the truck's tailgate and wrenched the tire iron free of the accumulated rubble in the bed. He dashed back to the bus in a frenzy, driven by the increasing terror of the trapped children and the spreading smoke and flames. He managed to wedge the tire iron in between the door and the bus frame and somehow found the strength to force the door open. Screaming children, most seeming to be of middle school-age, began scrambling out of the opened rear door. Mike stepped aside momentarily, then climbed in the smoke-filled bus to look for any who might still be inside.

He found three huddled in between seats and hustled them to the back of the bus. Then he saw the bus driver, slumped unconscious half-way out of his seat. He grabbed the small older man by his belt and dragged him to the back of the bus and handed him to others who had begun rushing to the scene. Then one of the children shouted, "Grace! Where's Grace?" Then several other children also began shouting, "Grace is still in the bus!"

Mike grabbed one of the older children and demanded, "Where was she sitting?"

"In the front, I think."

He turned back to the bus and clambered in, feeling the scorching heat from the flames and the choking, acrid smoke. He called "Grace! Grace!" as he worked his way forward. Then he bumped into an arm hanging down from one of the seats near the front of the bus. He froze for a moment, believing he was smelling the smell of death. Then in panic he followed the young girl's arm to the rest of her limp form, yanked her up and stumbled for the back door, gasping from the overpowering smoke from the bus.

He leapt to the street and rushed to the easement grass, gently laid the girl down and began calling her name. He slapped at her face, trying to coax consciousness. She remained comatose, her face beginning to turn a purple hue of gone. He pinched her nose, forced opened her mouth and began driving his air into her inert body. After a few forceful breathes he shifted to her chest, demanding with each push, "Dammit, Grace, get some air in you!"

He worked on the girl's chest, oblivious to the noise of the other children, staying focused for any sign of life. Miraculously, Grace gave a weak sound of coughing and began to drool a thin liquid from the side of her mouth. Instinctively, Mike stopped pressing on her chest and turned her on her side so she couldn't choke on her own vomit.

Grace continued to breathe and choke spasmodically, then raised her arm to her chest, crying "That hurts! Momma!"

The children standing around her began to cheer. Mike sat back, mentally exhausted by what had transpired in the last few minutes. He slowly became aware of the crowded, noisy scene around him. He and the children were surrounded by fire and rescue vehicles and at least three police cars. A fire emergency technician put a hand on his shoulder. "Good job, man. We'll take it from here."

Mike nodded and stood up, mentally drooping from the sudden depletion of adrenaline he had survived on for the past ten minutes.

He stumbled away, shaking his head in disbelief as the whole scene developed around him. He felt a strong grip on his arm and heard a voice say, "Come on, Sarge. We got lots of people who'll take care of things here."

Mike looked up to see the face of retired First Sergeant Meadows, a frequent drinking companion at the VFW and a patrol sergeant with the Jacksonville Beach Police Department.

"Shit, First Sergeant. Get me outta here. I don't need all this."

"Got ya', good buddy. Where's your truck?"

Mike looked around, then numbly nodded at his truck, still parked a dozen yards behind the bus.

After a few questions about how the accident happened, Meadows said, "Okay, Mike. Go get in your buggy and di di outta here. I'll stop by your place in a couple of days and get an official statement. You did a great job tonight. Saved a lot of lives. You really are a hero."

CHAPTER 38

Sgt. Meadows showed up early, stomping up the apartment stairs as Mike was finishing his third cup of coffee. The past two nights had been a restless battle between exhaustion and intense emotions. The emotions had won, as he relived the bus accident in a tangled nightmare with dangling dogtags rattling an accusing dance of guilt in his face.

He answered the knock on the door from Meadows with a twist of the door lock, then walked back into the kitchen, trying to ignore the presence of the First Sergeant.

"Mike, you doin' okay?" Meadows moved into the small kitchen space, picked up the coffee pot to weigh its remains, then glanced expectantly at Mike for a cup. Mike nodded toward the cabinet where he kept spare cups.

"Okay, Mike," Meadows said, as he filled his cup. "Let's get this crap outta the way. Tell me what happened with the bus crash," he said, pulling out a pad and pen.

"Hell, you know what happened. The bus crashed after some asshole cut in front of it. Everybody got out okay. I think. What about the kid named Grace? She gonna be okay?"

Meadows put his pad away, saying, "You're about as helpful as cow shit in a pasture, Mike. I'll make something up. The little girl, Grace, looks like she's gonna make it, thanks to you. She's got a concussion, a broken arm, and a couple 'a cracked ribs. But she'll be okay. The driver's gonna be okay, too. And he keeps wanting to know who pulled him out of the bus. And the pastor of the church keeps demanding to know who they have to thank for saving all their children."

"You kept your mouth shut, right, First Sergeant?"

"You know I did, Mike. But it's gonna get out. You're not exactly a stranger around here."

"Shit. I don't need this."

“Too bad, Marine. The world needs its heroes. And you fit that definition. You gotta’ deal with it, Mike.”

Mike stared away into the distance, twirling his empty cup in a wobbly pattern without direction. “Where’s she at? Where’d they take her?”

“Who? Who you talkin’ about?”

“The kid. Grace. Hell, I don’t even know her last name.”

She’s at Beaches Baptist. Supposed to be there about a week. Her last name is Phillips. Grace Phillips.”

Mike abruptly stopped breathing, staring at Meadows in shocked silence at hearing the girl’s full name. “Did you say Phillips?”

“Yeh. Grace Phillips. Why?”

Mike shook his head in confused denial. “No reason, I guess. Just reminded me of someone I knew.” In truth, hearing the name Phillips had pounded his brain with the memories of Philly in the sawgrass of ‘Nam. He could not get past the incredible coincidence that one Phillips had died in his arms so long ago, and now another had returned from death’s door, each calling for their momma.

He looked stupidly at Meadows, who had quickly sensed his confusion, but not able to make any sense of it. “Mike, what the hell is going on? Are you gonna be okay? Are you crashing on me?”

“No, I’m okay. But I’d like to go see her. It’s important. Can you arrange it? Can you get me in to see her? Today?”

“Mike, there’s no problem with you seeing the girl. What’s the big deal?”

“I need to see her.”

“I’ll set it up. But you know what, Pallaso? You’re really nuts sometimes. Meet me at the hospital’s front door at three this afternoon and I’ll get you in to see her. Now I don’t know what’s going on in your head, but you make damn sure you’re sober.”

CHAPTER 39

After Meadows left, Mike wandered about the apartment, trying to shake free from the irony that the young child he had pulled from the bus had the same name as Philly. What was the connection? Was there a connection, or was it nothing more than the continuing crumbling of his brain?

By early afternoon, Mike couldn't stay still any longer and drove to the hospital. He sat, moodily, in the truck cab running over the events of the last forty-eight hours. He hoped there wouldn't be any more public involvement for him and chastised himself for even trying to see Grace. Still, his mind wouldn't let him ignore the fact that the girl and Philly had the same last name. It was leading him down a path that had no beginning or ending or meaning he could comprehend.

He jumped at a sudden rapping on his truck window, seeing the smiling face of Sgt. Meadows. He rolled down the window to hear Meadows say, "I figured you'd be here early. Just surprised you're still out here 'stead of already banging on that kid's door. You were tighter than a tiger in a cage when I left this morning."

"Can we go in now? Is it too early?"

"Yeah, we can go in now, but first, I think you need to see this," Meadows said, and held up a copy of that day's beach edition of the Jacksonville Journal, with a front-page headline that read:

LOCAL ARTIST SAVES 15 CHILDREN AND DRIVER FROM BURNING BUS.

Mike stared in bewilderment at the paper, then grabbed it and began reading the story:

Michael Pallaso, well-known artist living in Jacksonville Beach, became a hero to fifteen young children and an injured driver as he saved them from a crashed and burning church bus Sunday evening in Jacksonville Beach.

Witnesses said they saw Palasso wrench open the rear door of the wrecked bus as flames began licking from the bus, enabling most of the frightened children to escape. Then according to witnesses, he leapt into the bus and found two more children huddled in the wreck, whom he led to safety. He then reentered the bus and brought out the unconscious driver. Finally, after hearing the children say one of them was missing, he ran back into the bus to search for the missing child. Witnesses said he reappeared shortly, carrying the unconscious child to the easement, where he began administering CPR. After a tense few minutes, the injured child began to recover. At that point, police, fire and rescue arrived to care for the children and driver and extinguish the burning bus.

Meanwhile, Mr. Palasso disappeared, and no one at this paper has been able to contact him.

Mr. Palasso has lived in Jacksonville Beach for several years. He is a decorated Marine, wounded in Vietnam. He began his artistic career with a wildly successful one-man show of his jarringly beautiful canvases and has since been called the second Jackson Pollock, the world famous American abstract expressionist from the 1950s.

Mike re-read the article, feeling an increasing anger he couldn't define, except as an invasion of his privacy. He tossed the paper across the truck's cabin with palpable anger, then said, "Fuck. Who's the big mouth? You, Meadows?"

"You better back off, Sergeant. I already told you I haven't said anything to anybody! From what I've heard, a reporter for the Journal was at the accident scene and talked to someone who knew who you were. What's the big deal, Pallaso? You hiding something? Don't want someone to know you are here ? Little late for that, buddy. Now, you want to go see Miss Phillips or not?"

Mike sat in silence for a moment, not sure what he wanted. He knew his seclusion was blown, but as comforting as it had been, he felt a compelling need to see the girl, to know she had survived. He cracked open the truck door, pushing Meadows aside. "Let's go."

"You're still wired tight. She doesn't need that, Pallaso. You pull yourself together, or I'll yank you outtta there. Got it?"

"Got it, First Sergeant."

"Just so you know, her parents are here and they know who you are. They know you're coming."

"Understand. What floor's she on?" Mike said impatiently as he began searching for an elevator.

"Second. God-dammit, Pallaso, take it easy. Her parents don't need to see a wild man, and neither does she."

An elevator finally arrived and Mike began pushing the second-floor button in impatient demand. As the door opened, a couple began to enter, then quickly stepped back to let Mike and Meadows step off. The woman said in surprise, "Oh, I know you. You're Mr. Pallaso. You saved our daughter," and she grabbed Mike in a crushing hug. "Thank you. Oh, thank you."

Meadows, quickly sensed Mike's confusion. "Mr. and Mrs. Phillips, This is Mike Pallaso. He wanted to come up and see how Grace is doing."

Mr. Phillips grabbed Mike's hand and shook it vigorously. "Man, we owe you so much. You saved our Grace. There's no way we can thank you enough."

Mrs. Phillips interrupted. "John is right. There's no way we can thank you. But I know a young lady that wants to try. Please go in and let Grace tell you how thankful we all are."

Mike could only nod, knowing he could find no words to explain to these people why he was there to see Grace.

Mrs. Phillips moved with him to the door to Grace's room. "Grace, there's someone here to see you," and gently pushed Mike through the door.

The young teen appeared swallowed up by the hospital bed, bandages and casts as Mike stepped to the foot of the bed. He was startled to see how physically diminished she appeared, yet there was a surprising alertness in her eyes.

She looked thoughtfully at Mike, then said, "You're the one. I remember the beard. I didn't like the beard because it scratched my face when you kissed me. And it hides your face."

"Maybe I'm just too lazy to shave."

"No. I think you're hiding from something. Sometimes I feel like hiding, too. But I can't grow a beard. So I have to smile even when I feel like crying."

Mike felt like he had just stepped into quick sand, listening to this young girl who seemed to have lost the need for any filters between thoughts and words. Her survival seemed to have triggered her need to speak the visual and mental reality that had been revealed to her by the proximity of death.

He stepped to the edge of her bed and offered his hand,. "I'm Mike, and I know you are Grace. I guess you could say we're kissing cousins."

She giggled as she grasped his large hand with the fingers of her heavily-cast right hand. She held on to his hand for a moment, saying, "Momma said I should be sure and thank you for saving my life. So, thank you."

"I'm glad I could be there. So, tell me about yourself, Grace. How old are you, what grade are you in, and what do you do for fun?" Mike couldn't believe he was actually pumping this girl for hints of Philly. That he was actually thinking his spirit might be imbedded somewhere in her.

"I'm almost fourteen and if I stand up tall and straight I'm almost five feet two. I'm in the eighth grade. For fun, I like to draw, especially animals. And no one's ever saved my life before."

"Well, I guess we're even then. I've never saved anyone's life before, either. But I like to draw, too and paint, although I'm not very good with animals. Maybe I could see some of your drawings sometime."

Grace nodded. "I have a whole book of drawings. And I got some blue ribbons for some of them in my class. My daddy says when I'm fifteen he's going to get me a horse for my birthday. Did you ever have a horse?"

"No. We didn't have room for a horse when I was growing up. But I like them, and I'd like to see your drawings. When you get better, can I come visit and see them? Maybe we could even paint one of your drawings."

She visibly brightened at the suggestion. "You mean with artist paint and brushes and everything?"

Mike smiled, feeling the tension in his neck and chest begin to ease hearing the life and excitement in this girl who had been almost lifeless only days before. "Sure. I'll teach you how to use all that stuff, and we'll paint a beautiful horse. But you have to get well first. You can't paint with a broken arm."

She smiled smugly. "Silly. I'm left-handed."

"What?! So am I! But you still have to get the rest of you well, okay?"

She yawned and slowly closed her eyes. "Okay. But you have to shave so I can see your face."

Mike stood looking down at the girl who had suddenly appeared in his life. Thoughts of Philly began to recede into the back of his mind, displaced by the knowledge that he had saved this young person. Was her life, somehow a rebirth, a moment of redemption for some of the madness of 'Nam? He didn't know, couldn't untangle the confused knots in his brain. He only knew that a peace, one he hadn't known for years, had begun to settle over him. He reached down and lightly brushed hair from her eyes.

At that moment Grace's mother walked into the room and smiled at the sight of the bearded young man gently touching her daughter's face. "How did she do? Did she behave herself?" She laughed. "Sometimes she engages her mouth before she puts her brain in gear. She can be impetuous."

"No, I think we got along well. I hope you don't mind, but I told her I'd come visit when she got better, maybe even give her some painting lessons."

"Oh, that would be wonderful. We'd love to have you come anytime you wish. Here, let me give you our address and phone number." She gave him a sheet of note paper, saying, "We live in Atlantic Beach, out towards Mayport. Call when you're ready to come and I'll give you directions." She reached out and touched his arm. "We will never be able to repay you. We are so grateful you were there to save her life."

"Mrs. Phillips," Mike said cryptically, "She may have saved my life as well," and turned quickly to the door, leaving her with a look of puzzlement.

CHAPTER 40

On his way back from the hospital, Mike spotted a drugstore and impulsively pulled in. He returned moments later from the store carrying a bag containing a razor, shaving cream and hair clippers. Back at his apartment he began the painful effort of stripping six months of hiding from the world. When finished, a strange face stared back at him, one he had not seen since before he had begun spiraling down into his self-imposed hell. The 'face staring back at him seemed puzzled, as though seeing an alien world for the first time, unable to see anything recognizable.

He struggled to comprehend what was happening to him because of the bus accident, and more specifically from the events with Grace. He wrestled with the absurdity he felt from thinking the children from the bus he had saved, especially Grace, might actually represent a chance for redemption for all those he had lost in Vietnam. But despite the irrationality of such thinking, he continued to circle back to it, reaching for expiation, even now, after all these years later.

He reached into the cabinet for his bottle of bourbon, wanting to quiet his mind with the opiate he kept always within arm's reach. But after opening the bottle, preparing to take a familiar first swallow, he stopped midway to his lips, and resignedly put the bottle down. He could no longer ignore the recurring need for true absolution.

Something was happening in his brain. Forces, alien thoughts over which he had no control, had invaded him, demanding he seek clarity. Thinking Phillips might be speaking to him through Grace could well be just the reasoning of a mad mind, but he could no longer take the risk of denying the possibility that it was a moment of truth. He put the bottle away untouched, collapsed on his rumpled bed and finally slept.

The next morning he woke early, feeling surprisingly energized. He felt the strange nudity of his face but ignored it as the calmness from his meeting with Grace continued to settle over him. He quickly fixed a rare breakfast of eggs, bacon, and toast which he consumed ravenously, then rushed to his truck to drive to the local art supply store. Soon he left the store carrying a supply of oil paints, brushes, a palette and several framed canvases.

He knew it was too early for Grace to be home from the hospital, and too early for him to invade their privacy with his need to reconnect with the injured girl. But his restlessness drove him to search his apartment for distraction, which finally resulted in his beginning a charcoal image of Grace, with her curious, demanding eyes, heart-shaped face, and eyebrows in fixed arcs of expectation.

Soon he had his palette thick with oils of pink, white, blues and yellows and began filling in her face with an amazing likeness from his memory of both her quiet features of near death and the aliveness of her resurrection in the hospital. And without distorting her likeness and with only his fading memory, he saw a vision of Philly's last breath in the sawgrass of Vietnam.

At the end of the third week following the bus accident and his completion of Grace's portrait, Mike could contain himself no longer and called the Phillips to invite himself over. He was met with bubbling enthusiasm from Mrs. Phillips who invited him to come right over, plan to stay for dinner, and gave him detailed directions to find their home.

He checked himself in the mirror, still feeling strange to see his shaved face staring back at him. Then he gathered up his presents for Grace, including her portrait, and pointed his truck in the general direction of the Phillips' home. He had no problem following Mrs. Phillips' directions and soon arrived at a pleasant tree-lined driveway that led him back to a multi-acre property looking like a horse farm surrounding a comfortable ranch-style, single story house.

Before he could knock, the door was opened abruptly by a smiling Grace, her eyes darting back and forth between his shaved face and the packages in his arms. "Did you bring the paints and brushes? What's in the wrapped package? Are we going to paint today? I like your face without the beard!"

"Grace!" her mother called as she opened the front-door wide. "Where are your manners?" Mr. Pallaso hasn't even had time to come in the house." She smiled broadly at Mike and reached for his hand. "Please come in, Mr. Pallaso. We are so glad to see you and please excuse Grace's lack of manners."

"Please call me Mike. And I'm very pleased to be here and to see Grace looking so well. How much longer with the cast, Grace?"

"Two more weeks! And then I'm free to do whatever I want."

"With permission, Missy." Mrs. Phillips said, winking at Mike. "Now, Mr. Pallaso… uh, Mike, come on into the kitchen and put those packages down. Would you like a beer, or we have something stronger if you like. And please call me Rebecca, and Grace's dad is John."

"Okay, Rebecca. Please don't go to any trouble for me, but a beer would be fine. And maybe Grace and I could see what's in these packages."

"Maybe you should. She's been dancing around here like a one-legged chicken since she heard you were coming. Grace, help Mike carry the packages into the den while I finish getting this roast ready. Daddy should be back shortly, then we can all sit down and visit."

Mike followed Grace into the den, each of them carrying an arm-load of the packages he had brought. Grace began ripping several of the packages open, chattering away as she did so: "I know what this is," she exclaimed. "A palette for mixing paints. And look at all these brushes. And there must be a dozen tubes of paint. When can we get started?"

"Easy, Grace. Maybe we'll get started after dinner. Right now though, you promised to show me your drawings. Where are they?"

"In my room. I'll get them," she hollered and dashed away. She arrived back shortly carrying several drawing pads which she proudly handed to Mike.

Mike began thumbing through the pages, noting with some amazement the artistic talent this young teenager showed. The many drawings, depicting horses in various poses, showed her focus on meticulous detail, resulting in a surprising focus on accuracy and realism.

She stood impatiently next to Mike as he slowly turned the pages, anxiously watching his eyes for signs of approval. Mike finally closed the last of her books, conscious of her nervousness. He looked at her face, screwed up tightly in painful impatience, and said, "Beautiful, Grace. Truly beautiful. I wish I could draw horses like this."

She collapsed on the sofa next to him, letting out a long-held breath. "I'm glad you like them. I was afraid you might think they were just little-girl pictures."

"I don't think you were really afraid of that, Grace. An artist knows when her work is good, and you are certainly an artist. Now, let's look at what else I brought to help you get started painting." He pulled out an easel, set it up, and then placed a framed canvas, about two by two-and-a half feet on it.

"Now, what's the first thing you think we should do?"

She shrugged. "I don't know. The canvas looks sorta dull. Should we paint it?"

"Exactly. Hand me that can that says Titanium White, and one of the big brushes. Now here. You brush this on the canvass."

She began brushing the paint on, tongue sticking out of the corner of her mouth in concentration. Watching her, Mike felt the same calmness settling over him that he had been experiencing since leaving her at the hospital. Like she was some kind of amulet. He thought it ludicrous to think that, but held on tightly to the feeling for stability.

"There," she said, proudly as she put a final stroke on the canvas. "How's that look?"

"Looks fine. Good job. Now would you like to see what a finished painting might look like?" He began to unwrap the portrait he had done of Grace, then paused as John and Rebecca entered the room. John came over to Mike and shook his hand firmly. "Welcome. So glad you could come see us. Grace has been beside herself with excitement."

"I've been pretty excited myself. I've looked forward to seeing her healing up."

"So how's the lesson going? I see a canvas set up already."

"We're just getting started, looking at some of the mechanics of painting, but I was about to show Grace what a finished painting can look like." Mike unwrapped the portrait of Grace he had done and handed it to her, as her mother and father gathered around her.

"Oh, my heavens!" Rebecca gasped, while John stared at the beautiful likeness of his daughter. Grace stood in rigid surprise, her face contorted in quiet concentration as she studied the face staring back at her, almost with an artist's critical appraisal.

"Where did you get a picture of me to copy?" she asked.

"Didn't have a picture, except the one up here," he said, pointing to his temple.

"Mike," John finally said, "the painting is so perfect. You have captured our Grace just as we often see her, with those beautiful black eyes looking off at somewhere or something only she seems to see. The only thing you missed is her tongue sticking out of the side of her mouth."

"I'm glad you like it. It was fun to do, even if I did feel sort of rusty. It's been a while since I've done any serious painting. But Grace what do you think? Do you like it?"

She continued to study the portrait, tongue sticking out the side of her mouth in typical concentration before finally replying, "Yeah, I like it a lot, but there's something different about it, like something a little strange staring back at me, something I don't see in the mirror. I mean the eyes are mine, but, oh, I don't know…"

"Grace, "Rebecca admonished her. "Where are your manners?"

"Yes ma'am. Than you, Mr. Pallaso."

"You're welcome," he answered reflexively while his mind wrestled with her comments about something strange in the portrait. He thought back to what he had been feeling as he painted her face, the vision he had of Philly's last breath. Mentally he shook himself and said, "I'm glad you like it, Grace. And if it's okay with your mon and dad, why don't you call me Mike? After all, kissing cousins should be on a first-name basis," and winked at her with their private joke.

Her face turned crimson as her parents looked at her with puzzlement, waiting to understand what they had just heard.

Mike interjected quickly. "It's just a little private joke we had in the hospital, referring to when I was giving her CPR. She said my beard had tickled her face when I kissed her."

The Phillipses laughed in embarrassment at the thoughts that had tumbled unbidden through their minds at the phrase 'kissing cousins.' Rebecca said, "Grace calling you Mike is fine. Now I need to go check on the roast."

Mike and John smiled at each other, both feeling the happiness of the moment filling the room.

John said, "Let me get some fresh beer. Be back in a second."

"Grace, why don't you get your sketch book and sketch one of your favorite horses on the canvas now that it's dry. Try to keep it the right size for the size of the canvas."

She looked at him with raised eyebrows and he nodded reassuringly that it was a good next step. With that she sat down with her latest sketch book and began thumbing through its pages, tongue in its usual place. Soon she chose one and began a careful outlining of a horse's head, its ears pointed forward in a curious expression.

Moments later, Rebecca called, announcing dinner. Mike and Grace reluctantly rose and moved to the dining room table, where platters of delicious smells lured them to find seats. John placed a fresh beer at Mike's place and then, with everyone seated, Grace reached out and took Mike's hand, momentarily surprising him until he realized all were holding hands as John said a prayer. He was even more surprised to hear Grace whisper, "And God bless little John," at which all said "Amen."

Mike had no time to consider Grace's addition to the prayer, as plates of roast beef, mashed potatoes, carrots, peas, and rolls began to be passed, but it lodged in his brain .

After dinner, when the table had been cleared, everyone joined in the family room to watch Grace put the final touches on her sketch of the horse's head she had drawn on the canvas. Mike gave his approval and then talked briefly with Grace about next steps, the most important of which --to Grace-- was putting paint on the canvas. She was beside herself with excitement, picking and then discarding various brushes, and grabbing tubes of paint with a clear intention of loading the palette.

Before Mike could interrupt, Rebecca said, "All right, Miss Grace. Back up. Look at the time. Tomorrow is school and it's time for you to get your shower and get to bed."

"Mother!" she protested. "I need to paint my horse!"

"No. What you need to do is go get ready for bed. Now tell Mike good night, kiss your father, and scoot."

She stood in front of the canvas, turned away from her mother, holding onto the palette and a hand-full of tubes in a rigid, semi-defiant posture.

"Grace," John said softly. "Say good night."

With a great sigh of resignation she said "Yes, sir," gave him a perfunctory kiss on the cheek, then turned to Mike, mumbled "Good night," and stalked off to her bedroom where she closed her door with slightly more force than was probably necessary.

Mike and the Phillipses smiled at one another and Rebecca said, "Sorry, Mike. As you can tell, our daughter is turning into a full-blown teenager. Speaking of which, can you believe she'll be fourteen this Wednesday and John has a special surprise for her. Tell him, John."

"What do you know about horses, Mike?"

"I know the back end from the front, but that's about all. Why?"

"Don't know if you've heard of an Appaloosa, but it's an unusual looking breed, full of splotches of color, some of them looking like they'd been painted by a drunk artist. Here, I've got a picture of one."

Mike mentally flinched as he took the photo, hearing John's reference to a drunk artist. Looking at the horse and its random daubs of browns, blacks and whites, he saw the similarity to his own abstract canvases and admitted they, like the Appaloosa, looked like the work of a deranged artist.

"Anyway," John continued, "that's a picture of the surprise Grace is going to find in our barn on her birthday. She's a four-year-old mare that I found, fully saddle-broken and well-trained. She's used to kids and is gentle with them. Cost me an arm and a leg, but it'll be worth it to see the look on Grace's face when they meet. Especially with the near miss with the bus crash. Hope you can join us on Wednesday, Mike."

"I wouldn't miss it for anything. Thanks for including me. Look, I got to be running, but before I go, you mind if I ask you something? It's about what I heard Grace say at the end of the prayer we said at dinner. Something about 'little John'. She seemed pretty intense. Was this a pet or something?"

John's face closed with pain, eyes slipping away to stare off in silence. Rebecca, her own face clouding over with watery eyes, reached out and gently touched John's arm. She said to Mike, "Little John was… is our second child, John Andrew Phillips, Jr. We lost him two years ago, when he was six, to leukemia. He and Grace were so close. She mothered him, even when he didn't want it. Like us, Grace was devastated when we lost him. Now, even after two years, not a day goes by that John and I don't grieve for him. We tried everything, every doctor, but nothing was good enough. We keep asking ourselves why we are still living, and he is gone.

"However, lately, after the bus accident, I think we've begun to realize that our place is here with Grace. We have to focus on her, no matter how strong our guilt is for losing John. And we've seen a change in Grace since the accident. She seems to be coming out of the shell she's been in. I don't know what's going on in her head, but she keeps talking about John as though he's still here, keeps telling us that he's okay."

Mike sensed the grief consuming the room. It had an all too familiar fragrance, like dried blood, and he felt a momentary loss of equilibrium as though a shell had burst overhead. He held his hands together, elbows on his knees, staring at the floor lost in a place of his own remembered grief. Finally, he said, "I'm sorry. I didn't mean to upset you. I'm really sorry for your loss. Now I better go before I find any other way to put my foot in my mouth. John and Rebecca, thank you for including me in your family."

They rose as he did, she giving him a strong hug while John gripped his hand with both of his. They stood arm-in-arm in the door as Mike cranked his truck, waving a final good-bye as he drove down the pine-bark covered drive.

CHAPTER 41

Driving back to his apartment, Mike found himself in a surprisingly calm state of mind. The warm interaction he had enjoyed with the Phillipses and with Grace had been one of the most pleasant times he had experienced in a period too long to measure. Strangely, he felt some comfort knowing that they seemed to be dealing successfully with their loss of little John, that they were able to move on with living, if for no other reason than for Grace.

It was a stark reminder of how he had failed so miserably, for so long, in dealing with his own sense of loss, first from Vietnam, then Peter, then Cindy--how he had indulged in a year-long period of self-pity.

When he arrived back at his apartment, he saw the ignored accumulation of mail spilling from his mailbox and resolutely decided to clean up the mess it was making at his door step. He gathered up the pile and began glancing at the individual pieces, quickly separating them into piles of *ignore*, *must do* -such as final notices on overdue electric, phone and water, and *curious*, for later attention. This final category included several letters from Zacharias and Cavanaugh he had previously ignored, certain they would again be chastising him for his self-destructive, drunken existence. There was one other letter, addressed to him in a strong cursive style, with no return address save *Cindy.*

He sat down heavily on the couch in the living room, clutching the letter in apprehension. Why, after all this time was she writing to him? Was she dredging up what should have been long-dead ashes? Or were they not dead, but only smoldering, waiting for a wind of loneliness to ignite them again? And with that thought, his lingering fear that he might kill --with caring--surfaced. He grasped the envelope in both hands, tempted to rip it in half before he could be enticed to see its contents. But longing proved stronger than fear, and he ripped the envelope open and began reading:

Dear Michael,

You're probably as surprised to be reading this as I am to be writing it, but the truth is you've never been far from my thoughts. Even though I didn't see it at the time, I've finally realized that we were always ships passing in the night. That we were too far apart to stay together. I was always intent on getting to the 'edge' and you had already been there, horribly scarred by the experience.

The reason I'm writing is to tell you I saw the story in our local paper about your saving all those kids from the burning bus. What a wonderful thing you did! I'm glad you weren't hurt, but knowing you, I know you didn't give a thought about your own safety. Anyway, I'm so proud of you, as I'm sure you know the Zachariases and John Cavanaugh are as well. In fact, I've had a chance to talk with Mr. Zacharias since the bus accident, and he helped me better understand the pain you brought back from Vietnam and how it was driving you, not just with your art, but in your relationships with others. And he said something pretty profound: That he hoped the fact that you saved all those children might convince you to put away those guilt-ridden dogtags, that you might realize you are not the angel of death after all. I'm sure he's anxious to tell you that as well, but in the meantime, I agree with him. It's time for you to come out of the darkness.

As for me, I think I've found a way to get to my 'edge.' Thanks to my Dad's influence and my hard work, I've been accepted into NASA's Astronaut Candidate training program! I start training next month. I get goose bumps just thinking about it. Maybe I'll finally get to the stars! Anyway, wish me luck.

Mike, I hope I'll be able to see news about your new paintings soon. It will tell me that you are healing. You will always have a special place in my heart. I hope you know that. And I hope I'll have a special place in yours.

Love,
Cindy

He read her letter over and over until the words blurred as he tried to grasp all the emotions it had generated in his mind. At once, he felt a vague disappointment that he had received a kind of 'Dear John' letter, albeit sweetly written. He also felt oddly freed by her words, freed to move on with his life, and finally, he was uplifted by the thoughts from Zacharias she had shared with him, that maybe he wasn't 'the angel of death' after all.

Impulsively, he picked up the phone and began dialing Zacharias' number, only to stop half-way through, torn between wanting to hear the warm voice of his friend and mentor and fearing the emotions that would likely surface. He reluctantly hung up, staring at the phone. He could feel the earlier calmness of the evening beginning to crumble, replaced by the too familiar anxiety from the past. Shaking his head in frustration, he rose quickly, not bothering to change clothes, and trudged out the door toward his sanctuary of sand and waves.

A three-quarters moon hung in the night sky, laying a pale luminescence across the rolling waves of an incoming tide. While running down the beach was his usual pattern of escape, tonight he chose to simply sit at the edge of the waves rolling into shore, ignoring the rapid wetness soaking his pants.

Hypnotically, he allowed the lapping of endless waves help cleanse his mind of the old anxieties that had threatened to overtake him at the apartment. Instead he focused on Zacharias' words: Maybe he wasn't the angel of death after all. Didn't the saving of those kids, especially Grace, prove something? He bathed his mind in the possibility that life, the future, had meaning.

A breeze began to blow from the west, awakening him to the soaking water he was sitting in. With a calmness he was just beginning to feel he rose and began plodding back to the apartment, intent on nothing more than a collapsing night in his bed, hoping to sleep without the memory of past pain.

CHAPTER 42

Mike woke to the jangling phone, squinting at the early morning light streaming through his bedroom window. He stared bleary-eyed at his table clock, registering a little after 8:30 as he stumbled to reach the phone.

"Hello?" he mumbled as he sat heavily on the couch, shaking his head in an effort to throw off the cobwebs.

"Mike, it's Rebecca Phillips. Hope I didn't call too early, but I wanted to make sure you knew we want you to be here for Grace's birthday celebration on Wednesday. We're having fried chicken –one of her favorites—for dinner. We're planning on an early dinner so there'll be plenty of time for the horse surprise, so if you can, come about 3:00."

"That sounds great. And I'd like to get Grace a present for her birthday. Any suggestions?"

"Oh, Mike, that's not necessary, after all you've already done."

"No, I really want to."

"That's really sweet of you, Mike. How about something with a horse theme? Maybe a cowgirl shirt she can wear in the fall. She would need a junior size small. And if doesn't fit we can always exchange it for one that does. But really, Mike, you don't have to…"

"I know, but it's something I really want to do. Thanks for the suggestion, and I'll see you Wednesday."

"Thanks, Mike. We look forward to seeing you. Have a good day. Bye."

He sat back, still feeling blurred-eyed, trying to sort the emotions in his head. He had slept like the dead, something he had only previously accomplished with an over-abundance of booze. Now, he felt light-headed, but free of the pain of waking to the demands of breathing another day's air. Now, he felt alive, breathing the air of peace he had begun sensing as he left the Phillipses, and later, on the beach with the soothing wash of the waves. Today, he promised himself, he would be free of booze, focused on a present for Grace, and maybe a call to Mr. Z.

With a fresh cup of coffee in hand, he soon had his truck heading out for shopping. He eventually settled on a local clothing store where he found a long-sleeved, button-down shirt covered with horse heads and lush green fields. As a bonus, he also found a short-waisted jean jacket in her size --perfect , he thought, for riding in the dew-soaked fields of a fall morning. Best of all, the store offered a free wrapping service which he gratefully took advantage of, despite the fifteen-minute wait.

When he arrived back at the apartment, he first applied a razor to his growing stubble. As he scraped away, he was still surprised by the nakedness staring back at him, with the thin ridges and crow's feet of a face weathered in the present by remnants of a past still demanding its place in his life.

Finished with the ordeal of shaving, he dressed for running the beach, anticipating the challenge of running full-tilt down the hardened sand of low tide. Only, for the first time in many months, he felt the invigorating rebirth of life with new meaning.

CHAPTER 43

Mike arrived on Wednesday at the Phillips' promptly at three, eager to see Grace's reaction to her coming surprise. As he stepped out of his truck Grace came out of the front door, giving him a quick hug, but focusing on the package he was holding behind his back.

"What's that, Mike? Is that for me? Can I see?"

"Later, Little Bit," Mike laughed. "When your Mom says it's time to open presents."

At that moment Rebecca came out the front door, wearing an apron and wiping her hands on a kitchen towel. "Hi, Mike. Glad you could make it. Grace, where are your manners? Take Mike's present and put it in the family room."

"Yes, Ma'am," she said, reluctantly, then stamped up on the porch, hollering, "This day is taking forever. Mike, are you going to look at my paintings?"

"Of course. I'll be right in." He looked at the frown on Rebecca's face, filled with obvious exasperation and laughed. "Believe it or not, I still remember how tough it was to be a teenager."

"I know," she smiled. "I remember. Still, I may kill her before the day's over." She linked arms with Mike as they headed for the house, giving him a singular moment of sweetness in his soul.

"Wow. The chicken smells delicious. Hope there's enough so ya'll can have some."

"There may be enough, although you and Grace may fight over the last piece. Now, you better go look at her paintings. They really are extraordinary, even if I am her mother. I'll bring you a beer."

Dinner was a mixture of endless babble from Grace and amused glances among Rebecca, John, and Mike, made even more enjoyable for Mike by Rebecca's crisp fried chicken, mashed potatoes and gravy. He felt gathered in by the family and the events of the afternoon, unashamedly basking in the tranquility surrounding him.

After hastily-eaten birthday cake, Grace bounced up from the table and announced, "Now we open presents!"

"Okay." John agreed. "But before we do, Grace, do me a favor and run out to the barn and bring me one of those empty buckets."

"What?" she exclaimed. "Why do I have to do that, right in the middle of my birthday?!"

"Please, Grace. It's part of your birthday surprise. I'll explain later. Now go."

She stomped out, mumbling to herself, and they heard the kitchen door slam with teen-aged irritation. They jumped up and quietly sneaked out the back door in time to watch her kick her way down to the barn door. As she neared the door, she stopped suddenly, obviously having heard the soft, impatient fluttering that horses tend to make when aroused. She stood for a moment, silent as a statue, then hesitantly opened the door and stepped inside. Her scream was immediate, as was the mare's neighing, frightened by her sudden excitement.

She rushed out of the barn door in disbelief, then dashed back in as though she couldn't believe what she had seen. John, Rebecca, and Mike, all laughing, ran down to the barn, walking in to see Grace and the mare staring at one another in a mixture of animal curiosity and wordless teen-age delight. John stood behind Grace, hands on her shoulders and whispered softly, "Happy Birthday, Baby."

She swung around and hugged him with a tremendous squeeze. "Really? Is he really mine?"

"She. And yes, she's really yours. Now there's a bucket over there with some carrots in it. Why don't you take one and introduce yourself to your new friend?"

She dashed to the bucket, stopping on the way to hug Rebecca, who had been watching the scene play out with tears on her cheeks. Mike felt choked up not only by the event, but by being a part of it.

Grace hesitantly approached the mare, holding out the carrot at arm's-length so she could examine the offering. Shortly she began nibbling the carrot while Grace looked back at the adults with surprised delight.

"Look, she likes it. And I think she likes me, too."

"I think she likes you. Would you like to take her out for a walk?"

"Oh, yes! And can I ride her, too?"

"You can ride her tomorrow. I have a gentleman coming after you get home from school who's going to teach you how to ride her and care for her. He'll be coming for several weeks to help you learn how to be a cowgirl. In the meantime we'll take her out and give her a walk, and you can be thinking about a name for her."

CHAPTER 44

Mike left the Phillips that evening feeling emotionally washed out but invigorated by the experience of watching Grace blossom before his eyes --coming alive with the excitement of meeting her horse and the ensuing emotional summersault as she basked in that momentous change in her life.

As he opened the door to his apartment, he thought he could smell a renewal of his own life. A feeling that all the pain and suffering he had indulged in over the past year was slipping away.

He spied a new letter in the mail from Zacharias. But rather than putting it aside unopened, as he had with all the others, he sat down on the couch and slowly peeled the envelope open. Inside were two pages filled with Zacharias' neat hand- writing, beginning with,

Michael,

I hope you are reading these scribblings from a meddling old man, knowing that they are written with love and caring. It has been a long time since you left Dalton-- and us-- and I know you have suffered greatly from the pain you have experienced from Vietnam. I know this past year, since the break-up with Cindy, has been particularly hard. My spies have let me know you have tried to disappear from life, living an existence devoid of meaning until your wonderful experience with the children on the bus.

And that is what I want to focus on. I want to tell you, as I told Cindy recently, that your saving those children in the accident proves that all this guilt you have been carrying around from the deaths of those you cared about-- with the belief that you are some angel of death, is totally wrong. No angel of death could ever have accomplished what you did with those children.

Knowing this, I want you to return from the darkness that has swallowed you, to begin your life anew. Let me be philosophical for a moment-- as you know I can be --and quote two of my favorites: Aristotle and Seneca. Aristotle said, 'The ideal man bears the accidents of life with

dignity and grace, making the best of circumstances.' And Seneca said, 'Sometimes, even to live is an act of courage.'

I had to rely on these words when we lost Peter, along with the support of my friends and family. And that is what I am urging you to do. There is a reason for everything that happens in our lives, even though we are too blind or ignorant to understand. I believe, in your case, God has given you a talent to expose the cruelty and stupidity of this world through your art, despite the pain from which it is born. Your behavior over the past year has denied the world of your message and it has blinded you to your obligation to give that message new life.

Don't be selfish, Michael. Don't take yourself away from all those who love you now, and those gone whose memory you are obligated to keep.

Enough babbling. Come home, son.

All my love,

Nicholas

Mike sat on the edge of the couch, elbows on his knees, head bowed, holding Zacharias' letter. Over the next few minutes, he re-read the letter several times, feeling the warmth of Zacharias' words wash over him. They came as an affirmation of the rebirth he had been experiencing over the past few weeks.

He rose, walked to the phone and dialed Zacharias' number, unconscious of the lateness of the hour. Zacharias answered almost immediately, as though he had been expecting the call.

"Mr. Z…"

"Michael, what a wonderful surprise. It's so good to hear your voice."

"Mr. Z. Not sure why I called. Just read your letter and wanted to let you know I appreciated it."

"Which letter was that Michael?" Zacharias laughed. "I've sent several."

"I know, Mr. Z. It's probably the last one you sent, I guess after the bus accident."

"I understand, Michael. It was the one after the accident which gave me the wisdom to tell you what I believed it represented… a transformation of sorts, a beginning of a new belief in yourself, not as an angel of death, but as an object of healing."

Initially, Mike couldn't find the words to respond, feeling only their warmth wrapping themselves around him as he settled back on the couch in a cocoon of peace. Finally, he roused himself to say, "Mr. Z. I'd really like to see you. Any chance you might be coming this way anytime soon?"

"Funny you should ask, Michael. I'm planning on being in your area in the next few weeks. Perhaps we could spend some time together then."

"That'd be great, Mr. Z. Just let me know and I'll be ready. Even clean up the apartment."

"Fine, Michael. I'll let you know the details soon. In the meantime, get the rest I know you need. I can't wait to see you."

"Me either," he replied as they both hung up.

Mike continued to sit as he rummaged through the thoughts and emotions running through his mind. The peace he was feeling overwhelmed him but at the same time he remained tenuously fearful it might evaporate. Eventually, though, he fell asleep on the couch, anesthetized by the new-found peace.

CHAPTER 45

Several weeks later, after not hearing from the Phillipses, Mike took it upon himself to drive unannounced to their house, finding himself missing the comfort of being with them. He hoped they wouldn't mind his unannounced visit but felt the need to surround himself with their friendship.

As he approached the house, he saw Grace sitting astride her new horse, listening patiently to a weathered gentleman dressed in jeans and boots. He held the horse's bridle as he talked, and it seemed as though he was talking to both rider and horse. Mike shut off his engine and quietly opened the cab door, not wanting to interrupt the rapt conversation going on in what he recognized as a new hastily-constructed corral.

Rebecca, hearing his truck stop, walked out of the house and gave him a warm hug. "What a wonderful surprise, Mike. And you're just in time for dinner."

"Good," he laughed. "I was counting on that. No, I stopped because I hadn't seen you folks in a while and missed you. And I wanted to see how Grace was doing with her new horse."

"She's doing really good. She and her teacher seem to be bonding well, and she and Asterope are getting along as well."

"Asterope?"

"Oh, Asterope is her horse's name. I'll let her explain where she got the name, but I think it comes from Greek mythology."

"Greek mythology? Why am I not surprised? That complex daughter of yours has more sides to her than a circle. Can't wait to hear how she got from mythology to her horse's name."

Rebecca grabbed his arm. "Come on back to our new eyesore, otherwise known as a corral. I think the horse lesson is about over and I know Grace will be delighted to see you. Also, I want you to meet her trainer, Ed Trent. He's marvelous with horses and kids. He's brought Grace along so quickly. I've talked him into staying for dinner, so you'll have a chance to get acquainted. John managed to catch some trout this weekend, so we're having fried fish, grits, hush puppies and coleslaw."

Mike held out his arm to her. "Okay, give this a little twist and I'll try to find a place in my busy schedule to sample some more of your cooking."

"You goof," she laughed, and punched him in the ribs as they walked back to the corral. "Grace is going to be so excited. She's bonkers with her horse, and just about as bad with her painting. She's done a marvelous job capturing Asterope on canvas, and I know she can't wait to show it off."

As they reached the corral, Grace looked up, and seeing Mike, jumped from her saddle and launched herself into his arms. "Mike. Oh, Mike! Come see my horse. Her name is Asterope. And I can ride her! She's beautiful!"

Mike gathered her up in his arms, laughing as she hung around his neck. "Okay, cowpoke, let's go meet Miss Asterope. But first, introduce me to Mr. Trent."

Grace slid down from his arms like a greased monkey, then dragged him over to where Trent was holding the mare's bridle. "Mr. Trent, this my special friend –he saved my life—Mike Pallaso. Mike, this is Mr. Trent. He's teaching me how to ride Asterope and to take care of her."

Mike and Trent shuck hands, firmly, eyeing each other with knowing stares. Mike said, I've seen you before. When were you there?"

"Yeah, I've seen you before, too. Sixty-seven, sixty-eight. But I read about you a couple of months ago. Seems you got our little Gracie and some others out of a tight spot. I'm pleased to shake your hand."

Mike marveled at the mark each had, like an invisible tattoo on the forehead with rank, serial number and place in an evil history. He said, "Con Thien, Khe Sanh. And you?"

Trent said, "Miss Gracie, time to walk Asterope a bit, then we'll brush her down and give her some grain. Off you go."

Grace left, reluctantly, wanting to hear these new men in her life, but used to the discipline of Trent's commands, she walked obediently with the horse trailing her.

Trent turned back to Mike, watching Grace walking the mare, then said, "Army, First Cav. We were on Peanuts, one of the fire zones protecting Khe Sanh. You?"

"Khe Sanh, just before you guys got there. Sorry we missed you."

"Yeah, sorry we couldn't help more. After that –go figure the Army—I got transferred to a transportation unit to help the South Vietnamese move supplies in the Mekong Delta by mule no less—I guess 'cause I could spell horse. Anyway, that's where I spent the rest of my thirteen, chasing mules. Learned a lot about horses and mules, so here I am now, a long way from New Jersey."

"Yeah, Georgia for me. But this place grows on you, I guess. Think I heard John drive up. Guess we need to go in and pretend to help with dinner. Buy you a beer?"

"Uh, I'll take a coke. Be in in a minute. Just want to check on Gracie and the horse."

Mike nodded and walked around to the kitchen door, wondering at the coincidence of meeting Trent, another veteran of Khe Sanh. He knocked on the kitchen door and stepped in as Rebecca and John both hollered, "Come on in."

John met him with a freshly opened beer. "Becca said we had another free-loader for dinner. I heard Grace screaming a few minutes ago so I guessed she knows you're here."

They clinked bottles, took healthy swallows, then slapped one another with manly pats on the back.

John said, "Been a while. Thought you'd forgotten us."

"No chance of that. Just got busy with my painting again. Been away from it too long. Trying to knock the rust off, you know."

"So, how's it going? The painting I mean."

"Not sure. Haven't been able to get my rhythm back yet, but I think I'm beginning to feel the creative juices flowing again. Anyway, I thought seeing you folks again, especially the young cowpoke, might help me get my battery charged. Rebecca tells me she's heavy into her painting-- in fact, I understand she's done a canvas of Asterope. What a strange name for a horse."

"There's no telling with that child. I'm sure she'll fill you in at dinner. I assume you've met Ed? He and Grace have really connected. He's the most patient, caring man I've met."

"Yeah, we've met. Turns out, we have a history of sorts --Vietnam. Hope we have a chance to talk later."

At that moment, Grace rushed into the kitchen, breathless with excitement, followed by a grinning Ed. "Mike," she gushed, "guess what Asterope did? She kissed me!"

"Kissed you? Ugh. I've been kissed by a lot of things, but never a horse. What did it taste like? Was it as good as my kiss?"

"Silly. I gave her an apple, holding it in my teeth. And she gave me a kiss when she took the apple. I love her."

Ed hid a laugh behind his hand, winking at the adults. "We're working on getting to be friends with Asterope. I think we're making progress."

Mike said, "Speaking of Asterope, I need you to tell me how you named her. Maybe we can talk while you show me your painting of her."

"Okay, come on. My painting's in the family room. Promise you won't laugh."

"Grace, I can't promise I won't laugh at anything you do, but I know your talent for drawing horses. You're a winner. Why don't we let Mr. Trent be the judge if you've captured the real Asterope."

"Okay, Mike," she said impatiently. "Now you and Mr. Ed come on." And grabbed each of their hands, dragging them into the family room. The canvas sat on a sturdy easel, covered by a canvas cloth. With a flourish, Grace threw back the cloth to reveal a beautiful, realistic portrait of the standing mare, complete with the drunken pattern of white, brown and black colors of her breed.

She was beautiful, Mike murmured under his breath. He was especially captured by the mare's translucent brown eyes, seeming to be staring back, ears forward, with curiosity, and wisdom, almost human.

"Well, Ed. You need to break the tie, cause Grace and I think it's a beautiful painting."

"I don't know nothin' about painting, but I know a horse when I see one. She's a beauty. Guess it's unanimous."

Grace jumped up and down, clapping her hands in shameless delight. "See, I told you I could paint a horse. Right, Mike?"

Mike nodded sagely, still examining the painting. He could see some areas for improvement, but overall remained awed by the young woman's natural artistic talent. He made a mental note to get John and Rebecca to enroll her in an art class he knew about at the beach.

"Grace, what a beautiful painting of Asterope. Now, how did you choose such an unusual name for her?"

"We've been studying mythology in class, mostly about the Greek gods. Asterope was one of the daughters of Atlas –she's also called Sterope, but I liked Asterope better; anyway, Asterope is one of the seven daughters of Atlas, and one of the other gods –Zeus, I think, sent the daughters to the heavens where they became stars gathered together as Pleiades, a group of stars in the heaven, and one of them was Asterope."

"And what made Asterope special to you that you chose her name for your mare?"

"I don't know. Just liked the sound of it. Anyway, the Greeks believed that when the Pleiades appeared in the spring sky, they were the source of light that signaled the renewal of life in the spring. People sorta believe funny things about life, especially what the stars mean. Anyway, I liked the sound of Asterope, and thought of her racing across the sky, bringing light and renewal of life. Sorta like you bringing life back to me."

Mike sat in disbelief at what he had just heard: he, being compared to a myth of bringing life back, when so much of his history involved death. He was not prepared to contradict Grace or further pursue the discussion. Instead, he turned to the portrait of Asterope, pretending to begin a critical analysis of the painting. In fact, he found few flaws in her work.

"Okay," Rebecca called from the dining room. "Dinner's ready. Come on while the fish is hot."

When they were all seated, with Grace directing Mike and Ed to sit beside her, she led the blessing that Mike noticed included Asterope as well as John Jr. Afterwards, they all quickly filled their plates with fried trout and all the side dishes and conversation was limited to murmured thanks to the cook and sighs of contentment. As the meal progressed, Grace chattered excitedly about her day's events, primarily about her training with Asterope. Ed added a comment occasionally bolstering her account of how she and Asterope were bonding. It seemed that Asterope had begun following Grace about the corral without a bridle as long as she had a carrot or apple in hand.

The dinner proved a pleasant diversion for Mike, freeing him further from the past and enabling him to look forward with renewed energy to his painting. He still marveled at the effect Grace and her family had had on him since the bus wreck.

After dinner, Grace directed them out to the barn to check on Asterope, who greeted them all with a fluffing of lips and an expectation of a carrot treat. She paid particular attention to Grace, who rubbed her nose with affection as though they had become bosom buddies.

As they stood by the mare, Mike said, "Folks, it's been great, but I need to get going. Rebecca and John, how 'bout walking with me out to my truck. Got an idea I'd like to get your thoughts on. Ed, hope to see you again soon, and Grace, you know I'll be watching you and your painting, and of course how you and Asterope are doing. Now, let me have a hug before I go."

She gave him a big squeeze, then turned back to the mare. Mike and Ed shook hands, then Mike, Rebecca, and John turned and walked to the truck.

"Okay, Mike," John said. "What's your idea?"

"I'd like to get Grace enrolled in an art school I know about here at the beach, if it would be okay with you. MY treat. She's got an amazing talent, and the art school director would be able to help her find a niche for that talent and help her become more disciplined. Maybe she could do it this summer."

"What a wonderful gesture, but you don't have to pay for something like that," Rebecca said. "Right, John?"

"Hell, no. But I agree. I've seen her paintings and can't believe a child of mine can do what she does with a paint brush. If you think art school would help tighten her talent, then we'll get her enrolled. Just get the details for us and we'll take care of it. Summer sounds like a good idea."

Mike said, "I'd like to make the arrangements, including paying for it. I know the director and I'm sure she'll give me a good discount, especially when she sees some of Grace's work."

Then he said, feeling embarrassed, "I think I owe Grace for my life. I can't really explain it, but before the wreck I was going down fast, not caring whether I lived or died. Now I'm feeling life seeping back into me, thanks to Grace –and you two."

"Mike, you know we owe you more than we can ever say for your saving Grace and for all you've done for her since then," John answered. "We'll talk more about who pays for what. We'll talk with Grace, and if it's something she'd like to do, then you can go ahead and set it up.

“Okay,” Mike said, and turned to his truck feeling the flushed heat from his confession. “Thanks again for dinner, Rebecca. It was delicious. Now I’m outta’ here.” He cranked the truck and waved as he drove off, feeling light-headed with contentment at the way his life seemed to be turning around.

CHAPTER 46

The next few weeks were busy but strangely relaxing for Mike. He spent his time trying to clean up the apartment and setting up his studio with fresh canvas, new paints, and sketches of paintings he might do. He continued to spend time with the Phillipses, especially Grace with her budding art, watching the teenager blossom as a young and enthusiastic horse-woman. In between, he spent long reaches of time running the beach, not insanely away from pain, but toward a promise of life renewed.

One morning, a month or so after his phone call to Zacharias, as he approached his apartment after a run on the beach, he looked up in surprise to see Zacharias and John Cavanaugh sitting on his small veranda, coffee cups in hand. As he climbed the apartment steps Zacharias and Cavanaugh raised their cups in mock salute.

"Hope you don't mind," Zacharias said, "but the door was unlocked, so we thought you'd be back shortly and helped ourselves to some coffee."

Mike stumbled up the last steps and then stood awkwardly trying to comprehend what they were doing on his porch. "Where… where'd you come from?" he asked as Zacharias and then Cavanaugh reached out to shake his hand.

"Sit down, Michael, before you fall down and act as though you're glad to see us," Zacharias chuckled.

"I told you I had some business down here," Zacharias continued. "That's taken care of, so now we're checking on you. Couldn't keep John away."

"That's right, Mike," Cavanaugh added. "We're here because we were tired of wasting money on stamps and unanswered phone calls. Quite frankly, I'm here to try to redeem our investment in you."

Mike leaned against the veranda railing, feeling more than a twinge of anxiety at the demands on him that their appearance suggested. Was he really ready to face the future—a future in which he would need to accept obligation and responsibility? Despite his anxiety but realizing how much he enjoyed the warmth of their presence, he said, "I can't tell you what it means to have you here. I've missed you and feel stupid that I've pushed you away for so long."

"Michael, we understand," Zacharias said. "But that's in the past. Now, you've made your atonement for the things you felt you were guilty of. As I said in my last letter to you, saving those children must make you understand that you are not the angel of death you believed you were. There is no need for you to push those who love you away. You can bring no harm to them, only to yourself."

Cavanaugh added, "That's right, Mike. Now it's time to get back to your art. I can tell you there is a still a large demand in the art world for more of Mike Pallaso. I took the liberty of snooping around in your *studio,* and based on the paltry work I saw, it's clear that you haven't been focused on your art for a while. I hope that's going to change. In fact, I've some ideas for another showing in the future. Call it 'Pallaso Reborn'. As you know, I have galleries in Chicago and DC in addition to Atlanta. Once you've been able to create some new canvases, say maybe ten or twelve, I'm thinking we can have showings --if you agree—in all three galleries. What do you think?"

Mike couldn't absorb all he was hearing. He felt like his head was a ping-pong ball being batted back and forth by these two over-powering friends.

"Slow down, guys. I'm still trying to deal with finding you sitting on my veranda, drinking my coffee. Much less with all your ideas and advice to make me over again. John, I can't begin to imagine producing even one decent painting, much less ten or twelve, although the thought of doing it is exciting. But you're talking about at least a year, probably more, even assuming I could try. And we're not talking about an assembly line. You know how fickle the creative juices can be. I may not have any juices left. A lot has happened in the last two years."

"Yeah. But would you be willing to try?"

"I need to think about it –a lot. A lot depends on whether Mr. Z is right. I can't be sure I won't turn back to my old ways. Logically, I believe you're right, Mr. Z. There has been a change in my head ever since the bus accident. And I'm beginning to sleep through the night, don't need the alcohol. I'm beginning to feel alive again –maybe like John says, 'reborn'."

"But here's the irony. Maybe my art, the old art, was good because of the passion my mental pain caused me. If that pain has somehow been dissipated, who's to say any future work will be any good?" He leaned against the veranda railing, arms crossed, face perplexed as he looked to each of his friends for understanding.

Zacharias laughed softly, then said: "Michael, of course you could be right. But what if the changes in you will simply make room for a new passion. You haven't lost your sense of the pain and loss that that horrible war created. Your new passion should develop from a need to help the world understand how stupid man is to believe that war is a solution for anything. You have the same creative, artistic talent you've always had. Now may simply be time for bending that talent in a slightly different direction."

"I appreciate all you have both said and what you're trying to do to help me. I really do. I guess I just need time to think about it."

"We understand, Michael," Zacharias said. Then in a sudden change of direction, he casually asked, "That old truck of yours still run?"

"Sure," Mike replied, puzzled. "Why?" He knew Zacharias well enough to suspect the sudden change of subject was deliberately mysterious.

"We need to run an errand and hoped you might be able to give us a lift."

"Okay. Where'd you need to go, and when?"

"It's a place in Atlantic Beach. I think I can show you the way. And now would be fine."

"Right. Let me grab a quick shower and some clean clothes, then we can go."

Zacharias nodded, and Mike went in the apartment, still bemused by Zacharias' mysterious manner. As he left. Cavanaugh said, "Nicholas, you are a devious demon. Why can't you tell Michael what's up, instead of stringing him along?"

"Michael has a lot to absorb right now. Most of it good. I don't want him to get too overpowered by good, to the point he begins to think he'll need bad to balance things out. His mind is still pretty fragile."

Cavanaugh nodded his acceptance of his friend's logic, even though he didn't fully understand it. A few minutes later Mike reappeared dressed in clean shorts and a non-descript tee-shirt. He rattled his car keys with pretended impatience, but in reality, curiosity drove him to find out what Zacharias was up to.

Zacharias and Cavanaugh rose and they trooped down the apartment stairs behind Mike, who hurried to clean off the front seat of the truck. The three of them then crowded in, and with a hesitant growl from the aging engine, drove out of the apartment parking space.

"Okay, where're we going?"

Zacharias pulled a penciled map from his pocket, then said, "Get on A1A, go north to Atlantic Blvd, turn right at the intersection and go two blocks to a street called Beach Drive. Turn left there."

Mike shrugged, trying to cover his curiosity with indifference and followed Zacharias' direction. When they reached Beach Drive, Mike remarked, "This is the ritzy part of Atlantic Beach. It's so rich I couldn't even afford to carry out the garbage."

"We're only going a couple of blocks, Michael. There, up ahead, where the sold sign is."

"All right, Mr. Z. What the hell is going on?"

"Michael, this is my new vacation home."

"What? Wow," Mike exclaimed as he took in the two-story cedar-shingled house, with columns surrounding the front entrance of double doors. It had a porch wrapping around the entire house except on the north side where it ended at a three-car garage. The second-floor rooms each had its own balcony.

"Wait until you see the back, Michael. It has an enclosed veranda with a spectacular view of the dunes and the ocean.."

"It's beautiful, Mr. Z. Does this mean you and the family are leaving Dalton and moving down here?"

"No, Michael. This is just a vacation home, for maybe two or three weeks in the summer. The rest of the time, I will need a house sitter. I thought I might be able to talk you into taking that on."

Mike looked unbelievingly at Zacharias. "What the hell? I'm no house-sitter. First you tell me I need to get back to my painting, then all of a sudden want to make me your house-sitter? What the hell is going on? Why would you make me into a housekeeper?"

"Michael, it's not free. I expect a hundred dollars a month from you to stay in my house. And you'll be responsible for electricity, plumbing, up-keep, and landscaping, and any changes inside, like setting up your studio."

"Bull-shit, Mr. Z. We both know this is charity. It won't cost me a fraction to stay here compared to what I'm paying in that cheap-ass apartment!"

"Michael, did I mention that staying here will involve a rent-to-own agreement? Eventually, this home could be yours, if you keep up the rent. By the way, it comes furnished. It was part of an estate sale."

"Dammit, Mr. Z! What the hell's going on? Why are you doing this?"

"Michael, I didn't mean to upset you but let me take you back to that first moment in the cemetery at Peter's grave. Your sudden appearance was a transforming moment for me. At that moment I was dying with my grief at Peter's loss. Seeing you, as Peter's best friend, and recognizing you needed help with your own demons, made me think that life had to go on. That your appearance might have been a message from Peter, that somehow you were a reincarnation of his spirit, there to tell me that the world hadn't ended, only changed.

"In effect, you became my adopted son, as you have been ever since. That's a long way of telling you that this is the house I would have given to my first born, and which I am now giving to you. All you have to do is accept your obligation to Peter and all the others to make this world understand, through your art, the craziness it is infected with."

Mike leaned his head back on the car seat, eyes scrunched closed in disbelief as he tried to process all he was hearing. He tried to imagine all the implications of how his life was changing, even more than it had already changed since the bus accident.

He shook his head, searching for clarity, then said, "Mr. Z, you've got to know I'm blown away by all this. I want to tell you how grateful I am, but I can't find words. To know you think of me as a son is beyond comprehension. Your belief in me hurts my heart with happiness.

"But I'm also pretty afraid I'll fail you, and you, John. I know my head seems to be healing, but I'm a long way from well. The demons in my mind may not have disappeared, but they're only hiding, waiting to pounce the minute I let my guard down. Can you understand what I'm saying?"

Zacharias held his shoulder firmly, looking deep into his eyes. “Michael, we do understand. We understand there will be missteps along the way, but you are beginning to heal, and John and I will be here for you if you need us. Now why don’t we go see where you think your studio should be?”

CHAPTER 47

Three days later, Mike dropped off Zaharias and Cavanaugh at the airport for their flight back to Atlanta. He knew he would miss them but wasn't really sorry to see them go, as exhausted as he was by their continuing, enthusiastic suggestions on how the future would unfold. For the new house, Zacharias laid out plans for renovations, including an ambitious studio design for Mike with ocean-wide windows for the morning sun to inspire his artistic muse. For his part, Cavanaugh had continued to hammer him with details of his vision for the exhibits of Mike's new works and his impatience in wanting to see the rebirth of the new Pallaso's art.

On his way back from the airport, Mike impulsively decided to stop by the Phillipses since he hadn't seen them in a couple of weeks. As he drove up the road to the house he saw Grace riding Asterope at a trot along the fence, looking as though she and the horse were one. When he pulled even with rider and horse, Grace saw him and pulled Asterope to a halt , hopped from the saddle, rushed to climb over the fence, and jumped on the running board.

"Oh, Mike," she gushed, "I'm so excited to see you. Where have you been? Do you see how beautiful Asterope is? Would you like to ride her?

"Hi, Kiddo. I'm glad to see you, too. And no, I don't think I would fit on that saddle as good as you do. I'd just rather see you ride her. Now, are your mom and dad home? I wanted to see if ya'll would like to come see my new house and maybe have a party."

"A party? You have a new house? Come on! Asterope and I'll race you to the house." With that she was down off the truck, vaulted the fence and jumped into the saddle on the docile mare, beginning a quick gallop to the house.

Grace and Asterope were at the house before he could even put the truck in gear. She jumped off the saddle and went tearing to the house, fingers raised in a victory sign. "Mom, Dad, guess who's here!"

John and Rebecca heard Mike's truck and came out on the porch. John hollered, "Oh no. It's the free-loader again. Fridge empty, Mike?"

"Rebecca jammed him in the ribs and hurried down the steps to grab Mike in a tight squeeze, whispering loud enough for John to hear, "Ignore him. We're both delighted to see you."

Well, I'm glad to see you again too, but tell that husband of yours that's no way to greet a Marine. We get our feelings hurt easily. The least he could do is offer me a beer."

John guffawed and joined them in a hug. "So, where you been, Marine? We were beginning to think you'd deserted."

"No. I had some surprise guests. And by the time they left today my world had been turned upside down. In a good way I guess, but I'm still trying to get my mind around what's coming."

"Well, come on in and tell us about it," Rebecca said. "We're fixing hamburgers on the grill, if John doesn't burn them like last time. And Ed is here. I know he'll want to see you. In fact, why don't you and John grab a beer and go supervise Ed and Gracie putting Asterope away for the evening?"

John and Mike, beers in hand, walked out the kitchen door and headed for the barn. They walked in to watch Grace busily brushing Asterope down in her stall while the horse munched contently on some grain. Ed stood to the side observing his protégé at work, obviously feeling no need to provide guidance. He looked up to acknowledge their presence. "Mike, good to see you. You're all Little-Bit's been talking about for the last ten minutes, when she wasn't talking the horse's ears off."

"Was not, Mr. Ed. I was telling Asterope how beautiful she is and how glad I was to see Mike, and about his new house, and the party. Besides, Asterope likes me to talk to her, don't you, girl?"

Hearing her name and the warmth of her new friend's voice, the mare turned her head back to Grace, trying to lip her face. "See, she likes me to talk to her."

"Okay, Gracie," Ed said. "That's enough brushing, and enough grain. Let's let her settle down for the night. Hang up her saddle blanket so it can dry and put away the saddle and bridle."

"Here," Mike said, "Let me help."

"No, Mike. Mr. Ed says I have to do it myself. It's part of learning to care for Asterope. I'll get it."

Ed grinned. "She's a good student, gonna be a good horse woman."

Mike shrugged, Grace beamed, and John managed to hide a smile of pride. Then, when the barn chores were done, they all trouped off toward the house. John went ahead of them saying he needed to check on the charcoal for the hamburgers.

"So, what's this about new digs Grace was spouting about? And a party to boot? You fall into a pot of gold?"

"It's sorta complicated. It's not exactly my place. A friend of mine just bought a summer home and wants me to be his house sitter for a while. I'll explain it more after we eat. By the way, you're invited to the party. Hope you can make it."

"I'll check my calendar. In the meantime, let's go see if we can keep John from burning the burgers."

After dinner Mike said, "Okay, here's what I was thinking. Maybe this coming Saturday we could all get together at my new place in Atlantic Beach, the one I'm now housesitting. I could show you around, show you some of my paintings, and cook some ribs for dinner. And Ed, if you think it's doable, maybe you could trailer Asterope there, and Grace could ride her on the beach."

Rebecca said, "What a fine idea. We'd love to come. And Ed, you can make it too, can't you? And we have the loan of a horse trailer, don't we, John? So, the horse can come with us, too."

John nodded enthusiastically. "Sounds like a great idea. Ed, you've got to come with us. Grace, think you and Asterope would like to ride on the beach?"

"Yes!" she shouted.

"Okay," Mike said. "Plan on coming about noon on Saturday. I'll show you the place, Grace can ride Asterope on the beach and I'll try not to burn the ribs on the grill. Now I need to go before I fall asleep from the two hamburgers I scoffed down. Grace. Come give me a hug."

Grace eagerly obliged, and Mike felt his ribs begin to protest as she wrapped her arms around him. "Thanks, Kiddo," he said. "I'll see you Saturday. Ed, I look forward to seeing you, too. John and Rebecca, how 'bout you walking me out to my truck."

As they walked out of earshot, Mike said, "I was wondering where we are on Grace and the art school. Have you had a chance to see what her thinking is?"

"Yeah," John said. "We've talked about it but haven't pushed her too much. She's back and forth on the idea. I think she's afraid an art teacher might not believe she can be a good artist."

"Okay. Maybe I can talk with her this Saturday. I really want to encourage her. If you're okay with that."

"Of course." John said. "We just don't want her to feel like we're pressuring her. We want it to be something she feels good about. And I know she trusts you, so yeah, talk to her."

"Good. If it's okay with you, can I sneak by and get some of Grace's work ? I'd like to share it with Mrs. Craft, the art school director."

"I'll gather some up tomorrow and drop them by for you," Rebecca said. "I'll call and get your address."

"Thanks, Rebecca, and for dinner, too. Now I'm outta here."

CHAPTER 48

Mike thought the Saturday gathering went well. Rebecca, John, and Ed were impressed by his new digs. Grace and Asterope, along with Ed and his horse, rode the beach with abandon, returning an hour or so later, with both horses and riders lathered. He managed not to burn the ribs, and together with the potato salad, coleslaw and watermelon Rebecca insisted bringing, they all had a delightful meal on the veranda overlooking the ocean. Despite a stomach swollen by his over-eating, he felt expansive in his role as host and guide through the mini-mansion.

As they toured the house, he brought them to his new studio, where they viewed some of his recently finished paintings, as well as some half-finished that he had promised Cavanaugh he would try to produce for the up-coming exhibits he had agreed to.

He watched intently as they all studied the paintings. Some they viewed non-committedly, while others drew surprise at the intensity of his work. He was particularly aware of Grace's reaction to the work, noting first her insight into the mechanics of the art, but more intently at her overall reaction to the paintings.

Finally he said, "So, Grace. What do you think?"

"I can't like them. They're too gloomy, too sad, too dark."

"Grace," Rebecca admonished. "Mike has obviously worked hard on these paintings. And I think they're wonderful."

"No, Rebecca. I asked Grace what she thought, and she gave me an honest answer. And in fact, I agree with her. These paintings come from a continuing torment in my brain from a period too dark to ignore. But I'd like to get beyond that darkness, to finally find some hope, some light in my mind. Unfortunately, I'm not there yet. Don't know if I ever will be. But I'm going to try. No, Grace. Thank you for your eyes, your perception, and your honesty." He put his arm around her shoulder and gave her a reassuring hug.

"Now," he said to John and Rebecca. "Have you had a chance to talk about what we discussed earlier? I'm ready to arrange things if everybody is in agreement?"

"Grace. Mike's talking about art school. Have you decided if that's something you'd like to do this summer?"

"Yes, ma'am. I mean, I think so. I just don't someone to think my work is stupid or something."

"Don't worry, Grace. I've already shown some of your work to Mrs. Craft, the director of the school, and she's anxious to meet you. She think's you have a wonderful natural talent and she'd love to work with you to help you develop it."

"Okay. I'd really like to try the school this summer."

"Then it's a done deal. John and Rebecca, I'll take care of the details like we discussed."

As they were leaving the studio, Ed held back. "Mike, I've been where you've been, and I think you've captured all the pain I've brought back from that place. I appreciate what you're trying to do with your painting, but I agree with Grace. We have to get on the other side of that darkness before it buries us. Just thought you needed to know that your art will reach a lot of us who are feeling the same kind of pain." He reached out for Mike and they engaged in a silent embrace of understanding.

CHAPTER 49

The next day, after contacting Mrs. Craft at the art school to finalize arrangements for Grace's enrollment, Mike began working at an energized pace to complete the paintings he had promised Cavanaugh. To his surprise, and reinforced by the visit from Cavanaugh, they all contained new dimensions of artistry he had not seen before in his work. In a phone call to Cavanaugh, he told him of his progress, including the new depth he was seeing in his work. Cavanaugh responded with enthusiasm, reminding him of his prediction that they would soon be exhibiting the new Pallaso.

While they were talking, Cavanaugh laid out detailed plans for his proposed exhibits which would include his studios in Atlanta, Chicago and D.C. He and Mike agreed to shoot for ten finished paintings for the exhibits, to be completed during the next six months.

The plans were contingent, of course, Cavanaugh added, on agreement from those sure to purchase his paintings to delay taking possession until the exhibits were completed. Cavanaugh said, "Don't worry, Michael. When word gets out that new Pallaso works are imminent, people will be clamoring to purchase them, and getting their agreement to delay possession will be minor."

"Oh, by the way," he added, as though an afterthought, "I'd like you to plan on being at all three galleries with your paintings. You know, sort of a press-the-flesh opportunity for your admirers."

Mike was caught off guard by this last bit of planning. He couldn't initially absorb the idea of leaving his safe beach haven for at least a month of non-stop activity in the art world, as he was prone to think of it. In the end, he could only agree in mute acceptance, knowing that it would be useless to object to Cavanaugh's determined plans.

Weeks later, Mike finished the last of his promised paintings and arranged to have them shipped. Cavanaugh quickly put the final touches on his plans for the exhibits, making sure Mike was committed to being present at each one. It proved a grueling time for Mike over the next few months as he traveled to Atlanta, then Chicago and Washington with the paintings. He met hundreds of strangers, all clamoring for his attention. And he had to sit through numerous interviews with various writers and critics, including Anthony Beloise, who greeted him quietly but friendly, asking more about his state of mind than his art.

Altogether it was an exhausting period, and despite Cavanaugh's support, and his accounting of amazing sales figures, Mike finally arrived home, feeling as though he had just completed Marine boot camp.

Despite his exhaustion, he ran to the beach, first diving into the ocean waves, then running for miles on the firm low tide sand, feeling a renewal beginning as he finally climbed over the dunes to his veranda. That night he was able to sleep as soundly as he had in a year, waking groggily to a soft breeze and a bright sunrise.

He rose, showered, and realized he had no food for breakfast. He dressed in a casual mix of shorts, tee-shirt ,and sandals, and walked leisurely to a nearby café and consumed a huge breakfast of eggs, sausage, grits, toast, and coffee. He spent the rest of the day puttering, straightening up his studio, sweeping sand off the veranda, and shopping for essentials. As evening approached, he decided on impulse to visit the local VFW, promising himself sternly that he would only have a celebratory beer.

To his surprise and consternation, he found the VFW closed for renovations. Feeling a vague sense of disappointment, he drove back to Atlantic Beach where he thought he remembered there was an Irish pub of some sort. Thinking he could kill two birds with one stone, he decided to go in and try the pub food along with his beer.

There he met a beautiful auburn-haired, green-eyed young lady behind the bar. She smiled as he sat down, saying "Hi, I'm Molly. What can I get you?"

MIKE AND MOLLY
CHAPTER 50

As was her habit, Molly woke at the hint of dawn. She listened to the building sound of the waves being driven by the nor'easter and felt the strengthening breeze through the bedroom curtains.

She marveled, as she always did on waking, at the serenity and happiness of her life, living with her man in this house. Then she remembered Mike's announcement about the Parkinson's and couldn't dismiss the worry and the constant awareness that life could be challenging.

Annoyed at herself for the brief negativity, she quickly rose, threw on some shorts and a brief top, and went into the bathroom to brush her teeth and comb her hair. As she brushed she looked critically at the small bridge of freckles across her nose. Mike said he loved them and counted them every day to remind him of how lucky he was to have a beautiful Irish lady.

She viewed them more critically but decided that she wasn't too bad for fiftyish, with a firm bottom, decent legs, and breasts that still stood up on their own.

As she walked to the kitchen to start breakfast, she thought about how she and Mike had first met. She was tending bar at one of the beaches' Irish pubs, to which Mike had become a fairly steady customer, usually nursing a draft beer and munching on free nuts from a saucer on the bar. He had seemed a decent sort, not given to much conversation, but friendly enough.

In her abbreviated autobiography to Mike, she mentioned that she was a born-and-bred beach lady, a child of an Irish working-class couple who had moved to the beach community a couple of years before Molly was born. She and her younger sister Reba had spent their entire youth as beach bums, loving every minute of it.

She admitted to Mike that, much to her father's bemusement --and amusement-- in her wanderings around the beaches' neighborhoods she had had a penchant for finding lost and homeless animals –mostly dogs and cats and bringing them home with her. In tolerant exasperation, her father once claimed that her name must mean *Finder of Lost Ones* in its Gaelic origins.

Finally, she casually mentioned she was three years past a failed relationship, and since then had avoided any serious involvement. She walked away briefly to serve another customer, wondering as she did so why she had mentioned the failed relationship and avoiding any subsequent serious involvement. She admitted, ruefully, the last thing she wanted was to discourage Mike. Dumb, dumb, dumb, she thought.

CHAPTER 51

This brief story of her young life took several evenings of telling , in between serving other customers at the bar, cleaning glasses, putting out fresh bowls of nuts, and wiping up imaginary wet spots on the bar. And each time, in quiet interludes, she always seemed to gravitate to Mike's spot at the bar.

To Molly, there was something oddly appealing about Mike. Looking back, she wasn't sure if it had been her life-long drive to rescue the needy or something more –perhaps a need of her own. In any event, from her observations he was carrying a great deal of baggage, but somehow still seemed to have the strength to handle it. He was quiet as he sucked his nightly beer but still seemed interested in the world around him.

As the weeks progressed with his frequent visits, they both became aware of a growing attraction between them. When she wasn't doling out pieces of her life, he was hesitantly dropping small pieces of his own, that he had some interest in art, had lived in the beach community for several years, most recently in a house on the oceanfront.

One evening, as she was wiping an imaginary spot in front of his place he said, "You know, as much as I've enjoyed hearing your life story, I really don't know much about you. Who is the real Molly Sullivan? What does she do when she's not pouring beer for the likes of me?"

She laughed. "I don't change much when I put on this apron, like you don't change when you sit on that stool. I'm still the same person. Right now, during the day, I volunteer at the local animal shelter, try to make it to the gym, and love to read good books. And I even try to write poetry. Who knows? Maybe I'll even try to get something published one day."

Mike sat silently for a moment, then said, "I knew since we first met that you were much deeper than you let on, that you had a kind of mystery about you that would be fun to explore. I would love to read some of your poetry one day."

Molly felt herself blush and realized she had started wiping the counter in front of him with unneeded vigor. "I'm afraid you might be more than a little disappointed, both in exploring that mystery you think you see and also with my poetry. Now, you're about to get tested. Just so happens I have a poem in my pocket I just finished this afternoon and I'm going to let you read it. But you have to promise not to laugh out loud, and you have to be honest. And kind."

With that, she handed him a folded sheet of lined note paper, then quickly moved down the bar to wait on several other customers.

Mike watched her go with admiring amusement, then unfolded the paper and began reading:

I surrender
I surrender to the ocean waves that
Come from eternity to carry my footsteps
Away.
I surrender to the light of the sun that comes
To wash away my night fears.
I surrender to the perfect love that comes with such quiet power
To still the fear that sneaks unbidden into my heart,
The fear that I will not know all the glory that is yet to come.
I surrender, God, to all the mysteries you surround me with,
Accepting that I will never fully know their meaning.
But I would rather live in ignorance then have to live
Thinking you are not there for me when I
Have stopped wondering why I have put footsteps on the sand.

Mike looked up and spent a moment watching Molly moving efficiently behind the bar, refreshing peanuts, refilling glasses, wiping the bar and laughing quietly at customer remarks. She looked up briefly, sensing his eyes on her, met his gaze briefly, then moved to respond to another customer's call. Mike absently took a sip of beer then bent his head to read the poem again. As he thought about the poem and its intention, he was struck again by the depths of this beautiful woman and the growing feelings for her, feelings he thought would never surface again after Cindy.

Molly finally moved back in front of Mike, with a questioning look as he handed the folded paper back to her. "Remember, I said be kind."

He laughed, then looked deeply into her eyes. "I thought the poem was beautiful, deep and very moving. I would like very much to read more of your work. But first," he said, smiling, "I'd like to make use of another of your talents."

"What are you talking about?" she laughed.

"Well, Miss Molly, 'Finder of Lost Things,' It looks like I've lost my beer. Think you could find me another?"

"Well," she grinned, "you actually made a joke! What other surprises do you have?"

"First, find me my beer. Then I'll show you a courageous act of derring-do."

She laughed and walked off to draw him a draught of Harp. She returned, with his glass. "Now what is this courageous act of derring-do?"

"For courage," he said, as he took a large swallow of beer. "I was wondering, when you got off work, if you would like to have an early breakfast with me?" He managed to say it without mumbling, looking directly into her delicious green eyes.

Molly returned his gaze, searching earnestly for any signs of insincerity or shallowness, none of which she really expected to see. Finally, she said, "I'd love to have breakfast with you. It's the least you can do after I have given you my life's story and let you read my poetry. We close at one, and I should be finished by two. By the way, where are we going for breakfast?"

He laughed as he climbed off his stool. "I thought we'd try the Waffle House. It's the best I can do at that hour of the morning. See you at two."

As she watched him leave, she laughed to herself. "At least he didn't say his place," although she admitted she wouldn't have necessarily turned that down. In fact, she thought, it took him long enough to ask her out –a lot longer than she had wanted it to.

She finished the evening waiting on other customers, a little impatient and distracted, thinking to herself that at least she should be dressed okay for her first Sunday morning date at a Waffle House. She wondered if they would have a brunch menu.

Breakfast that morning had stretched into a full day at the beach, including lunch at his house on the ocean, and a couple of hours napping on matching chaise lounges on the veranda while listening to Mike's rather eclectic collection of jazz, country, classical, Sinatra tapes, and a beautiful album by a Greek artist named Nana Mouskouri.

Finally, in the evening, he offered her a tour of his studio and the finished canvases he had stored there. She was struck by the huge artistic talent he seemed to have, but also by the angry, painful focus of his work.

Mike didn't solicit her opinion, but watched her closely as she walked among his paintings. He noted when she stopped to stare at a particular piece, realizing that she stopped longest at the pieces that he knew he had felt the most passionate about. Finally, when he was almost ready to demand her reaction, she had said, quietly, "You must have experienced a lot a pain in your life."

"Why do you think that?"

She paused for a moment, then looked at him intently. "I'm clearly no art expert and certainly not a psychologist, but I feel like I see a great deal of pain and suffering in your work. Am I wrong?"

Mike had turned away from her, obviously in denial at first, then turned, slowly took her hand and led her out of the studio, onto the dune crossover where they could watch the moonlit waves rolling softly on the beach. They stood for a time, not speaking but nevertheless seeming able to communicate silently, in a quiet comfort that neither had experienced before.

Finally Mike asked, "How old are you? I know it's none of my business, but you seem much too wise and deep for someone so young."

She said, "Almost twenty-six. Not so young, though, that I can't feel pain or anger in others when it seems so obvious. I certainly feel like I sense that in your work. I also think you hide it very well, even control it, but it seems almost blatantly obvious in your painting.

Sensing a unique level of sympathy in Molly, Mike found himself beginning to relate those moments in his life that had produced the most pain. He told her, hesitantly, about Vietnam and the friends he had lost there. He told her about his friend Pete and finally, told her about the first love in his life –Cindy-- and how he had sent her away, fearing that she might be another victim of his angel-of-death persona, at which point he had wished for the relief of death.

Molly hardly knew how to respond. She couldn't find words that might ease the pain he had revealed. She knew, however, that what she was experiencing was an important moment in her life with Mike, but she didn't know how to hold on to it. She finally said, "How about me? Do you think I'm in danger because you might care about me?"

"No. I do care about you, would like you to be a part of my life, but I no longer fear I'm the angel of death for those I care about. The changes in my head began with a bus wreck and a young lady named Grace." He went on to relate the changes that had occurred, the events that had lifted him up from the depths of darkness.

She marveled at his willingness to open his heart to her, knowing that from this moment on he would be a single focus in her life. "Thank you for sharing that with me. I remember reading the article about the wreck and what you did to save those children, but I didn't put it altogether until now. I'm feeling blown away by this moment."

"I've never shared all of that with anyone before. I'm not sure where it came from, but being able to talk about it with you seems awfully important to me. It's probably time I took you to your car, but I don't want to lose this special something I'm feeling here with you. Do you think we can hold on to it?"

Molly answered, "Yes. I want that very much."

When they arrived back at the pub to get Molly's car, they stood for an awkward moment, then she reached up, touched his cheek and kissed him gently on the lips. She whispered softly, "I expect to hear from you shortly," and drove off.

She heard from Mike the next day, and a year later he surprised her with a proposal and an engagement ring. Molly remembered she had jumped up, staring at the beautiful ring he held out to her. "Oh, Mike. It's so beautiful." With that she had hugged him, saying over and over again, "I love you" and "I'm going to be Mrs. Michael Pallaso."

They were married shortly after, followed by a three-week honeymoon in Europe, visiting Dublin, London, Paris, Rome and Florence. It was a trip they repeated on their tenth and twentieth anniversaries, and one she hoped they could make again, as a way of reminding themselves of all the special moments they had spent together. The years had been filled with joy, comfort and a happiness Molly couldn't have dreamed of.

THE PRESENT
CHAPTER 52

As she set about making coffee, Molly noticed a note from Mike on the counter. "Don't let the guys leave before I get back from my run. Love, M."

Shortly, she heard stirring in the bedroom where Paul and Keith were staying. She went to the bedroom door, knocked softly and announced, "Breakfast in fifteen minutes, gentlemen."

Paul opened the door. "Morning, ma'am." Then added, "You don't need to go to any trouble for us."

Molly replied, "Don't be silly. Breakfast is no trouble. Come out when you're ready, and I'll start the eggs and pancakes. And it's Molly, not Ma'am."

Paul nodded, saying softly, "Thank you, Molly."

In a few minutes, both men walked into the kitchen, dressed in their clean clothes, wearing their backpacks, looking anxious to go.

"Sit down, fellows," Molly said, pointing to the kitchen table, "and I'll pour you some coffee. The food will be ready in a jiffy."

Shortly, as promised, Molly placed dishes piled high with eggs, bacon and pancakes before them, then joined them with her own mug of coffee. Keith and Paul began slowly picking at their food, eating little Molly noted, unlike how she thought grown young men normally would.

After pushing their half-eaten food around for a few minutes, each put down their forks. Paul said, "Where's Mike? We wanted to tell him thanks before we leave."

Molly sensed their discomfort and eagerness to leave. Nonetheless she smiled, and said, "He and Lady are taking their morning run on the beach." She glanced at the wall clock. "He should be back in about fifteen minutes. He left a note asking that you stick around until he returns. I hope you can wait."

Both nodded their agreement, then after a few minutes of awkward silence, Paul said hesitantly, "Last night you mentioned that Mike has had some of the same nightmares that Keith and I are having. I figure he must have been in Vietnam. "What was it like for him over there?"

Molly laughed with a hint of exasperation. "I've been with Mike for twenty-five years, and I've had to pull Vietnam from him like teeth from a gator, so I don't know the whole story, but I'll tell you what I know. Mike was in Vietnam for about a year, the last half of which was in a place called Khe Sanh, around 1968. He was wounded there and was medically discharged.

"From what he has told me, he had a pretty rough time getting mended at Walter Reed, and after his discharge he had a really bad time getting back to civilization. He turned to alcohol in a big way after he got out of the hospital. Then somewhere along in his alcoholism, a good wise man talked him in to going back to his art and using it as a way of purging his Vietnam experiences.

"From that point on, Mike was able to use his artistry to fight the pain in his mind, and in the process began to be recognized as an artistic talent some have compared to that of a famous gentleman named Jackson Pollock. I have to warn you though, that his paintings are very abstract and can be painful to see."

She paused, then continued. "One other thing you should know about Mike, because I think --and he even admits-- that he's fearfully affected by the experience of losing those he has loved, to the point he was on the verge of giving up his art and becoming a recluse.

"He thought it was the only way he could avoid the pain of losing anyone else he might care for. He lost so many friends in Vietnam, including his best friend. He also lost his mother and father prematurely, and worst of all, he lost his first love, when they couldn't overcome the sickness in his head. With all those painful experiences, he became convinced that somehow he was to blame. Of course, I don't believe it, but the pain has seemed to always be at the fringe of his subconscious."

Paul and Keith had sat quietly listening to Molly. They were both intrigued by her recounting of the mental pain Mike had brought back from Vietnam, feeling a resonance with the pain they were feeling. Both felt a flickering optimism that they, like Mike, might find some relief. Still, they were skeptical and waited impatiently for Mike's return so they could continue their directionless wandering.

To hide his impatience and fill the time before escaping, Paul murmured, "You must be proud to be a part of his life. But where do you fit into what you've described as the fear he has about losing people he loves? Isn't he afraid of losing you?"

"You're right, Paul. He's a remarkable man and thank God, a very important part of my life. He's as good as they come. As to why I'm different? First of all, we've been together for almost twenty-five years, and I haven't gone away. Second, we know we love each other deeply, the kind of love that can overcome almost any fear.

"Third, by my father's conviction-- and my own admission, I'm a finder and keeper of lost things –animals, people, whatever. My father used to call me the Shepard. So, I guess I've spent a good part of our time together watching over Mike, trying to read his moods, anticipating the rough times and how I might be able to help ease him through them.

"Finally, over the last few years, I think I've seen a change in Mike. He seems to have mellowed in his approach to life, seems to be calmer, more accepting of what life is offering him. Now, I sense he is looking for something --a finish, if you will-- that gets his vision beyond the pain, anger, and fear that seems to have dominated most of his work."

CHAPTER 53

"But enough about us," she said. "I don't mean to pry, but you know, I don't even know your last names or where you come from."

Keith and Paul sat awkwardly quiet for a moment, then Keith volunteered, "My name is Hargraves, ma'am. I come from a small town in Tennessee, called Clarksville."

"Clarksville." Molly said. "I think I've heard about that. Isn't it near an army post?"

"Yes, Ma'am," Keith replied. "Fort Campbell. My father was posted there. He retired as a major in the Military Police."

"Oh," said Molly. "So you come from a military family. Your father must be very proud of you. But with a father in the army, how did you come to be a Marine?" she asked.

Keith didn't respond for a long minute, then mumbled, "That's sort of a long story."

Realizing she might be treading on soft ground, she nodded, then quickly said, "And what about you, Paul? And remember, it's Molly, not ma'am."

Paul nodded with a slight smile. "My last name is Rogers, and I come from a small town up in the northwest part of North Carolina, called Boone. I went to school there, tried to play football at the university there -- Appalachian State-- got hurt, then joined the Marines."

"Sounds like you guys have left a lot out," Molly said. "Care to fill in some of the blanks? Hey fellas," she continued, "I'm not trying to pry, it's just that I'm interested." And yes, she said to herself, I am being nosy, because that's what us Finders of Lost Ones do.

Paul picked up his narration, finding Molly's interest compelling. "Boone," he said, "is a great little town, if you don't mind being surrounded by hills and small mountains, and slushing through snow in the winter. My mom and dad divorced while I was a junior and then he left to go to Florida to follow his job in construction. The next year my mom got real sick with cancer and then died while I was still in high school. After that, I moved in with my mom's sister. After I graduated, I tried to play football for Appalachian State, but got cut when I hurt my shoulder. I kicked around for a while in Boone, working in my uncle's cabinet shop, then, like an idiot, decided to join the Marines for the adventure. And here I am," he finished soberly.

"And here you are," Molly agreed and added, "and we're glad you're here with us."

Then she said, "Keith, I think I interrupted your 'long story'. I'd love to hear some of that story if you don't mind indulging a nosy old lady."

Encouraged by Molly's warmth and interest, Keith picked up his story with the admission that he and his father had a tough relationship while he was growing up.

"With his military background," Keith explained, "I guess dad tended to be a strict disciplinarian. He insisted that we -I was the middle of three kids-- all adhere to his rules regarding school, homework, chores, and whatever other regulations he could think of to make the family run the way he wanted. My older sister was lucky enough to escape this mess. She got a full scholarship to the University of Tennessee in Knoxville. And my younger sister was just finishing middle school, so I think he let her slide a little.

"Me," he continued, "I guess I was his biggest target. By the time I was a senior, we were always butting heads. He didn't think I helped around the house, wasn't keeping my grades up where he wanted them, and I guess I had an attitude that made me try to defy his rules. We were constantly in combat. Being in my family was a bitch--sorry ma'am. It wasn't much fun being his son.

"Anyway, at my mom's urging, after high school I enrolled in the local college and promised to find a part time job. That seemed to be okay with the old man as long as I kept grades up and helped around the house.

"But he continued to ride me about my grades and finding a job and my attitude didn't get any better. My college grades got really bad and I finally flunked out after a year. Dad blew his top and said I'd have to find a full-time job, or join the army. Finding a job in Clarksville was almost impossible, and after a couple of months of no job, Dad demanded I go talk to the army recruiter. That was when –I guess in defiance--I went and found a Marine recruiter, and so here I am."

"Sounds like you guys have had a few challenges getting started. Hopefully, things will start to calm down a bit." She didn't state her real thoughts --that war had damaged them with some tragic and painful experiences that were still consuming their minds.

All three sat quietly for a moment staring into empty coffee cups. Then, as Molly started to rise to clean off the breakfast dishes, Paul said, "What about you, Molly? What's your story?"

Molly laughed. "There's nothing important to say about my life, other than meeting and falling in love with Mike. I was a born and bred Irish Catholic girl, raised as a happy-go-lucky beach bum, always managing to get into and out of trouble around the neighborhood. I got a degree in sociology from the local college and currently I manage the beaches animal shelter for the Humane Society."

She finished by admitting to some gardening around the house, making it to the local gym three or four times a week, trying to write poetry, and trying to keep Mike out of trouble. She was interrupted by the sound of Mike and Lady climbing the patio stairs, with Mike laughing, as usual, about the mess Lady was going to make in the house with all the sand she had collected during the beach run. For her part, Lady stood impatiently at the kitchen door, looking for her usual doggie treat, tail wagging in expectant happiness.

CHAPTER 54

"Good," Mike exclaimed as he walked into the kitchen, "you two're still here. I want to talk to you about some help I need for a few days. Pay is good and bed and board are included. Think you might be interested?"

Paul and Keith looked at one another, baffled by the suddenness of the offer. Then Paul, speaking for both himself and Keith, said, "We appreciate all you've done for us, Mr. Pallaso, but we don't want to take advantage of your kindness, and we don't need any charity."

After an awkward moment of silence, Mike then said in a somewhat brusque tone, "First of all, it's Mike, not Mr. Pallaso. Second, this isn't charity. I got a problem, and I think you two can help me out." With that, he handed his cup to Molly for a refill and said, "Come with me" to Paul and Keith.

Mike led them from the kitchen into his large studio, which had once been the house's three-car garage before Molly had insisted he give up the room in the house he had been using. He turned on the overhead lights. "Have a look around, guys, and then I'll explain what help I need."

Paul and Keith slowly walked around the studio, gazing at painting after painting, seeing but not truly understanding what appeared to be someone's vision of an abstract hell. In each painting there appeared to be an almost manic blend of colors –primarily crimson, black, yellow and blood-red—mixed together with explosions of spiraling swirls and slashes.

Keith suddenly ran out the studio's back door onto the veranda, with Paul close behind. He began vomiting his breakfast, while Paul stood behind him, looking ashen-faced, trying to give Keith support.

Mike followed and stood in awkward silence. Molly, hearing the sudden commotion, came from the kitchen with a wet towel for Keith to wipe his mouth. She gently rubbed his shoulders, murmuring soothing words of encouragement. Paul stood apart, sympathetic to his friend's obvious pain, but knowing Molly would best be able to help him. Lady was there as well, nosing Keith's hand as he fought to compose himself.

Finally, after sitting on the edge of the veranda for a few quiet moments, head bowed in his hands in embarrassment, Keith managed to say, "Sorry. Can't seem to hold it together. I think it would just be better if I left."

Mike --angry at himself and frustrated at his inability to be of help-- stood staring at the rough waves rolling onto the shore. Out of the corner of his eye he noticed the empty look in Paul's eyes.

The ministering that Molly and Lady had been giving Keith seemed to be helping, so Mike cleared his throat and said, "Ok if we talk about the help I need from you guys, and how we might be able to help one another?" He saw the narrowed, warning look he was receiving from Molly, but he signaled his understanding of her strong caution and plunged on.

"Look," he said to Paul and Keith, "the only thing I've tried to do for the last forty years is put paint on canvas. Some people seem to think what I've done is pretty good, so I've been able to make a decent living at it. But when I thought I was ready to do something really good, along came the devil, in the form of something called Parkinson's disease. Bottom line is, it makes my hand and arm shake. I can't put paint on the canvas like I once could. It's likely only going to get worse. But I still have this vision and a driving need to put it on canvas. And that's where I think you guys can help."

"Tell you what," he continued, "let's take Lady for another walk on the beach while I tell you what I've got in mind. If you don't want to buy in, okay. I'll pay you for your listening time and get you wherever you need to go. What do you say?"

Keith and Paul looked at one another for a moment, then with a shrug nodded okay, vaguely curious about Mike's offer.

Molly, still not sure what Mike had in mind but confident that he was trying to help the young men, also nodded her assent, then announced to all, "Okay, I've got to get dressed and go into work. Mike, you best get Lady her morning biscuit, and when you get back, I don't want to find any sand or dog hairs in the house. In fact, you will probably need to hose her down."

"Yes, ma'am," he said with a smile.

"And don't forget," she continued, "Tom is coming over for dinner tonight. We're having Shepard's Pie. I'll see y'all this evening." And with that, she went inside, leaving Lady and the men to start on their walk.

CHAPTER 55

By early afternoon, Molly had pretty much finished at the shelter for the day, having spent a good portion of her time evaluating new arrivals. They had taken in a half dozen dogs and twice that many kittens and cats.

Molly took a final walk through the kennels and cages housing the various animals, stopping to reach in and pet tail waggers or meowing kittens as she thought about possible homes each might fill. Finally, she said good night to the evening volunteer supervisor, walked to her car, and then remembered to call Father Tom to remind him of his dinner date with them.

She also wanted to let him know that Paul and Keith would be with them and to make him aware that they both seemed to be having problems with post-traumatic stress from combat. She hoped, based on his work with Wounded Warriors, he might have some thoughts on how she and Mike might help them. She wanted to suggest he not reveal himself as a priest in order to keep Keith and Paul from being inhibited in front of him if they chose to talk about themselves or their problems.

As she waited for the rectory secretary to try to run down Father Tom, she laughed at the memory of how she and Mike and Tom, as he insisted they call him, had first gotten together and became close friends.

It had started at the Irish pub where she was tending bar, soon after she and Mike had begun to gravitate towards one another. Tom, whom she then knew as Father Thomas McGee, the new parish priest at St. Paul's Catholic Church, was a more than occasional visitor to the pub, where he enjoyed a draft or two of Harp a couple of times a week. He dressed in disguise, as he called it, without his collar, when he came to the dimly lit pub, which he admitted to Molly allowed him enough anonymity to recharge his batteries.

In the course of their getting acquainted across the bar, she had learned he had graduated from Boston College with a degree in psychology, did a stint --as he described it-- as a lieutenant with the

Marines in Vietnam, came home with many unanswered questions about what he had experienced, and slowly gravitated to the church and the priesthood. It was clear from listening to him, that his transformation –his conversion he called it- had involved a great deal of personal anguish, and she marveled at the peace and serenity he now seemed able to enjoy.

One evening, as Tom sat at the bar, she mentioned to him that she'd like him to meet a friend, a fellow Marine, because she thought they might enjoy getting to know one another. She enticed him with an offer of another draft of Harp --on the house-- to move down the bar to the empty stool next to Mike.

Mike, with noticeable indifference, nodded to the well-disguised priest as Molly introduced them. He straightened up with a bit more interest when Molly mentioned that Tom had been a Marine and served in Vietnam. In silent acceptance, he clinked mugs with Tom with a quiet salute to the history they shared.

Inevitably, questions began between them about when were you there, what unit were you in, where did you serve, etc. Both responded in monosyllabic tones with the barest of information, quickly signaling to the other their reluctance to talk about their experiences.

The evening ended with a fairly warm expression from each that they were glad to have met and had a chance to talk, with vague mentioning that they hoped to get together again. They shook hands, after which Mike said good night and walked out.

Tom noticed the small look of disappointment on Molly's face as Mike left. He picked up his tab to let her know he was ready to leave and as he handed her payment, including a tip, said teasingly, "Sweet on Mike, are we?"

She handed the tip back, telling him to put it in the poor box, then said, "Awfully nosy for a priest, aren't we?"

Tom gave her a full Irish laugh, then smiled smugly. "We priests have to be nosy, else how would we find out what people are really coming to confession for? Anyway, he seems like a fine fellow. But how could he not be, being a Marine? I wish you both the very best. May God bless you and give you happiness." With that he turned, saying "Time for evening prayers," and walked out.

Once Mike and Molly became a pair -- as Tom liked to tease-- they found increasing times when they got him over for beer and dinner. Tom enjoyed the casual release from his priestly duties, and he and Mike soon began engaging in a spirited exchange of friendly insults that only men could understand.

Slowly, they began to share their Vietnam experiences, during which Tom revealed that he had led a Marine Force Recon unit and had spent more time communing with snakes and spiders than he had chasing the Viet Cong. Unspoken, but understood by both men, had been the knowledge that Tom and his unit had experienced and lived in the most perilous times in 'Nam.

On about Tom's third visit with them, Mike revealed in obvious delight, that he had known for several months what Tom's true profession was, confessing gleefully that he had heard Patrick, the owner of the pub, greet Tom as 'Father' one evening. He took great delight in teasing Molly and Tom as though they had committed a grievous sin of deceit.

They laughed guiltily, and admitted they were concerned about his acceptance of Tom's secret of bring a priest. They were afraid he might shut down in the presence of beliefs that could be in conflict with his own spiritual doubts.

Mike shrugged off their concerns, visually signaling to them that he had things under control.

Taking advantage of the closeness that seemed to be occurring in their relationship, Tom said, "Mike, I've seen your paintings, and I gotta' confess they're disturbing beyond anything I might have imagined. In my mind you have certainly captured the emotions and pain I know I brought back from 'Nam, that fortunately-- for my sake-- led me to God.

"But what about you? What gives you peace? Are you able to grab hold of some belief system to help you deal with the pain your paintings seem to suggest?"

Mike, unwilling to let the conversation move him beyond his comfort zone, said, "Sorry, but I'd rather not go there. Truth is, I'm not religious. I'm still trying to figure things out about God, and religion, and all that shit."

Tom nodded. "Well let me know when you get it all figured out. I'd like to know."

Mike and Molly shared puzzled glances, both looking at Tom as he shredded the label from his beer. "What's that mean, Tom?" Mike, said. "Thought you had it all squared away, wearing that collar and everything."

"Yeah, I know. I oughta' have it straight. But did you know the Christian religion, the whole Christian concept is one big paradox? Nothing but contradictions in man's logical thought?"

"You 've lost me," Mike said, reaching for another beer. "You're goanna have to get closer to us peasants."

"Think about it. We're asked to believe that the God of the universe, if there is one, that nobody's ever seen, and has only been heard from by a tribe of ignorant people from a place called Israel, chose to send his Son to be a poor itinerant carpenter in a backward country conquered by a rough country of killers, and he becomes the well-spring of God's redemption of us humans from our sins. And the paradox continues. The meek will inherit the earth; if you want to be first be last; if someone slaps you on one cheek, offer them the other; if Christ puts mud on your blind eyes, you'll see; leprosy disappears if he but touches you; If he says rise, you live again. And if you wish to live, you must die. And the paradox goes on and on."

At this point, Molly intervened with quiet laughter. "Okay, you two. I have coffee with Bailey's for anyone interested. Then, if you are so inclined, we can take a walk on the beach. It is such a lovely evening and there's almost a full moon. The only rule is we leave the serious stuff here."

The rest of the evening was spent in comfortable silence, and when Tom left, he gave Molly a tight hug, thanking her for the wonderful corned beef and cabbage meal, and Mike a shoulder squeeze for the new friendship they knew they were enjoying.

Shortly after, before he proposed to Molly, Mike told Tom of his plans and asked if Tom would marry them. Tom agreed immediately, and after the proposal he worked with Molly on the marriage details.

Finally, interrupting Molly's reverie, Tom came to the phone somewhat breathlessly, and said, "And how is the beautiful Mary Kathleen Sullivan Pallaso this fine Wednesday evening? And how is that ne'er-do-well husband of yours, the one who scams people into buying the globs of paint he throws on cloth and calls art?"

"You mean," she laughed, "the one who accuses you of being a rogue Irish thief, talking the poor innocent people into filling the poor boxes with your retirement money?"

"The same," he responded. "The one the Lord has saddled me with as a test of my Christian faith and endurance."

"Well, he's doing as well as can be expected, given his penchant for getting in trouble. But I called to remind you of your Christian duty to come have dinner with us this evening. We're having Shepard's Pie, which of course you know, Mike insists on calling Italian lasagna."

Tom laughed. "I don't know how the Holy Father endures being surrounded by the ignorant Italian masses. Anyway, you can be sure I will be there. I assume dinner will be accompanied by some good Irish beverage as well."

"You can be certain of that,"' Molly replied. "Also, I wanted you to be aware that we have a couple of young men staying with us, both recently discharged from the Marines --veterans of combat in Afghanistan-- and both who seem to be suffering from their experiences over there. I feel pretty sure each is suffering from some degree of PTSD.

"Mike saw them walking near the Mission House the other evening and, believing they were homeless, invited them to come have a meal with us and bunk in for the evening. Mike and I both think they need help, but we're not sure how we can make that happen. Mike is trying to talk them into working with him on one of his painting projects, but we don't know how that might work out.

"Anyway, if you don't mind, come in disguise, have dinner with us, and see what you think we might be able to do to help them. I think they might be more willing to open up with you if they don't know you're a priest, just another Marine. Are you okay with that?"

"Of course," Tom replied. "You know me. I'll do anything for a free meal that doesn't involve a casserole from the ladies of the church. I'll see you guys around six, after a couple of visits at the hospital."

KEITH
CHAPTER 56

As Mike, Keith, and Paul started out on their walk, the tide was low, and even though the breeze out of the northeast was brisk, it seemed a pleasant time for a walk. Walking three abreast with Mike in the middle, he began his explanation of what he had in mind by trying to help them understand his art.

"What you saw this morning," he said, with a look of silent apology to Keith, "was my most recent work --although I haven't tried to paint anything in the past two months. But it's a continuing theme that has driven all my work for the past forty years. It is, I admit, full of anger and pain and fear that I brought back from 'Nam. I admit my painting has always been an attempt at a type of self-administered therapy to try to purge my mind of that pain.

"It was an effort first suggested to me by a very wise friend who I'll never forget. Anyway, what he said to me was there's no difference between today and yesterday unless you can empty your brain of yesterdays. He said I had to find a way to throw the memory of those sounds and visions from yesterday from my brain onto my canvases. Only then would I have room in my brain for all the beauty and peace and love that the world still had to offer.

"So, over the years, I have attempted to follow his advice, as hard as it has been at times, and finally I have been able to purge most of the pain from my mind and today I have replaced it –given new birth to my mind—with the images of Molly and Lady, and sunrise on the beach, and the sound of laughing children. And that's how I stay sane –how I have stayed sane all these years."

"So what does this have to do with us?" Keith protested. "We're not painters, and besides, I don't see how your paintings can help me! All I see when I look at them is the pain in my mind staring back at me. All the senseless suffering and killing, for what purpose? Where in your paintings is the color of peace, the shape of freedom from pain?"

With this Keith had stopped walking and stared out to sea with tears running down his cheeks. For a moment Mike feared he might go running into the surf, searching so desperately for the peace he was chasing. Mike walked back to him, placed his arm around his shoulders and pulled him to his chest and held him while he sobbed.

When Keith had calmed and had let Lady lick his hand and nosed it to be scratched, Mike said, "Brother, believe me I feel your pain. And I'd be lying to you if I said it all goes away. But maybe there's a point of calmness and peace possible. And you don't have to be a painter to get there.

"When I said the same thing you said about my painting to the friend I told you about –that my paintings were only showing the pain, fear and horror that was in my mind—he said two things to me. One, that my painting was a therapy, a way of emptying all the horror and death out of my mind onto the canvas, and that that therapy was what was most important. And two, it only mattered what other people thought of my painting if they walked away hating the pain and suffering it portrayed, and looking for a soul-saving alternative."

Keith nodded his understanding if not his agreement. He resolutely squared shoulders and moved as if to continue the beach walk.

Mike sensed the on-going battle in Keith's mind and stopped him, saying, "I know we're not supposed to, but let's take a seat on that dune over there and see if we can take a breather."

With that, he led them to a fairly barren spot on one of the dunes, wondering whether anything he was doing made any sense. But once they were seated, he said, "Now, before I continue telling you what I need your help with, I want you guys to know I really do know your pain. And my gut tells that your helping me with my painting will help you deal with that pain.

"I think a place for us to start would be for each of you –if you're up to it—to talk about your experiences in Afghanistan, and the things you are carrying around with you. Mentally, it might be like what I was able to do with my painting, emptying my mind through the images I threw on my canvases. Sorta like a purge. How about it, Keith You feel up to throwing some paint on your canvas?"

With great reluctance Keith, after a long stare out to the horizon, tried to clear his throat, then said, “I lost my best friend in a place called Sangin….

CHAPTER 57

As the Boeing 757 began what felt like its final approach, the intercom opened up with the raspy voice of the Company Gunny, Jim Watson, saying, "Listen up, people. We're coming into Manas Air Base, in the Country of Kyrgyzstan --or however the fuck you pronounce it. It's also known as the gateway to hell! Well, that's just fine, 'cause we're here to kick the devil's ass! Do I hear an Oorah?"

Despite the long and tiring flight, the plane rocked with a loud "Oorah!

"All right, people, when the doors open move out quickly with your gear into platoon formation. You'll be released and directed to a chow hall shortly. Squads stay together. We'll reassemble at 1630 to load up on C-130s for the flight into Dwyer airbase, assuming they can find the fuckin' place. After that, we'll load up on choppers for the final leg into the Battalion's Forward Operating Base in a quaint little place called Helmand Province. Captain Pierce will brief you further at that point. Word of warning: the weather is shitty cold, so dress accordingly, and remember, you are Marines!"

A loud "Oorah!" responded, followed by loud murmurings of profanity and crude jokes.

As the plane touched down, Keith felt a nauseous lump in his gut and experienced a confusing mixture of excitement and fear. He locked eyes with his buddy Rod Milton, who had a similar expression on his face. Finally, they bumped fists and shrugged in resignation for what was to come.

Once off the plane, the company gathered as directed into respective platoons and squads, after which they were dismissed and pointed to waiting duce-and-a-halves for the trip to the mess tent. Keith couldn't decide what time it was, or for that matter, what day it was. He knew he was hungry, so he figured he had a one in three chance of getting the time right. When they arrived at the mess hall, the squad leaders had them sound off their names, then gave them a stern warning to eat, reassemble in thirty minutes, and don't fuck off.

The meal was hamburgers, hot dogs, baked beans, cold slaw, and some kind of cake with peaches. Keith, Rod, and the rest of their squad went through the chow line, loading their trays and found a table together. The first few minutes were spent in silence as they shoveled the heavy fare into their starving mouths. Finally Rod said, "Sergeant Thomas, you been here before, right?" The squad leader nodded with a sour face designed not to encourage further questions, saying "Yeh, so what?" But Rod persisted, asking, "You were also in Iraq, right. So how do they match up?"

Thomas glared at Rod, then said flatly, "Same shit, different day. They all want to kill your ass. You best remember your training, Marine. All of you. Keep your weapon clean, your head down, and don't do stupid shit. This place we're going to –Sangin-- from what I've been told, is a viper's nest, like all of Helmand Province. The British got their asses kicked there. But we are Marines, so like the Gunny said, we are here to kick some ass! Now go find the pisser and then meet me outside. You got five minutes."

As he moved through the latrine, Keith thought about the briefing they had received back at Pendleton on where they were going –a village area called Sangin –and how matter-of-factly the briefer had warned them it was a dangerous place.

He had pointed out, as he displayed a google-type overhead shot of the area, that the town of Sangin was surrounded by trees, thick foliage and high growing crops that severely reduced the view of the terrain outside the village wall. He further pointed out the rolling hills that surrounded the village, all of which made it a dangerous set up for enemy fire into the village, especially for sniper fire. In addition, he pointed out, the village had a warren-like, honeycombed construction made up of all kinds of inter-linked, high mud walls that surrounded mud compounds in which the village inhabitants --probably including Taliban-- lived.

It was a geography that favored the enemy, allowing easy access into the town's center from almost any direction. The briefer didn't need to point out to his captive audience it was going to be impossible to cover every potential gap the Taliban could use to push their way into town. Keith remembered the briefer mentioning the terrain was such that when the

Marines were running patrols into and around the town they'd be tempting targets for IEDs and ambushes.

The company commander, Captain Pierce, had thanked the lieutenant who had given the briefing and then told the company that there'd be further briefings on how they'd be countering the tough terrain and enemy tactics, then had dismissed them to get ready to leave Pendleton.

CHAPTER 58

The C-130s moving the battalion to Dwyer left about on schedule without serious incident and arrived within the scheduled timeframes to meet up with the choppers to take the battalion to the FOB. As Keith's company off-loaded from the choppers, he was struck by the desolate appearance of the FOB. It was orderly to Marine standards, but still seemed like a moonscape. The cold was numbing and a desert wind was blowing strong enough to choke his lungs. Not for the first time Keith wondered what he was doing here, what turn he had missed leaving Clarksville, Tennessee.

However, he, like the rest of the Marines in Echo Company, had no time for thinking beyond Marine thoughts as Gunnery Sergeant Watson called them into platoon formation then brought them to attention as the Company Commander, Captain Pierce, stepped before them. At his direction, the Company stood at ease and then he called them to circle up around them.

"Oorah," he hollered, to which the company responded resoundingly, "Oorah!"

"All right, gentleman," he began. "We're where we're supposed to be, where Marines are needed. And we'll do as we've been ordered to do. Let me fill you in on those orders. Yes, we'll find and kill the enemy --the Taliban--but we'll do more. We'll pull the real Afghanis to us--the people who're trying to live a decent life, to educate their children, to find some happiness without the Taliban boot on their necks. This is a critical part of our mission–to gain the trust of these people and help them rebuild their country.

"We don't have an easy task, but we're Marines, and we'll find a way. Let's start with our Rules of Engagement. Yes, you'll kill the enemy, as sure as you know him. The problem is, he'll likely look like everyone else in this tough country. We need to know how to identify the Taliban. If you see people firing on you, no brainer. If you see someone carrying a weapon, no brainer. If you see someone who looks like they're planting an IED, no brainer –grease 'em!

"However, it won't be that simple. There'll be times when your gut tells you you're looking at the enemy, but you can't be sure. You *will* hold your fire. If an adult Afghan starts running toward your position, use your translator to tell the individual to stop and to lift his top and show his gut. If a child is running towards you, use your translator to make the child stop –do not fire or otherwise try to stop them. If you can't do anything else, take cover. In short, our first job is to find and kill the enemy, but our other job is to win the hearts and minds of the decent people in this country, and we will do both!"

Capt. Pierce looked around at the men. "Your platoon leaders have already met with their counterparts with Alpha Company, who we're replacing. They'll direct you to your positions and give you a briefing on what our plans and expectations are for the rest of the night. I expect each of you to conduct yourself as a Marine and to carry out your duties as I know you can. Platoon leaders, take charge."

The company broke down and gathered with the individual platoon leaders. Second Lieutenant Jackson, a recent graduate of the Marine OCS and Advanced Infantry Training, had Keith's platoon take a knee, then began briefing them on what the night would bring. "Listen up," he said. "We're going to occupy the southwest quadrant of the FOB. We'll have two squads on and two off, in four- hour shifts. Squads One and Two will take the first shift, Three and Four the second. We start at 1900 hrs., after Alpha Company has had a chance to get their stuff together and move to the choppers. Squad leaders, get with your counterparts in Alpha and get the lay of the land and a feel for what we might expect for the rest of the evening."

Keith's squad, the Third, moved with their gear to the stone hut that occupied the southwest portion of the FOB. As they moved into the hut, they were passed by a squad of Marines from Alpha Company, who mumbled wishes of "Good luck, keep your head down," and an occasional "You'll be sorry."

By now, all Keith and Rod wanted to do was find a warm place to bed down and give in to the utter fatigue they were feeling after the long trip from Pendleton. What they found was a hard mud floor, no heat, and the sounds of creatures scuttling around on the walls of the hut. They knew they needed to get some sleep before their shift started, but all they could think of was the hard cold floor, the freezing night, and their frozen toes. They ended up gathering together in an effort to share body warmth but no one spent a good hour actually sleeping.

CHAPTER 59

It was almost a blessing when Sgt. Thomas began kicking their butts when their shift was scheduled to start. By now, the cold had settled into a bone-chilling, breath-stealing, ground-hugging fog of misery, especially for the Marines who had just left sunny southern California twenty-four hours ago. Keith and Rod, together with the rest of the squad, stomped around the hut, trying to get feeling into their toes, then followed Sgt. Thomas out to their posts on the southwest quadrant of the FOB. They passed the First Squad, whom they were relieving, with each squad walking in an arm-swinging, head down motion, not even acknowledging the other Marines as they fought the numbing cold.

Sgt. Thomas directed the squad to several firing holes in the lower floor of the guard tower. The 4th Squad would man the second level. Looking out of his firing hole, Keith could see nothing and he and Rod exchanged glances that said, What the fuck are we doing here? Sergeant Thomas, sensing the confusion in his people, moved from firing hole to firing hole, propping each man up with quiet warnings to stay awake, keep their ears open, and let him know if they saw or heard anything.

The rest of the night passed in agonizing slowness, with the Marines giving only empty attention to their posts while trying to find ways to save their toes, ears, and hands from imminent frostbite. Finally, slow signs of dawn began to spread across the grassy, tree-lined plain that marked the boundary of the FOB from the rest of the countryside. As light began to penetrate the area, Keith could see what appeared to be a river or canal off in the distance. And off to his right, far in the distance, he could see the outline of what he assumed to be a village.

At the full flush of dawn, Sgt. Thomas relieved the squad from their guard posts, told them to get some food, a change of socks, and get ready for a patrol into the village of Sangin at 0900. He told them to expect it to be a hot patrol, with plenty of efforts by the Taliban to test them.

"The patrol's job," he reminded them, "was to challenge the Taliban, and to let them know the Marines were here to kick their asses." And he continued, "remember the ROE: If they fire on us we kill 'em. If they are carrying a weapon we kill 'em. If they are planting an IED, we kill 'em."

On hearing this, Keith began to feel his juices flow and a mixture of nausea and anxious excitement filled his head. After a quick MRE meal of what passed for egg and sausage together with a coffee-like concoction that Rod put together, he and Rod began checking their M-16s, making sure their armored vests and combat harnesses were secure, that they had extra ammo clips, and their hydration camels were full. When fully loaded up, they were each --as was every Marine--about eighty pounds heavier.

CHAPTER 60

At a little past 0900, Keith and his squad followed Thomas through the FOB gate where they were met by a team of three Explosive Ordinance Disposal specialists, accompanied by an eager explosive-sniffing German Shepherd.

"Okay," said one of the three EODs, a Sergeant Balms. "We're going to lead you guys into this rabbit warren. We've swept a path this morning that'll take you to about the center of town. The path is marked with small yellow flags. Don't move outside them flags. This here," pointing to an Afghani interpreter, "is –shit I can't pronounce his name—we call him Reggie--, but he'll be able to help you talk to the people in the town about where the Taliban might be, not that you'll get any straight answers. Any questions?"

"Yeh," Rod, hollered. "What's the pooch's name?"

"He ain't no pooch!" Sergeant Balms replied reproachfully. "He's the best fuckin' bomb sniffer in the Marine Corps. And he'll save your asses more times than you can count. He's a Marine, and he decides what name he'll answer to. Right now, he goes by Snoopy, especially if I got a biscuit in my hand. Any more silly–ass questions?"

Hearing none, he turned and began walking down the dirt road toward the village, not bothering or caring to see if the squad was following.

Keith was struck -- feeling his own fright—at how utterly fearless Balms and his fellow EOD specialists appeared.

The squad fell in behind the EODs and started its first patrol toward what someone called Indian Country. The patrol angled slightly right, and began moving toward the jigsaw puzzle of mud walls and compounds that made up the town of Sangin.

They moved in single file down the side of a dusty road –more a path than anything-- with Sergeant Thomas' harsh warning to maintain proper intervals and to keep their eyes open. The town had supposedly been cleared by Alpha Company of occupying Taliban, but the cluster of mud huts and walls that the town consisted of made that impossible to verify.

CHAPTER 61

As the squad began moving toward the town, they suddenly heard several blups of automatic rifle fire behind them, most likely from AK-47s. Marine return fire was sporadic, then there were shouts of "Corpsman," followed by frustrated hollering and cursing from the Marine squad that apparently had been the target of the enemy fire.

Sgt. Thomas immediately put the squad in a defensive position on the upslope of a ditch paralleling the dirt road they had been following. The EODs sat down to wait in bored indifference. After a few terse questions on the radio back to the Company, Thomas clicked off, stared silently off in the distance for a moment, then hollered, "All right, listen up! Second Squad just lost a man to sniper fire not fifty meters from the FOB. Any you clowns think this is a cake-walk better think again!

"We're gonna hold our position here for a few mikes till we get the word to move on to the village. Keep your eyes peeled. You see anything holler out but no shooting 'less I say so! "

Keith hunkered down with the rest of the squad, more intent on keeping his head down than trying to see anything beyond the edge of the muddy road they were hiding behind. Eventually, however, he began searching the terrain in front of them with morbid curiosity, wondering if he might see evidence of Taliban moving towards them. What he saw, instead, was a stand of skeleton-looking trees along the edge of the far canal. They looked, in his hyper state of anxiety, to be waving their wind-driven, leafless limbs in mocking, taunting gestures of death at the Marines.

Finally, Sgt. Thomas hollered, "Okay, off your asses and move out smartly! We're still headed for that fuckin' town, and the first chance we get, we're gonna' kill some of these assholes! Peterson," he called to one of his fire team leaders, "you and your people take the point! And maintain decent intervals, damnit!"

Oh shit, Keith thought, as he tried to swallow the dry spit in his throat, Why do we have to be up front? Nonetheless, he and Rod began cautiously trudging after Peterson, making sure to step exactly in the point man's footsteps, following the EOD team. And so the squad moved toward the edge of the village walking behind Sgt. Balms and his EOD team as they neared a narrow path running between two mud walls, marked with the beginning of the yellow flags.

The walk down the marked path, surrounded as it was by high, thick mud walls, produced its own brand of gut-wrenching fear for the patrol. Every turn, despite the lead of the EOD team, felt as menacing as anything the squad had yet encountered.

Finally, after several anxious minutes of creeping down the path between the walls, they entered what appeared to be the village marketplace, a series of crude stalls paralleling the main dirt road where the venders were selling and trading various goods. Despite the warming temperature as the sun rose toward the center of the sky, Keith continued to feel chilled and almost claustrophobic in the small marketplace.

The area seemed moderately busy, particularly around the stalls involving food. A fair number of villagers, seemingly indifferent to the Marine patrol's presence, bartered in a singsong cadence over prices for limited quantities of scrawny vegetables, squawking chickens hung upside down, and tethered bleating goats. The only other activity seemed to be at the stalls farthest from the center of the marketplace, which Reggie said was where opium prices were being argued.

Besides the Marines, only the chickens and goats seemed to sense the malodorous perfume of fear in the village.

Thomas gave the squad a silent hand signal to kneel in defensive positions while he, Sgt. Balms, and Reggie sought out some of the villagers who might be willing to talk about the whereabouts of the Taliban. Those villagers were reluctant, to the point of belligerence, to give any information regarding where or how many Taliban were present in the village. Their reluctance seemed a mixture of fear of the Taliban and a resentment over the presence of the Marines.

Suddenly, as Sergeants Thomas and Balms and Reggie began walking back through the market place to the squad's position, a whooshing fusillade of vicious rifle fire began raking the marketplace. "Sniper! Sniper!" Balms hollered as he and Thomas hit the ground and started trying to crawl toward cover in amongst the nearest stalls. The villagers immediately began ducking and walking rapidly in different directions in a curious dance of resigned acceptance, some even stopping long enough to cover their stalls, as though a sudden rainstorm had begun.

The squad, too, tried to take cover around the stalls while looking around wildly, attempting to find the source of the firing. Thomas shouted, "Anybody see anything? Anybody got a fix on where the fire's coming from? Anybody hit?" A mumbled chorus of "No, Sergeant" responded, after which Thomas whispered loudly, "Hold fire! Fire teams, each pick a sector; look for any movement! Anything out of place! And keep your fuckin' heads down."

At that point, Sgt. Balms started whispering softly, "Snoopy, stay." Then he shouted, "Anybody see my dog?" There was no response at first, either from the squad or the other EOD team members. They were all focused on trying to spot the snipers and keeping their heads down.

Then Reggie whispered fearfully --obviously not wanting to be the bearer of bad news-- "Sergeant Balms, sir, Snoopy over there under opium stall. He not moving."

Balms, who had been squatting behind a pile of tattered cloth and rags, stared uncomprehendingly across the dusty marketplace road at the still, lifeless form of Snoopy. "No!" he shrieked. "The fuckers killed my dog!" And before anyone could stop him he leaped up, ran across the road and knelt down by his unmoving friend, frantically trying to will life back into him. Then, in uncontrolled grief and anger, he stood and began firing his M-16 at nothing but the empty groves that surrounded the village.

Thomas and the other EOD team members rushed to his side and roughly threw him to the ground, holding him firmly until he began to calm. Finally, wiping tears from his face, he demanded to be let up.

Crouching low, Keith brought his poncho over and offered it to Balms to use if he wanted to carry Snoopy back to the FOB. Balms took it without speaking, then said to Thomas, "It's up to you, Sergeant. You want to continue this patrol we're good with that. I think the sniper was out there" – and pointed to a stand of low trees about a hundred meters to the east of the village wall— "but probably is long gone by now. My team will continue to scout ahead for your people as best we can without" --he hesitated--"the dog."

Sgt. Thomas stood unmoving in the middle of the market for a moment, trying to process what had just happened. Then it dawned on him that –like him-- the rest of the squad was standing out in the open, making easy targets. It was, he thought, as though they all felt like the price for the day had been paid by the dog.

Mentally he shook himself back to reality, nodded at Balms that the patrol would continue and then began shouting at the patrol to get their head out of their asses and assume proper combat discipline.

The patrol continued, moving slowly through the warren-like perimeter of the village, stopping at strategic points to try to question villagers about possible Taliban activity. Without exception, the villagers they questioned denied any knowledge of the Taliban. Instead they used the encounters as opportunities to complain bitterly about the invasion of the Marines into their village. They listed in rote fashion, damage to their compounds and market stalls, the theft of their goods by Marines, and numerous other issues for which they demanded compensation. Generally, they expressed their displeasure at the disruptive nature of the Marine presence. All of this was being provided in translation by Reggie, which Thomas and the rest of the patrol had been warned to take with a grain of salt.

CHAPTER 62

At the end of their six-hour patrol, Thomas turned his squad back toward the dusty road leading to the FOB. They continued back through the village paths, following closely the flags set by Sergeant Balms and his EOD team --which had been rechecked. During the entire patrol, after the market place sniper fire, Balms had continued to carry the lifeless body of Snoopy.

As the patrol approached the gate to the FOB, Balms and his team stopped, gave a desultory wave to Thomas and his squad, and moved on to the separate encampment maintained by the EOD detachment. Thomas dismissed his squad inside the gate, sending them to get chow, get cleaned up and squared away, while he reported to the lieutenant. He would find them later with assignments for the rest of the evening.

Keith and Rod and the rest of the squad moved to their quarters where they met up with the rest of the platoon. Scuttlebutt had it that Lance Corporal Porter, 3rd Platoon, had been hit and killed by sniper fire within minutes of his squad leaving the compound. No other details were available, other than he had been hit in the head. In addition to Porter, three Marines from the Second Platoon, Echo Company had been wounded by an IED near the canal while patrolling near a small makeshift bridge. Subsequently, the bridge had been destroyed by an EOD team.

Sergeant Thomas reappeared shortly after the squad began to settle in, advising them that they would be moving out at 0700 hours for another patrol into the village. An EOD team would accompany them.

And so began a repetitive, fear-filled pattern for the squad, and all of Echo Company, trying to engage an elusive, ghost-like enemy. An enemy that seemed always to know where the patrols were headed and able to appear suddenly in ambush with a deadly IED explosion followed by bursts of AK-47 and RPG fire.

In the first five days, the company lost eight killed and fifteen wounded. Most were the victims of IEDs. The company commander,

Captain Pierce, numb with the punishment the company was taking, had no immediate ideas how to counter the Taliban tactics. Nor could he and his platoon leaders find any workable solution to the plunging morale the young Marines were experiencing.

Withdrawal, advised by some in the chain of command, was never seriously considered. Instead, reinforcements from two companies from another battalion were brought in to support a fundamental change in tactics: From now on, two squads, rather than one, would move out together for more firepower. Huts or compounds suspected of supporting the Taliban, especially with the manufacture or planting of IEDs, were summarily destroyed, despite the original maxim to try to win the hearts and minds of the people.

By the end of their fourth month in Sangin, the Marines had lost fifteen KIAs and forty wounded, most by well-hidden IEDs near the paths the Marines were forced to take around the village and through the paths they had to take within the village itself. This despite the increased success that the EOD teams had been having in finding planted IEDs. The numerous daily explosions by the EOD teams to destroy hidden IEDs were a comfort to the Marine infantry units but a sober reminder of all the IEDs that had not been found and were waiting to kill or maim them.

CHAPTER 63

Despite their constant grind of patrols through the treacherous terrain of the village and surrounding countryside, Keith's squad remained remarkably free of casualties. They had been involved in numerous firefights, many instigated by heavily armed, tenacious Taliban units in ambush settings. But many had been started, almost spasmodically, by the squad when they thought they had spotted Taliban in the groves around the village or the Marine FOP or across the Helmand River.

As Sergeant Thomas tried to explain to Captain Pierce, it was like trying to fight ghosts. You knew they were out there waiting to kill you, but you just couldn't zero in on them. Yes, Sir, he knew there was a lot of wasted ammo, but the men were so hyped at wanting to get at the enemy that they couldn't keep their fingers off the trigger. And when the Marines did see people defiantly staring back at them across the fields or the river, their natural assumption was that it was the enemy and it would only be a matter of time before the bastards would try to kill them.

For his part, Keith had reached a point at which there seemed to be no future, no meaningful past. He lived only in the present, made solely of mud walls, sporadic AK-47 rounds wheezing overhead, RPG explosions, or Marine fire in heavy, hollering return, punctuated by the ear-splitting explosions of IEDs.

One evening, as he and Rod were half-heartedly bartering over who got what from the evening MREs, Keith suddenly asked, "Are you afraid? You know, about being over here and maybe getting killed or losing your legs or some shit like that?"

Rod looked at him for a minute, then said, "Man, I'm too stupid to be afraid. In fact, I think I'm addicted to war –to the excitement, the challenge. The feeling I get when I pull the trigger on the 16 or the SAW, it's like the first swig of a 100 proof Jack Daniels. It sets me on fire. What about you?"

Keith was quiet for a moment, trying to find the words to explain what was going on in his head. Then he said, "I don't know. I think I'm scared --not just of dying or getting blown apart, but dying and not knowing why. I'm confused. Why are we here, what good are we doing?"

"Man," Rod responded, "you're too deep for me. How'd you end up in the Marines anyway?"

"It's a long story. But I love the Marines. I love the straight ahead, kiss my ass, take the objective no matter what attitude that means being a Marine. But that doesn't help me answer why we're here. Why are Marines being killed, or worse, blown apart? If I'm gonna die, I want it to be a bigger reason than stepping on a mine in some god-forsaken country whose name I can't even pronounce!

"And what about the people here, the ones we're supposed to be helping? Do you think they care that we're here?"

Rod started laughing, not so much at his friend, but at the whole situation they were in. He interrupted himself as he managed to burn his fingers on the MRE package of so-called beef stew he was rescuing from the small fire they had built to cook over. Licking his fingers, he looked at Keith with a slowly dawning understanding of his friend's angst and frustration.

"Look. I guess I feel your pain, but this shit we're doing is what Marines've been doing for two hundred years –going where no one else is crazy enough to go to pull someone's nuts out of the fire. And nobody remembers the names of those places except the Marines who went there and died there.

"And the people here, they couldn't give a shit about us being here, or why, as long as they can still put meat and bread on the table. Whether it's us or the fuckin' Taliban that makes that happen, they couldn't give a fuck. Now, give me some of that delicious spaghetti you're fixin' and I'll let you have some of my gourmet beef stew."

They ate in friendly silence, with Rod occasionally glancing up at Keith, concerned that his friend was not handling the constant pressure they were under. And he admitted to himself that what he had told Keith about his feelings wasn't totally honest.

He also wondered why their being in some place called Sangin could possibly be important enough that --he had heard-- over twenty-five Marines had been killed, and another seventy-five wounded, some with horrific injuries from those fuckin' IEDs. He chose not to share those thoughts with his buddy. Instead, yawning loudly, he signaled his intention to try to catch a few minutes of sleep before the next round of patrols started.

Keith finished eating and began to try to find a spot with as few lumps as possible to lie down on. He couldn't remember the last time he'd been warm since coming to this god-awful country, but he'd learned to deal with the night cold using layers of clothing, ponchos and various other covers so he could at least contain his body heat. He'd learned to change socks, but the boots stayed on.

He thanked God or whoever was responsible for the bone-numbing fatigue he was feeling that he knew would win the battle with the cold and let him sleep. As his last thought, he tried to count the days left until their deployment would be over, over-shadowed by the constant fear that he wouldn't make it to that last blessed day.

CHAPTER 64

That morning, Sergeant Thomas assembled the squad, checked that they were all present and accounted for, packed up for the day's activities, and – after pretending to listen to their habitual grumbling-- said, "Listen up. This morning we're heading for the village, with the 1st Squad from Lima Company, 2/9.

"Our orders are to check out some of the compounds on the northern edge of the village. Supposedly, there's an IED factory in there somewhere, and we're gonna find their asses and shut 'em down. They're not gonna be happy, so keep your asses alert. EOD units have tried to clear the way in, but these bastards ain't using metal in the IEDs so it ain't easy finding the suckers. Lima's squad will be taking point. Now keep your head outta your asses and let's keep this clean."

The patrol, led by Lima's squad and following an EOD team with dogs, moved down to the village using a familiar path along the eastern edge before beginning to cut in behind a long, serpentine series of mud walls. In places, the walls were over six feet high, making it almost impossible for the Marines to know who or what might be on the other side.

As drilled in their heads countless times by Thomas, the patrol maintained required intervals of ten to twelve yards as they snaked by the compound walls. Keith and Rod's fire team occupied the middle of their squad, with each man keeping constant watch as they walked the treacherous paths, each haunted by the eerie silence that pervaded the early morning, each constantly sweeping the area with roving eyes, trying to see the unseeable.

Keith walked with what had become an unchanging combination of pain and nausea in his gut, with a gnawing fear he tried desperately to deny. Rod, who walked ahead of Keith, strutted with a quiet confidence that said he was where he wanted to be –where he belonged. Every few minutes he would look back at Keith with a wink of encouragement and a thumbs up to his friend.

Suddenly, as Rod partially disappeared around a slight curve in the mud wall, a thunderous explosion blew out from the wall as he passed, shattering the morning silence with a world-stopping, paralyzing flash that Keith had never experienced. He was momentarily blown backwards by the force of the explosion, landing on his heavily laden backpack, dazed and squirming without success to right himself like a capsized turtle.

Finally, as he began to get himself turned over and his hearing tried to return, he felt a numbing fear for his friend. Then calls for "Corpsman up," began to sing out ahead of him, along with cries and curses from the wounded. Shrugging out of his pack and combat vest, Keith ran forward only to be stopped in mid-stride by the sight of his lifeless friend, pulverized and broken by the force of the explosion he had taken full-on. Keith fell to his knees by his friend, unable to believe the horrible reality before him.

By now, corpsmen began to pass by him and Rod, moving towards other members of his squad and those from the Lima squad who had obviously been wounded by the explosion. Thomas, who had been at the rear of the patrol, moved by Keith, stopping briefly to put his hand on his shoulder, quietly acknowledging his pain, then moved on towards the front of the patrol to try to assess the situation.

Already, the corpsmen were calling for immediate medivac choppers to move the severely wounded. It appeared there were at least a half dozen wounded --including the squad leader from Lima Company-- some with obviously critical injuries, who needed to be moved to Dwyer Airbase for more extensive treatment. Thomas quickly contacted Echo Company, briefly explained the situation, gave the patrol's map coordinates, and requested immediate chopper evacuation for the wounded. He was quickly acknowledged in the affirmative, told that choppers were already lifting off and reinforcements were saddling up.

Thomas then ordered the unwounded survivors from the two squads to set up a defensive perimeter out in the adjacent field for the medivac choppers, to anticipate possible ambush by the Taliban.

He told two squad members to get Rod into a body bag, then took Keith away for a few feet to try to help him get under control. He spoke calmly to Keith, acknowledging the loss of his friend, but reminding him that he was a Marine, had a responsibility to his other Marine buddies, and that they all had to keep on keeping on.

Keith was hardly able to acknowledge Thomas, but training and discipline prevailed, and as directed, he went to get his combat vest and rifle and took up a defensive position in the field to await the choppers.

CHAPTER 65

The next six weeks were a spasmodic, walking nightmare for Keith. He slept little, if at all, moved with a zombie-like motion through his duties, spent each day staring off into empty space, with no notion of the passing of time. He saw only the sinister, skeletal trees waving off in the distance mocking him as he and the rest of the squad continued making patrols around and through Sangin. He moved in a bubble of isolation, feeling an inner trembling that his next step would be on an IED and almost hoping it would be so, just to end the pain.

One of the most difficult tasks he had shortly after Rod's death was attempting to sort through and pack up his personal belongings. His charge was to make certain nothing would go back to his family that would embarrass them or the Marines, but each and every item he touched put a crack in his heart, leaving him with a desolate sense of pain. He wept silently as he packed up the few belongings, wondering how anyone or anything could justify Rod's loss.

Six months after returning to the States, Keith's enlistment was up. He had been sent through several medical evaluations on his return by his command structure, primarily based on Sgt. Thomas's observations and concerns. But Keith had been able to disguise his pain enough to pass through his examinations, motivated primarily by his fear that his discharge might be held up by some obscure medical diagnosis.

On the day of his discharge, he elected to catch a Greyhound bus to Clarksville, where he endured a tearful reunion with his mother and sisters, and a firm handshake from his recently retired father. Clearly his family was overjoyed at his safe return, while Keith quickly began to feel the stress of their joy, oblivious as they were to the pain he carried with him. Added to the stress was his father's not too subtle questions about what he was going to do now, with the addition of suggestions about what he might do education or job-wise.

Two weeks after arriving home, Keith penned a terse note explaining that he needed to get away for a while and left early one morning before dawn for the bus station. There he bought a one-way ticket to the first city name that came to him, and shortly boarded a bus for Savannah, Ga., where soon after he'd met and hooked up with Paul.

PART THREE

STREAKS OF MORNING LIGHT

THE PROJECT BEGINS
CHAPTER 66

Mike sat still on the dune as Keith finished his story. He knew there were no words that would wash away the pain. He remembered all too well his own pain and how his mind had been impaled by his own 'Nam experiences. He could only hope that being able to talk about Afghanistan had helped loosen the band of pain that was squeezing Keith.

"Thanks, Keith. I know it was hard for you and just want you to know that we –Molly and me, and Lady—are here for you. We don't have all the answers, but you have a safe place to land if you need it."

Keith could only nod his thanks. Still, he felt a calmness begin to settle in around him as they sat on the dune, Lady at his feet, and the knowledge that Mike and Paul seemed to understand what he had been going through.

Mike had been keenly aware of the tension that had surrounded them as Keith recounted his experiences. But now he felt slightly more confident that it had been a good strategy. With that sense, he turned to Paul. "What about you? Care to talk about your time in Afghanistan?"

Paul stared silently for several minutes at the rolling waves moving in with the rising tide. Then he stood abruptly, turned back to Mike and said, "I know you are trying to help, but I can't talk about Afghanistan. I'm not able to deal with the pain now, if I ever will." With that, he began walking back toward the house, leaving Mike and Keith and Lady to hurry and catch up.

For several minutes, they walked in silence then Mike said, "Look, I know you guys are going through some tough times, but I could really use your help. What if we just give it a try for a couple of weeks, then if it's not working, feel free to take off. Same deal, room and board, the house is yours, and I'll pay $50.00 bucks a day. What do you say?"

Without directly responding, Paul said, "Guess we better get back and get Lady cleaned up. Molly sounded pretty serious about no mess. Then we'll see how it goes. Keith?"

"I'm okay with it," Keith said, and then, "Come on, Lady. I'll race you back."

He and Lady took off at a good pace, even running down through the edge of the surf with Lady barking her excitement.

Mike and Paul followed at a slower pace, but both feeling fairly calmed by the ocean wind, the surf, and Lady's enthusiastic barking.

CHAPTER 67

By the time Molly arrived home, Lady was clean, the house was straightened up and vacuumed, and Keith and Paul had both showered and changed. Mike had also showered and was having a beer when he heard Molly drive up. He went out to greet her, at which point, after a short kiss, she handed him a twelve pack of Harp bottles and a large bag of salad mix. She followed him in, carrying a bag filled with five Shepard's Pie dinners she had picked up from the pub.

"Ah," said Mike, "nothing like a home-cooked meal."

About fifteen minutes after Tom said he would arrive, which was about average for him, the doorbell rang, announcing his presence. Lady barked with delight and Molly called out, "Come in."

As Tom walked in, Mike hollered, "Who left the door unlocked?"

Tom said nothing, just walked in and held his hand out in an accusing, empty gesture. Mike filled his hand with a freshly opened bottle of Harp and sighed in feigned resignation. "I figured the poor would be here since it was meal time."

Tom ignored him, walked into the kitchen, and said in obvious anticipation, "Ah, Irish lasagna. My favorite." By now, Mike had followed Tom into the kitchen, watched him give Molly a hug, then walked over and tilted his bottle of Harp in silent welcome.

Mike observed Tom's disguise of jeans, sport shirt, and boat shoes, then said, "Thanks for coming, Tom. We really appreciate your willingness to help. Com'on, let me introduce you to the guys."

He led him into the large den where Keith and Paul sat watching a local news program. "Fellows, I'd like you to meet a good friend of ours who'll be joining us for dinner. Watch what you say, though, 'cause he's also a Marine and can't handle rough language."

The two young men smiled, stood up, and shook his hand. "Hi, guys. Mike tells me you're also Marines, which doesn't say much for our character, but at least we have that in common. Even Lady seems to be willing to overlook our poor decision making." He laughed as the collie demanded his affection with her probing nose.

Shortly, Molly called from the kitchen. "Food's ready." All four men stood up and filed out of the den to take seats at the round kitchen table.

Everyone filled their plates with salad and Shepard's Pie, took a fresh bottle of Harp, and commenced eating in hungry silence. Eventually each man gave a deep, satisfied sigh of fullness, took a last swallow of beer, then tried to out-do each with their compliments to Molly for a superb meal.

Molly laughed, telling them they were all full of blarney, that they knew full well the Shepard's Pie was from the pub, the Harp was bottled in Ireland, and the salad was store bought.

"Nevertheless," Tom protested, "you set a beautiful table. That's something Marines always relish."

"No more of your b-s, Thomas," Molly said. "Now who wants coffee?"

When all were settled around the table again with coffee cups in hand, Tom said, "Mike tells me you guys got back from Afghanistan not too long ago. I heard it was pretty rough over there. Anything you care to share --one dumb Marine to another?"

The two young men remained pensively silent for a moment. Then Paul finally said, "No, sir. There isn't much to tell. It was pretty rough, but Mike says you were in Vietnam, so you pretty much know what it was like."

Then, attempting to change the subject, he said, "So, Tom, what about you? What do you do?"

Without blinking an eye, Tom said, "Once I got back from 'Nam, my old man, knowing that a Marine had no chance of making a living in civilian life, decided to set me up with a decent income --he was loaded-- and a place to live. He told me to go find some way to try to make myself useful. So, ever since I've been bumming around, doing stuff like helping build Habitat houses, helping people find jobs, visiting old folks' homes, working with an outfit called Wounded Warriors, and just listening to people talk about their problems. I guess you could say I'm a fairly well-to-do ne'er-do-well."

Confused by Tom's non-description of what he did, Keith and Paul failed to notice the silent choking afflicting Mike, or Molly's less than dainty covering of her mouth to hide her glee at the unabashed Irish forgery spilling from Tom's mouth.

The meal ended in quiet satisfaction, with each man lending a hand at cleaning up. Finally, Tom announced his need to go while he could still maneuver the beach streets without gaining unwanted attention from the local gendarmes. He shook hands with Keith and Paul, gave Molly a tight squeeze, and ignored Mike's less than helpful suggestion that he help him out to make sure he got in the right car.

As they stood at Tom's car, Mike asked, "So, what do you think? Any way you think we can help these guys?"

Tom replied, "I'm not sure. They're both as brittle as dried branches and look like they could snap at any time. Keith looks pretty fragile but probably will respond to plenty of TLC in the right dose. Paul I'm not so sure of. He seems definitely to be coiled really tight and he might pop at any moment. He seems to be carrying a really big burden.

"Molly says you're trying to get them to help you with an art project. It's worth a try, but I'd love to also see them get involved with the Wounded Warrior project, get some individual counseling, group therapy, et cetera. In the meantime, giving them a comfortable environment, a safety net, if you will, has to help. I'll keep in close touch and we can all --you Molly, and I— monitor them closely. In the meantime, try to keep them busy."

He gave Mike a brief shoulder squeeze, saying "God bless you, brother," and drove slowly away.

Mike came back into the house with a large, mostly fake yawn on his face, for the benefit of anyone who might be interested. Then addressing Keith and Paul, said, "Assuming you're still interested in my work proposal, I'd like to get an early start on tomorrow's project, right after Lady and I take our morning run. Anyone caring to join us is welcome, starting at 0630 sharp. Otherwise, we'll get started around eight after breakfast."

Paul and Keith quickly got the message, and they, along with Lady, said their good nights and retired to their guest bedroom.

Molly grabbed Mike around the neck as Paul and Keith disappeared and whispered into his ear, "You're about as subtle as a turd in a punch bowl, you gufus. Didn't it occur to you that they might have wanted to stay up and talk for a while?"

Mike hugged her tightly, whispering back to her, "Didn't it occur to you that I had more interesting things to do tonight besides talk? Besides, we did a lot of talking this afternoon, and they're probably tired of it by now. I know there'll be more conversations in the next few days, so we'll just have to be patient."

Molly squeezed back. "Okay, mister. Now, come tell me more about what you have in mind for the rest of the evening." With that, they walked arm in arm back to their bedroom, laughing softly like two young kids.

CHAPTER 68

The next few days were a puzzle for Paul and Keith as they tried to fathom what it was Mike was willing to pay them for. He started with getting them to help straighten up the studio. They carefully sorted and stacked both the finished and unfinished canvases, then cleaned off the work table so there was room for paints and brushes, space for sketching on sheets of butcher paper, etc.

Next, Mike began showing them how to construct framing to which the new canvas would be attached. He told them the dimensions he wanted to experiment with, then showed them the pieces of framing they would be working with.

By now, Paul and Keith were exchanging knowing glances regarding what they were sure were make-work projects Mike was inventing to keep them occupied. Then, to their surprise, Mike rolled out a long sheet of butcher paper, fastened it to the work bench, then began sketching in very broad sweeps, almost unintelligible images, which they assumed were representations of his vision.. It quickly became clear from his obvious frustration, that his sketching was distorted by the shaking of his hand, as though there was an uncontrollable disconnect between the images in his mind and what his hand was able to receive.

With a surprising calmness of equal parts acceptance and resignation, Mike threw down the piece of charcoal. "Now, do you guys understand what's going on? I can't get my arm and hand to work right with my mind. So, the question is, what do I want from you? How can you help me?"

Paul and Keith both nodded, puzzled at their lack of understanding of what Mike thought he needed from them.

Noting their obvious confusion, Mike continued. "Bottom line, my idea is for you to be the hand for my mind, the funnel through which my vision can make it onto the canvas. But more than that, maybe you can help me get my head around the direction and meaning of the message I want for this final piece.

"I told you about my friend, Nicholas Zacharias and the help he gave me in dealing with the pain I brought back from 'Nam. But only now, after all these years, am I beginning to understand the most important thing he told me. Keith, you may have hit a spot in my mind when you said, 'Where in your painting is the color of peace, the shape of freedom from pain?'

"Then I remembered Nicholas saying 'You must take the sounds and memory of those days, and then throw them from your mind onto the canvas. Then you will have room in your mind again for all the beauty and peace and love that the world still has to offer."

Mike looked at them. "I've become convinced there has to be a place of calmness and peace, where hate is replaced by love, darkness by light, and fear by peace. And somehow, I want to show that in my work.

"Only problem is, I can't get my hand to cooperate with my mind, and that's where I need your help. I don't have any clear vision of what I want this work to show, but I have this very strong feeling that you guys can help me see my vision more clearly and to make it the reality I have been missing all these years. So, will you stick around and help me?"

Paul and Keith looked at Mike still puzzled, wondering how they might be of any use to him beyond picking up the scraps from his work. Still, they remained mesmerized by the passion in his voice, each searching for a place where they might play a part.

Mike continued. "You probably think we've done nothing but make-work these past few days, but what I needed to do was clear the deck, to start all over, to be fresh as we tackle this new beginning. I know that doesn't make much sense, but I learned long ago that doing the mechanics helps clear the mind and gives vision and creation room to grow. Now we're almost to the point where the real work will begin.

"Paul, with your background in cabinet making in your uncle's shop, I'd like you to begin making the frames. In the meantime, Keith, you and I will go pick up some supplies, including some canvas paint. Then I intend to introduce you both to brushes and paint and begin picking your brain on our vision and how it can be made meaningful on our canvas. Okay?"

Neither Paul nor Keith knew enough about what was going on in Mike's mind to question or challenge, so as good Marines, they settled on "Aye, aye, sir."

"Good," Mike said. "Let's get to work," and walked out to his truck. He felt as drained as an empty sink, not even remotely close to knowing how he could realistically expect to fold Keith and Paul into a creative process still fuzzy in his own mind. Still, he thought, one step at a time.

CHAPTER 69

Over two weeks passed, during which Mike, Paul, and Keith tried to find common ground over shape, size and content of the planned artwork. It was a frustrating time for Mike, who had relied before only on his own sense of proportion, color, and image to shape his creative direction. Now these two young men, whom he had enlisted mostly out of immediate concern for their recovery, had assumed a demanding role in trying to visualize the direction the art should take.

The operative phrase seemed to be 'from darkness to light,' but no one, including Mike, could visually describe what that was supposed to look like and still stay within the form that had been the hallmark of his art. It seemed to be a major road block for all of them, as though each was fighting image demons of his own.

Following his years-long habit of letting mechanics bridge his creative chasms, Mike directed them back to the physical drawing board, constructing variations of framing for the canvas they could not yet visualize. Together, they used the construction as a physical means of confronting the mental frustrations blocking their creative progress.

First, they attacked size as a barrier, putting together comparatively huge frames, possibly spanning ten by twenty feet. Then they argued over how the frame should hang, vertical versus horizontal. It took most of an afternoon of physical exertion interspersed with wild, out-of-the-box visual ideas to imagine what the movement from dark to light should look like.

Finally, out of physical and mental exhaustion, Keith threw up his hands. "Why are we being trapped by squares and rectangles? Maybe we should try circles or trapezoids, whatever the hell they are." At that point, they stood like statues, staring at the frames they had attempted to construct and at each other.

Suddenly Lady, who had been lying on the tile floor of the studio while Mike, Paul, and Keith worked on the framing, lifted her head, pricked up her ears, and gave a sound half way between a huff and a woof.

Then she rose quickly and padded to the studio's back screened door leading to the driveway as Molly stepped from the driver's door and opened the sliding door to the back of her car.

Lady, both excited and anxious, pawed at the screen door and finally barked her impatience. Molly laughed and said, "Patience, Lady. I've brought you some new friends." With that, she lifted out two almost identical collie puppies from the car, each on a leash. The puppies, looking to be about four months old, were remarkably like Lady in color with the same mixture of tan, black and white fur. One was male and the other female. They were almost uncontrollable at the sight of Lady. They tugged mightily at their leashes as Molly tried to control them.

Finally, she dropped the leashes and they ran wildly to the door where Lady stood. When Molly opened the door to let them in, they immediately began trying to lick the fur from Lady's face. For her part, Lady gave each of them a lick, then proceeded to smell and lick their behinds. The puppies quickly rolled over onto their backs while Lady sniffed them, then they jumped up and began running around her, trying to pull on her ears and biting at her tail. They quickly calmed down, however, after a menacing growl from her.

As Molly reached down to unclip the puppies' leashes, Mike looked from the canvas he and Paul had been framing, saying. "Now what have you done, woman?"

Molly laughed. "They were abandoned at the Humane Society. Apparently their mother had been killed by a car. So what better place to give them a home than here. Besides, I thought Keith and Paul might like to have a companion of their own. I hope that wasn't too presumptuous," she added for Paul and Keith's benefit.

They were already on their knees, scratching the puppies' heads and roughly rubbing their fur. In turn, the puppies were going wild at the attention they were receiving, licking and play biting their new friends' hands.

Molly handed each of them a leash. "Please take your new best friends for a walk on the beach and wear them out a little bit. I could use the rest."

Dutifully, Paul and Keith clipped on the leashes and encouraged the puppies to follow them out the door to the veranda. They crossed the bridge over the dunes and began running with the puppies down the beach.

Standing with his arm around Molly's waist as they watched the young men and the puppies, Mike said, "You never cease to surprise or amaze me. I think bringing the puppies was a great idea. Both Paul and Keith have been needing a distraction from what we're trying to do with the painting, and so did I. It's turning out to be such an intense experience for all of us. This should give us all some release. Only thing smarter you have done is get hooked up with me."

Molly smiled, then gave him a wicked pinch in the side. "You're the smart one, and the lucky one, hooking up with me." Then she reached up and licked his ear. "Now, Mr. Smarty, we better figure out where we are going to bed and feed these animals. By the way," she added, "they're not house broken, yet."

NICHOLAS
CHAPTER 70

About three weeks into their work on the project, Keith was moving some unfinished paintings into a safe corner of the studio when he came across an almost finished portrait of a gentleman he had not seen before. He was intrigued by the eyes, which seemed to reflect sadness but also strong courage and compassion.

He showed it to Mike. "Who is this?"

Mike sat for a moment staring at the painting, then said, "Someone you would have wanted as your closest friend. This is a half-finished portrait of Nicholas Zacharias, the friend I mentioned to you guys. This was one of several attempts I tried to paint him, one that I'm still working on. Please put it away carefully. Then go put the second coat of white on the canvas we've got set up on the easels."

As Keith walked away, Mike remained sitting, thinking about the sad call he had received those twelve or thirteen years ago.

"Michael," Mrs. Zacharias had said, with a tearful catch in her voice, "I wanted to call and let you know that Nicholas passed away last night."

Mike was speechless, feeling as though someone had stabbed him in his heart. "What?" he stammered. "What happened? I just talked to him last month and we talked about you all coming down soon to visit Molly and me. I don't understand!"

"I know, Michael," she replied. "Nicholas had pancreatic cancer and knew he wasn't going to survive. He knew for the past year, but he forbade me to tell anyone except the girls. It was his wish that life would go on normally for everyone. But he specifically asked me to let you know as soon as he passed and to remind you of how much he loved you and would miss you.

"He also asked that you come to his memorial service, which I have planned for Saturday of next week. Can you and Molly come?"

"Of course, we'll be there, probably by Wednesday. Now what can we do in the meantime?"

"There really is nothing to do, Michael," she said. "You know Nicholas. He had everything planned out. Just come and be with us as part of the family."

"Of course, Mrs. Z. You know we will. Thank you for including us. God bless."

"God bless you too, Michael," she replied quietly, and hung up.

After several minutes of painful silence, trying to adsorb the sad news from Mrs. Zacharias, Mike had slowly risen and begun searching through his collection of completed and partially finished canvases.

Eventually, his hand closed on two fairly large canvases, neither of which he had finished. They were portraits of Nicholas Zacharias.

Mike's favorite showed the face of the man who had given him the courage to continue living through the pain he had brought back from Vietnam. It was the face of a man who reached out to others in the midst of his own pain at the loss of his only son. It was also the portrait that Mike had been unable to complete without his own pain showing through.

The second showed Nicholas in a more positive and fulfilled point in his life. He was happy in the work he was doing, the satisfaction he received from his giving to the community, the love of his family, and his joy in life.

With sudden resolution, Mike determined to finish the second painting and get it framed before he and Molly left for the memorial service. He thought it would be the better of the two paintings to give to Mrs. Zacharias because it captured more fully the happier, more upbeat memory of his friend. Mike worked tirelessly for the rest of the day to finish the portrait, stopping only long enough to give Molly the news and let her make preparations for their trip to Dalton.

Early that Wednesday morning Mike and Molly left with his completed portrait of Nicholas carefully wrapped and packaged in the trunk. Molly insisted on driving, knowing how hard Mike had worked up to the last minute to complete the gift for Mrs. Zacharias.

CHAPTER 71

About eight hours later, Mike and Molly pulled into the circular driveway of the Zachariases' residence in Dalton. The front door opened suddenly as the two daughters --grown women now-- walked quickly to the driveway to greet Mike and Molly. Mrs. Zaharias followed only slightly less quickly.

It was a poignant moment of strong hugs and tearful kisses before Mrs. Zacharias pulled back slightly and beckoned everyone into the house. Mike couldn't help but notice several cars already parked in the driveway, wondering how many friends were already here and just how large a crowd they would be dealing with before the night was over.

As they walked into the foyer, Mike suddenly knew he was hearing the deeply resonant voice of John Cavanaugh telling some off-the-wall story involving some artist or other. Cavanaugh had been Mike's representative and agent since his first painting sold, and though they talked often on the phone, they had not seen each other in at least two years.

Mike grabbed Molly's hand and pulled her with him into the large family room toward Cavanaugh and the group of amused people he was entertaining. With a unique sense of his surroundings, Cavanaugh interrupted himself with an, "I'll be damned, Mike Pallaso," and lunged over to give him an enormous hug.

They stood together for an intense moment, then backed away far enough for Cavanaugh to say quietly, "I knew you'd be here, Mike. We're still reeling from Nicholas' death, but knowing how close you two were, I knew I'd see you. I'm so sorry for our loss, but I know he's here with us even now."

Cavanaugh then looked at Molly. "My dearest Molly, I can't believe you're still married to this nut case of an artist." He gathered her hand in his and kissed her cheek, murmuring, "I remain immensely jealous of Mike that he has captured such an angel as his wife."

Molly laughed at the blarney "As always, John Cavanaugh, you are full of it. But knowing what a true friend of Mike's you are, I'm willing to ignore the more outlandish stories and simply say thank you for all you have done for Mike."

Mike said, "John, we're so glad to see you, even in this very sad moment. I know Mrs. Z 's glad you're here for her."

"You gentlemen visit. I'm going to find a glass of wine and see if Mrs. Z needs any help with the food, "Molly said.

CHAPTER 72

"My God, Mike," Cavanaugh said as Molly walked away. "You're such a lucky man. She's a beauty."

"I know, She's the light of my life. By the way, is that Beloise over there?"

"Yes. Let's go talk with him. He has a new job you might be interested in hearing about." With that he raised his arm in a circling motion to catch Beloise's attention.

Beloise walked quickly over to Mike and Cavanaugh and shook hands with Mike. "Mike, I'm glad to see you again. John has kept me up to date on your painting and, of course, I've had a chance to see some of your recent work. He tries to keep some of your art on display at the gallery, but frankly, it doesn't stay very long before someone demands an opportunity to own it. It's good to see you again, even at this sad occasion."

Mike appreciated Beloise's comments but was a bit puzzled by the warm reception from the usually taciturn critic. Seeing the puzzled look on Mike's face, Cavanaugh said, "Mike, I am pleased to tell you that I have, after much discussion, finally been able to talk Andrew into taking over the directorship of my galleries. He'll be spending most of his time in Atlanta, but will also oversee my other five galleries around the country. Andrew has also agreed to take an active role as your representative. Assuming those arrangements are satisfactory with you, the commission arrangements would remain unchanged."

Over the years Mike had happily left the handling of his finished work in the very capable, trustworthy hands of Cavanaugh, so he saw no reason to disagree with Beloise's involvement, especially since Cavanaugh seemed so pleased with the arrangement. He nodded and shook Beloise's hand again. "I'm very happy for you, Andrew, and look forward to working with you."

"Thanks. When it's convenient, I would like to come down and visit you at your studio and see what you might be working on."

"Great idea," Cavanaugh interjected. "Perhaps we both could come down and visit."

"Fine," Mike said. "I have two pieces I've about completed. Why don't I let you know when they're finished and you can come down then?"

Both men agreed. Then Cavanaugh added, "There is one more thing I wanted to mention to you. A few weeks ago, when he finally admitted his illness to me, Nicholas indicated that he wanted to donate the three original paintings you had given him to either the Metropolitan Museum or the National Gallery. He said he had discussed it with Mrs. Zacharias and she agreed.

As an alternative, I suggested that he consider loaning the paintings to either of the museums for a period of time --say ten years or so-- and that way the paintings would still be part of his estate. He agreed, and I'm in the process of contacting both museums regarding their interest. I wanted to make you aware of this, to make sure you had no objection."

"No," Mike said immediately. "Those paintings belong to Mrs. Zacharias and she can certainly do whatever she wants with them. There's just one request I'd like to make. If she or her estate ever decides to sell the paintings and I'm still alive, then I'd like the opportunity of first refusal to purchase them. But we can certainly talk about that at a better time. Now, I have a special gift for Mrs. Zacharias and her family, and I want to go find a quiet place to give it to them. You, of course, are more than welcome to be there." With that he left to go find Molly, whom he suspected was talking with Mrs. Zacharias.

CHAPTER 73

After making Molly and Mrs. Zacharias aware of his plans, Mike went to the car and retrieved the portrait of Nicholas. Mrs. Zacharias had suggested they use the smaller formal living room, in which Molly had gathered the family and Cavanaugh and Beloise.

When all were gathered, Mike unwrapped the portrait, apologizing as he did so, for what he felt was a work that failed to do Zacharias justice. When he finally displayed the painting, there was a hushed silence. Then Mrs. Zacharias rushed to his side, wrapped her arms tightly around his neck, and tearfully whispered "Thank you, thank you."

She and Mike placed the large portrait on a sideboard so everyone could view it. Zacharias's daughters softly touched the edge of the frame, murmuring at the wonderful likeness of their father. The rest of the group stepped up to gaze at the painting. Cavanaugh squeezed Mike's arm and whispered, "What a marvelous gift you've given the family."

Mrs. Zacharias continued to hold on to Mike's arm as they gazed at the painting, laughing softly. She told him she thought she could even see the devilish twinkle Mike had captured in Nicholas' eyes.

"I want the rest of our guests to come see this beautiful gift, Michael, but before that, I wanted to give you this." She handed a sealed envelope with his name on it written in Zacharias's elegant scrawl. "Nicholas asked me to give this to you after he passed. I have not read it, but I know it must contain words of his deep affection for you."

Mike took the envelope almost reverently, gazed at it for a moment, then gave it to Molly for safe keeping. He hugged Mrs. Zacharias. "Thank you. I'll wait to read it when I won't embarrass myself and of course, I'll share it with you."

As the afternoon wore on, it became obvious that Mrs. Zacharias was beginning to feel exhausted and the guests began leaving with goodbyes and promises to call or stop by soon.

As Mike and Molly were saying their goodbyes, Mrs. Zacharias stopped them. "Nicholas had been anticipating you and Molly coming up to see us for some time and has had a major renovation done in the garage apartment, your first studio. Please, won't you stay there while you are here. It will be almost like old times, and I know Nicholas would want you here."

Mike and Molly agreed, sensing how much it seemed to matter to Mrs. Zacharias. With one last hug and a promise to see her in the morning for breakfast, they quickly walked to their car, gathered their bags, and went up to the apartment.

While Molly wandered around the remodeled rooms, noticing the already-made bed, new bathroom and kitchen fixtures and appliances, Mike sat down and pulled out the sealed envelope from Nicholas. With a slow motion, he opened the envelope and removed the folded note inside. It was handwritten in the old easily recognized style of Nicholas, beginning with:

My Dearest Michael,

If you are reading this, then, sadly, I am gone. Not sure where, but I know I will be free of the pain from the last few months and feel sure I will be able to put my arms around Peter again, and maybe even share a beer. However, I will surely miss all the beauty and wonder of this world. I used to walk outside at dawn with a cup of coffee and watch the beginning of a brightening sky, sensing God's promise of peace and goodness.

And he has delivered despite the last few months of pain. I don't regret the pain --well maybe a little--, because I think it has helped me look forward to the next step in my journey. Anyway, rest assured, I am in good spirits, bolstered by the good life I have known on this earth, which is why I have chosen to try to write this farewell to you, whom I regard as my son. I firmly believe God sent you to be by our side at our darkest moment, when we lost Peter. In ways I can't begin to understand, I believe you came to us in our hour of greatest need, not to replace Peter, but to remind us of why love is so important in our lives. You came to us in a moment in which your need was perhaps greater than ours, and it was a need to which we could respond, when sadness over our loss of Peter otherwise threatened to crush our lives forever.

I know this might not make much sense, but blame it on the rambling thoughts of a sick old man who imagines he is hearing the Lord whispering in his ear.

In any event, I just wanted you to know how proud we are that you have been such an important part of our lives. I am so pleased to know that not only have you survived the pain you brought back with you from the war, but that you have thrived in your recovery.

That is not to say you don't still have pain, but I know that you are on the right path to overcome it and to fully appreciate the life and the world you now enjoy. I ask you –no, perhaps beg you—to look at the world that surrounds you. Look at the beauty of God's sunrise, look at the endless expanse of his sky. Think of all the love that surrounds us, unbidden but still there in the help that people give to others in need, the happiness so many have at seeing the good fortune of others, and the sadness we all feel when pain or sorrow strikes another.

I guess what I am trying to say to you, however poorly, is that good strongly outweighs the bad in this world, and we must always keep that in mind when we deal with pain or sorrow in our own lives.

Enough babbling. Stay strong in your commitment to find love and happiness in this life. Believe in the message of your art to help others seek goodness over evil. I love you, my son. God bless you and give you peace.

Nicholas

P.S. You remember the promise I made to you about some day deeding the home in Atlantic Beach to you. Enclosed is the deed to the property. May you and Molly enjoy it as a lasting memory of my love for you.

Mike silently handed the note to Molly and turned away, needing to be alone with his thoughts. After reading the note, Molly walked to him and placed her arms around his back, understanding his pain and sense of loss. He turned to her, took her in his arms, and buried his tear streaked face into her shoulder. They stood together for several moments, then Mike pulled away and wiped his eyes, saying in a quiet, almost reverent tone, "I love that man. I know he helped bring me back to life."

"And I love him, too," Molly murmured, "because he brought you to me." She kissed him gently and then led him to bed, where they lay in each other's arms until sleep overtook them.

PAUL AND TOM
CHAPTER 74

After several days working with Mike and Keith, Paul came to Molly one evening saying hesitantly, “Didn’t you say you were Catholic?”

Somewhat surprised by his question, she said, “Yep. Born and bred. Why?”

He answered, “I need to talk to a priest.” He admitted that he had been raised Catholic but had lapsed as a young man. But now he felt in desperate need to find a priest and go to confession. He asked her if she knew someone he could talk to.

Hearing his distress, she reached for him and held his hand. She whispered, “I know a great priest, and I’ll be happy to set up a chance for you to meet with him, probably tomorrow. Okay?”

Embarrassed, he mumbled his thanks and slowly walked to his room.

Molly called Tom the next morning, let him know that Paul was looking for help and asked if he would be able to see him. Tom said he’d make room in his schedule and told her he could see him at 4 P.M.

She went down to the studio and quietly told Paul what she had arranged, gave him directions to the church, and handed him the keys to her car. He reacted hesitantly, but Molly assured him he was expected and that he needed to go meet with the priest that afternoon.

Molly had let Mike know of her conversation with Paul the evening before and what she had arranged with Tom, so he ignored the exchange Molly and Paul had in the studio. At a few minutes before four, Paul announced he had an errand to run and excused himself.

CHAPTER 75

When Paul walked into the cubbyhole of an office to which the rectory receptionist directed him, he was shocked to see Tom sitting behind an old door now serving as a make-shift desk. "Christ," Paul said, in utter confusion.

Tom said, in his characteristic droll manner, "Not hardly. I'm just a poor substitute. I apologize for the earlier deception, but neither Molly, Mike nor I knew how you and Keith would respond to a turned-around white collar. And besides, selfishly I wanted a break from all that goes with the collar.

"Anyway, I'm glad you're here. I knew from meeting you last month that you were dealing with some heavy pain, so please come in and let's talk. And if it helps any, remember that I've been there too."

Paul walked tentatively into the office, feeling confused by Tom's presence and his own emotions. He said, "I wanted the opportunity to make a confession, but now I'm feeling weird. I was looking for relief but now I don't know what I want."

"Paul come sit down. I can tell you with absolute certainty that the Lord has forgiven you for whatever you think you've done. Confession is just a ritual to help us get past the things we feel guilty about.

"The real issue, the one you and I may need to talk about, is why you're feeling so much pain. My part is just to help you examine that pain and help you understand its relevance to what God might have planned for you."

Paul stared at Tom with blank eyes, trying to find understanding and comfort in Tom's words, but felt no relief. His impulse was to get up and leave, feeling he wasn't going to get what he came for, although admittedly, he didn't know what that was. Instead, he finally just said, "You know, Father Tom, I think you're full of shit. How can you know what's in my head, and even if you do, how do you know God forgives me?"

In a surprisingly candid reply, Tom said, "You know, Paul, I may be full of shit, and, no, I'm not sure I know why God would forgive you for what you think you have done that needs his forgiveness. But I know he has. And I can tell you for sure he's forgiven me for the things I've done.

"But before we get into that, why don't you tell me what happened in Afghanistan and why you think you need help in dealing with it. For your information, I have things going on in my head from 'Nam that still eat at me, so don't think either I or God will be much surprised. But if you keep this bottled up inside your head, I can guarantee you it will rot your soul. Now tell me, what went on in Afghanistan?"

Paul sat for minutes, without responding to Tom, then abruptly began his narration, as the words spilled from his mouth.

CHAPTER 76

His company landed in a place called Marjah, a small town located somewhere in Helmand Province, where the Taliban were strong in numbers and determined to take the fight to the allied forces supporting the Afghan government. The Marines' mission was supposed to be to clear out the Taliban so an Afghanistan government could be reestablished in the area.

The choppers dropped them into the middle of the town about 0100 hours and surprisingly, they met no resistance. Paul's company was nervous as they spread out in defensive positions because they'd been told to expect heavy resistance and especially plenty of IED activity. After an hour or so of scouting the center of town by small patrols, Capitan Burke gave the word to settle in, beef up their defensive positions and bed down for the rest of the night. Patrols through the town would start at dawn.

Paul was one of the team leaders in the 3rd Squad. The squad located an empty building that appeared to have been a school of some type, and they decided to bed down there for the rest of the night. The floor was hard, cold cement, but the building walls helped keep out the freezing winter wind.

They spent a restless three or four hours trying to get some rest after the initial excitement and fear began to wear off. It didn't help any that an eerie chanting began over speakers that each Muslim town seemed to have to call people to prayers. Only, according to the platoon's Afghan interpreter, the voice was announcing the Marines' invasion and calling for all true believers to come kill the infidels. The ritual message continued endlessly, so that getting any sleep was almost impossible.

During the next few weeks the Marines were constantly fighting in a series of confusing battles with the Taliban. At times it seemed like they were having some success driving the insurgents out of Marjah. But just when they thought they could relax they would suddenly be caught in some ass-freezing ambush, usually triggered by killer explosions from well-hidden IEDs. Then all hell would break loose from concentrated small arms fire and rocket fire. The whole battalion was taking bad casualties, with KIAs sometimes outnumbering the wounded. And sometimes the wounded were hurt so bad you wondered how they kept living.

Frustration was grating, from the top down, with a feeling that the Marines were fast losing control, to the point that patrols often ignored the Rules of Engagement. Compounds and mud huts even slightly suspected of harboring Taliban were attacked, with the result that non-combatants were frequently injured.

There were meetings –called Shuras—almost daily, between village leaders and some of the Marine officers to discuss alleged problems caused by the Marine forces. A good deal of money was paid to the complaining villagers to try to placate them and more than a little was probably paid to some that were really Taliban or their sympathizers. In any event, the unhappiness, anger, and bitterness of the complaining villagers, whether real or not, allowed them to walk away with full pockets.

Paul's squad stayed on constant search and destroy patrols. The results were marginal. The Taliban stayed mostly out of reach, almost like ghosts in their ability to disappear suddenly during furious firefights and blend in with the villagers.

Taliban snipers were another constant danger. They would be hidden about two hundred yards out, in groves of trees, or down in brown fields of winter grass. Harassment fire from these locations was almost continuous, usually in the early mornings or as patrols were returning in the afternoon.

The fear of being shot dead by some unseen enemy was paralyzing for the Marines and at the first shot they would frantically dive for whatever cover they could find. Then eventually, usually only after being cursed at by their squad leader, they would begin trying to take some counter-action to find where the sniper was.

The Marines were filled with anger -- at themselves for their fear and at the damn Taliban-- especially if there were casualties. Often that anger would drive them to charge toward the area where they thought the sniper fire originated, firing their M16s, SAWs and grenade launchers with undisciplined frustration. Enemy dead were often over-claimed, two or three times over what could be verified.

CHAPTER 77

The result was the Marines were feeling overcome with anger and frustration because they couldn't get the enemy to stand and fight. They couldn't fight like Marines were trained to fight. They walked around with itchy trigger fingers, but at the same time with a nagging fear that their next step might be on an IED. Almost no day went by without a sudden explosion, usually followed by ambush fire, sniper fire, and more hollering for corpsman.

One afternoon, as his squad was returning from patrol, one of his fire team hollered, "There's one of those fuckers, and he's carrying a weapon." Paul's team began pointing at a figure running across the back of the field the patrol was paralleling, and it seemed clear he was carrying what appeared to be a rifle.

"Get him," Paul hollered to his team, aiming his M16 at the running target. There was a roar of shots and several shouts of "Got him."

By now, his squad leader had moved up to the team, hollering, "What the fuck's going on, Rogers? Who gave the order to fire?"

"Sergeant," he yelled, "we saw a guy carrying a weapon running across the back of the field. I gave the order to fire. It looks like he's down."

"Goddammit, Rogers," he hollered. "I give the orders around here. Now get your people out there and clean up this mess."

"Aye, aye, Sergeant," he hollered, still feeling the adrenaline rush, and led his fire team in a quick zig-zag run to where they thought the downed enemy was.

As they reached him, one of his team members dropped down next to the still body and hollered, "He's still breathing. Christ, he's just a kid!"

Hearing this, Paul felt his chest freeze up and he began trembling. "Corpsman up," he hollered by reflex, and ran to kneel by the kid. It was obvious he had taken at least two shots to the chest as well as one to his arm. He was moaning softly from the pain.

At that point, the corpsman arrived, began a preliminary examination, then said, "He's probably not gonna make it. We need a Medivac chopper right now or there's no chance."

Paul relayed the chopper request back to his squad leader, then knelt in helpless anger as he tried to figure what to do next. At that instance, one of his fire team called, "Here's his weapon. Aw fuck, are you kidding me? It's a pellet gun! It's not even loaded!"

Paul felt his stomach lurching in sickening revulsion. His fire team stood around in stunned silence as the rest of the patrol crept up. As word passed around through the patrol, whispered conversations began with the majority saying the kid shouldn't have been out running around with a rifle in his hand.

Soon Paul knew his team and he were in deep shit. Almost at once the brass began shouting communications up and down the Marine Regimental Command with demands for immediate evaluation of what had happened, when and why. The situation got even worse when they got word that not only had the kid died, but he was the youngest son of a top village elder, one who had been shouting angrily since day one about the Marines being in his village.

Paul's squad leader and he began to get increasingly harsh questioning, beginning with those from their platoon leader, running through the company commander--Captain Burke-- and finally, the battalion commander. Basically, they focused on whether ROE had been followed. After hours of grilling, the command structure reluctantly agreed that Paul and his team had acted okay, at least as far as the ROE, and that what had occurred was simply regrettable and unfortunate.

Paul didn't feel that way. He kept imagining the kid's eyes looking up at him, seeming to ask over and over, why did you do this to me? He was sickened to the point he couldn't sleep or eat, but he knew he had to hide his feelings because he was a Marine, and Marines weren't supposed to feel guilt when the enemy died. Except the boy hadn't been their enemy.

Before it was all over the Marines paid a large amount of money to the boy's father, who nonetheless continued his grievance against the Marines. Since then, Paul could still constantly hear the father's accusing voice and see the child's sightless eyes staring at him.

CHAPTER 78

As Paul ended his story he looked helplessly at Tom, wanting him to understand his pain and his need for relief.

Tom, wise with his own experiences, placed a hand on Paul's shoulder. "You can't go on carrying this burden of guilt and grief by yourself. Let me help you work through it, whenever and for as long as you feel it might be helpful. Where would you like to begin?"

Paul responded without hesitation. "I came here for confession. I want to have someone hear my confession. It seems like you're it."

Without further discussion, Tom reached for his stole, crossed himself, blessed Paul and invited him to sit beside him.

Paul sat hesitantly, and with tear stained cheeks said, "Bless me, Father, for I have sinned. It has been years since my last confession. My sin is that I took a young man's life, a young boy of twelve, without justification. I am heartily sorry for my misdeeds."

"Did you know that the young man was innocent of trying to harm you? Would you have taken his life had you known he was just an innocent child?"

"No, Father. I never wanted to hurt innocent kids! I just wanted to stop the crazy shit that was going on around me."

"Paul, God understands your pain and forgives you. Now he wants you to forgive yourself and to move on with your life in a way that honors the young man whose death you grieve for. Now go in peace, Paul, and promise me that we can talk further on this. I have every belief that God has other plans for you that will begin with your willingness to forgive yourself."

"Wait, Father. What about my penance?"

"Ah, your penance," Tom replied. "I want you to say three Hail Mary's before you go to bed tonight, and two 'I don't think Father Tom is totally full of shit'."

With that he blessed Paul with the sign of the cross. “I strongly urge you to come and talk with me as frequently as that slave driver will turn you loose. Just tell Emily, our secretary, when you can make it and she’ll put it on my calendar. We can probably talk better around a bottle of beer than in this cramped place.” And with that, Tom showed Paul to the door and walked him to Molly’s car.

CHAPTER 79

Several days later Tom walked into the rectory office in the afternoon following his routine visit to patients at the beaches' hospital, his mass at the assisted-living facilities for the elderly, and a quick peanut butter and jelly sandwich lunch. Emily handed him a fist-full of messages, all of which seemed to demand his immediate attention. He mentally sorted them, based on his knowledge of the sender's real versus imagined need, and finally settled on a short message from Paul, which stated he really needed help –at least needed to talk—as soon as Tom might be available.

Tom called the cell phone number Paul had left with Emily and heard the resigned, stoic hello from Paul. "Paul, Father Tom, here. Think you can get away this afternoon? I was thinking how good a Harp might taste around four."

Paul's terse response was, "Four is fine. I appreciate it."

When Paul arrived at the pub, Tom was already sitting at one of the isolated tables, sipping on a mug. Hillary, one of the waitresses who seemed to be almost a fixture of the pub, saw Paul walk in and took him immediately to where Tom was sitting. As she approached the table with Paul, Tom gave her a nod with his half empty mug, and she hurried quickly away to fetch drinks for the two of them.

Tom reached out and shook Paul's hand as he took a seat, noting as he did so, the characteristic tell of darting eyes that Paul displayed, as though he was already looking for an escape hatch.

As Hillary brought the beers, Tom decided on a direct approach. "I'm glad you called, Paul. But this is your nickel, so what's going on?"

"I didn't feel any real relief from the confession, and don't know where to turn to get away from the confusion in my head. Thought maybe you could help, but, to tell the truth, I don't know how you or anyone can."

Tom reached across the table and squeezed his hand. "First, have a sip of good Irish beer, then let's see where we go from here. We may not get very far, but at least we might know if we're on the right path.

"Let me start us by telling you a little bit about my own coming home from the pain of that stupid war we had going on in Vietnam --the one that cost almost 60,000 American lives, plus God knows how many Vietnamese and other poor folks.

"I was angry because there seemed to have been no good reason for decent people to die, feeling guilty because I had a heavy hand in those deaths, and unable to find a source of comfort or reasonable explanation. Truly not the poster boy Marine.

"I first looked for relief in alcohol, but before I drowned in that, I met a gentleman who had also been in Vietnam --a Catholic priest-- who had said the last rites over thousands of humans –Americans and Vietnamese.

"He heard my confession –over a bottle of Harp, by the way-- then asked me what I thought the root of my pain was. Was it my guilt over the hand I had had in the war effort—my role in the killing and maiming of other humans-- or was it something even deeper? He asked that question seeming to have gone through the same painful questioning I was experiencing.

"Later I understood his question about something deeper bothering me. He was talking about guilt over my loss of faith in God. But at the time I could only challenge him in my frustration with why God had allowed the killing to happen. Why had he allowed his own creations to behave as they had since the beginning of time?"

"Yeah!" Paul interrupted. "That's my question too. If there is a God, why has he allowed us humans to do what we do to each other, like my killing a twelve-year-old kid?"

Tom held up his hand in silent understanding, but also asking Paul to let him continue.

"In response to my question, this wise and patient priest, whose name was John O'Brien, started by saying that, despite everything he had seen and experienced on earth, he believed in a loving creator, who gave us life with a purpose beyond our understanding."

"Yeah, well, it's way past my understanding, too. Makes no sense."

"I understand. But stay with me. He told me about a remarkable experience he had as a young man of seventeen. It seems he was hit by a car as he was riding his bicycle, resulting in critical injuries, including a fractured skull with brain damage. He was in a coma for over a week, then began to recover, far beyond his doctors' expectations.

"He had no memory of the accident, but had a fascinating memory -- a near death experience I believe it's called today. In it he recalled floating around the edges of many universes – not just ours—conversing with millions of people, not in a language, but through some common thought process. In his memory, he even believed he had spoken with God and Christ.

"He said he had never experienced such peace and love and calmness, anticipating being able to stay in this endless paradise he was in. Instead, he miraculously recovered and with that recovery began to believe he was sent back to life with direction from God to deliver his message of peace and love.

"So, I guess we have to get hit by car, get our brain scrambled, to understand this God of ours."

Tom took a swallow of beer, then sat back in tired resignation. "Paul, I don't have a ready answer for you, except to repeat the old saw that God acts in mysterious ways.

"Anyway, to continue, Father O'Brien gave no argument of logic when we talked. Instead, mostly based on the memory of his extraordinary near-death experience, he simply stated with absolute certainty that the miracle of the universe could only have been created by the one true God we profess to be our creator. And he believed it is this loving God who has an ultimate plan of perfection for mankind, even if we can't yet visualize it.

"But anticipating my next challenge, Father O'Brien said he knew that such a belief begs the obvious question: How in the midst of such designed perfection can mankind's terrible cruelties towards one another exist?"

"Yes!" Paul almost shouted. "That's what I want to know!" he said, squeezing his near empty mug.

Tom, again holding up his hand in time-out fashion, signaled to Hillary for refills. He worried a little that Paul's intensity might be the wrong combination with more Harp, but he hoped it might help ease the young man's desperation.

"Why don't we slow down a bit. This is heavy stuff. And I'm not sure we're ready to lift it all at once."

At that point, Hillary appeared with two fresh mugs of beer, set them down, then placed a bowl of nuts down between them. Tom and Paul both nodded their thanks. Then Tom said, "Let's look a little deeper at our questions about the disparity between God's plan of perfection for us and our continuing cruelty and hatred towards one another.

"The one important word we've left out of this discussion is faith--the faith we need to have as part of our belief in our loving God. In our discussions, Father O'Brien introduced me to one of the lesser known prophets in the Old Testament, a man called Habakkuk. Father O'Brien said he reminded him of me and my questions about God's plan for us. In a similar way you remind me of Habakkuk as well. Let me take a minute to get this month's missal from my car to show you what I mean."

Paul silently acknowledged his agreement, reaching absently for a small handful of nuts.

CHAPTER 80

Tom returned shortly with his missal then turned to the Sunday in which a quote from the book of Habakkuk was featured as the first lesson. "Let me read a part of this to you," he said. "I think you will see the similarity I am talking about." He began to read:

How long oh Lord.
I cry for help, but you do not listen.
I cry out to you, Violence
But you do not intervene.
Why do you let me see ruin?
Why must I look at Misery?
Destruction and violence are before me.
There is strife and clamorous discord.
Then the Lord answered and said:
Write down the vision clearly upon the tablets
So that one can read it readily.
For the vision still has its time;
Presses on to fulfillment, and will
Not disappoint;
If it delays, wait for it,
It will surely come, it will not be late.

He handed the missal to Paul who, when he finished reading, looked up questionly at Tom. "So, we just have to sit on our hands and wait for God to take care of things?"

"That's not the worst definition of faith I've ever heard. But you might need to add belief that he *will* take care of things.

"Now I hate to cut this short, but I'm going to need to call a timeout in a few minutes 'cause my other priestly duties are calling. But I want to get together again soon. Can we meet day after tomorrow, here, about the same time?"

Paul nodded reluctantly in agreement, and taking a last swallow of beer, started to get up.

"Wait," Tom said. "In the meantime, I want to give you something --a diagram-- if you will, that Father O'Brien shared with me many years ago regarding his concept of God's plan. It may help us try to understand how the young boy's death could possibly be part of God's plan for us.

"Here's what Father O'Brien showed me," Tom said, pulling out a pen and a bar napkin. On the napkin, he drew a long straight line, from one side of the napkin to the other. "This," he said, "according to Father O'Brien, is an infinite continuum that represents God's plan for mankind. At this far-left point on the continuum," he said, making a mark with his pen, "is the instant in infinity when God began time. It marks the beginning of the universe we know, and the infinite number of other universes we can't know."

Then, pointing again with his pen about a quarter of an inch farther down the right on the straight line, Tom said, "This point, according to Father O'Brien, was the beginning of man. This is where you and I, and the billions before us, started as fragile beings, wandering like blind men into the light of God's world from a dark cave.

"We were created by God with the potential for perfection, but not necessarily with the ready capacity for understanding what that potential might represent in his plan. Maybe that's why God warned Adam and Eve to stay away from the tree of knowledge, because we weren't ready to understand his plan for us.

The next major point on Father O'Brien's diagram was here," and wrote a capital 'C' on the line. "Obviously representing Christ. And clearly a pivotal point in Father O'Brien's mind in God's plan for mankind.

"Finally –although that doesn't seem to be a word in God's vocabulary—at the end of Father O'Brien's line is the sign for eternity. God has no ending. Nor does his plan for mankind, based on Father O'Brien's vision.

"Now," Tom said as he folded the napkin and handed it to Paul, "Take this with you, and we can talk about it as deeply as you want the next time we meet, which I hope will be soon. But be warned, even after all these many years, and as old as he is, Father O'Brien and I have not stopped talking about it yet."

With confused fatigue, Paul nodded okay as they stood and walked to their cars.

CHAPTER 81

In the next two days, Paul moved about in rote fashion, helping put canvas frames together, taking his young collie puppy for long walks, or sitting silently at the dinner table as conversation passed around him.

The talk at the table bounced from issue to issue, mostly warm and friendly. But Molly noticed that Paul remained on the fringe, looking distantly into a depth he wouldn't share with the others.

As had become their habit, the group left the hastily cleaned table and began their evening beach walk with Lady and the puppies, amused as usual at the antics of the animals jumping in and out of the waves at the shore.

Half-way through their walk, Molly took Paul's arm, slowing them back from the rest. "How are your talks with Tom going? I hope they're helpful, but I can't help but notice a change in you since they started. And if I'm being nosy, just tell me."

Paul continued to walk, enjoying the comfort of Molly's hand on his arm. "You know, Molly," he said, "Father Tom is a strange guy. He's not like any priest I've ever known. He's –I don't know—so different."

"You mean irreverent?"

"Yeah. But more than that. He seems to be able to see right into your heart. No judgement, no lessons, no demands, no requirements, you know, like obeying the Ten Commandments. He's just there for you."

"Sounds like you're experiencing a good relationship with Tom. Oops," she laughed, "Guess I'm not supposed to just call him Tom."

"He doesn't care what you call him. In fact, he said we'd get rid of Father in our talks unless we're talking about God. He's the most caring, gentle person I've ever known, and talking to him has really been helpful. It has begun to give me some comfort and release.

"That reminds me. We're scheduled to meet tomorrow afternoon. Any chance I can borrow your car for a couple of hours?"

"Of course. In fact, why don't you plan on taking me and the puppies to the shelter tomorrow morning --they need to get checked out—and then you can pick us up when you're finished with Tom in the afternoon. Tell him we're having non-vegetarian pizza for dinner if he'd like to join us."

"Thanks, Molly. Keith and I really appreciate all you and Mike have done for us. I just hope there'll be a way we can thank you."

She pulled at his arm. "Come on. We're getting left behind. And Mike and I just want you guys to get better. That will be our thanks." With that, they began jogging after Mike, Keith and the dogs.

CHAPTER 82

Paul arrived earlier than normal at the pub and Hillary took him immediately to the corner table he and Tom had staked out for their visits. She returned shortly with two mugs of Harp and a large bowl of nuts, followed by a tired looking Tom.

Tom's first action was to take a large swallow of beer, then smile. "So where were we? I hope you brought Father O'Brien's heavenly diagram, 'cause I'm not sure I have the mental energy to reproduce it this afternoon."

Paul pulled the folded napkin from his pocket but said, "Listen, Tom, if you want to do this another time, I'm okay with that. You look pretty beat."

Tom waved him off and took another swallow of beer. "No, Paul. I'm fine. Some days are more challenging than others, even for a do-nothing priest. I buried a good friend –a good and faithful servant—this morning, long before it should have been his time to go. Messed up my mind a bit. Then, on top of that, we spent a good portion of the day with plumbers trying to unstop an ancient toilet in the rectory. And I don't want to hear any rude remarks about a certain old priest being too full of shit for an old toilet. So, where are we?"

Paul had a hard time controlling his laughter. "You were going to explain how, in the midst of his design for perfection, God has allowed the imperfection in mankind to occur."

"Not so. There's no way I can be held accountable for explaining his plan. The best I can do is tell you what I think is occurring as part of that plan."

"Okay. But I need to hear something that can make sense out of what I did to that kid."

"All right," Tom replied, taking another swallow of beer and a deep breath. "But first, let's try to define this perfection I think God plans for us to reach. All we have to do is look at the example that Christ set. I think

God sent Christ, not just to sacrifice himself for our sins, but also to set an example of perfection for mankind to understand and follow.

"If you think about Christ's brief time on earth, the core of his presence was love –unconditional, all forgiving, sacrificial, compassionate, caring love for others. I believe that's the essential definition of God's plan of perfection for his children to achieve: the ability to love him and each other unconditionally. And given our inherent human imperfections, it suggests a long journey for us to travel, with many failures for every step forward we achieve."

Paul nodded. "But why? Why would he not give us the ability to love as Christ does? Why would he create us imperfectly, and allow us to hate and kill one another for our entire existence?"

"Okay. I promised I'd give you my theory about that. Actually, it's a theory that's evolved from my many challenges to Father O'Brien on the same subject. It goes like this: God created us with the potential to achieve perfection, but he didn't want it to come too easily, else how could we know the value of our existence? He wanted man to be able to fully appreciate the gift of perfection as a result of our journey through the trials and tribulations of being mortally human.

"In other words, how could we know the true value of his perfection if we had nothing to compare it to – like the pain of our humanity? How could we truly value light if we had not experienced darkness? How could we appreciate reaching our heavenly goal if we had not experienced the challenge of the journey to reach that goal?"

Paul sat for a long moment trying to absorb Tom's words. Finally, he said, "I guess I understand what you're saying about God's plan, but how does that square with the death of an innocent twelve-year-old? How does that square with all the evil shit that man has committed, including what we did to Christ?"

Tom sat still, listening to Paul's frustration, feeling his own at not being able to give adequate answers. "Paul, I'm not smart enough to give you good answers to those questions. I'm not even sure the Pope has all the answers. Some very tough questions.

"I can't tell you why or how that young man's death is part of God's plan for us. It's a very complex and challenging issue, especially if we try to find a rational explanation of how the death of the young Afghan boy can be part of that plan. Your part in his death could very well be part of

God's plan for your own journey. It could be that your grief has helped lead you to redemption. The fact that you are so disturbed by your role in the young man's death is certainly proof of that. We're all God's children, so we continue to be given the chance to do better.

"Now, all I have told you is what I told you at the beginning: I don't know the answer to your question. All I can do is speculate, and trust that God, in his infinite wisdom, has a reason for all that happens."

Paul nodded in quiet acceptance, then in a significant change of direction, said, "What made you decide to become a priest?"

"Wow! A heavy question. Why did I decide to become a priest? Okay, thanks to Father O'Brien, I began to believe Christ's compelling promise that there is life hereafter. That this life we are trying to lead is just a step along the way. Of course, Father O'Brien, in the sneaky way of the Irish, helped move me along in my decision-making, and so here I am.

"Now what other questions do you have that I'm sure not to know the answer to?"

Paul sat in quiet contemplation, curling his hands around his near-empty mug. "Do you have a Bible I can borrow? It's been a long time since I tried to look at one."

Tom clinked his near-empty beer mug against Paul's. "Happens I do have one on the back seat of my car. If you can get the pages unstuck you're welcome to it. Now, I need to go drain my brain and then go get on with my priestly duties."

They rose together, with Tom promising to meet Paul at his car. In a few minutes, Tom reappeared, opened his car and handed Paul his Bible.

"Thanks, Tom. I'm sorry to be such a pain in the ass. I'll get this back to you soon. Oh, by the way, Molly told me to tell you you're invited for some non-vegetarian pizza tonight if you can make it."

Tom smiled. "Tell Miss Molly that I accept her invitation and I'll be there around six, bearing liquid refreshment provided I can find a package store that doesn't recognize me."

CHAPTER 83

Although Paul felt as though his brain had been through a mix-master, he was happy to see Molly and the puppies. He handed the car keys to Molly and climbed into the passenger seat with the two boisterous pups jumping all over him, vying for his attention as they drove away from the shelter. Despite all their wildness, he felt himself begin to relax, to let his mind go into a calmer state.

Seeing the Bible in his hand, Molly said, "How was the session with Tom? I hope he's behaving himself."

Paul laughed as the puppies continued to try to lick his face. "The man is a marvel of understatement. I hear passion in the tone of his voice that he covers with his jokes about himself and what he's involved with. But I don't think I've met anyone as devoted to what he's doing, other than Mike when he talks about his painting."

Molly thought of Mike and his pain over the past few months as he had tried to paint a final canvas. She knew that involving the guys in that effort had started out as a way of trying to help them with their problems. But much to hers' and Mike's surprise, the guys' involvement had helped more than they had expected in lessening their struggles with the PTSD. And as they became more engrossed in working with Mike, he had convinced them that they would play a crucial role in creating a painting that would be a fitting climax to his art.

"Well," she said, "both men are pretty passionate about what they feel, but I'm glad if Tom is able to help you find some peace. As for Mike, I know what a blessing your help has been to him. He has said more than once how good it feels to have you guys around, almost like having sons. I certainly share those feelings. We're so glad you have happened in our lives."

Paul sat quiet for a moment, feeling choked up. Finally he said, "Thanks, Molly. That really means a lot." Then, to get past the awkwardness he was feeling, he changed the subject. "By the way, Father

Tom asked me to tell you he accepts your invitation to join us for pizza and that he will be happy to bring an Irish brew."

Molly laughed. "I'm so glad. He always lights up our table." As they turned into the driveway, the puppies, joined by Lady from inside the house, began whining and barking. "I'll drop you guys off, then I'm off to find a huge non-vegetarian pizza or two to fill your huge gullets. Maybe you and Keith could walk the dogs while I'm gone to help get them quieted down."

As Paul grabbed the leashes for the two wild puppies, he leaned back into the car. "Thanks, Molly, for all you and Mike are doing for us." She blew him a kiss, then quickly backed the car from the driveway, waving as she left.

CHAPTER 84

Dressed casually, Tom arrived in his usual ebullient mood, carrying two six packs of Harp. Mike took the beer, saying, "What a cheapskate. Only twelve bottles for five adults. You Irish Catholics. No wonder so many of you moved to America."

"We moved here," Tom responded, "to try to improve the diversity ratio with all the Italians here. Obviously, we failed. Besides, I thought it was bring your own night. Twelve bottles should just about take care of me."

"All right, you two," Molly laughed. "Take your beer and insults out of my kitchen while I get this pizza warmed up and a salad made. And tell Keith and Paul to wash up because I know they've been rolling around with the dogs."

Tom and Mike, each with a newly opened beer, wandered into the large family room where Keith and Paul lay spread out on the couches absently letting the fast- growing pups nibble on their fingers as they watched an old movie.

"Okay guys. Molly says go get cleaned up. We're eating in five."

Once they were alone, Mike said, "How do you think they're doing? I know you've spent a good deal of time with Paul, and Molly says you have sat in on a few of Keith's group sessions with the Wounded Warriors."

"Well," Tom said, "I have a few thoughts. Why don't you and Molly and I take the dogs for a walk after dinner and we can talk more privately then."

Dinner was a jovial, relaxing event with everyone seeming able to stay and be happy in the present moment. As usual, part of the conversation centered around the Project, as the painting had come to be called, and the frustration each was feeling that the others refused to accept his creative idea as the best. But the exchanges were tempered by good humor and the shared belief that they were just on the cusp of creative breakthrough.

As dinner was ending, Mike announced that the young people had KP duty that night, while the grown-ups and the dogs were going for a walk. He ignored the fake grumbling and rattled the leashes to call the dogs. Then he, Molly and Tom walked out onto the veranda and headed for the beach.

Mike released the dogs from their leashes as the evening began to darken, then they ambled through the wet sand. Tom took up the conversation about Paul and Keith. "You know, I think you two have really been good for these fellows at a moment in their lives when they were both really walking close to the edge. You've provided them with a haven that, if not actually saving their lives, still gave them a chance to rest and find some peace.

"Now as to how I think they are currently doing. I have the feeling that they're still walking pretty stiff-legged through life, expecting any minute to be assaulted by pain they can neither understand or control. I think both are eaten up by guilt –Paul because of the death of the young boy, and Keith because he survived Afghanistan and his best friend didn't.

"Bottom line, however: I think they're both making progress. And, Mike, I have the feeling that your so-called project has taken on a life of its own, that its completion represents a moment of healing for Keith and Paul that will play a significant part in their recovery."

He went on, "Have you noticed the animation with which they discuss the project? It's as though its completion represents an essential breakthrough in their ability to deal with their pain? Perhaps I am reading more into it than it deserves, but somehow I don't think so. What do you two think?"

They walked for a few paces, then Mike said, "I think you're right. The changes I've seen in them over the past several weeks have been pretty positive. What I don't know is whether that can continue, how much back-sliding they might experience, and where do we –-they—go from here.

"I agree that the importance of the project seems to have captured their interest and enthusiasm, but, you know, the creative process can be pretty frustrating. I just hope we can begin to make some positive strides before frustration begins to kill their enthusiasm. What do you think, Molly?"

"I agree with both of you," she responded. "I think they both have found some peace here with us. I haven't seen the level of anxiety recently that they both had at first, although I can certainly still hear the restlessness in their sleep and the occasional nightmares.

"But all in all, they seem to be spreading their wings and trying to get back to some degree of normalcy. Like you, though, I keep holding my breath, afraid they might slip back. The reading I've been doing on PTSD says there's still a lot of guesswork on what causes it and how best to treat it. But, Tom, if you think they can continue to benefit from living with us, then I'm all for keeping it going. I'm pretty fond of those young men, and I'm hoping hard that we can be helpful to them."

CHAPTER 85

Paul and Tom met Wednesday in what had become their usual table at the pub, each sipping from a mug. "So, tell me, Paul," Tom said, "what words of wisdom that I don't have are you seeking today?"

Paul smiled slightly, then, in a very serious tone, said, "What does one have to do to become a priest?"

Tom only just avoided choking on his beer at the question out of left field, before he recovered enough to say, "First, you have to be crazy! It's a demanding, life-long, personal-sacrifice profession that has no end. And it takes years of dedication and work to even get to the point where sane people are willing to call you Father. If you're talking about yourself, then the biggest favor I can do for you is to talk you out of even thinking about it!"

Paul remained silent for a moment, then said, "But you did it. Why can't I?"

"You're right, Paul," Tom responded, "and I guess the obvious conclusion would be that if Thomas McGee can do it so could anybody. But I have to tell you, there isn't a day goes by that I don't question that decision-- that I don't have to pray every night for God to give me the strength to continue in his service.

"So the first question you have to ask yourself is, Why? What's driving you to even think about becoming a priest? Is it that dead twelve-year-old child in Afghanistan that's motivating you? If so, I can tell you with pure certainty that guilt is the worst motive you can have. You can't go into this business unable to believe that God has forgiven you for whatever you believe you did to cause that young man's death.

"You have to believe with all your heart that God has already forgiven you, and in doing so, has begun a transformation in your life. A transformation that you have to believe involves a renewed faith in his love and unique plans for the rest of your life. And lastly, I can guarantee you that the path you might try to follow won't be an easy one. Now, let me pause for a moment to ask God's forgiveness for trying to talk someone out of trying to be one of his disciples."

Paul didn't move or otherwise try to react to Tom's discouraging sermon. He simply swirled his beer with patient silence, then said, "Okay. I understand it would be hard, but what would I have to do? Tell me the steps involved and let me make my own decisions."

"All right. First, you have to have the bishop's blessing. He's got to believe that you believe you're making a right decision, and it's something he will keep questioning. Second, it takes about eight or ten years of schooling just to meet the basic educational requirements. From what you've told me, with your small amount of time at Appalachian State, you'd be starting pretty much at the bottom of the ladder.

"It would be a long climb, including getting some kind of bachelor's degree, then a long bout of religious training, and so on. Like I said, it would be a long, painful journey just to get to the start of a long challenging life of priesthood. A good number of young men have started on that journey only to find the climb too tough."

"So," Paul said, "where do I go from here?"

After a long moment of silence, Tom said, "If you want me to, I'll talk to the bishop and see if he's willing to meet with you."

"Okay. Let's do it. And thanks, Father, for caring enough to try to talk me out of taking the first step."

They stood together and Tom gave Paul a strong hug, whispering, "God bless you. I will let you know when things have been set up. In the meantime, I suggest you contact Appalachian State and get a copy of your records."

They shook hands and walked to their cars.

CHAPTER 86

Bishop William Burns waved Tom into his modest office as he was finishing up a phone call that Friday afternoon and pointed to the couch.

Tom took the offered seat and let his eyes wander around the office. He noted with a comfortable familiarity the untidy room he had grown accustomed to over the past twenty-plus years.

"Well, Tom," the bishop said smilingly. "To what do I owe this curious visit, when you should be visiting the sick or putting a roof on a Habitat house?"

Trying unsuccessfully to maintain a reverent manner, Tom shrugged slightly. "Bless me, Father, for I know I've sinned. I may even have had more Harp than I should have in the last few weeks."

"I'm sure you have, although if it were not for my diabetes, I might not consider it a serious sin. Now what's truly going on, besides your parish's contribution to the Bishop's Fund being down by four percent from last quarter?"

"Bill," Tom replied in familiarity born of years of friendship, "I think I may have a nibble on your prospective priest trot line and I wanted to get your thoughts."

"First of all, you need to work on your analogies, especially when they involve your bishop's effort to find new young priests to fill the shoes of some slowly aging protectors of the faith in this diocese. Now, beyond that, tell me about this nibble you so ineloquently describe."

"I've been working with a young man, a mental casualty of Afghanistan, who has moved from a great weight of guilt from that conflict to an honest questioning of his faith and belief, and subsequently, to an earnest desire to serve Christ. It hasn't been easy for him and I expect there will be slippage. Still, he's begun asking serious questions about the process to the priesthood, what he needs to do, education-wise, how he can deal with the doubts in his faith, and so on.

"With your permission, I'd like to encourage him. Would you agree to meet with him, and if you're agreeable, allow me to help him get on a beginning course of action and see where it takes us?

"I feel like this young man has a great deal of potential. I have some money in my discretionary account, and between that and his veterans' benefits, I think we can see him through undergraduate studies –at least the first couple of years in- one of the state universities. I'm thinking the University of North Florida because it's local and I expect he will need a lot of sheparding. Of course, it would require your considerable influence to get him past several of the entrance hurdles. He is from out-of-state and only has a year or so of college credits."

"Tom, do you really feel this is a positive course of action or is it just a sympathetic reaction on your part to someone who may have had some of the same painful experiences you've had?"

"Bill, this young man, whose name is Paul Rogers, first came to me suffering from a great deal of pain over the death of a young Afghan boy for which he felt responsible. Through our many conversations, it was obvious that he was looking for some way to atone for the boy's death. Regarding his interest in the priesthood, I have admonished him strongly that guilt can't be a path to the priesthood, that he must believe God has forgiven him for the young boy's death. I believe he has the faith to accept that.

"And, besides," he said with tongue in cheek, hoping to deflect other possible objections, "when have you ever known me to take an action without giving it a great deal of thought and prayer?"

The bishop's laugh was boisterous, and as Tom had hoped, he waved his hand in resignation. "Make an appointment with Janet and I'll be happy to meet with this young catfish. Be sure and get me some biographical details before we talk. Now you best get back to your parish and figure out how to make up the deficit in your contribution to the Bishop's Fund."

Paul's interview with the bishop, which Tom had finagled to happen quickly, was both frightening and inspiring for him. He found the bishop kind and understanding, but very serious in his questions, challenging Paul's future plans and the depth of his faith.

Paul, for his part, and through the coaching of Tom, tried to answer as forthrightly as possible to the bishop's interrogation.

At the end of the session, the bishop gave his conditional approval of Paul's involvement in the exploration of the priesthood. He told him that he expected him to involve Father McGee closely, especially in his education and his involvement in the parish activities. The bishop also indicated that he would use his influence to see that Paul was accepted at the local university for his first semester, and that he expected Paul not only to enroll but to secure on-campus housing. And clearly, superior grades were expected.

Paul left the session with the bishop feeling drained but momentarily satisfied that he was heading in the right direction. He called Tom to share those feelings. Tom congratulated him on his success, saying he would see him at Mike and Molly's that evening to raise a Harp in celebration.

THE WALL
CHAPTER 87

As had become his habit of late, Mike woke about three in the morning, and after struggling to go back to sleep, finally got up quietly and with a cup of day-old coffee, moved to the studio.

He stared with impatient eyes at the large collection of different shaped and colored canvases that he, Keith and Paul had struggled with, trying to find a creative consensus. He knew their struggles seemed to be part of a healing process they were going through, yet at the same time, it seemed to be creating a mental struggle for each of them.

For him, it was a desire to create a work that would give closure to his years-long efforts to find peace through his art. For Keith and Paul, it seemed to be only a beginning point, trying to find a breakthrough from their struggles to a new beginning. Regardless, the process had become a challenging process for them, and he wished for a moment to have the fresh insights of Nicholas Zacharias for guidance.

As he wandered through the studio, his eye caught sight of an unfamiliar canvas hidden back in one corner. It was clearly not his work, but it had a look about it, as though it might have been an unusual copy of his style. The colors were those that he might have chosen, but their style and treatment, an impressionistic variation of the swirls and slashes that had been his trademark, were refreshingly different. It was unfinished but clearly had a promising direction.

Mike stood studying the painting, then heard a snort, as though someone was either waking up or shifting in sleep. He walked quickly to the back of the studio, where he saw Keith asleep slumped over at one of the drawing tables.

Mike shook his head in quiet understanding, as he remembered the countless nights he had spent in exhausted sleep after working through most of the night on a piece. He had no idea that Keith had been going through similar experiences.

He thought about retreating and letting Keith sleep when he spotted a sketch pad next to his head. He slipped the pad up and began flipping through the pages. There were several sketches of Lady, looking remarkably like her in her inquisitive moods as she tried to insert her nose into whatever was going on. Then there was a very good likeness of Molly in one of her pensive moods. Mike was stunned. He had no idea that Keith had this artistic talent and wondered how he had been so blind to it.

As he began walking away to let Keith continue resting, he noted several prints from Google on the table that looked surprisingly like photo shots of the Marine combat base at Khe Sanh. Now he was really puzzled and shook Keith who woke up with momentary confusion. Mike said, "Sorry, but if you got a minute, I'd like to talk. There's coffee in the kitchen."

Mike sat on a stool in the kitchen as Keith walked in. He poured a cup of coffee and handed it across the bar to him. With a smile on his face and in his voice, Mike asked quietly, "Where'd you get the talent I saw in your sketches of Lady and Molly. And when were you going to let us in on the secret?"

Keith sat with some embarrassment, feeling hungover from lack of sleep. "I don't know where my ability comes from, but since I was a kid, I've always liked to try to draw the things I saw. My dad thought it was a waste of time, so he never really encouraged me. Said if I liked to draw maybe I could be an architect or a draftsman.

"Anyway, with his attitude, it wasn't something I felt like pursuing. We didn't see eye to eye on much, and anything I could do to get him to get off my back was what I did. Stupid, huh?"

"You're not the only one who's had a problem getting along with parents. But that's beside the point –you've got some strong potential. How would you like to go to an art class here at the beach? I know a good one, and with your natural talent, you could do some fantastic work. What do you say?"

"That would be great, but I can't afford to do something like that right now, and we've got your painting to work on."

"You let me worry about that. We'll find the time you can break loose for classes and I'll take care of the cost. I'll get my money's worth out of you before it's all over. In the meantime, why don't you go hit the sack and get some rest. We'll probably have a busy day today."

"Okay," Keith responded, and began to head for the bedroom. "And thanks for the offer of the art class, Mike. That'll really be great."

"Wait," Mike said. "Before you go, what's up with all the aerial photos of Khe Sanh I saw in the gallery. Where'd those come from?"

"Well, Paul and I googled the fight at Khe Sanh. We were just trying to get into your head a little bit, to see if we could get a better idea of what you went through over there, to see how it might have gotten into your art. It was just one more thing we were trying to do to figure out how we could make a breakthrough on the structure and vision you're looking for. We didn't mean to pry."

"Not a problem," Mike replied, smiling inwardly to himself. "Did it help any? Did you learn anything?"

"Not really, at least not yet. And we were afraid the photos might stir up some painful memories for you."

"Not to worry. I'm pretty much over that now. But thanks for thinking about me. Now go get some rest. We'll talk some more later this morning."

CHAPTER 88

Mike sat for a few moments finishing his coffee after Keith left. He hadn't been totally truthful with Keith. Yes, he was much better about Vietnam than he had once been, but he still had his moments. That reminded him it was about time for another visit to the Vietnam Memorial in Washington, a practice he had begun years ago, soon after the memorial had been completed in '82.

When he first heard about the memorial's planned construction and the effort to raise money to pay for it, he'd made a substantial donation. Since his initial visit, he had felt a continuing need to go back periodically to remember those he had lost in that ugly war. He wondered if now might be the right time, that maybe stirring old memories might help give him a fresh perspective on the art they were struggling to create.

Maybe he could even take Keith and Paul, if they were feeling strong enough to handle the emotional impact of standing at the memorial. He decided to talk to Molly and Tom about it. Now he felt like trying to run the beach to clear his head, even though he knew the Parkinson's was beginning to make his runs harder. He called for Lady and they headed for the dune walkway as the sun began its rise.

About fifteen minutes into their run, Mike slowed to a stop and watched as the brilliance of the slowly rising sun began to overpower the last of the lingering grey and white overnight clouds. It was, he thought with his artist's brain, almost an explosion of bright orange color, seeming to blast through the clouds in a demonstration of its power and majesty. The sun's sudden brightness was so great it laid down its reflection on the waves lapping onto the shore at his feet.

He thought, in the imagery in his mind at that moment, that the splendor of the sun's initial rising could almost be a mirror of some of his paintings, but without the violence. Rather, its quiet, overpowering beauty signaled the birth of a new day without the destruction and brutal endings he had been attempting to portray in his paintings all these years.

At first it seemed to be a contradiction --that the beauty, peace and comfort of the day's beginning could so closely match the image of pain and fear he had brushed on his canvases. Then, as he continued to watch the day's birth, he began to feel a mental stirring that maybe it wasn't a contradiction.

Instead, he thought, maybe he was just seeing different faces of the same coin. Or like the two faces of the Roman god Janus, he was seeing nothing but a continuation of the same forces that created both death and life. He realized, with growing certainty, that in his efforts to empty his mind of all the pain of war, he had failed to see the power of life to renew itself, like the rising of the sun each day.

He knew finally that that transformation was what he had been trying to visualize as the missing piece of the Project. Now, if he could only visualize the shape of that image.

CHAPTER 89

He and Lady finally finished their run and quietly tried to enter the kitchen for her treat and fresh coffee for him. As he was pouring a cup, Molly walked in and greeted him with a soft kiss, at the same time shaking her head at the sand he and Lady had brought in. Mike tried to ignore her pointed rubbing of a toe across the sandy floor, saying "What's for breakfast?"

She laughed. "Nothing until you sweep me a path to the stove and fridge."

"Yes, ma'am. Then I want to get your thoughts on something I've been thinking about, maybe involving the guys."

Later that morning, while Paul and Keith had taken the dogs for a run on the beach, Mike sat down with Molly and began to talk about his growing need to go visit the Wall again.

Molly didn't question his motives, knowing that Vietnam remained a scar on his brain that occasionally needed to be rubbed, even after all these years. They had made the trip several times since the Wall had been built.

"I understand. I'm ready to go when you are."

"I know, and I appreciate your understanding all these years. But you know, there's something more going on in my head this time. Yeah, I need to go visit the guys again, but somehow in my mind, the Wall seems to be calling me for other reasons as well. Not sure I can explain it, but it seems to have something to do with the vision we've been struggling with for the painting.

"I'm probably not making much sense, but the tug seems extra strong. And I'm also thinking about taking Paul and Keith with us. Not sure why, but I'm thinking their seeing the Wall might help them in their healing. What do you think? Am I crazy?"

Molly's reaction was mixed. She had always been highly tuned to Mike's occasional struggle with his lingering trauma from Vietnam and tried to support him any way she could. She had seen the positive effect the visits to the Wall had had on him and knew it was important. But she worried about Paul and Keith and what their reaction to seeing the Wall might have on them. She just wasn't sure whether their healing was far enough along that they could handle the Wall's emotional trauma.

"I think it might be a positive thing, especially if, in their minds, it's tied into the painting. But I think you ought to discuss it with Tom. You know, from his working with the Wounded Warriors program, he has a wonderful insight into the struggles young men like Paul and Keith have. And he knows Paul and Keith personally. I trust his judgement and would like to know what he thinks."

"You're right. I plan to talk to him. In fact, I'll call him this morning. Thanks for your help, Babe. I'm glad you got lucky and found me."

She smiled and pulled his ear. "You're the lucky one, finding me when I didn't have enough good sense to pour salt in your beer. Now go call Tom while I check on flights to DC."

CHAPTER 90

When Mike called and announced who he was, the parish secretary greeted him warmly and told him she'd hunt up Father Tom immediately if he didn't mind waiting.

Tom answered within a minute. "I've got to change the screening criteria for this office. What's up, bro?"

"Maybe you just need to take a long sabbatical. It'd probably double the church population."

"Ouch! I'm feeling mortally wounded! What's on your mind, Sergeant?"

"I need your advice. Think you might have a few minutes this afternoon? I'm buying."

"In that case, I'll make the time. When and where?"

"The usual Irish swill, I guess. How 'bout we shoot for three?"

"Ok. I'll see you there. Want to give me a clue what's going on?"

"No big deal, but it involves the guys. I'll explain over Harp and nuts."

"Three o'clock then," Tom said, and hung up.

Mike was only a few minutes in before Tom, but it gave him enough time to order two Harps and a bowl of nuts. Tom arrived, looking like he had just run five kilometers, quickly scooted in across the table from Mike and took a long swig of beer. He sat for a moment, sighed heavily and then said, "This job would be a lot easier if people stopped sinning and getting sick."

"Then what would you do for excitement, besides swilling beer at my table? Seriously, you doing okay?"

"Yeah. Just feeling my age. So what's on your mind?"

"Molly and I are getting ready to go see the Wall again soon. You know how I get the itch once in a while. And I was thinking about seeing if Paul and Keith wanted to go with us and wanted to ask what you thought. See if you thought they could handle it."

"Why now? Aren't you and the guys in the middle of your painting project?"

"Yeah. We're in the middle. Stuck right in the middle, trying to work theme and vision into a meaningful canvas. Truth is, I'm --we're-- feeling pretty frustrated now, trying to find the right creative direction. My intuition tells me we're moving in the right direction but the vision just won't take on any clarity.

"Thing is, I've probably been dealing with this problem throughout my art, but been too blind to realize it. There's something vital missing in the message I've been trying to get across. Now, when I'm trying to put a period to my art I still can't grasp what that is, or how it should look on canvas. And I'm afraid it's affecting the guys to the point I might be losing them. They've become really involved with this project, but I'm worried that they might begin to slip back into their pain.

"For some reason I can't explain, I've started feeling that seeing the Wall might help me get my head straight, that it might help me get what I'm trying to put on canvas clearer in my mind. Don't ask me why or how. It's just a feeling I'm having. And I was thinking seeing the Wall might help the guys get refocused, might help them continue to heal by seeing the pain so many other guys experienced."

"Interesting thought," Tom said, "but, it could backfire. They might freak out from all the reminders the Wall represents. I'm guessing that's what's got you worried."

"Yeah. I really don't know which way to turn. Seeing the Wall feels pretty important to me right now, because of the painting if nothing else. I'm just not sure of the guys. Just don't know how it might affect them."

He stopped and swallowed the rest of his beer, then said, "So what do you think?"

"I think you've got a tough problem. Not Gordian-Knot tough, but still tough. It makes me think of a quote from one of Robert Browning's poems. He said, 'Ah, but a man's reach should exceed his grasp, else what's a heaven for?'"

"Not sure I understand. What's that supposed to mean?"

"It probably means different things to different people, but I think it means to achieve anything worthwhile you've got to be willing to attempt things that may turn out to be impossible. That maybe the effort may be as important as the outcome. But clearly, if we don't bust our butts trying, we'll never get where we wanna be.

"You're in the 'bust your butt' phase, and the creative side of your brain is telling you to go to the Wall to try to find a breakthrough. Another part of your head is saying what about the guys? Would their creative focus get sharper at the Wall, or will being there have a negative effect on their healing process?"

"So? What do I do?"

"I definitely think *you* need to go to the Wall. And *you* need to explain what's going on in your brain to the guys and give them a choice of going or not. I'm as blind as you when it comes to PTSD. It's a tough problem to get your mind around. It can take a weird turn. Tell them your concerns and let them try to decide. If you couch going to the Wall in terms of trying to use it to help get clarity for the painting's direction, that might help them decide to go or not."

"Yeah, that's a good idea. I have a good idea, too. Why don't you come with us? It's really a moving experience if you've never seen it. And maybe it might even help you find some closure for all the demons I think still run around in your head once in a while. Plus, if Paul and Keith go, you could help us see how they're doing."

Tom stared at Mike quietly, and slowly drained his beer. "I don't know, Mike. I've got so much going on in the parish right now. Not sure I could get away."

"That sounds like excuses. We could go up one day and be back the next evening. The parish would probably breathe a sigh of relief without you for twenty-four hours. And the plane fare and hotel are on me. What'd you say? If the guys go, will you go? And even if they don't, come with us anyway. I could use your support."

Tom remained silent, slowly peeling the label from his bottle. "I'm not sure this is going to be a good idea, but okay. I'll talk to the bishop, and assuming he says it's okay, I'll go, provided the guys agree to go too. When're you planning? It'll need to be in the middle of the week."

"Molly's working on the schedule now. We'll make sure it works for you. I'll let you know what the guys say this evening and after you get all clear from the bishop we'll make final arrangements. I'll want to go soon."

They shook hands warmly and went their separate ways. Mike called Molly to let her know what was happening and asked her to round up Paul and Keith for a family conference that evening.

When he got back to the house, he delayed going in, taking a short walk on the beach. He wanted to get his mind clear about why he was going to the Wall now and why he wanted to take the guys with him. He had always experienced some anxiety before he made the trip, but now he was feeling extra tight and he wasn't sure why.

He watched the waves struggle to the shore against a brisk westerly wind It reminded him of how he was feeling, dealing with the painting, as though he wasn't going to make it. But then he thought about the sudden burst of energy, of renewal, that going to the Wall seemed to have given him in the past. He thought, as he turned back toward the house, that he would follow his instincts.

CHAPTER 91

That evening after dinner, he and Molly sat down with Keith and Paul. Mike started by telling them about his periodic visits to the Vietnam War Memorial and how it seemed to help him deal with his lingering pain. He posed the thought that the Wall -as he chose to call it-- had become more than just a remembrance of Vietnam for him, but served as a reminder of all the pain, loss and suffering that all war had created.

He finished by saying, "Molly and I are planning on going to the Wall next week, and I wanted to see if you guys would go with us. I thought maybe it might help us get some fresh ideas for the painting."

Neither Keith nor Paul seemed able to respond at first. They stared at each other, then looked hard at Mike, visibly bothered by the thought of what might be a radical change in the comfort of their routine.

Keith asked hesitantly, "What's it like? I mean seeing the Wall. Up close, I mean. I've read about the Wall and seen pictures of how upset some people are when they go there. I don't want that. On the other hand, I'm really tired of living with fear, of feeling paralyzed half the time by all the crazy things going on in my mind. If seeing the Wall would help get my head straight, then I'm willing to go. And if it helps us figure out what we want for the painting, that works for me, too. I'll go."

"Good," Mike said, then turned to Paul. "I'm not pushing, but how do you feel? Think you might be okay making the trip?"

"I honestly don't know. I feel like my sessions with Father Tom have helped turn me around, although like Keith, I've still got the demons in my head. But also, like Keith, I'm tired of being afraid, of not feeling sure I can stop feeling handcuffed by what happened in Afghanistan. If going to the Wall might help me get free of the past, then, yeah, I'll go."

Molly got up from her chair and moved over to sit between Keith and Paul on the couch. She put her arms around their shoulders and pulled them close.

"I think I know how you're feeling, guys. Mike and I have worried about whether your going to the Wall was a good idea, but I've seen the good effect it has had on him.

"Somehow he comes back with a feeling of renewal in his life and in his painting. I know the Wall is for his war, but it may have the magic to help purge the pain of all war from all of us. And finally, we'll be going up there as a family, so we can help support each other. Father Tom's going with us, so we'll have his support as well. Now, Mike, call Tom and find out when he can go, and I'll make plane and hotel reservations."

CHAPTER 92

Tom got his schedule cleared for Wednesday and Thursday of the next week and Molly got a flight for Wednesday afternoon and a return flight for Thursday afternoon. At Mike's insistence she got first class tickets round trip. She also got reservations at a hotel in downtown DC that would put them in walking distance of the Wall.

As their flight approached Reagan, Keith turned to the other four and said he'd done some reading about the memorial. He quoted the Wall's dimensions, saying it had two sloping sides, each measuring about 246 feet long and met in the center at an angle of 125.9 degrees. Where the two sides of the wall met at the center each measured eight feet, and then tapered down at their ends to about eight inches. He said each side had seventy-two panels on which the names of those killed or MIA were recorded. Over 58,000 names were listed.

Hearing the bare statistics laid a sobering pall over the group, and each withdrew into an introspective silence. As the jet lowered its wheels and began its final approach, Molly searched Keith and Paul's faces for signs of anxiety. Remarkably, neither looked unusually troubled and knowing she was watching over them, they managed a slight smile of reassurance for her.

Their hotel was only about three miles from Reagan and their taxi delivered them with surprising efficiency through the Washington traffic. It was after six p.m. before they finally finished registration and found their rooms. They agreed to meet in Mike and Molly's suite and make plans for that evening and the next day at the Wall.

They sat around in the suite's living area drinking bottles of Harp Molly had ordered from room service, while Mike sketched his thoughts about how they would spend their time. He let them know that Molly had already made reservations for dinner that night at one of the hotel's restaurants.

"Guys, regarding our visit to the Wall tomorrow," he said to Paul and Keith, "I want to remind you –all of us—that it can be a heavy place emotionally. At any time anyone feels the need to back away, do it. We're here as a family and there'll be plenty of support.

"I also want to remind you that for some reason I don't really understand, the Wall has become an important part of my thinking about the vision and shape of the painting. I know how hard we've all struggled with this problem, and I think you two have a big part of yourselves invested in what we're trying accomplish. So, we need to approach the Wall as maybe a source of inspiration for us. There's pain there, for sure, but if we can get beyond the pain, maybe we'll find some help with the vision for the painting.

"Keith, I'd like you to make some sketches of the wall. They don't have to be precise. Just let your creative instincts take over. Paul, I need you to take some photos of the Wall. You'll need to capture it in pieces that we can put together for a complete picture. Go ahead and take some close ups as well so we can have a good physical vision of it. I'd like to get an early start tomorrow morning, so let's plan on meeting for breakfast in the lobby at eight. Now, let's go get some dinner and relax."

CHAPTER 93

To save time and because of Mike's anxiousness to get to the Wall, they elected to take a taxi to the Memorial. Keith and Paul stared at the various capital buildings like awe-struck tourists from the hills of West Virginia.

"I never knew how beautiful the Capitol is," Keith said.

Paul was equally blown away, especially as they began to drive through the cluster of memorials to the heroes of war and the proud moments of pain captured forever in bronze and stone.

The taxi stopped at the edge of the Vietnam Memorial just as the sun began its trip from the Washington Monument, with its rays beginning to splash down the easterly arm of the Wall. It was a luminescent moment, with the highly-polished marble wall beginning to mirror the sun's rays.

As the taxis drove away, they were left standing at the foot of the west arm of the Wall, staring down its endless length.

Mike took Molly's hand and moved slowly down the path in front of the Wall, finally stopping at the panel for 1967 and 1968. Memory quickly brought him a name where he paused, head bowed, and gently rubbed his fingers over the letters of his Pete's name. Molly stood with him, softly rubbing the back of his neck. Eventually, he moved from Pete's name and found those of Philly, Fisher, and all the other lost members of his squads.

Tom, Paul, and Keith watched Mike and Molly standing at the wall, each isolated in his own thoughts. For his part, Tom had felt a welling up of the emotional anxiety he had not experienced for over forty years. He knew he had been uncharacteristically withdrawn and reticent during the trip up and felt the guilt of not being more supportive of the rest of the group, especially Paul and Keith.

He worried about them now, even as he felt the long dormant demons from Vietnam begin to stir in his head. Finally, he mentally crossed himself, forced a placid look to his face, and turned to the two young men, saying, "How 'bout it, guys. Want to take a walk with me down the wall?"

Paul and Keith were both staring around them with anxious eyes, their bodies tense. They looked as though they were getting ready to walk their first patrol around the mud walls of an Afghan village, and reacted to Tom's invitation as though he had just told them to saddle up and move out. With reluctance, they followed Tom's lead and began a slow trek down the mirrored wall and back into a painful history.

They stopped with Tom at the panels that marked his Vietnam tour and stood silently as he looked at all the names engraved there. He didn't try to find individual names but rather rubbed his hand softly over the wall, saying a silent prayer for all the dead.

CHAPTER 94

Mike and Molly saw Tom, Keith, and Paul approaching down the walk in front of the Wall. When the three reached them they continued together down toward the east end of the wall, with Molly's arms linked with Keith's and Paul's.

Mike sensed the anxiousness in the young men. "How you holding up, guys?"

Keith admitted he was feeling intimidated by the wall and its surroundings. "I'm almost feeling trapped, like I'm surrounded by ghosts, like maybe Rod is here and I'm about to step on an IED with him."

"Do you need to leave? You know we can. We're in this together and we need everyone to feel okay about what we're trying to do."

"No. I want to see this through. Like I said earlier, I'm tired of feeling like a prisoner of what's in my head. Maybe this is the best chance I have to get better. Besides, you gave me an assignment. I intend to do it."

Mike nodded, then said, "What about you, Paul? You doin' okay?"

"Hangin' in there. It feels like a strange place to be. One that feels like peace one second and pain the next. Can't explain it, but it's like walkin' into a quiet cave one second and then the next there're thousands of screaming bats flying at your face. But I'll handle it."

At that point Tom took over. "Fellows, at first my reaction was the same as yours. I confess I've been feeling some of the same anxiety. But I've been countering those feelings by imagining we're surrounded not by ghosts, but by the healed souls of those whose names are inscribed on the Wall. I'm trying to feel their calming presence and think they're reaching out to those of us still living to assure us that all is well and that they've moved on in their journey, living in God's presence."

For moments, none of the group talked or moved, nor did they see the small group of visitors to the Wall who had stopped to listen to Tom's words. Finally, Mike said, "Okay. We all together? Ready to go to work?"

Keith and Paul, seeming to come out of a hypnotic state, nodded and looked expectantly at Mike.

"All right. Paul, if I were you I'd start your photos on the east wall where the sun is strongest and work your way to the center and then down the west side. Sort'a lead the sun's rays as they begin to move down the Wall. And don't get too far away. I'd rather you be close enough to capture details of the Wall in the segments you're shooting. When we get back we can overlap the segments to make a complete picture..

"Keith, when you're doing your sketches, let your creative juices flow. Keep in mind that this wall is an abstract in itself, trying to capture in a symbolic way all the pain and suffering of Vietnam, in the names of those who didn't survive.

"Look, keep in mind we're trying to capture our vision for the painting. I'm convinced it's buried in these walls.

"As for me, I'm gonna be wandering around, trying to see if I can feel that vision. Holler if you need me."

"Wait, Mike," Molly said. "What are Tom and I supposed to do while you guys are doing all the creative work?"

"Take care of us. We're going to need your support while we're here. It could get rough. To begin with, maybe you could find some coffee. I'm beginning to feel the need for some nourishment. And Tom, please keep an eye on us. We may be walking on some shaky ground here and spiritual support from you could help get us through."

With that, the group broke up, getting ready to carry out their assignments. Molly managed to find a vendor truck nearby that served coffee and pastries, which she diligently delivered to the rest of the group. She satisfied herself that Keith and Paul seemed to be holding up and began looking around trying to think of some way to keep busy and out of the way.

She noticed that the number of visitors to the Wall had begun to grow, many obviously searching for names of lost ones. There were veterans, of course, and families remembering loved ones, even after so many years. Flowers and notes dotted the base of the Wall, and many hands touched names in silent effort to penetrate the marble surface for reconnection.

In ironic contrast, the Wall echoed with the happy sound of restless young children running around or wandering away, clearly vexing their parents and others who were trying to reach into the painful past of the

Wall. Without conscious thought she moved to the Wall and began to engage some of the children in greeting and light conversation. Soon she had a small group of young children gathered around her, eager to tell her their names, where they were from and what their favorite songs were. Many knew the same songs and with little urging from Molly began to sing. The small group quickly grew with the children happily sitting in a circle, talking and singing together while grateful parents turned back in relief to give their full attention to the Wall.

Eventually the group of children broke up as their parents and grandparents called them to leave. Many spontaneously gave Molly a peck on the cheek as they left. Soon she found herself alone wondering at the curious silence that had settled around the Wall and the strange peace it provided. She rose and began following a circling path around the monument grounds.

Tom had watched Molly in what he knew was her natural element, marveling at the peace and love she continually gave to those around her. In contrast, he felt himself growing increasingly anxious being in this place at this time, despite what he had said earlier to the others in his impromptu homily.

He realized, with growing awareness, how all these years he had blocked out the pain he had brought back from Vietnam, using his priesthood to seal off the reality of that pain-- how he had managed to fool himself into believing that the memories of that time and place had been dissolved by his faith.

Instead, he thought, they had remained hidden in silent ambush, waiting to create cracks in his faith. He lay on the grass in front of the wall, staring sightlessly at the building patterns of clouds, thinking about the 58,000 plus lives surrounding him and feeling the doubt that they could possibly fit into a plan by God for man's eternal perfection.

As he watched the clouds, with their enormous clustering in the sky, he thought, not for the first time, that as large as they were, the clouds were only a microscopic drop in the vastness of the universe. And he questioned again where in this unmeasurable vastness his belief in a loving God fit. And where in that vastness did the deaths of over 58,000 lives rest?

At the height of his wavering of faith, he slowly began to realize that in the very vastness of the universe lay the answer to his doubt: He felt a gentle revelation building in his mind, telling him that those souls, and all who died on earth, were just beginning on a journey of God's design, one that fit squarely as a vital piece into his eternal plan. He closed his eyes and said a prayer of thanksgiving for the resurgence of faith he knew God was giving him. Then he rose and went looking for Keith and Paul to make sure they were dealing okay with the weight of this place.

CHAPTER 95

Mike had found a quiet place to sit alone on the grass about twenty-five yards in front of the wall where he thought he might be able to stir his creative juices.

He thought about the years-long battle he had fought with the demons of war and how important his painting had been in beating back those demons. Yet in all those years he had been unable to achieve total freedom. He still struggled to understand fully why the pain of war still lingered. For reasons he had never understood, he had been unable to get fully beyond the darkness that threatened his sanity.

If not for people like Zacharias, Cavanaugh, and most of all Molly, he knew he would not have survived. Yes, his painting had been a therapeutic blessing, but even with it he had not totally healed his mind. Something vital was missing, and now as he was approaching the end of his art and a new struggle with Parkinson's, he was desperate to find completeness.

The Wall. Ironic, he thought, that despite its inscriptions of war's pain, he had come to it hoping it might provide the inspiration he needed.

He closed his eyes and opened his mind, straining to hear what the Wall was trying to tell him. Then he felt a soft hand on his shoulder and opened his eyes to see Molly sitting down beside him. He leaned over and kissed her hand and thought her presence was like the morning sun driving away the blackness.

"Where you been? I saw you playing with the kids, then suddenly you disappeared."

"Just went for a walk, absorbing the beauty of this place and wondering how beauty could be a part of what it's saying to those who come here in sadness. "What about you? I saw you sitting here alone looking like you were lost in another world."

"I was. But you came and brought me back to the only world I want to be in, the one you're in."

She leaned over and kissed him softly, then took his hand and held it tightly. "That's where I want you, too. Don't ever go away."

They sat together in comfortable silence, and Mike thought back to what she had said earlier about the beauty of this place in the midst of the pain it represented. She was right. Despite the darkness of so much death, the Wall had an ethereal quality about it that seemed to lift the spirit to a higher plane. Thinking that, he felt a trembling in his gut, a moment of creative understanding, a clarity of vision. He stood abruptly, pulling Molly with him and began a slow visual exploration of the Wall.

"What is it, Mike? Are you okay?"

He nodded his head, but placed a finger to his lips. After a moment, he said, "Where is everyone? I think we can go now."

"Okay. You stay here. I'll go round everyone up." She quickly moved off, intuitively sensing Mike was experiencing an important visual breakthrough and didn't want to interfere with that process. When she had gathered up the three guys, she tried to explain what she thought was going on without making Mike sound like Van Gogh in one of his less lucid moments.

CHAPTER 96

"Well if you guys are finished," Tom said, "let's find a cab and get back to the hotel for lunch. I'm starving. And we'll let Mike have his quiet time if he needs it. Don't know about you, but I could use a beer."

Everyone agreed. They joined Mike and soon were heading back to the hotel. A subdued Mike sat quietly on the ride back, listening to the various discussions about the Wall. When they arrived at the hotel, he said he'd skip lunch, but wanted to see the photographs and sketches Paul and Keith had made. With them in hand, he excused himself and went to the room, while the rest of the group headed for the restaurant.

On the plane ride back, Mike remained withdrawn, continuing to study the sketches and photos and occasionally looking up to stare off into space. The rest of the group gave him as much room as possible. They spoke in muted conversations, but mostly they relived the visit to the Wall in their own minds.

Paul and Keith had returned from the experience of the Wall with a slowly growing sense that they, and their PTSD, had passed a crucial test: They had survived the trauma of the Wall's message.

Tom sat in a state of grace, strongly believing that the Wall had been God's message to him. That it had helped him restore his faith with the vision that all death, regardless of cause, was transient in God's universe..

Molly's thoughts were all on Mike. She understood and supported the dogged search he was going through. At the same moment she feared he was winding down in energy, possibly because of the Parkinson's but also perhaps in frustration trying to find that elusive culmination for his work.

At the airport, Tom left to find his car, promising to be in touch shortly. Molly, with typical foresight, had memorized where their SUV was parked and soon had them heading for the beach. She stopped at the animal shelter to pick up the dogs, which created bedlam for the rest of the ride as the three animals tried desperately to voice their joy at being rescued from their prison.

It was almost seven when they reached home, and Paul and Keith, still feeling stuffed from lunch, protested when Molly mentioned dinner. Instead, they opted for some fruit and a run with the dogs on the beach.

Molly opened two bottles of Harp and called to Mike. "You haven't eaten anything since breakfast. Can I fix you some eggs and bacon?"'

"No, I'll get something later. Right now, I think I'll take a walk." He kissed her and quickly left. He knew Keith and Paul had headed north with the dogs and chose to turn south, feeling the need to be alone.

CHAPTER 97

Mike began to relax as he stepped out onto the wet beach sand, interrupted only by the sudden awareness that his left foot seemed to have a problem moving as his brain instructed. Reluctantly he acknowledged the Parkinson's effect as the doctor had predicted, but with determination, mentally demanded the foot to work properly. For the moment, it obeyed and he continued his walk.

The calmness he was feeling faltered from the sudden reminder of the limited time Parkinson's might be giving him. But he chose not to be intimidated by the presence of the disease, opting instead to focus on the visions he had sensed at the Wall.

Looking at the majesty of the Wall, he had begun to understand that in all his paintings he had never been able to get past the darkness of the war. He realized that, until today, he had never been able to see that there might be a path out of that darkness.

All he'd been trying to do all these years with his art was empty his mind of the pain, never realizing that it had left an emptiness where hope, love, light and peace could fill the void.

Finally, feeling the stubborn left foot complaining about his pace, he sat down on the wet sand and with his artist's eyes, began watching the beach birds flying in their continuing search for food. He was particularly fascinated by the acrobatic terns, as they flew above the waves, hanging almost motionless against the wind before diving suddenly to snatch a morsel from the receding water. Occasionally they would drop briefly on the wet sand, then lift effortlessly into the air for some destination only their bird minds knew.

They had no problem he thought, as the poet Browning had suggested for man, of their reach exceeding their grasp. He, on the other hand, for all these years, had blindly been unable to grasp where his artistic reach had tried to take him. Now, for the first time he believed he was at the creative cusp, that he was on the threshold of finding a way to fill the gulf between where he wanted – no, needed—to go and his ability to get there with his art.

With the growing darkness, he rose and traced his steps back to the house, making sure there was no limp in his gait for Molly to notice as he opened the door to the kitchen. He was met with the delicious aroma of Molly's warmed up chicken and vegetable soup, and he marveled anew at her many talents.

Keith and Paul sat at the kitchen table eating what Mike suspected were second helpings. He walked to Molly and kissed her cheek. "That smells almost as good as you. I think I might have a small bowl, that is if our guests have left any."

A large slurping noise greeted him, as both Keith and Paul good-naturedly acknowledged his snide comment with their last spoonful of soup.

Hearing the noise, Mike began to feel the tension of the day releasing and a calmness overtake him. He glared at the young men in mock anger, then laughed with the feeling that the world was tipping back into its natural orbit.

Molly placed a large bowl for him next to hers and tapped the table for him to sit. He sat, raising a fresh bottle of Harps to his young protégés. "It looks like we all survived the Wall. More important, I've got these new visions for the painting running around in my head and I feel a breakthrough coming. I think we all need to get a good night's sleep and be ready to go first thing in the morning. You guys okay with that?"

Keith and Paul nodded their agreement, thanked Molly for dinner, and headed to their room.

Mike and Molly both felt the exhaustion of the past two days overtaking them and turned in early. As they lay together, Molly gently brushed his face with her fingers. "Are you okay? I haven't seen you so knotted up in years like you were today."

"I know. The best way I can describe it is like there's been a large blind spot in my vision all these years, and now suddenly it seems to be clearing up and I'm suddenly beginning to see things differently. Only the vision's not perfectly clear yet, so I guess I've felt excited, frustrated, and impatient most of the day.

"But I'm feeling calmer now. It's like I told the guys at dinner: I feel a breakthrough coming. Now I just need to get my mind quiet and wait for the vision to gel. Probably doesn't make much sense, but bottom line is I'm feeling better and sorry If I worried you."

She reached for him and held him firmly for a moment. "Okay, Mr. Pallaso. Just checking. I love you. Now get some sleep."

CHAPTER 98

He woke shortly after midnight, feeling a wide-awake restlessness. He remembered portions of a puzzling dream in which he had been standing in front of the Wall when suddenly several large birds landed on its top. Only rather than bird heads they had human heads and he suddenly realized they had the smiling faces of Pete, Philly, Fisher, and other comrades he had lost in 'Nam. They would take turns suddenly lifting effortlessly on spreading wings, soaring into a cloudless sky, then quickly returning to settle down again on the wall, still with smiling faces looking at him.

He sat on the side of the bed for a moment, then resolutely rose and, throwing on shorts and a tee-shirt, plodded quietly out to the kitchen. With a large cup of left-over coffee in hand, he turned to the studio and switched on the overhead lights.

He stood for a moment, looking at the photos and sketches Paul and Keith had left on the workbench. He thought he understood why he would dream about the Wall. Their visit had been somewhat traumatic, more so than with earlier visits. But he couldn't make sense of seeing the faces of his friends with bird bodies.

With a resigned shake of his head, he began to move the eight by ten glossies of the different parts of the Wall Paul had printed until he had a reasonably accurate composite picture of the total Wall. He tried to gain some visual clarity of the images that continued to flit evasively through his brain.. What could the Wall represent in relation to what had become the demanding visual theme of the painting --the movement from the pain of darkness that had consumed all his earlier work to the light of peace?

Restlessly, he looked at the free-hand sketches Keith had made, seeing again what he had seen when he'd first looked at them. Somehow, Keith had captured the Wall not as stone or marble, but as something organic and breathing.

For a brief moment Mike looked back and forth between Paul's composite photographs and Keith's sketches. Then the elusive image that had been flitting through his brain suddenly solidified in his mind's eye and he quickly reached for a sheet of blank butcher paper and a piece of charcoal. Demanding stilled obedience from his shaking hand, he began sketching the vision spilling from his head.

After an exhausting half hour of which he had no conscious memory, he threw the charcoal aside and stood transfixed at the image he had created. Yes, yes, a voice in his head kept repeating. He had finally found the missing piece from his art work, and it was like nothing he had ever imagined.

Rummaging around on the worktable, he searched for tubes of paint whose color would match his vision. He haphazardly spread globs of the colors he had chosen on an old used palette and with a stiff brush began to dab the shapes and colors of his past on the bottom of the sketched sheet. With frenetic haste, he smeared the explosive colors of Khe Sanh, deadly blooms of crimson, yellow and black, mixed with the dark wetness of jungle greens.

Then, at the top he began to spread the morning brightness of daybreak, filling it with brilliant yellows, freshening blues and softly fading white. The middle he left uncolored, knowing as the centerpiece of the painting it could not be hurried with shape or color.

CHAPTER 99

After an exhausting two hours, he tossed the brush and palette on the table. He carefully gathered up the painted butcher paper, the composite photos and Keith's sketches of the Wall and left for the kitchen as the morning light began to invade the studio. He smelled fresh coffee brewing and knew Molly had already started the new day. She stood at the stove frying bacon, and he gathered her up in his arms and nuzzled her neck.

"Is that the milkman? I thought we agreed you wouldn't come on Fridays."

"I couldn't stay away from you or the bacon you cook. It's hard to tell which smells better!"

"Well, you'd better leave before my husband gets up, but not before you take the dogs out for their morning business." With that, Molly turned in his arms and brushed a kiss on his lips. "Hi, stranger. Where've you been all night? I missed you."

"I've been painting a masterpiece, maybe the only important one I've ever painted."

"Wonderful! Where is it? I need to see it."

"Not now. I'm still trying to get my mind around it. I'll let you see it after breakfast, when I show it to the guys."

"Oh, all right. In the meantime, go get cleaned up, get the paint off your face and wake the boys. Breakfast will be ready soon."

"Yes ma'am." He kissed her softly, rubbed a thin line of blue paint on her cheek and left quickly for the back bathroom.

Keith and Paul sat at the table finishing their coffee, watching Mike curiously as he fidgeted impatiently with his coffee cup. "What's up, Mike?" Keith asked. "You look as tight as a drum."

"Yeah. I've been up most of the night thinking about the painting, and if you guys are finished, I've got something to show you."

"We're done," Paul said with heightened interest. "So show us what's going on."

"Yes, please," Molly said, "before we all go crazy."

"Okay," Mike said, and began clearing a space at the table. "First, here's a composite of the Wall I put together from Paul's photographs. And here's a couple of Keith's better sketches. Now, look carefully and tell me what you see."

Both Paul and Keith looked quizzically at the composite and the sketches. "I see the Wall," Paul said. What am I missing?"

"Don't mean to be dense," Keith said, "but I'm like Paul. I'm missing what you're talking about."

"Look at the shape of the Wall," Mike said impatiently. "What does the shape remind you of?"

Both looked hard at the photos and sketches, eager to solve the puzzle Mike was presenting. Both sat back in frustration, shaking their heads in defeat.

"A bird. It looks like it could be a flying bird," Molly said.

"Yes! Exactly!" Mike exclaimed.

Paul and Keith once again looked closely at the photographs and sketches, finally nodding their heads in agreement. "You're right," Keith said. "It could be a bird, but why is that important? What does that have to do with the painting?"

"I'll show you." Mike spread out the piece of butcher paper in front of them. "It's the piece we've been missing in trying to see how we visually move from the images of the pain of war that're screwing up our minds to the peace that will free us from that pain. What I'm visualizing, in an abstract way, is the Wall, with all the pain it's carrying, rising like the phoenix from the ashes, renewing itself!"

Keith, Paul, and Molly sat in silence as they tried to absorb Mike's description, looking hard at the butcher paper images, then trying to put them together with what they had heard from Mike.

"Beautiful," Molly whispered. "You've done it!"

Paul and Keith nodded in awe, both feeling a wave of triumph and odd relief.

"So where do we go from here?" Keith asked in a mixture of excitement and anxiety. "What are our next steps? How do we put this on canvas?"

Mike sat back, feeling a pleasurable sense of exhaustion and vindication at the buy-in from his artistic conspirators and Molly's keen insight. "I don't know exactly. First, we need to decide visually how the wall transforms into a phoenix. How do we do that? For instance, what colors do we use to portray that transformation? How far can we move away from reality with our abstraction in displaying the bird without losing the reality of the Wall? Or does it matter?"

"Feathers," Keith said. "It's a bird, so it's got to have feathers. And the Wall has over fifty-eight thousand feathers. We need to use dogtags as the bird's feathers.

Mike sensed a moment of creative genius developing "Go on, Keith. What are you thinking? What about color?"

Keith creative juices swelled. "We use the names from the wall, not as names, but vertical 'feathers', as they might appear on a dogtag. And we color them changing from deep crimson, to a light red and finally to white as they near the top of the bird's wings. Abstractly, of course."

Mike sat in quiet admiration, feeling excitement growing as he thought of next steps. "I think you've nailed it, Keith. But keep in mind that what we're trying to create is an abstract expression of our thoughts and feelings, consistent with my other work.

"I don't want to go too far in trying to mirror reality. In other words, some people might be able to gain a glimmer of what the painting represents, but it needs to stay subtle. I want to cause the viewers to walk away from the painting with a desire to explore what they've experienced for deeper meaning. Not everyone, if anyone, will understand the underlying message of moving from darkness to light we're trying to create here, but they should be driven to question. Think about producing this painting for John Cavanaugh to look at."

"Jesus, Mike," Keith said. "I don't what you've been snorting this morning, but I want some."

"Me too," Paul said. "But the real question is, can we three pull this off? God knows, Mike, you're going to have to guide us all the way on this, from start to end. I feel like I just got off the chopper at Marjah, with no bearings and little sense of where I'm going."

"Okay, guys. Sorry about spouting off like that. Keith, I still think you nailed it. Next steps are simple. I want the painting to be big, bigger than anything I've done before. I'm thinking maybe fifteen by twenty or so feet. We can get started on the framing for that this morning. And because of the size, I'll want to use hard board rather than canvas. Come on. If you're ready, let's get started. Paul, let's go to get the supplies we'll need. We'll need to stop at the art store for hard board and other hardware. Keith, spend some time sketching what you think the bird, or its abstract representation, should look like. We'll be back in an hour or so. Ready, Paul?"

"Lead on, Merlin. I'm right behind you."

CHAPTER 100

Mike and Paul were back in a little over an hour, with the truck bed loaded with sheets of ash hard board, framing wood and paint. Keith came out to help unload, but when Mike asked about his sketches he seemed reluctant to share them.

"Come on, Keith. You're the next step. Let's see what you got."

"It isn't much, Mike. I can't read your mind, so I wasn't sure what you expected."

"I expected you to be creative, that the accumulation of all we've worked on would come together in your mind to help solidify your vision. So give it up, my friend. Let's see what you got."

With that all three walked into the studio where Keith had laid out three variations of the Wall transfiguring into a rising phoenix. Mike stared at them intently, moving from one to another without comment.

"Okay. Quick, Keith, which do you like best? And why?"

"I like the first one I did, the one on the left. I like it because I think it best shows the lifting of the Wall as a bird might look lifting from its perch, effortlessly, with a downward surge of its wings pushing against the wind. And I feel like that one best captures the instant when the Wall transforms itself into the phoenix."

Mike stood still as he listened to Keith, finally nodding his head in agreement. "You're right, Keith. That's the best one of the three. I think all we need to do is work on the feathers. You were right to say we need to add the feathers, but how we do it will be vital to the image we're creating. I agree that they should symbolize the dogtags as the feathers, maybe starting as dark crimson and purple at the bottom but turning bright colors near the top edge of the bird's wings, beginning to blend in with the skyline colors of the top of the painting. Let's work it out with sketches on a good-sized canvas. Any thoughts?"

"Yeah," Keith said. "I've been thinking. There're 72 panels on each side of the wall. So let's do the feathers in groups of panels, 72 on each side. I don't mean we actually duplicate the panels, but we can make each section different from the other, say with the most or largest feathers in the largest panels, like the largest panels on the wall have the most names.

"We can also vary the colors of the feathers in each panel. And there's no way we can put 58,000 feathers on the bird-- we just put enough to abstractly represent the wall as a flying bird.

"Any of that make any sense?"

"Yeah," Mike said, slowly. "I think I see where you're going. In fact, I'm making you the bird man, the feather man. Paul and I will help, of course, but you'll have to keep us straight. Why don't you work on the design of the feathers, and Paul and I'll take care of putting the frame and hard board together. Later this afternoon all of us can and roll on the base white. Come on, Paul. Let's let the artist get back to work.

"Oh, wait. Keith, here's a card with the name and number of the art teacher I told you about. Her name is Grace Phillips and she's expecting your call. Ya'll work out the details about getting together. Maybe you could even talk about the feathers."

"Thanks, Mike." Keith stood looking at the card, not sure what change it might represent in his life. But surprisingly, he found himself looking forward to this new challenge, virtually free of the paralyzing anxiety he had brought back from Afghanistan.

CHAPTER 101

Molly lay stretched out on one of the chaise lounges on the veranda, enjoying the afternoon shade when Mike walked out to join her. She turned her head when hearing the door close, smiled and said, "Didn't think I'd see you so soon. So how's the Project coming?"

Mike leaned down to kiss her and brushed her hair from her eyes. "It's going great. Tomorrow, I think we'll start trying to paint. We ended up quitting early this afternoon. Paul went with Tom to do some hospital visits, and Keith is meeting with Grace Phillips to talk about starting art classes. Anyway, I thought we could spend a few minutes together. I'm feeling pretty wound up and need you to keep me centered."

Molly reached for his hand and brought it to her lips. "I hope I am your center. In any event, I have something I want to get your thoughts on. We're coming up on our 25th anniversary, and I've been talking to Tom…"

"And," he interrupted, "you thought we might exchange our vows again and have a big party."

She gasped, "How did you know?"

Mike laughed. "You're not the only one talking to Tom. We've already agreed on the time and place, and I've put together a list of people to invite. You can look at it and add or subtract however you wish. I thought we'd have the party here and get the Irish to cater for us. We're about six weeks from our anniversary, so we ought to have enough time."

Molly leapt on him, pinning him on the chaise lounge he'd been sitting on. "You devil! Here I was thinking I'd have to drag you kicking and screaming to agree, and now you've taken away half the fun! I love you, you big lummox. Now, I'll take care of the details. You just make sure you're cleaned up, including washing behind your ears. Now where is that list of guests? I'll need to start sending out invitations tomorrow."

Mike gently disengaged himself. "Just a minute, while I go find the list."

In a brief moment, he returned with his hand-written list, handed it to her, and then said, "And you might also want these," producing two roundtrip airline tickets for first class. "I thought we'd start out in Rome, and work our way back through Florence, Venice, Paris, London and Dublin."

"Oh Mike," she whispered, wrapping her arms tightly around his neck. "I'm blown away. I love you so very much."

"Good, I'd hate to think I went to all this trouble for nothing. Come on, let's take the dogs for a walk while we decide on where we're going to eat tonight."

COMPLETION
CHAPTER 102

"Okay," Mike said, several days later. "Here's where it gets tough, putting paint on. Now we've got to get creative, trying to paint our images.

"Keith, did you get a chance to talk to Grace about the bird and its feathers?

"Yeah. She thinks we're on the right track. We talked about not letting the feathers overcome the rest of the painting, that it sounded to her like there were going to be several focal points, all important, and the feathers should just be a small part of the bird's rising."

"Yeah, that probably makes sense, although the feathers do represent all the people lost and their escape from the darkness. I guess, in the end, they help give life to the wall as it renews itself from the ashes. We can talk about it some more, but you still have the lead. We'll end up making changes, but that's what oil paints are for. And keep in mind we don't need to focus on creating recognizable forms, just create images that engage and grab the imagination of those who might be looking at the work. It's not slight-of-hand --it's an effort to create a gut reaction in the viewer that also excites the brain."

"Jesus, Mike. You'll have to be with us all the way if we have any chance of getting this done," Keith said.

"Yeah," Paul added. "We don't have a clue of even where to start."

"We can do it," Mike said determinedly. "I'll make you an extension of my mind and my hand. Keith let's start with a sketch of the bird, probably centered between the top and bottom and side to side."

The next three weeks were exhausting, full of starts and stops, with Mike's voice directing, demanding and criticizing each step of the effort. Miraculously, the painting began to come together as Mike had envisioned it but with subtle embellishments by Keith and Paul that added to the quality of the effort. Finally, at the end of Friday afternoon of the third week, the three stood together looking at what seemed to be the finished painting.

"The bird is flying, lifting from the ashes," Keith murmured. "I think we nailed it,"

"Yeah, I think you're right. I owe you guys, more than I can say."

"No," Paul said. "We owe you. You and Molly may have saved our lives. I sort of feel like our bird. Reborn."

With that, they threw the many brushes, scrapers and sticks they had used during the painting process into a large bucket of paint thinner and walked out into the late afternoon sunshine.

Mike called Molly to come see the finished product. She then called Tom to come over when he had a moment.

After Tom's arrival--minus his disguise-- and many minutes of looking at the painting by everyone, Tom said, "Quite a moment. A significant step forward, a beautiful step forward in our journey. Now how do we celebrate such an event?"

"Well," Mike said, "I know a place a few blocks from here that makes the best tasting gelato at the beach. All we have to do is follow Lady. She knows the way." With that, he rattled the leashes and the three collies ran to the studio door. In a moment, the five adults and three dogs were parading down the street in a quiet moment of celebration.

Later that evening, after several Harps and generous amounts of Irish lasagna, Tom stood, saying he needed to leave, and asked Mike to walk with him out to his car. At the car, Tom reached into the back seat and pulled out an oily rag in which was wrapped a Marine-issued Beretta pistol and a full magazine. He handed them to Mike. "Paul asked me to give this to you, thinking you'd know how to get it back to the Marines, that thanks to you and Molly, he didn't need it any longer."

With that, he got in the car, waved as he drove away, and said to a stunned Mike, "God bless you, brother."

Made in the
USA
Columbia, SC